BREAKING BRANDON

(Fate #2)

Also by Elizabeth Reyes

The Moreno Brothers Series
Forever Mine
Always Been Mine
Romero
Sweet Sofie
Making You Mine

The 5th Street Series
Noah
Gio
Hector
Abel

The Fate Series
Fate

BREAKING BRANDON

(Fate #2)

Elizabeth Reyes

Breaking Brandon

(Fate #2)

Elizabeth Reyes

Copyright © 2013 Elizabeth Reyes

All Rights Reserved. This book may not be reproduced, scanned, or distributed in any printed or electronic form without permission from the author. Please do not participate in or encourage piracy of copyrighted materials in violation of the author's rights. All characters and storylines are the property of the author and your support and respect is appreciated.

This book is a work of fiction. The characters and events portrayed in this book are fictitious. Any similarity to real persons, living or dead, is coincidental and not intended by the author.

To Emily, my "soldier girl," I LOVE that I had you "shaking in your combat boots!" ;)

CHAPTER ONE

Brandon

Then

The demanding knock on the door should've been his first clue that something was wrong. Brandon stood from where he'd been sitting staring at his ailing, sleeping father and walked out of the room, closing the door behind him. It couldn't be his mom. She had a key, and she always came in through the garage door anyway.

Glancing out the door window, Brandon was surprised to see who it was. He opened the door and smiled. "Hey, Sal." He started to unlatch the screen door. "Damn, how long has it been?"

Sal pulled the door open roughly. "This isn't a social visit, Billings."

The murderous glare in Sal's eye surprised Brandon. Of Sofia's three brothers, Sal had always been the calmest one. They all lived up the street, and he'd known them most of his life, but he had a feeling what this was about. So he stepped out onto the porch, closing the door behind him.

"Okay, so *why* are you here?"

"I think you know *exactly* why I'm here: that stunt you pulled on my sister last summer."

"That wasn't a stunt—"

"Bullshit!" Sal stepped closer to him, and again, the anger radiating off him came as a total surprise. Sal wasn't even the bulldog of her brothers. *What had Sofie told him really happened?* "You knew the moment you invited her back to your house what your plans were."

"No, I didn't. I just—"

"Yes, you did!" Sal's raised voice, startling Brandon further, and he hoped this conversation wouldn't wake his dad. "You knew damn well that because of Angel, Alex, and me she'd never been put in that kind of predicament." Moving even closer, Sal got right in his face. "You took advantage of my sister, motherfucker, and I swear to God you're lucky it's not Angel or Alex here having this conversation with you. But know this: just because I'm not doing to you what they wanted to do doesn't mean I won't. It's in the past now, and even so, I'm here instead of them because if I'd let one of them do this, you'd end up in the hospital and I'd be bailing them out by the time this was all over. I don't know how long you're in town this time, but get this straight, Billings. You get one warning. One. You stay the fuck away from Sofie, or I'm coming after you personally."

"Sal, I swear to you—"

"I don't wanna hear it." Sal said, already walking away. "I don't give a shit what your reasons were. Bottom line is she told you she was in a relationship. So you knew what you were doing wasn't right, but you did it anyway."

"Does she feel this way too?"

Sal turned around at the bottom of the porch steps. "Do yourself a favor, and forget about what my sister thinks about *anything* where you're concerned. She knows I'm down here right now, and she knows after today your ass *will* stay away from her or you'll be answering to me."

Brandon watched Sal walk away, knowing full well he meant every word. Even before he'd come back to this godforsaken neighborhood with all the memories of his fucked childhood, the reality of knowing he never had a shot at the only girl who'd ever pulled him out of his bitter existence had been a tough pill to swallow. He knew this was the final nail in that coffin. Not only did he have to finally accept that he and Sofie would never be but her brothers were making him out to be a monster who took advantage of her.

He walked back in the house, closing the door a little harder than he should. Fuck Sofie and her brothers! He'd never given a shit what any of them thought of him, and he wouldn't start now.

~~~

Finally, Brandon's mother gave up trying to coax him out of his room. He swallowed down another swig of good ole Jack Daniels straight from the bottle, and Brandon's mind repeated the same thing it'd been repeating for the last hour. He'd been sitting there, reflecting on his miserable life on that New Year's Eve. The only home he'd ever known, aside from the ones he'd lived in since he enlisted, was being sold. In less than a week, he'd be moving away for good. The father he'd lived to impress his entire life, and never had until just recently, had only a few months, maybe weeks, to live. He and his mother would be alone soon as he'd wished for so many years growing up; only it wasn't what he wanted now. Damn it.

He'd finally proven to that man that he was worthy of his love. His dad had finally said the words he'd yearned to hear his entire life. *I'm proud of you, son.* And now he was dying? This was bullshit!

He'd never been one to cower down, no matter how bad things got. And no matter how fucking unfair his life had always been, he wasn't one to feel sorry for himself, but in the last few days, he'd been close to breaking.

The image of Sofie's beautiful face came to him, reminding him just how unfair life really was. The kiss they shared last summer hadn't been *just* a kiss, and he couldn't stop wondering how different things might've been if he'd just taken it slower.

Growing up, Sofie was the only one, aside from his mother, who'd shed a little light on his wretched existence. His senior year they'd grown close. He lived for that one hour each day he got to spend with her in his Geometry class. Being a loner his whole life, because he dared not get close to anyone who might ask him about his personal life, he'd never made a bond with anyone—until Sofie.

Senior year he'd been certain he felt something from her—seen it in her eyes when they spoke all through class. She felt what he'd been feeling.

But she was too young, and his loser ass was in no way good enough for her. Besides that, she'd been, and apparently still was, surrounded by her three older, ridiculously overprotective brothers, who would make sure he knew it. He never forgot her, not even when he left to the Marines for years. He thought of her the whole time, thought of what might've been. So last summer when he came home on his leave, he'd decided since she was older and he'd made such an about-face with his life he'd go for it. He was determined to prove to her and her brothers that he was worthy of her.

Seeing her for the first time in years had been breathtaking. She was even more beautiful than he'd remembered. Then she dropped the bomb. He was too late. She was already in a relationship. It made sense too, who she'd ended up with. Eric was her brother's best friend since they were all kids. He'd had access to being around her by default all those years. Of course the guy had staked his claim on her the moment she was allowed to date.

Not only had Eric always had a better chance because of his friendship with her brothers he had something else—he was Hispanic. Brandon didn't think Sofie or her brothers were racist against white folk or anything, but he'd seen it all through high school. Girls like Sofie tended to stick to their own kind. Her family was very traditional. At all the parties they'd thrown all year long, there had been mariachi bands playing traditional Spanish music. Hell they owned and ran a

Mexican restaurant. If her family had a choice between the rich college Hispanic guy they'd known and trusted all their lives and the loner white boy from that house up the street where the cops were often called for domestic disturbances as a suitor for their little princess, naturally Eric was the hands-down winner.

Still, even as she'd told him about her and Eric, Brandon was convinced he saw something deep within her. There was something still there. He'd seen it in those big beautiful eyes and felt it when he'd finally kissed her last summer. She'd been as willing as he was. That's why a few days after Sal's visit he'd followed her to the beach where she ran. He had to make sure she didn't believe the bullshit her brothers were trying to feed her now.

He'd gone there with a tiny bit of hope. Maybe if he got the chance he had last summer to get close to her, he could do it differently. He'd take it slower this time. He was certain he saw the possibility of her falling in love with him—the possibility that maybe he could convince her to leave Eric for him. It would be worth not reenlisting and staying here to fight for that chance. If he thought there was even the faintest hope, he'd do it in a heartbeat. So he'd offered to apologize to her brothers and to Eric—try and get on their good side so that he could at least have a chance.

Even though she assured him she never told her brothers he took advantage of her, that it was the conclusion they came to on their own, she did agree with her brothers that what she and Brandon had done was wrong, a mistake, and that he needed to stay away from her now. But her response to him wanting to try to make amends with Eric and her brothers had left him once again with uncertainty and a bit of optimism.

"The damage is done, Brandon. We had a chance to be friends, and we blew it. Eric was actually okay with me running with you until . . ."

As tiny as it was, Brandon was still clinging to that glimmer of hope—hope that maybe she was regretting having blown their chance as much as he was.

Taking another swig of the whisky, Brandon pondered that. Maybe if he told her how he felt about her, she would admit to her forbidden feelings as well. Was her response her way of cryptically trying to tell him she blew it too?

We blew it.

"We blew it," he whispered bitterly.

But would she be saying that if she knew how he really felt? Would she be so quick to dismiss any further chance if he told her?

He sat up, his head spinning a little, and he laughed stupidly then immediately frowned. How the hell was he supposed to tell her now when he had to sneak around and follow her like a creeper just to have a conversation with her? Even she had cut him short the other day at the beach.

Flinging the pocket knife he'd been flipping open and shut across the room, he stood up. Life sucked! Out of nowhere, Sal's words suddenly slammed into him. *Stay the fuck away from Sofie, or I'm coming after you personally.*

"Fuck no!" He took another swig of from the near empty bottle. "No, Sal. I won't stay away from her, not until I tell her how I feel!"

He set the bottle down on his desk and charged out the door. The entire hallway moved from side to side as he walked through it.

"Where are you going?" His mother's anxious eyes searched his.

"To see a friend," he said, walking past her.

"Brandon, you're drunk!"

For some reason that made him laugh. "Yeah, I guess I am."

"You shouldn't go out like this." His mother warned.

"Don't worry. I'm not driving," he said as he pushed through the front door.

The cool fresh air hit him like smelling salts, and he shook his head. Until that moment, he hadn't realized how buzzed he really was. Even drunk he knew this was a *bad* idea, but he continued his long strides with even more conviction. The entire cul-de-sac where Sofie lived was packed with cars. Of course, he expected nothing less. At every party her family had ever had, they'd had a ton of people. A New Year's party for them would be huge.

There were a few men just outside her front door as he walked up the circular driveway. He recognized Sarah, Sofie's brother Angel's girl, tying balloons around the mailbox out front, so he approached her.

"S-sarah."

She turned, and he actually saw the color in her green eyes pale. "Brandon?"

"Can you get S-sofie for me? I need to talk to her."

She shook her head. "She's not here." Turning to the front door, she glanced back at Brandon, quickly lowering her voice. "You shouldn't be here, Brandon."

He knew this wouldn't be easy, but he was determined. "I know she's here." His struggle to keep from slurring was pissing him off. "You guys are having a party. Where else would she be? Can you . . .? Can you just get her for me? I—" The sidewalk suddenly shifted underneath his feet, and he stumbled sideways but recovered quickly. "I *need* to talk to her before I leave."

"I'm telling you the truth. She's at the restaurant." She gasped, looking behind him. Just as he turned, he saw Angel turn back toward the garage. "He almost saw you. You better go. I'm serious. They're all here, and they *do not* want you around Sofia."

"I'm not leaving until I talk to her." Sarah's eyes opened wide, and she shook her head. "They can't do this, Sarah. When I leave, it's forever. There are some things I need to say to her first."

Her eyes looked even more anxious now, and she continued to speak in her lowered voice. "This is *so* not the time or place—"

The front door slamming against the wall as it was pushed open made Sarah flinch and got their attention. As usual, Sofie's hotheaded brother Alex looked incensed as he charged down the porch steps. "Why the fuck are you here, Billings?" he demanded, his hands already fisted at his sides.

Brandon stood his ground. He was sure it was the alcohol, but seeing her larger-than-life raging brother charge toward him with no hesitation and knowing that he'd no doubt be in a world of pain soon didn't stop him from speaking up. "I wanna to talk to S-Sofie."

"You're out of your mind!" Alex sped up.

Brandon shook his head. "I won't leave until—"

Alex's fist hit him just under the eye, and he stumbled back. "You won't leave?" Alex roared as he landed another fist to Brandon's mouth, making him fall back onto the hood of the parked car just in front of Sofie's house. "You think I'm letting you anywhere near my sister, asshole?"

Brandon blinked, shaking his head again. He'd always thought the expression "seeing stars" was just that, an expression. But he was literally seeing stars or bright specs flashing as he continued to shake his head again, blinking as he tried to clear his sudden double vision. Just as his vision was coming together and he could see straight, he noticed the amount of people who'd poured out of Sofie's house. Sal, Angel, and some of the other men who were out there now held Alex back, but he could see it was a struggle.

"Get out of here, Brandon!" Sal yelled as Alex nearly came loose.

Even with the metallic-like taste of blood in his mouth, Brandon knew he was asking for it by staying, but he wasn't leaving, not until he got his chance to talk to her. "I won't leave!" he yelled, holding himself up against the car. "I wanna see Sofie!" He slurred, pounding on the hood of the car and pointed at the house. "Get her out here!" He turned up to the window on the second floor he knew was hers. "S-sofie!"

Alex came loose suddenly, and Brandon heard Alex's mom cry out.

"Lo va a matar!" she shrieked. *"Paren lo!"*

"God damn it, Alex!" Sal reached out for Alex with both hands. "He's not worth it!"

Alex grabbed Brandon by the throat, squeezing so hard Brandon's ability to breathe was instantly blocked.

"She's damn right. I am gonna kill him!" Alex growled as he slammed Brandon down against the car.

Between Sal, Angel, and several of the other men there, they finally pulled Alex off Brandon, and he held on to the car for dear life, gasping for air.

"Ya pues, hijo! Calmado!" Alex's dad tried in vain to calm him as they all held him back.

As Brandon continued to gasp and cough, he looked up at Alex. "H-hit me." He gasped. "Hit me all you want!"

"You see. He wants me to!" Alex yelled, trying to get loose as they pulled him further away.

"I won't leave until I talk to her," Brandon said, rubbing his neck.

This time he said it with a little less conviction because he was beginning to feel as if he might pass out. Sal said something to Sarah, who rushed into the house.

The hope that maybe Sal had told Sarah to go get Sofie was squashed with the next words out of Sal's mouth. "It's not happening. Look around, Brandon." Sal pointed at his brothers and everyone else out there. "Do you really think you're gonna get to talk to her?"

"Like hell he is," Alex yelled.

Brandon glanced around. It wasn't just Sofia's family out there anymore. Everyone who lived in her cul-de-sac was out in their front yards, watching the spectacle. Then he looked up the street and saw his mom standing there in tears with her hand over her mouth. Brandon's shoulders slumped in defeat. As much as he felt like looking Sal in the eyes and telling him that he *would* talk to Sofie before he left, he wouldn't give Sal another reason to make his mom cry.

Even as calm as Sal was acting compared to Alex and as drunk as Brandon still felt, he'd sobered up enough to know saying something like that to him right now would land another fist on his already aching face. Some of the other guys in her family looked as if they were being held back now too. Brandon couldn't care less about the physical pain. If his mother weren't standing there, he'd gladly get pummeled just for the satisfaction of being able to tell all these fuckers he wasn't giving up.

Pushing himself away from the car, he stumbled on his first steps.

"Brandon," Sal said as he walked by him, his voice slightly lower and calmer now. Brandon didn't turn to him, but he did stop. "Do *not* come back. You hear me? Stay the hell away from Sofia if you know what's best for you."

With a humorless chuckle, Brandon continued to walk but said nothing. Both Angel and Alex yelled out similar threats, but Brandon was done listening. They couldn't keep him from her forever.

CHAPTER TWO

Waiting by the pharmacy for his dad's meds, Brandon stood there, feeling numb. When he'd taken the emergency leave to come home, he'd known his dad was bad, but he had no idea things had progressed this much.

His parents hadn't even realized it either. When they put the house up for sale, the plan was they'd all move to Georgia together. Using the money they got from their astronomically-priced California home, Brandon would buy a house in Georgia with cash. His mother would live off whatever was left from the sale and his dad's pension. Considering the home prices in Georgia, there'd be plenty of money left over. Now his dad's condition had taken such a turn the doctors said he was too ill to travel. The meds Brandon was picking up for him today were the last he'd ever pick up from a pharmacy for him because in a few days his dad would be admitted to a hospice where he'd live out the rest of what was left of his life.

Brandon wouldn't even be there, since there was no way to know how long for sure his dad would be around and his leave was only temporary. Already strings had to be pulled to get a leave during the holidays on such short notice.

His reaction to seeing his dad's condition decline so rapidly was not what he had expected. Brandon was certain he'd never felt his heart so heavy, not even through all he'd been through as a child. He'd always been able to just hold it all in and suck it up for his mom's sake. She was going through enough as it was. She didn't need to be brought down any lower by seeing his pain and fear.

He was determined, like all those times growing up, to be strong for his mom's sake. Even though he'd been determined on New Year's Eve to see and talk to Sofie, in the last few days, watching his dad deteriorate before his eyes, he needed to focus now on his parents. He needed to get his dad situated in a hospice before he left. The house needed to be sold because his dad wasn't going to be around for long. Then he needed to step up and look after his mom as his dad had asked him to when he could still hold a conversation without going into an agonizing fit of coughing.

It was all he was focusing on now, even though a small stubborn part of him still wished he could've talked to Sofia one last time.

His number was called, and Brandon stepped up to pay for his father meds. He stared at the pharmacist as the man gave him some brief instructions, but Brandon barely heard anything he said. He paid and walked numbly through the store.

The moment he saw her car he froze. Sofie pulled into a parking spot and got out of her car. Brandon walked back into the store, not even sure what he'd say or how he'd approach her. All he knew was she was alone and this could be his last chance ever to speak with her.

He stood behind one of the magazine racks so she wouldn't see him immediately and watched as she walked in and passed him. Watching, he waited until she'd stopped somewhere. When he saw her stop in the shampoo aisle, he was hit with brief reminder of how good her hair had smelled that day he kissed her. He'd come up from behind her, and, aside from how incredible it felt to have her body pressed against his, it was the first thing he'd noticed.

Gulping, he walked toward her slowly. The closer he got, the more he knew exactly what he wanted her to know. After his drunken fiasco in front of her entire family, he knew if things weren't impossible between them before, they were now. But he still had to tell her.

"Hey, Sof,"

The moment she looked up at him she flinched. "Brandon!" Those beautiful eyes that had once smiled at him so warmly stared at him completely alarmed before looking around. "Did you follow me?"

"No, I was on my way out when I saw you pull in."

"I can't be around you. You have to understand—"

I know, Sof," he said, cutting her off because he didn't want to hear about her being so fucking forbidden to him anymore. "I just hoped I could speak with you before I left. Do you have a few minutes so we could go somewhere more private?"

"No!" She practically gasped.

Looking into her eyes this close again did something to him. She'd been the only one who could elicit these kinds of feeling in him. But now he felt something else—tortured. Any hope he had with her was gone. Yet he still needed her to hear what he had to say so he could just let it out and it wouldn't be inside him anymore, tormenting him.

He glanced around, feeling desperate, and an emotion so unfamiliar began to overwhelm him. "Can you give me a second then, here?"

Sofia stared at him, still looking very apprehensive. "Make it fast."

His emotions nearly betrayed him before he spoke, but he held it together and told her. "My old man is dying."

The look of apprehension on her face was immediately replaced with that of surprise then complete sympathy. Brandon told her all about his father's lung cancer and how they'd be selling the house. Then he apologized for all the troubles he'd caused her and grief he put her family through on New Year's Eve.

She didn't comment on his apology; instead, she stared at him, her eyes completely distraught, and shook her head. "I'm so sorry, Brandon. I had no idea."

He explained he was just there to pick up his old man's meds, showing her the bag, but that he was glad he'd run into her because there was more he needed to tell her.

Sofie stared at the bag of meds for a moment then back at him a bit confused. "Tell me what?"

It felt wrong telling her right there in the middle of a drug store. "Are you sure we can't go somewhere else to talk?"

"No way, Brandon," she said immediately, and he knew there was no way she was going to budge.

He'd have to tell her here or forever hold it in. "I'm in love with you, Sof."

The moment he heard his whispered words he knew he'd made a mistake because he had to swallow back the giant-sized boulder in his throat that had been building the entire past week as he watched his dad slowly withering away. But it was too late now. It was too late to take it back, so he held it together, determined to finish. "I thought I was in high school. Last summer only confirmed it. I almost didn't re-enlist because of that kiss."

Her eyes welled up, but she said nothing. She didn't have to. Her shaking head was enough, but the expression of pity on her face was just another blow to his already aching heart.

"Don't worry. I know it's impossible. I just needed to tell you before I left." He swatted the one fucking tear that escaped the corner of his eye away. "I needed to say it to you if only once. I'm glad I got the chance." He didn't wait for her to respond. He couldn't. He had to get out of there *now*, but he couldn't resist the urge to touch her just one last time, so he reached out and squeezed her shoulder. "Good-bye, Sof."

That was it. He couldn't stand there for even another moment and look into those stunned eyes, eyes that said without a doubt he'd been completely wrong. She'd never felt for him what he he'd been so delusional enough to think she might.

Pushing through the front doors of the store, he nearly growled. He was infuriated that he'd been so close to losing it in front of her, something he'd vowed years ago he'd never do, not when he'd had to watch his mother suffer at the mercy of his father's rage, not when his dad turned that same rage on him, not even when he found out his father was dying, and certainly not over feeling his heart crushed by the only girl he'd ever had feelings for.

Nothing had ever been so clear and so fast. He felt like a complete idiot now. All this time, he'd secretly been banking on the possibility that, deep inside, what he thought he felt from Sofie last summer had been real. Even when she'd taken it back just before he left again, making it clear she'd only been curious, his delusional heart was convinced she was just covering up—clearing her conscience.

The painful truth had never been so infuriatingly clear. She'd only been curious about what it'd be like to be with someone like him, someone she'd never take seriously in real life. So she'd used the opportunity with his desperate ass to indulge that forbidden curiosity.

Throwing his dad's meds on the passenger seat, he banged on the steering wheel. He'd almost done what he held back from doing all his life—something he'd promised his dad he wouldn't even do at his funeral—for a girl who never gave a shit about him. He'd almost broken down.

He finally understood what his father had meant all those years. That kind of deep emotion—the kind he felt suffocating his heart at that moment—was sacred. It was something that should remain deep inside. *No one* had a right to know you were feeling it but yourself. Showing it was a sign of weakness. That's exactly how he felt at that moment, like the weakest most pathetic idiot on the planet. At that moment, he vowed once again he'd never let anyone—no matter what—witness this side of him again.

~~~

It wasn't even a week after he'd reported back to Georgia when he got the call. His dad had passed, and just like that, Brandon was back on a plane to attend the services. As expected, not too many people showed up. His father had never made many friends, and as hardened and difficult as he'd become over the years, any acquaintances he did have once upon a time had distanced themselves from him long ago.

Brandon took solace in the fact that he and his dad had finally begun to actually have a real father-son relationship, even though his dad had passed too soon afterward. He and his mom would move to Georgia permanently and start all over again. Maybe now he could rekindle that bond he once had with her. His mom had been the only one in his life to ever show him love. He'd felt it from her through and through. Brandon was determined to turn his life around—take away all the negativity that had built up all these years and live a normal happy life. Now that it was just he and his mom, he knew that could happen. She'd been waiting for this change as long as he had.

Days after the services, they somberly finished packing up the U-Haul truck with all their belongings. Brandon would be driving it across the country. He wished that on such a long drive he and his mother could be in the same car. It would be a perfect way to start getting to know each other once again—talk about their new life and the neighborhoods they'd be shopping for their new home—but his mother would be driving their mini-van across the country.

Brandon had been tempted to rent a trailer and just haul the van as well, not just because he was looking to really talking to his mom but because she'd always been a nervous driver. The longest drive she'd ever made was just over two hours up north to Los Angeles. Still, she insisted she'd be fine.

"We'll just take it nice and slow," she smiled, squeezing his arm before getting in the van.

She wasn't kidding about the nice and slow part. Eight hours later they'd barely made it a little past Tucson. He had a week to get back to the base. At this rate, it was going to take them twice that long.

As the clerk at the hotel they'd be staying at for the night looked up the room, Brandon leaned against the counter. "Maybe I should rent that trailer, Ma."

"Don't be silly. I'm fine."

Brandon shook his head. "It's not that. I think it would speed up the trip. I only have until Monday to report back. At the rate we're going, it'll be at least Thursday before we get there."

"You think so?" His mother frowned. "We had a bad start today. Tomorrow we'll get up super early and see how far we get. If you still think we have to by the end of the night, we can rent one."

Exhaling, he gave in with a nod. After getting their things in their room, they left again to grab something to eat. During dinner, his mother told him about his father's last dying wish. "Aside from the hope that someday you'd forgive him, he wanted grandchildren."

Chuckling humorously, Brandon shook his head as he scooped up a spoonful of mashed potatoes and ate them. He wouldn't say it because he was determined to leave that darkness behind him. Saying that was a joke, considering what a rotten father his dad had been his whole life, would definitely darken the mood. His father had taught him nothing about being a man much less a father. While he'd be eternally grateful to his superiors in the Marines who had showed him what honor and integrity were and had turned him into the man he was now, it wasn't enough, not enough to erase the only example of a father he'd ever had. It didn't take away that his father's blood ran through his veins and the fact that he may very well turn into him someday.

"He said he knows you never really got to experience what a bond between a father and a child should really be, so he wants you to experience it with your own child."

Fighting the bitterness he felt over that statement, he almost gave in to retorting like he wanted to. "Yeah, well just 'cause he fu—" He cleared his throat, taking a deep breath, and decided to start over instead. "I don't think that'll happen, but—"

"Why not?" His mother touched his hand and smiled weakly. "I'd love grandchildren too. And honey," she paused until he'd look her in the eyes, "despite what you remember of your father, he did have a heart. I know it's very hard for you to understand why he was the way he was. He had so many personal demons he was fighting, but he did love you. I know what you're thinking, Brandon." She squeezed his arm. "You *are not* your father. No matter how bad things got, you were always such a loving little boy, so mindful and sweet. Remember how you used to tend to me when I wasn't well?"

Her eyes dropped in pain, and Brandon knew why. He squeezed his hand into a fist. All those times he'd tended to her weren't because she wasn't well. Most of those times, she was hurt—injured because of his asshole dad. As if she'd read his mind, she looked up and patted his arm.

"Regardless of why you were tending to me, Brandon, whether it was because I was banged up or was nursing a cold, you were still so attentive and looked after me so thoroughly. Do you remember how you used to bring me flowers from the backyard every time?"

Brandon gnashed his teeth. He couldn't even look at her now. Yes, he remembered, so he nodded but said nothing.

"Look at me right now, Brandon," she said.

He didn't want to, but he finally did. His mother wasn't that old, but those eyes had lived through so much they were worn and tired beyond her years. Lowering her hand, she undid his tightened fist and slid her hand into his then looked up at him again. "Your father never did any of that. He didn't feel things like you did. I want you to remember that always. You have a wonderful heart capable of loving and feeling the things he never could admit he did. You'll make a wonderful husband and daddy. I know it."

Swallowing hard, Brandon looked away from her hopeful eyes and moved his food around on his plate. As much as he'd like to believe that, he just couldn't. Even though he'd hated his father for so many years for being so cold and having such an impenetrable exterior, a part of Brandon knew he was a lot like his father. He hadn't shed a tear when the man died, and something told him he never would again. It's why he wanted to start all over. He didn't want to become his father, but he knew he'd never change enough, and he wouldn't put another human being through what his father had put him and his mother through. But for the sake of avoiding the deep shit he had no intention of getting into on this trip, he shook his head.

"I don't think it's in the cards for me, Ma." He shrugged. "I'd just as soon concentrate on my career in the Marines— the only thing I've ever been good at. Everything else in my life so far . . ." He shook his head, swallowing in the bitterness. "Having my own family is not something I anticipate ever happening."

His mom was silent for few moments before picking up her water glass and drinking. "I think Shakespeare said it best when he said, 'What's past is prologue.'"

Brandon didn't look at her. Growing up reading books and poetry had been his escape. He'd read enough Shakespeare to know what that meant, but it didn't apply to his past. His was too fucked up.

"It's like fate, son. The past has set the stage for what's to come."

Again he laughed humorlessly. "Then that's pretty fucked to think about, considering what my past has been like."

His mom stared at him for a moment. The pained expression said it all, and he knew what she was thinking before she even said it. "I know I failed you—"

"No," he said, shaking his head and throwing his napkin down on his plate. "Let's not start with this again. You did your best. He was just too damn unpredictable and dangerous. You were only trying to protect me. I get it, Mom, okay? You stuck around because you were afraid he'd come after you and in the process hurt me. We both know it's what he would've done. Look," he said before she could start again. "I don't know." He shrugged, not wanting to look her in the eyes, so he stared down at his glass of water. "Maybe it will happen someday. I'll stay open-minded for you, okay?" he lied. "If I ever get the chance, I'll take it." He glanced up at her still very remorseful eyes. "Okay? Just promise me you'll stop blaming yourself for the past. You're right." He lifted his glass in the air to make a toast. "To our fresh start and to forgetting about the past."

"Yes." She squeezed his hand. "Always remember, Brandon, you had no control over what happened in the past. Arm yourself with the lessons that your past—good and bad—has given you, and take control of your future. It's time to leave all that behind and move onward, son." She smiled, lifting her glass quickly, but even seeing her immediate change in mood, he couldn't summon so much as the tiniest of smiles. He forced himself to at least not frown. "To our bright future," she said, clinking his glass.

Satisfied with their toast, his mother thankfully changed the subject after taking a sip of her water. She started talking about the neighborhoods in Georgia she'd seen online. This was a much better topic. He'd rather think of their new beginning.

Just as she promised she would, Brandon's mom was up before dawn. "Let's get moving, sunshine" she said, holding up her cup of coffee and smiling. "I didn't make you one because I know you hate the stuff."

Brandon nodded, grabbing their things and heading out. They were off to a better start this time. Yesterday, his mom had jumped on the freeway heading in the wrong direction, and it was miles before the next exit where she could get off and they could turn around. Maybe this did mean they'd make it there on time after all.

Everything was going smoothly for the first fifteen minutes until his mom swerved suddenly, and Brandon saw she'd blown a tire.

"Fucking great," he said through his teeth, looking into the rearview mirror.

He turned on his own hazard lights and followed closely behind as she made her way onto the tight shoulder. She made it there, but it took Brandon a few more minutes to park his much larger truck in a way that he wasn't sticking out into traffic. He glanced up at his mom as he continued to maneuver the big ass U-Haul, but he had to wait until there were no cars coming so he could twist out then back onto the shoulder. His mom stayed put in the car as he mentally ordered her to. She'd be no help coming out anyway.

Groaning at the thought of having to take everything that was so tightly packed in the back of the minivan so he could pull the spare out he decided right there he was done humoring his mom. They were getting a trailer as soon as he replaced her tire. He didn't have time for all this shit.

He did a double take when he saw the driver's-side door open and his mom start to get out. "Stay in the van!" he yelled, motioning with his hands, but his window was still closed, and she obviously hadn't heard him. "God damn it," he mumbled as his finger hit the button to lower the window.

Just as the window went down, he was startled by a truck's loud horn as it flew by him so close it shattered the side mirror loudly. Brandon lifted his arms and hands up in front of him in reaction. Between his arms, he saw as his mother, who'd already stepped out of the van, didn't even have a chance to react. She and the entire open minivan door were literally blown away by the truck's massive force.

~~~

"I don't need it, sir." Brandon stood at attention in front of Master Sergeant Hatch, who sat behind a desk.

Hatch stood now. "Son, you gathered your mother's remains in pieces just days after burying your father. Then you came straight here without taking a single day off."

"Sir, thanks to the Marines, I was prepared for that and much worse. And there was nothing I could do during the investigation but report to duty until it was over. Her remains were then cremated and sent to me. I didn't need to take time off."

Brandon wouldn't look at him, but he knew the sergeant must be staring at him as if he were one cold son of a bitch.

"They were the only family you had, and as far as I know, you have no close friends. You have to be feeling something, and you can't keep all of it inside you. It's not healthy."

The sergeant paused, but Brandon wouldn't respond to that. He felt nothing, and because of that, he was convinced now he'd already turned into his father. He was certain his old man would consider therapy weak too.

"You've got to let some of what you're feeling out, or it'll only build until you finally blow."

Brandon stared straight ahead, both arms to the side of him. Hatch had no way of knowing that blowing up—

breaking down—was not anything Brandon would ever do. If witnessing his mother torn apart then walking around gathering the pieces of her body hadn't broken him, he knew nothing ever would. "Sir, I'm fine. I don't need therapy."

He heard the sergeant take a deep breath then sit back down. "Have a seat."

Taking the seat across the sergeant's desk, Brandon saw the displeasure on the older man's face. "It hasn't affected your work, so I can't force you into therapy, but you will be evaluated." He lifted the folder in front of him and motioned it toward Brandon. "You have all the qualifications to enter DI school, and I've already signed off the go-ahead to start all the preliminaries, but you'll have to pass a psych evaluation before you're accepted. Now are you sure you wouldn't like to speak to someone before going through that? If you don't pass the eval, you don't get in. They don't give a shit that you just lost both your parents. You need to be one hundred percent ready, both physically and mentally, to get in."

"I'm sure, sir," Brandon said without hesitation.

The sergeant exhaled, pressing his lips together as he shook head. He wrote something in Brandon's file before handing it to him, wishing him luck then excusing him.

As Brandon walked out the door, he knew he had to get accepted. Failure was not an option. He was born to be a drill instructor, and since the Marines had been the only thing he'd been proud of—never let him down—this was what he'd pour his heart into instead: The Corps.

CHAPTER THREE

Regina

Then

Grasping on to the cold handle of the gun, Regina's body shuddered uncontrollably. Before tonight, she'd never even held a gun much less used one. Crouched down in a cold corner, she rocked back and forth, and the sobs came louder and louder.

Her entire body began to shake as thoughts of her family came to mind and what they'd say when they found out. Her father had a weak heart. Would this kill him? They'd all be devastated, no doubt.

"Why!" she screamed at the top of her lungs. "Why, Ryan? Why did you have to be so fucking selfish?"

Staring at her bloody knuckles, she chuckled grimly. All she'd wanted to do was break a few things to help ease the anger, and she couldn't even do that without hurting herself. A few things like some dishes and then a bottle had quickly turned into her smashing every piece of furniture she owned. She stood up sloppily, holding on to the walls for support. The blood on her hands was smeared against the expensive blossom branch tile she'd taken so long to pick out, and now all of this meant nothing. The anger inundated her again. "This is all your fault! Do you hear me?!" She held the gun up over her head. "You did this! You! I hate you! I hate you! I hate you!"

Falling against the wall, she pressed her face against the cold tile and sobbed. Her entire face was one slobbery mess. Never in a million years would she have guessed she'd become this pathetic person. *Never.* Yet here she was holding the gun that would soon seal her fate. That she'd had succumb to such weakness riddled her with shame. Yet this is what it'd all come down to.

The knock on the front door was completely unexpected, and she froze. She waited, and then there were more knocks.

"Mrs. Brady?"

Recognizing her neighbor Quinn's voice, Regina squeezed her eyes shut.

"No!" she muffled her own whispers against her fist. "Go away."

He knocked again. "Is everything all right? I heard you screaming, and Mrs. Shimley said she heard the sound of things breaking and crashing in there earlier. Are you okay? Do you need me to call someone for you?"

Still sobbing, Regina slid her body down the wall until she hit the ground with a thud. She couldn't even put two words together. She was crying so uncontrollably.

"Mrs. Brady, please answer me, or I'll assume you need help."

If he came in now, he'd see what she'd done. He'd try to stop her and ruin everything. The sound of the pounding on the door was now like a body slamming against it, so she scurried herself off the floor and rushed into the front room. Her thoughts were spinning. She couldn't let him in!

Something slammed against her door again, and the third time, the door crashed open. She stood there frozen, staring at a stunned Quinn breathing heavily. They stared at each other for a few silent moments, and then his eyes began to quickly look around the room. They opened wider and wider as he took it all in. She saw the moment his eyes noticed the gun in her hand, and she began to lift it, her hand shaking violently.

He shook his head, his eyes nearly bulging out now in terror. "Mrs. Brady—Regina—don't shoot, please!"

CHAPTER FOUR

Brandon
Now
Ronald Reagan National Airport
Washington D.C.

Taking one last look at the flight status board, Brandon frowned. As frustrating as it was, he was at the very least grateful that his flight still read delayed and not cancelled like so many of the others. That was one thing he wasn't going to miss about the East Coast: this frigid weather. He may not be thrilled about having to go back to San Diego, but the warm sunny weather was one thing he'd welcome with pleasure. He'd already checked ahead, and even in January, the temperature there was in the sixties. He thought about how he actually considered turning down the promotion just to avoid having to go back and possibly face his demons. He was glad now he'd come to his senses and didn't allow the past to dictate his future. He'd earned this promotion, and nothing and no one was keeping him from it.

Glancing out the snow-laced windows, he shook his head. "Good riddance."

The line at the deli counter had shortened considerably since he first arrived, so he decided he may as well grab something to eat. He still had a five-hour flight ahead of him, and from experience, he knew, unless you were in first class, the in-flight food sucked ass.

The dark haired girl who stepped in line just before him nearly knocked over her very expensive looking carryon as she rolled it along too hastily. Her other hand was at her ear, where she held her phone. Brandon didn't know much about bag brands, but he could tell just by looking at it, it was expensive. Everything about her said expensive from her long leather coat to her high-heeled sleek city boots to the equally expensive purse that hung on her shoulder. The sunglasses that sat on top of her head alone probably cost more than his airline ticket. She even smelled expensive.

"No, Daddy, I'm fine." Her bracelets jingled as she reached out for a tray. "I have a car service picking me up at the airport, and I'm all set up in a condo when I get there. Don't worry." Brandon stared at the side of her face dryly. It figured the princess was well looked out for. "Yes, I'm meeting *abuelita* at Flemings for dinner tonight if I make it on time. My connector flight was delayed. I'm in D.C. right now."

Grabbing a tray, Brandon glanced around at the choices of chips he had to throw on it, trying to ignore the girl's annoying conversation with *Daddy*. She struggled to push the tray along while pulling her carryon and holding her phone at the same time. Cradling the phone between her shoulder and her chin, she looked up at the lady behind the counter who was waiting to take her order. "I'll have a chicken salad with no tomatoes or egg with light thousand island dressing and a Coke Zero."

"The salads are premade." The bored-looking lady held out a premade salad in a plastic container. "We only have regular thousand and Diet Pepsi."

"No, I already told Mom I'd look into buying a car when I got there." Princess glanced up at the lady behind the counter and held up a finger. "You can't just give me your car, and besides I don't drive stick shift." She glanced back at Brandon and offered an apologetic smile for holding up the line. "Daddy, let me call you back. I'm in line right now.

Okay. Okay." She smiled at the lady behind the counter then at Brandon again.

Brandon stared at her unsmiling, taking in the small details of daddy's little princess. The lip gloss that she wore was barely there but enough to accentuate her already plump lips. They were subtle and flawless, as were her well-manicured French-tipped nails. She had dark features: dark, thick, shiny, near-black hair that flowed down halfway to her elbow and dark lashes that draped over those big brown eyes. The fact that this grown woman was standing here talking to an obviously overbearing daddy and that she referred to her grandmother in Spanish brought back the annoying reminder of . . .

"Yes, I promise," she said, finally sounding as impatient as Brandon was beginning to feel. "Okay, bye, bye. I love you too."

She hung up, smiling crookedly at Brandon, who again offered no smile in return. Turning back to the lady behind the counter, she waved the salad away and glanced around. "Is there some place here I can get a salad made?"

The lady behind the counter pressed her lips together, taking the salad back. "You can try Gordon's," the lady said, and with that, she was done with the princess, moving on to Brandon. "What'll it be?"

Brandon put in his order for a turkey sub and an iced tea, not noticing which direction the princess had gone. He ate quietly, sitting on the floor near a window overlooking the runway, his back against the wall.

He was over being bitter about having to transfer back to a place he'd vowed he never return to. San Diego was a huge city, and the truth was just as in South Carolina where he'd been a DI for the past four years, he'd be spending most of his time on the base anyway. Whatever time he spent off the base he'd be sure to steer clear of La Jolla.

"Well, I was just gonna go back to the same gym I always went to."

Brandon glanced up to see the princess on her phone again, standing in front of a seat in one of the nearest rows of seats to him. He studied her for a moment as she removed her coat, revealing the rest of her long high-heeled boots. They went all the way up past her knees. What she wore under them—skin hugging leggings and a gray sweater that draped over her round but tight little ass and hips—said a lot about how much time she must spend at the gym.

As his eyes made it all the way up to the scarf around her neck and back to the full lips that had caught his eyes the first time, he noticed she was watching him watch her. The expression on her face was an amused one. Brandon was anything but amused. Her lips curved into a smile, and he looked away. Pulling himself up, he gathered his trash. He threw his military bag over his shoulder and walked away, annoyed that he'd given the pampered princess yet another reason to feel better about herself, as if a girl like her didn't already have enough reasons to feel superior to those around her.

~~~

A few days after Brandon arrived in San Diego, he was all set. They'd given him a week to relocate. Who needed a full week? His things along with his Jeep were delivered the day after he arrived, and his apartment was already set up before he got there. They'd offered to put him up in the NCO condo complex on base, but as he did in North Carolina, he preferred living off base. It was the only time he ever left the base, but living on base meant closer contact with some of his co-workers. Everyone who lived on base spoke of the base as a small town-like place where everyone was a close-knit military family. He wanted no part of that. All the relationships he'd ever made in the Marines were strictly professional. Having no emotional attachment to anyone, even his fellow Marine brothers, was how he liked it. He lived and breathed the Corps, and if he ever had to, he'd take a bullet for any of them any day. He respected them all, and they could trust he was absolutely dependable, but there was zero attachment.

On occasion back in North Carolina, he'd had a beer with some of them at the local watering hole, and they'd talked work and sports. Mostly he'd listen, adding little to the conversation. He was used to the jokes about him being a hard-ass. Some of the guys even tried breaking him out of the character they accused him of being in at all times, but it never happened. It never would because it wasn't an act. He just had no desire to open up to anyone and talk about his personal life. As he told them all, he didn't have much of a personal life, so there was nothing to talk about.

Now that he was at a new base, he already knew the invitations to have a beer with his "brothers" were going to be inevitable. But just like back at his old base, he didn't want his lack of socializing to do just the opposite of what it was supposed to do—keep the attention off his personal life. It seemed the more of recluse he was, the more mysterious and interesting he became to those around him.

Already, he'd only been there a few days, and the questions had started. He'd been asked twice by a couple of his superiors why he lived off base if he was single. "Why fight the traffic every morning when you could just be here already?"

Another one of the single DIs had questioned if there were other motives. "Is it so the chicks here don't see who you take home every night?" The DI had laughed when he'd also asked, "You don't want them comparing notes?"

This morning, he was meeting with the previous Gunnery Sergeant in charge of the platoons and lower ranking DIs that Brandon would now be in charge of. He wanted to touch base with Brandon and show him around the building he'd be calling home for the better part of his weekdays.

"It's been under construction for some time," First Sergeant Carter said. "When it's all over, there'll be a new building over there with a bridge that connects to this one and an underground tunnel that will connect both buildings as well." He pointed at the area in question as they walked around some of the construction work just outside the building they were headed into. "In the meantime, it's been a pain in the ass. Make sure you save anything you're working on often because even though they're supposed to tell us when they'll be shutting off the electricity for a few minutes, they don't always do. Some of us have learned the hard way that we should've backed up our shit more often."

Carter shook his head as he walked on before continuing. "Some of the engineers have set up camp inside the building. Letting them borrow a couple of offices and conference rooms in the building took up less room than bringing in a temp bungalow for them." He looked back at Brandon. "Get used to seeing civilians in civilian clothing coming in and out of here." The sergeant turned back to where they were headed but continued talking. "It's usually during the week, but they're all on strict orders to wear their photo ID badges at all times. So if you see anyone in here without one, feel free to question him. In fact," he glanced back at him very seriously, "you're supposed to. Civilians without photo ID are not allowed in this building at all. Those photo IDs make them the only exception."

Brandon nodded, following the sergeant into an elevator as he continued to talk. They got off on the second floor, and Brandon followed him once again through the long hallway. A couple of plain clothes men walked out of one of the doors, and Brandon took note of how the sergeant scrutinized them but kept walking as they both were wearing large photo IDs around their necks. Brandon took in what the IDs were supposed to look like for future reference. The door to the ladies' room next to the room the other men had walked out of opened, and a woman also dressed in a plain clothes skirt suit walked out. The clinking of her shoes that echoed through the stark hallway as she walked caught Brandon's attention. Not often did you hear that on the base. He glanced down to take a look and saw the high-heeled shoes she wore.

The shoes had obviously caught the attention of the sergeant too because he actually stopped and looked her up and down then focused on her ID badge for a moment. Brandon stopped also and waited for the sergeant to proceed. That's when he recognized her. She slowed, staring at the sergeant a bit perplexed. It was the princess from the airport in D.C. Her long hair was up in a twist today, and she wore glasses now, but there was no mistaking those eyes and those lips. *What the hell?*

Glancing down at her badge, he read her name: Regina Brady. Below it was the name of the engineering firm she was with, her title, the title of her project, and some numbers.

Apparently satisfied, the sergeant nodded at her and started walking again just as Brandon and Regina's eyes met. He'd been wearing his fatigues at the airport as well, so he figured if he recognized her so easily, even as different as she looked now, she'd easily recognize him too. Her eyes confirmed he was right as they brightened and she smiled. Brandon held her gaze for a moment, his deadpan expression unfazed, before turning away and walking off without a word.

When they were a bit further, the sergeant turned back to him again. "She must be new. I haven't seen her before."

Without comment, Brandon walked into the room where his desk awaited. There were two other desks there, also occupied by two other sergeants who quickly stood as Brandon and the sergeant walked in and saluted them. The sergeant introduced them as Staff Sergeant Rodriguez and Sergeant Evans. Evans was obviously younger than Brandon, but Rodriguez appeared to be the same age as he was. Brandon, like any other soldier, immediately took note that he outranked them both.

The sergeant went on, filling him in on the minor stuff he would've figured out on his own such as where the break room was and the list of added duties he'd be required to do on top of the usual ones, now that he'd been promoted to Gunnery Sergeant. He also told Brandon his box with all his office belongings would be delivered to him later. Brandon listened intently and respectfully, annoyed that his thoughts had gone back to the princess from the airport. He'd been certain that she was Hispanic. Brady? Then he remembered that she'd referred to her grandmother as *abuelita*. The last name could mean only one thing—she was married.

CHAPTER FIVE

Regina

Now

Week two of this boring ass assignment hadn't gotten any better. Regina missed the lavish projects she'd gotten in New York already. This would never live up to the excitement of working on sky scrapers and one-of-a-kind buildings like the Ronnet Museum she'd worked on early last year. She'd taken this transfer only because of its location. Now she wondered if she'd made a mistake.

She thought working on the west coast and living on the beach would be an exciting change, the change she needed. But the job was turning out to be so boring. Of course, she'd been notorious her entire life for having the worst luck ever. Her family and friends had labeled her the female Charlie Brown. They thought it was funny. It never failed. If something could go wrong at the most inopportune time to any of them, no one had to guess which one of them it would be. It was never anything real bad, or maybe her family wouldn't think it so funny, just frustrating, mistimed, or inconvenient things like always being the last to be served at a restaurant when in a group or the restaurant no longer serving the specific dessert she'd craved all the way there. On the airplane, she'd been stuck next to the chattiest person on the planet when all she'd wanted to do was sleep.

Taking a deep breath, Regina folded her arms in front of her as she went and stood by the window of her makeshift office. Her sister had been right. There were a ton of soldiers here, which meant major potential for meeting someone. But as usual, as her rotten luck would have it, she was stuck working on the side of the base where it was mostly basic training with brand new, way-too-young troops who seemed terrified of doing anything inappropriate that might get them in trouble like flirt or even talk to a civilian—that and a bunch of hardnosed drill instructors and their even harder superiors. So far, the only one who had caught her eye seemed to be the hardest of them all, the same one she caught staring at her at the airport in Washington D.C. He'd blown her smile off then and then again when she'd run into him a few days ago.

Because they were on the same flight to San Diego and he'd been wearing fatigues, she figured since she'd be working on the base there was a small chance she might run into him again. But she never imagined it would be this soon and certainly not that they'd be working in the same building. At the airport, she'd thought she'd imagined the look of distaste she'd picked up from him—distaste for her. She'd chalked it up to him having a bad day or something. Their flight had been delayed over two hours. Even she'd been irritated by that. And certainly there could be no reason for him to dislike her. He didn't even know her. But the other day, the way he'd looked at her was even worse. For whatever reason, the man found her repugnant. Of course, that made him all the more intriguing than when she'd first laid eyes on him at the airport.

Sighing, she walked away from the window and sat down in front of her desk. For all she knew, the guy was married. He was certainly good-looking enough. None of that mattered anyway. Her excitement about working on a base full of soldiers had all been an act, just as this entire last year had been. She pretended she was excited about meeting men and getting on with her life. Of course, her family would never know the truth. She'd never forgive herself if she were ever the cause of anything that might send either of her parents back into the hospital. Between her dad's bad heart, and her mom's high blood pressure, she didn't dare tell them.

The day dragged on as the previous days had, and she finally made her way out of her office, down the elevator, and out to her car. Hitting the ignition button with one hand, she checked her texts with the other then pulled off her name badge. The radio turned on along with the car. She was so engrossed in reading a text from her sister it took a few seconds for the song playing to register, but when it did, she froze.

Would you know my name, if I saw you in heaven?

Immediately choked up, she hit the off switch, but it was too late. She felt herself drowning fast in that overwhelming grief and despair she thought she'd made progress dealing with. Choking back the tears because she was not about to fall apart right there or go into hysterics as she knew she could very easily do, she took a deep breath, fighting the anguish that bathed her so quickly and mercilessly.

She tried to think of something, *anything* she could channel her thoughts into instead. Her therapist had instructed her to do just that at times like this when she thought she might lose it. So she breathed in deeply and began channeling. She thought of her work, the designs she'd presented to her subordinates today, but it wasn't working, so she thought of her plans for that evening. She'd be going to the gym later, and then it hit her. Her Fitbit, the pedometer she used around her wrist to count her steps, the battery had died today, and she left it hooked up to her computer, charging in her office.

Glad it seemed to be working because she was already grabbing her keychain and pushing the car start button off, she opened her door. Taking more deep breaths even as the tears continued to spill from her eyes, she could feel herself calming. It'd been months since the last time she'd broken down as she almost had today. She'd consider this progress. This was the first time she'd been able to fight it.

Knowing her face must be a mess, she didn't care. It was late, and there were few people still walking around. She reached the door of the building just as it opened, and out walked the guy from the airport, who she now knew was a sergeant up there in rank. He stopped when he saw her, and she stopped too. They faced off for a moment, and the sudden puttering of her heart surprised her. She wiped the tears from her face even more regretful now about her sudden outburst because she was certain she must look a mess. This close his deep blue eyes were even more amazing than she first thought. The long dark sheath of lashes that draped over his eyes as he blinked almost in slow motion nearly took her breath away.

For an instant so quick it was over almost as soon as she thought she saw it, there was the slightest softening of his hardened stare as she wiped her eyes again. But then it went rigid again.

She started to reach for the open door, but he didn't move. "You're not wearing your badge," he said as stoned-faced as ever. "I can't let you in."

"But," she tilted her head, pinching her brows, "you know I'm authorized—"

"Only if you're wearing your photo ID."

Regina smiled nervously. He *had* to be pulling her chain. "Are you serious?"

She didn't think his expression could go any more severe, but it did, and she knew now he was absolutely serious. "Those are the rules, ma'am."

Her mouth fell open for a moment, but she closed it quickly when she saw his eyes drop down to her open lips. "I just need to get something I forgot on my desk—"

"Without your ID, you're not allowed."

Chewing the inside of her cheek in frustration, she squeezed her hand around her keychain. She was tempted to ask him if he actually had something against someone he didn't even know or if he was really just this big of an asshole. Afraid somehow that might get her in trouble, she refrained.

"Fine," she said through her teeth. "I'll go get it from my car."

She spun around, stalking off to her car, and she wondered if he'd even be there when she got back, making her need to walk all the way back to her car a waste of time. To her surprise, but even more puzzling, she was pleased to see him standing right at the door, waiting for her. At least he hadn't made a fool of her, making her go back to get a badge she'd wouldn't have anyone to show.

Walking up the stairs, she looked him straight in those intense eyes that still gave her no clue what his damn problem with her was. Even as she got closer and he stared her down as she imagined he did to intimidate his recruits, she hated how damn good he was at it. The determination to continue to stare back at him without looking away was beginning to wane as she got closer. He held out his hand, and she shoved her badge into it, noticing that even as she pushed down his strong arm hadn't budged.

His eyes were still on hers even as he held the badge in his hand, and it made her gulp, but she refused to look away. Finally, he looked down at her badge and studied it. She glanced at the badge he wore—*Gunnery Sergeant Billings*—but turned away quickly when he lifted his eyes from her badge and looked into hers. His expression was completely unimpressed, even though her title as an engineer had the words "Senior" and "Lead" in them. At her age, that was almost unheard of, but then she shouldn't expect him to know that.

"Make sure you always have this on you, Mrs. Brady," he said, handing it back to her, offering not so much as a tiny smile in exchange for having made her walk all the way back to her car. Then he just walked away, leaving her standing there.

Seriously? Not even a goodnight or have a good evening? Regina was beginning to wonder if the man *ever* smiled. She stood there, not sure if she should be mad or happy that he successfully yanked her right out of her depressed mood because now she was *pissed*. *Who the hell did he think he was anyway?* He may be a high-ranking officer, but she was *not* in the Marines. She had her own superiors to answer to, and *he* wasn't one of them.

Feeling completely annoyed as she made her way quickly to her office, she now hoped she'd never run into him again. Unlike the past few days where the anticipation of seeing the mysterious sergeant again made her feel like a silly school girl, she now had no desire to be anywhere near his self-important ass ever again. He may have every right to talk down to his recruits, making them feel inferior to him, but he had no right to look at her or make her feel that way.

Armed with a sudden feeling of resolve, she grabbed her Fitbit from her computer and put it on. The next time she ran into *Sergeant Billings*, because she knew it was inevitable, she'd give him that same hard look he'd given her from the very beginning. The look that practically said just the sight of her left a bad taste in his mouth.

~~~

After working out last night, Regina had called her best friend, Janecia. She was the only childhood friend who hadn't drifted away over the years. In fact, she'd been her best friend for as long as she could remember. She'd even vacationed the last few years in New York and came out and stayed with Regina a week out of the year. She also made shorter visits often for weekend getaways. The girl loved New York. She'd been sorely disappointed that Regina had moved back because she'd hoped to move out there eventually. Janecia was also the only one who knew about Regina's secret, but even she didn't know the whole story. Regina was taking that to her grave. Only Quinn, Mrs. Shimley, and Regina's therapist knew the whole truth, and the only one Regina had any intention of ever reuniting with was the latter.

Regina had been in San Diego over a week now and was beginning to feel like a hermit, something she'd never been. She'd gone straight from her place to work to the gym and back to her place. Part of the deal she'd made with herself when she decided to move back home was to do what her therapist told her she *needed* to do—move on. Live again. She was still very young, and there was so much she had yet to experience. Despite her doubts that she could ever find the kind of love she once had, she knew she could, at the very least, enjoy other aspects of her life.

Because she enjoyed cooking, trying out new restaurants was one of her favorite treats. She and Janecia had visited The Gaslamp Quarter a few times when they were younger, and she'd always said she was determined to go back there and try every single restaurant on that strip.

Now that she lived so close and Janecia was only a half hour away, Regina was ready to try and have fun meeting that goal. When she told Janecia last night, her best friend was, as expected, all for it. Since today was Friday, they'd get right on it, starting tonight after work.

Grabbing her Starbucks cup from the cup holder, she grabbed her things from the passenger side and got out of the car. She hurried up the steps of the building and inside, glad that her plan on getting to work extra early meant she'd miss most of the morning elevator commute. She was the only one in the hallway as she reached out and hit the button to retrieve the elevator. The elevator dinged, and she held her breath, hoping *he* wouldn't be behind the doors when they opened. Thankfully, a couple of other sergeants stepped out, but neither were him. She got in and pressed the button for the second floor, feeling a little anxious when the doors took a few seconds before starting to close. She exhaled slowly. Just as the doors nearly touched closed, they opened suddenly. Someone outside had hit the button and caught the elevator. *Great.*

Standing in the middle of the elevator as the doors opened completely, she was now face to face with Sergeant Billings. A nod so minute it was barely perceptible was the only greeting she got from the jerk. Lifting her chin and glad she was wearing her stupid badge, she took a step aside, ignoring the nod and him completely. The doors once again began closing. This time they closed all the way, and the elevator began moving. They reached their floor as the elevator came to a slow stop and not a moment too soon. Ignoring him was one thing, but ignoring how damn good he smelled was quite another. Regina needed to get out of that elevator before she was tempted to say something to him.

Just as the elevator came to a complete stop and the doors began to open, everything went black, making Regina gasp. Except for the early and cloudy morning's dim sunlight that streamed in through the small crevice of the barely opened doors, they stood there in near pitch darkness.

She felt Sergeant Billings move forward and block the only light they had as he tried to push the doors open. "It's just a power outage," he explained as he grunted, trying in vain to push the doors open. "It should be temporary."

Regina knew all about the power outages. They were necessary when working on parts of the construction near or around dangerously high-voltage areas. She also knew they saved the longer power outages for the early morning or late evenings when it was less inconvenient to those working in the buildings.

Of course! This shouldn't even surprise her sorry ass. It made perfect sense that she'd get stuck in an elevator with of all people *him.*

CHAPTER SIX

Brandon

Sensing her resentment the moment he walked into the elevator, Brandon had actually been amused by it. Now he wasn't sure what he was sensing from her. When the lights had gone off, he thought for sure it was alarm. Judging from the tears he'd seen last night, he'd already pegged her as an emotional one. Emotional equaled weak as far as he was concerned, so when he heard her gasp, he'd been sure he'd have his hands full, trying to calm her ass down. Instead, from what little he could make out in the darkened elevator, she was now leaning against the wall, seemingly undaunted.

"It's *Ms*. Brady, by the way."

Brandon looked up in her direction, barely able to make out the silhouette of the business suit that hugged her body. He saw her phone light up as she pulled it out of her purse. The moment the light illuminated her face, his eyes were on her lips. He remembered now even as he'd walked through the first-class cabin where she'd been sitting in her seat already enjoying a Bloody Mary how his eyes had been drawn to those lips then too.

On the plane, he'd watched as her lips wrapped around the celery stick that came in her drink. He hadn't quite been able to shake the visual almost the whole flight. Just like last night when she'd pressed her lips together because he'd pissed the princess off, she looked like she was pouting, but he could tell her extra full lips just made it appear as if she were. Since he'd first seen her here, she'd worn her hair up in that same twist and wore her glasses. Today was the first time since seeing her at the airport that her hair was down and the glasses were gone.

Before he could respond to her clarification, she was on her phone. "Antonio, I'm stuck in the elevator. Can you please have them turn the power back on so I can get out of here?"

Seeing those lips curve into a smirk should've had him fighting his own lips from doing the same. Even when she'd lifted that sweet chin and given him the cold shoulder earlier it had him fighting a smile. Instead her smile irritated him now.

"You did?" she said, her smile going even more playful—brighter. "Oh, wow. All the more reason to get me out of here as soon as possible. Now I really can't wait to get to my office. Thank you, sweetie."

Sweetie? Brandon finally pulled his eyes away from her lips, annoyed at himself for getting caught up in them. She was probably used to having guys like *Antonio* and all the other saps she worked with wrapped around her finger. Years of having Daddy wrapped made for good practice, no doubt. Any guy who'd never been around her type didn't stand a chance.

He noticed her putting her phone away, and he turned back to her. "Did he say how long it would be?"

"Few minutes," she said without looking up at him, but he did notice the bright smile had gone flat.

With the sun shining in the crack a little brighter now, he could even see her delicate eyebrow arch significantly as she sipped her coffee, scrolling through her phone, very noticeably avoiding eye contact. This time he did fight the urge to smile. Was the princess still pissed he hadn't fallen for that smile last night and given into her as she'd likely been certain he would?

The lights went on and the doors opened. Brandon was tempted for a weak moment to tell *Ms.* Brady to have a good day. Then he thought better of it. She might actually be *that* full of herself to think the only reason he'd not given into her last night was because he'd assumed she was married. Happy that he caught the almost slip-up, he walked out of the elevator, saying nothing more to her or even looking her way as he began down the hall.

He heard her step out behind him, and if he weren't mistaken, the tapping of her heels against the floor was a little louder than normal.

"Sergeant Billings?"

Curious and mildly pleased to hear her say his name, he stopped and turned to look at her. Seeing her once again in the light, he ignored the fact that she looked better every goddamned time he saw her. "Yeah?"

She took a few steps toward him. "Aside from the airport in Washington D.C., have we met before?" Her expression was visibly annoyed. "Or do you *think* you know me from somewhere else?"

Letting out a dry chuckle, Brandon shook his head. He'd hit it right on the nose. She really was struggling to figure out why he hadn't fallen all over himself to charm her from the moment he first laid eyes on her. Obviously, it's what she was used to. What a piece of work!

He was grateful for this added confirmation that she *was* a self-entitled little princess, because he needed it now that his eyes locked onto hers and they were even bigger and darker than he remembered. As she took a few steps closer and he got an even longer look at the fine details of those big brown inquisitive eyes, he had to focus on what he'd just confirmed. He suddenly needed the knowledge that he'd been right about her all along as a safeguard. It helped with the dislike he knew he needed to continue feeling for her. "No, Ms. Brady, fortunately, we've never met."

Her eyebrows spiked. Just like last night when he first ran into her and the hurt in her tearful eyes was so palpable, there was no hiding what she was feeling now. Utter annoyance. This time he pressed his lips together to refrain from smiling. Why the *fuck* did her annoyance with him amuse him so much?

"What exactly does that mean? *Fortunately*? You've obviously made some kind of assessment about me, yet you know *nothing* about me."

"That's right. I don't. And I'm sorry that my lack of desire to know more upsets you."

It pissed him off that even with his years of training in discipline he was incapable of keeping his eyes off those lips, especially when her mouth fell open as it did just then. Glancing back up at her eyes instead, he saw that little eyebrow lift again. "It doesn't upset me," she said. "It's just that. . ." She glanced around flustered. "I've just never—"

"I know you've *never*, Ms. Brady." He walked away, thinking he should be feeling smugger that she may as well have admitted she wasn't used to men not being interested. Instead, he felt somewhat disappointed he'd been spot on about her.

The sound of her heels clicking once again quickly and with conviction against the floor made him smile. But he wiped the smile the moment she came around him and stood in front of him, forcing him to stop. She stood so close that the subtle scent he'd picked up in the elevator overwhelmed his senses now. Whatever she used to wash those thick tresses was distracting as hell. "You don't know *anything* about me, Mr. Billings—"

"Sergeant Billings," he corrected her immediately rewarded with a very annoyed pucker of her lips.

Refraining from smiling, he considered for a moment that pissing her off might be a new amusing pastime. It'd certainly keep things safe if she disliked him as much as he wanted to dislike her. Unfortunately, it amused him a bit too much, so it was dangerous. He stared at her straight-faced as she took a deep breath.

"You don't know anything about me, *Sergeant* Billings. So whatever preconceived notion you *think* you've figured out about me is completely unfair, but you know what? I don't give a shit. As a matter of a fact—"

The lights went out again, and she glanced around for a second. Then their eyes locked once again in the dim hallway. Shaking her head, she didn't finish what she was going to say and started around him, but he moved in front of her, stopping her. It took her by such surprise her hand lifted, pressing against his chest. "As a matter of fact, what?" he asked, gulping as he stared in those startled brown eyes.

She held his gaze for a moment as her hand stayed put against his chest. Infuriating images of having her hands in other places assaulted him, and as much as he knew he should move aside and let her through, he couldn't bring himself to move away.

Clearing her throat, she finally took her hand back but didn't step back. The anger he'd seen in her eyes moments before the lights went off was gone. The stunned look in her eyes as she stared at him gave a hint of something else. For as much as she was protesting, she *did* care what he thought of her.

"As a matter fact," she started, and she was so close he could smell of sweet coffee on her breath. He'd always hated coffee, but at that moment he'd give anything to taste it. "I don't even know why I'm wasting my time. Think whatever you want of me."

She walked around him, and he let her by this time as he stood frozen in place. He had another moment of weakness where he considered taking it back—apologizing for prejudging her. But he'd already slipped once by showing even the remote interest in what she had to say. He had to get a grip. He'd only been around this girl a handful of times, and already his will to show complete indifference had been weakened more than once. Even seeing her cry last night had done something to him. Thankfully, he'd handled that as he should.

Today he'd nearly blown it.

Most days Brandon had glimpses of Ms. Brady either heading out to lunch or in the break room buying a soda or just like last night when he'd run into her as he was leaving. Today either Ms. Brady had gone out of her way to avoid Brandon or it'd been just coincidental that he hadn't seen her at all after their morning's insightful exchange. If it was the former, he should be glad.

In case her plan and admittedly his as well to avoid each other faltered and he did run into her again, he had every intention of going back to the way it was before that morning's incident. He wouldn't be exchanging so much as a smile with her. It just wasn't safe. Every time she'd smiled at him—the morning Sergeant Carter showed him to his office and last night when she'd smiled at him despite the tears still her eyes—he'd felt more than the only thing he should be feeling, annoyance. It was all he should feel just as he had at the airport. But since he'd arrived here, the annoyance of what that sweet smile did to him was being subdued by something else, something that felt dangerously wrong. And this morning, he'd confirmed it.

This was too close to what might lead to him to the temptation of breaking his number-one rule—no attachments. *None.* He'd done so well for so long he wasn't about to blow it now. Even the sexual encounters he'd had in the last several years he made absolutely sure were completely meaningless. He'd even figured out a way to keep the act itself especially cold while making the women he was with think it was all part of the performance. He never even slept with the same woman twice much less engage in the usual protocol of dating such as calling her again or even asking her out for another round. It was too risky.

His best bet was to hope he'd pissed her off enough she now hated him. That would eliminate any more of those sweet pouty-lipped smiles, smiles he wanted so much to hate. Today was proof he was losing that battle. The bad thing was Brandon wasn't even sure now what was worse, the smiles or her obvious contempt for him. For some reason, that seemed to amuse him almost as much as the smiles were beginning to soften him.

The thought of losing battles reminded him of something else and made him groan inwardly. He hadn't even been here a week yet, and already his anti-social ass had to go hangout with some of his fellow workers that night after work. He'd been warned before he even transferred that a few of the other sergeants had mentioned taking him out when he got here, kind of a welcome-to-the-team type of deal. That meant tonight he'd put on his social mask.

He was glad that for once the overly inquisitive and talkative personality of his office roommate Sergeant Evans had come in handy. He'd asked Brandon if he had any big plans for the weekend as soon as he walked in that morning, forcing Brandon to mention the trip he was making up to Los Angeles tomorrow. Later when Rodriguez arrived, letting Brandon know they'd be taking him out for drinks, his I-can't-be-out-late excuse that would get him out early tonight held far more weight.

He wasn't meeting his former drill instructor until late in the afternoon tomorrow, but they didn't have to know that. Tonight they'd be under the impression he had to be in L.A tomorrow *early*, which meant he'd have a few drinks and be done with this *welcome-to-the-team party*.

"Hey," Rodriguez said, standing up. "Either of you guys get a load of that sexy little thing working with the engineers?"

Brandon didn't even turn to look at him. He didn't have to ask who Rodriguez was talking about, because he already knew. Normally Rodriguez's banter about women and his admitting he was always horny were amusing. The guy could be funny. But Brandon had begun to worry about one thing.

Ever since the day he realized Ms. Brady would be working in such close proximity to him, nothing about what he was feeling for her was normal. Hearing Rodriguez speak of her now, the way he did, was anything but amusing.

Pretending to be too caught up in what he was reading on his screen to be bothered, Brandon listened anyway as Evans confirmed he *had* gotten a load of her.

"Yeah, yeah," Evans said. "The girl with the glasses."

"You seen her today?" Rodriguez asked.

"Nah," Evans responded.

"Holy shit!" Rodriguez said a bit too excited. "She must be going out tonight or something because her hair is down and she wasn't wearing glasses. I thought she was sexy before but *damn*." He lowered his voice a little since the door to the office was still half open. "Swear to God I'd risk my job and fuck her in the bathroom if she'd let me. I mean, shit, the girl's got it going on. I just about popped a boner, watching her walk down the hall."

Inappropriate. Technically, as Rodriguez's superior, Brandon could tell him so and end the conversation right there, but he never had before, and Rodriguez had always been this vivid with his stories. Since Brandon had only been here a little over a week, he didn't want to make a big stink about some raunchy guy talk amongst them. He always figured, since it was in the privacy of their own office and most of the stories Rodriguez told were of past conquests or women outside the base, it was no big deal.

"And she's gotta be at least a full C cup. Damn," Rodriguez laughed. "I'm getting a chubby just thinking about—"

"Well then, stop," Brandon said, sounding more annoyed than authoritative, so he cleared his throat before he continued. "She works in the same building. If someone outside this office," he motioned toward the open door, "gets wind of you talking like this, I may have to write your ass up. In fact," Brandon turned his chair around to face him, glad

Rodriguez had been stupid enough to make the comment about risking getting fired, "based on what you just said, I don't wanna see or even hear that you've been anywhere near her. Unlike you, I'm not about to risk my job. So to play it safe and not force me to keep an eye out for what you might be doing behind closed doors around here, I'd be more comfortable if we just make the *sexy little thing* off limits to you. Is that understood?"

Rodriguez and Evans exchanged humorous glances, and before either of them could ask if he was serious, because Brandon had never been more so in his life, he asked again, only this time he used that tone he was known for using out in the field. "I asked you a question, Rodriguez. Is that understood?"

The moment it registered in Rodriguez's face that Brandon was indeed serious was a little too satisfying. He didn't even care if they thought him an asshole. His reputation had preceded him, so these two shouldn't even have been surprised.

"Understood, sir." Rodriguez nodded, the smile he'd worn just moments ago completely gone. "And I apologize if—"

"No need for that." Brandon turned around to face his screen again. "As long as I don't see you anywhere near her, we're good."

That last part was even more satisfying than shutting Rodriguez up, but it was also a bit disturbing because Brandon knew making Ms. Brady off limits to Rodriguez was not at all for the reason he explained it was. His subconscious was already making decisions he didn't approve of.

His only hope now was that, after this, Rodriguez would change his mind about getting together for drinks tonight. Aside from knowing Rodriguez would be staying the hell away from Ms. Brady, which shouldn't be a good thing—yet it sure as hell felt good—getting out of his night with the guys would be the other good thing about this unanticipated confrontation.

Unfortunately, before the day was over, Rodriguez once again apologized to Brandon about his behavior and said he was looking forward to having drinks with him later that evening. So much for hoping he'd burned that bridge.

CHAPTER SEVEN

Regina

Trying not to do the middle school girl thing and squeal when Janecia walked up to the outdoor table where Regina was sitting, she still jumped up and hugged her tight. "Oh my God, it's so good to see you," she said as she continued to squeeze her friend.

Finally pulling away, Janecia laughed. "It's good to see you too, G. It's been just too long."

"I know!" Regina said, taking a seat and pointing across the table for Janecia to take hers. "It's been like over a year."

The sudden reminder of why it'd been that long had Regina picking up her drink and sipping it. Luckily, before Janecia could comment, the waiter brought Janecia's drink.

"I took the liberty of ordering for you," Regina smiled, glad for the change in subject.

"White Russian." Janecia smiled, pleased as she picked it up. "Still my favorite."

Wanting to avoid any talk of anything depressing, Regina went right into her plan of action for the night. "So I figured instead of full meals we can have a drink and split an appetizer then move on to the next restaurant and do the same." She glanced around the brightly lit and bustling street lined with restaurants and bars. "I think it's the only way we'll start making a dent in this place if we plan on trying all these restaurants eventually."

"Hey, we said we'd do this, and we're doing it." Janecia held up her drink. "To doing Gaslamp, girl."

Regina picked up her drink and clinked Janecia's glass. "Let's do this."

To Regina's relief, they caught up on the lighter stuff, and Janecia began telling her about the new guy she'd started dating. "Be warned he's a little different from some of the guys I've dated in the past."

Intrigued, Regina stirred her drink and leaned in. "Different, how?"

"Well, for starters, he rides a Harley."

Regina jerked back, feeling her heart sink. Janecia reached her hand out, quickly placing it on top of Regina's. "I said *he* does. I've already told him I'd never step foot on it."

Exhaling, Regina glanced around, feeling a little silly about her knee-jerk reaction. She still couldn't help asking, "You promise?"

Janecia smiled. "Yes, I promise. I just wanted to get that out there before you found out some other way." She took a sip of her drink and continued. "He's also not white collar or a college graduate like the guys I normally date. He's a longshoreman—hard labor man. He's a little rough around the edges and a bit of a hothead, but he can also be so sweet." She giggled. "And, girl, so sexy."

Regina smiled, trying to shake the thought of Janecia's new, sweet, sexy boyfriend coaxing her onto his Harley. Janecia went on, filling her in on how she met Clay as they finished up and paid their bill. They moved on to the next few restaurants, catching up on family gossip and laughing about old times. Regina was so glad she'd decided to do this. It was a good thing Gaslamp was so long and there were *so* many restaurants. It would take many returns here before they got through the whole thing. Having this to do with her best friend definitely gave her something to look forward to.

Beginning to feel a little tipsy as they left their fourth or fifth restaurant—she'd lost count—Regina decided at their next stop she'd be having water. They walked down the street, trying to decide which restaurant to hit next, and then she saw him. Sergeant Billings was at the bar of the very next restaurant in their route. This was the first time she'd seen him out of uniform. He wore a simple black long-sleeved shirt and a pair of black jeans. He stood by the bar with a couple of other guys and two girls. One of the girls was very obviously flirting with him, and then it happened.

"Well, I'll be damned," she said, staring at him as her heart did the weirdest flutter. She actually felt a tingly sensation. "The man *does* smile."

And by God, did it have to be such a beautiful smile? Even his eyes lit up sweetly, and at this distance, she could still admire how bright white and perfect his teeth were. Her heart fluttered in that weird way again, and the tingling spread through her insides.

Janecia turned to look in the direction Regina's eyes were glued to now. "Who?"

"Sergeant Billings," she said with no other explanation as they continued walking toward the restaurant. Just as they reached the entrance to the outside patio of the restaurant, Sergeant Billings looked up past the blonde he'd been smiling at, and his eyes met Regina's. Not only did his smile immediately dissolve but his expression went hard and rigid, turning into the very expression she was now beginning to think was reserved just for her.

"Well, *damn*," Janecia said, clearly noticing the icy change in his disposition as well. "Do you know him?"

"Sort of." Regina was finally able to look away and at the hostess asking them if they'd like a seat inside or out. "Outside." She smiled and followed the hostess to their table.

Taking the seat that would face the bar, Regina sat down. She wasn't sure why she hadn't just kept walking on to the next restaurant or one even further where she wouldn't have to deal with his lethal glare. What the hell was his problem? His "lack of desire to get to know her" was one thing, but the way he looked at her now said something entirely different. Obviously, he couldn't stand her, and Regina was at a total loss as to what she could've possibly done to warrant such severe detestation from a total stranger.

Janecia sat across from her, glancing back at the sergeant as she made herself comfortable. Billings had gone back to talking to the girl, but that annoyingly beautiful and playful smile she'd been privy to for too short of an instant was *gone*. "So what's his deal? He doesn't like you?"

"Apparently not," Regina said, looking down at the menu the hostess had handed them before walking away.

"Why?"

"I have *no* idea."

Regina filled in her friend about first seeing him at the airport and the first few run-ins she'd had with him, including last night when he'd made her go fetch her photo ID, knowing full well she was authorized.

"What a jerk!" Janecia frowned, glancing back at him again. "Maybe he's one of those guys who get a hard-on from playing the power card. Aren't most of those drill instructors like that? I mean isn't that why they go into that field in the first place?"

"My dad was a drill instructor back in the day, Janecia," Regina reminded her. "He's never been that kind of person, and he always said it was one of the most rewarding duties he ever had. I don't think it's that at all."

She glanced up at the sergeant but quickly looked away when she saw his head turn slightly in her direction. "I just don't know what to make of it. From the moment I first saw him at the airport, there was this disdainful way he looked at me. It's like there was just something about me that had immediately turned him off." She shrugged. "I asked him about it this morning."

Janecia's eyes opened in curiosity as the waitress arrived to take their order. They both ordered water, and Janecia agreed to the first appetizer Regina suggested. She was obviously more interested in hearing about that morning's happenings.

"What did you ask him?" Janecia asked as soon as the waitress walked away.

Frustrated and not even sure why she cared so much, Regina exhaled. "I started thinking maybe I did know him from somewhere. Maybe I'd blown him off in the past and didn't even remember, or maybe he'd mistaken me for someone else, so I asked him if it was either of those things." Feeling as little as he'd made her feel when he'd told her about his lack of desire to get to know her, she repeated his awful words to Janecia.

Her friend's mouth fell open. "You're kidding me!"

"Nope," she said, shaking her head. "For whatever reason, the man's decided he hates my guts."

Thanking the waitress for their waters, Regina sipped hers. Regina decided she'd keep to herself the fact that he'd stepped in front of her, forcing her to finish what she'd begun say. She also wouldn't say what being that close to those acutely blue eyes had done to her. She knew her best friend too well. Janecia would want to overanalyze it, and the truth was she was done thinking about the uptight sergeant. She'd already spent the better part of her day, trying to figure it out. Even when he was looking at her with what she assumed was unexplained indignation, he did so with such intensity that it was confusing as hell. But even more confusing was what she'd thought she'd seen in his eyes when he asked her to finish what she'd begun to say that morning. The guy shouldn't feel anything for her either way. Good or bad. He still didn't know much about her at all. Yet even tonight there was no hiding the ill will he had toward her.

"But it doesn't make sense. He doesn't even know you. And you're so damn cute." Janecia leaned across the table and whispered. "You think maybe he's gay?"

Laughing, Regina nearly spit up her water. Sergeant Billings gay? That still wouldn't explain why he would dislike her so much. One glance up and Janecia's theory flew out the window along with Regina's laughing mood. The sergeant was now whispering something in the ear of the same blonde he'd been smiling at so cheerfully earlier. "He might be married," she said, unable to move her eyes away from him and the giggling blonde.

Once again, following her eyes, Janecia turned to observe him and the girl. "Stop looking," Regina whispered.

Janecia did, even though Regina couldn't. Suddenly flustered with herself, she wondered why it hadn't occurred to her that he might be married or even in a relationship. Even more frustrating was why the hell did it even matter? The guy was obviously a jerk who didn't like her. It was annoying enough that he'd decided to hate her on little to nothing to go by, but even worse was the fact that, on just as little, she'd been taken enough by him to have given him and his unreasonable abhorrence to her so much thought.

"Sweetie?"

Regina swallowed hard, glancing away when she realized how intensely she'd been staring at the pretentious sergeant and his girl. "Hmm?"She took a very casual sip of her water but still didn't look Janecia in the eyes.

"Are you sure you're not leaving out anything about you and this guy?"

Now she looked at Janecia curiously. "No, why?"

Janecia lifted a very telling brow as she leaned over and put the straw between her lips. She took a drink of her water then raised a shoulder. "Oh, I don't know. Maybe because ever since you spotted him and his little female friend your mood seems to have taken a dive."

Regina scoffed, a little too loud and the waving of her hand in front of her might've been overkill because she nearly knocked her water over in the process. Janecia stared at her, clearly unimpressed, but Regina wasn't about to tone her response down because it *wasn't* an act. She *didn't* care. The guy was practically a monster to her. Why on earth would she even be looking at him in terms of anything other than someone she should hate? *Or* because she wouldn't lower herself to his level and hate someone she didn't even know, at the very least she should be irked with him for being rude. He could take his lack of desire to know more about her and shove it up his ass.

About to further protest Janecia's ridiculous insinuation, she was caught in his eyes as he began to walk off with the blonde hand in hand. As much as she knew she should look away, his eyes were like a magnet. It seemed the longer she stared at him the darker his stare went until he leaned over and kissed the girl deeply. That instantly snapped the pull he'd had on her, and she closed her eyes.

"You okay?" Janecia asked gently.

Regina opened her eyes, turning back to Janecia, feeling completely embarrassed. "Yeah. Yeah." She cleared her throat and smiled weakly at her very concerned-looking friend.

"You don't have to tell me if you don't want to, G. But clearly there's more going on."

After successfully convincing Janecia that she was fine and there was nothing else to tell about the stuck-up sergeant—or maybe not so successfully—her friend let it go anyway.

On her drive home, Regina came to the conclusion that nothing good could come from trying to figure out why this man, who might even be married, didn't like her. From that moment on, she decided her best bet was to avoid him at all costs, and when it wasn't possible to, she'd just ignore him completely. It was what he seemed to want anyway, so that was that. She was done giving any more thought to Sergeant Jerk Face!

~*~

Brandon

After a long day of supervising one of his newest DIs as he did his first evaluations of the newest recruits, Brandon made his way back to his office. He rode with Sergeant Miller in the golf cart they'd used to drive out to the field where the evals had taken place. Miller was in the middle of some long-winded story about his days as a DI when Brandon noticed Rodriguez and Ms. Brady just outside his office building, chatting. Slowing as he drove by them, they both turned to him. The big smile Rodriguez had worn up until that moment flattened, his face going even paler than it already was. Ms. Brady's smile wasn't as big as Rodriguez's, but it did seem to fade gradually at the sight of him.

Rodriguez nodded at both him and Miller then turned back to Ms. Brady and said something. In a flash, he disappeared back into the building. Brandon didn't even realize he was still glaring when he glanced back at Ms. Brady, who was still looking at him. Bringing his attention to his driving, he was alarmed at how unbelievably irritated the sight of Rodriguez yapping it up with her made him feel.

Instantly speeding up, he drove to the back of the building where he parked and he and Miller parted ways. It'd been such a long day. He'd planned on heading straight to his car and going home. Instead, he stalked into the building. With no patience to wait for the elevator and because he felt as if he needed to work off some steam, he hurried up the stairs.

Rodriguez had ignored a direct order. That was the only reason why Brandon felt so fucking annoyed. There was no other reason. Never mind the fact that the only other time Brandon had seen Ms. Brady all week she'd evoked the very same annoyance he felt now. That was two days ago, and she'd been laughing at something one of her engineer co-workers was saying to her.

Swallowing hard as he reached the top of the stairs, he turned the corner into the hallway just in time to catch Rodriguez waiting for the elevator. The second Rodriguez saw him he turned to him, taking a few steps away from the closed elevator doors.

"Sir, I can explain."

"Yes, you can and you will," Brandon said, his tone hard and full of authority just as he'd been trained by the very best. "Only not here, not like this." He got right in Rodriguez's face. "I want a full report on my desk tomorrow morning, explaining why you ignored a direct order from your superior. I wanna know *exactly* what you were talking to her about when you've been instructed to stay away from her entirely. And also want you tell me why the hell I shouldn't write you up."

The elevator door opened, and Ms. Brady stepped out, staring at them almost in question. Brandon looked away, refusing to make eye contact, and Rodriguez did the right thing, not even acknowledging her. They waited silently until she was out of sight. "I don't normally give second chances, so consider yourself lucky."

"Sir, yes, sir."

Brandon took two long steps into the still-open elevator and turned around to face Rodriguez, who wisely didn't dare step in with him. "First thing in the morning, Rodriguez," Brandon repeated the order through his teeth.

"Sir, yes, sir," Rodriguez said just as Brandon hit the close button, and the elevator doors closed, leaving a very staggered-looking Rodriguez outside.

This was completely unacceptable. Brandon needed to get a grasp on what she was beginning to do to him. The fact that Rodriguez had ignored a direct order was reason enough to piss Brandon off, but he shouldn't be getting this worked up over it.

The elevator doors opened, and he stepped out still feeling incredibly agitated as he walked out toward the front door of the building. Would he really write Rodriguez up if his report wasn't satisfactory or worse if he stupidly admitted to having been flirting with her? The thought of Rodriguez's remarks about what he'd do to her in the bathroom slammed into him.

Pushing the front doors open with a little more force than necessary, he concluded two things. Not only would Brandon write his ass up but he'd get the perverted asshole transferred to another fucking base.

Second conclusion? As much as he was trying to deny it, what this girl was doing to him was getting *way* out of control.

~~~

The next morning, Rodriguez's report was on Brandon's desk when he arrived, though Rodriguez himself was not there. Brandon knew Rodriguez would be out doing evaluations of his own all week. He was glad for that. He'd spent too much time thinking about what might be in the report, what he might learn about Ms. Brady, the woman he wanted nothing to do with. Brandon knew he'd be scrutinizing the report a little closer than normal, and it was better if Rodriguez wasn't there to witness it.

Along with the report was a letter of apology to Brandon for having disrespected him, though Rodriguez made it clear it was not his intention. The report stated that Ms. Brady had made the first contact as they stepped outside together. He went on to outline the conversation about the change in the weather and how Rodriguez felt it rude to just ignore her so he carried on with the harmless conversation.

Brandon rolled his eyes. He'd seen the playful smile Rodriguez wore as he'd driven close enough to see the exchange between him and Ms. Brady. From what little he already knew about Rodriguez, Ms. Brady had likely made a

comment as simple as "It's chilly tonight," and he'd run with it.
Skimming through the rest of the report, Brandon stopped only at the parts that caught his eye such as Ms. Brady saying she'd take this weather any day over the weather back east where she'd just moved from.
He'd wondered about that. According to her phone conversation with her daddy, it appeared she had family out here, so he'd assumed she was on her way home. But Sergeant Carter had also mentioned not having seen her here before, so there was the possibility she was only here temporarily. Now this confirmed she'd be here for good.
Brandon frowned immediately at the next part. With his very fair skin and light eyes, if it weren't for Rodriguez's last name, you'd never know he was Hispanic. He'd even made mention that the kids in the mostly Hispanic community he grew up in teased him about being the whitest Mexican they knew. Brandon remembered him saying that he liked blowing people away or using it to his advantage when trying to pick up women by speaking to them in his perfect Spanish out of the blue.
Apparently, the idiot didn't count on Brandon remembering that insignificant comment he'd made weeks ago, because in his report he included the part about answering one of her questions in Spanish. However, he wasn't stupid enough to mention whether or not she'd been *blown away*.
Last night after calming down, Brandon had no doubt he'd overreacted. He was even mad at himself for doing so. This really was getting ridiculous. If he wanted nothing to do with Ms. Brady, then why the hell did he care about seeing her with someone else? After finishing the meticulously written report, Brandon was now glad he had reacted the way he had. If Rodriguez hadn't blown Ms. Brady away yesterday, Brandon doubted that after his nearly explosive

reaction Rodriguez would be looking for another chance to impress her again.

Cursing himself, Brandon set the report down, remembering how he'd actually looked up the name Brady to make sure it in no way had any Hispanic ties. She'd made it clear that she was a Ms., not a Mrs. That meant one thing. Either she was part Hispanic and her father had Irish roots, which seemed unlikely given her looks, or she'd previously been married to a Brady. If it was the latter, then unlike with Sofie and Eric, Rodriguez or any other Hispanic guy shouldn't have a cultural advantage over Brandon about getting a girl like Ms. Brady, especially guys like Rodriguez using his Spanish to try and impress her. If she'd married out of her culture before, obviously it didn't matter to her.

Brandon shot out of his chair, more annoyed with himself than he had been last night. The fact that he was even thinking in these terms was absolutely unacceptable. He dropped the report in the trash and slipped his hat over his head. He had no business putting so much damn thought and even research into this. Damn it. He'd even told the woman he had no desire to get to know her better.

Shaking his head in frustration as he walked out of his office, he forced himself to think of what he should be thinking about: the day ahead of him. It would be a long one for sure. He had several meetings with a few of his stuffy superiors to discuss the evaluations he'd been overseeing all week. He'd concentrate on that instead.

CHAPTER EIGHT

Regina

Staring into the darkness outside her office window, Regina smiled, thinking about how nice it had been to see her family this past weekend. Saturday she'd gone into the gym then did some grocery shopping before going home and fixing herself some pasta. Eating alone in her quiet condo, she felt herself sinking into that lonely place again. She needed to get used her life as it was now. Here or in New York, this is how it would be forever. He was gone, and until she began to move on—find herself again, be the person she was once—she'd continue sinking. She needed to go back to being that girl who didn't need someone else to make her happy.

Sunday had been nice. Maybe she didn't need a man to make her happy, but her family, she definitely needed. Being close to them again felt right. She was glad when her mother told her that now that all her children were living close by she'd be having early Sunday dinner for the entire family at her place *every* week. That was even more to look forward to because seeing her siblings and their families had been wonderful.

Albeit her parents weren't *that* close, the just-over-an-hour drive each way to their home had also served a purpose. It'd given her time to think. Her job wasn't *that* bad, really. She just had to give herself time to adjust, and she'd already decided she wouldn't give the sergeant another thought. The only energy she'd put into anything where he was concerned was to avoid him completely. She had enough things to deal with and an entire new lifestyle to adjust to. She didn't need to be thinking about a man who, from what she'd seen Friday, was likely married or in a relationship anyway. Being around her family reminded her why she'd made this move in the first place. Knowing she was close enough that she could be with them often now made it all worth it. She wouldn't let a less glamorous job than her job in New York or some jerk working in the same building make her forget that.

For the past few days, she'd effectively managed to be upbeat about her job and hadn't once run into *him*. That is until yesterday, but fortunately it'd been brief, and both times he'd been just as cold and indifferent as ever. Screw him. She was done trying to figure out what his problem was. She'd seen the way he glared at the other sergeant she'd been speaking to. Unlike Sergeant Billings, Sergeant Rodriguez had been friendly and engaging. Yet Sergeant Billings had seen fit to look at him in that same rigid way she thought he'd reserved just for her. The simple answer could very well be he was just an asshole.

Done thinking about it, she brought her mind back to the more pleasant things about that week. Regina had finally come up with what her boss had been counting on when she pitched her the idea of taking this job—a way to get this lagging project moving along.

Standing from her chair, she smiled, feeling very pleased with herself. Today had gone better than she'd imagined. The impromptu meeting she had with the staff to run her idea by them had gone well also. Taking a deep breath, she grabbed her things and headed out.

All week she'd been taking the stairs instead of the elevator, except for yesterday when she'd seen him rush up the stairs. It'd been the only time she'd seen him do that. Usually, he took the elevator, so she'd stick to the stairs under normal circumstances. Taking the stairs added steps to her step count for the day, and she didn't have to worry about any uncomfortable elevator rides. Win—win. Tonight, however, because she got caught up putting her new idea into effect and had to make a few calls to some key people who could get it moving along, she'd been here much later than usual.

Since the building was just about empty, she figured her chances of getting caught up in the elevator with *him* were slim to none, so she made her way to the elevator. Unbelievably, halfway there, she heard slow ominous footsteps coming from behind her—the direction of his office—but she dare not look. It could be someone else. What were the odds that of all the other people on this floor it would be him?

Charlie Brown.

Panicking as the footsteps got closer, she thought of the stairs just around the elevator. She could keep walking and take them instead. She still had a chance. As she reached the elevator, she hesitated for a moment but then kept going. She'd rather walk down than risk ruining her otherwise pleasant day by engaging in another irritating encounter with that man. She stopped just on top of the stairs but out of view now of whoever had been behind her. Deciding she should wait and not go down just yet to avoid running into him downstairs, she did. But the footsteps hadn't stopped. What if like yesterday, he'd decided to take the stairs as well and came around the corner only to find her standing there like an idiot?

Going back and forth because the footsteps were still coming, she shook her fist, frustrated by her inability to make such a simple decision. *Head down or not? Geez!*

Maybe he just hadn't reached the elevator yet. Even if he did take the elevator, she still had a chance to make a mad dash down the stairs and beat him because he still had to wait for the elevator.

Regina took off in a hurry but immediately realized she'd be much faster if she took her shoes off. A few steps down, she took one shoe off then went for the other and lost her footing. Her heart jumped to her throat when she tried to recover and couldn't. Before she knew what was happening, she heard herself yelp from the pain of her ankle bending under her. Everything after that happened so fast there was nothing she could do to stop it. Her arms flayed out wildly, unable to grasp onto anything as her entire body went down. The things in her purse flew everywhere as it fell out in front of her, and she hit every step, unable to slow the fall until she finally hit the wall where the stairwell turned with a loud and painful thud.

Dazed for a few seconds, it took her a moment to grasp what had just happened. She shook her head and immediately regretted it because it made her head throb. She was so dazed she didn't even realize the loud clanking was someone running down the stairs toward her.

Looking up, she was face to face with Sergeant Billings, who immediately crouched down, the usual hardened expression now very concerned.

"Don't move," he said as she tried to sit up. "Lie down instead," he instructed her, and she did as he told her. "You might have a neck or spinal injury. You'll make it worse if you move."

Very slowly and gently, Regina moved her neck from side to side to assess whether her neck was really injured or not. She tried in vain to ignore the screaming voice in her head.

Of course, instead of avoiding him, you rolled down the stairs, bringing the most mortifying kind of attention to yourself. You didn't just trip or fall—you rolled!

"My neck feels fine," she said, wanting nothing more than to gather her things and get as far away from there as possible.

Over the initial shock and ignoring the pain now, Regina felt so incredibly embarrassed she couldn't even look at him as she tried sitting again.

"Look in my eyes," he said, and unwillingly she did. Was it possible they'd gotten even bluer?

As he held her from moving by her arm, she stopped. For the first time since he'd arrived, she got an up close less dazed look at him. Unlike all the other times when she'd seen him in his utility uniform, he now wore a service uniform with lots of medals, which only gave him an even more commanding appearance. Whatever cologne he wore smelled so good she had to fight the urge to close her eyes and just inhale deeply. She gazed into those very serious blue eyes.

"Can you tell me what your name is?" he asked.

Instantly, she was yanked out of the wistful state she hadn't even noticed she'd gone into. Her insides warmed with mortification or anger; she couldn't decide. But she was consumed by both emotions. Was he really going to act as if he didn't remember her?

She jerked her arm away from him. "You know who I am!"

Surprised by the tiny gleam in his eyes, she was caught in them once again, but she still glared.

"Yes," he nodded, and to her utter shock, he smiled softly. "I know who you are, Ms. Brady. I was just trying to assess how hard you hit your head."

"Oh," she said, and as if she couldn't feel anymore embarrassed than she already did, she now felt like a complete jackass. "Yes, I know my name. It's Regina." Even through her embarrassment, she was surprised by what a smile from him did to her. "I really don't think I broke anything," she explained as she once again tried to sit up, and he allowed it this time. "Nothing hurts that bad."

He stood up and offered both hands to her. "Stand up really slowly. You might be dizzy."

She reached up and took both his hands. The second she put weight on her right foot, the pain shot through her ankle, and she nearly went down again, but he caught her.

"Careful," he said as she fell into his hard chest.

The feel of his arms around her and that amazing scent of him as she leaned into him might've been more enjoyable if the sharp pain in her ankle hadn't spoiled the moment. She groaned instead. Suddenly the realization that she'd have to walk up or down a set of stairs in that excruciating pain came to her.

"Don't stand on it," he warned, pulling her arm around his neck and looking down. "It might be broken."

Holding on to him, she wobbled on her good foot. "I can hold on to the rail and hop down on one foot."

More surprising than seeing him smile earlier, she jerked her head up when she heard him chuckle softly. "That's not happening."

He already had one hand around her. He leaned down, and she felt his arm under her knees. In the next instant, she was cradled in his arms.

"Put your arms around my neck," he instructed her.

Before she could even begin to argue, he started down the stairs, and she wrapped her arms around him, holding on tightly.

~*~

Brandon

So her hair smelled better than he remembered, and she felt even better than he hated to admit he'd been imagining she would in his arms. She was injured, and even if the thought of holding her had crossed his mind before, *that* was the only reason he was doing this now. Just thinking about these things was reckless. He was beginning to think he saw something in the way she looked at him too—something curious—something he had no business even noticing and definitely no intention of looking into any further.

Brandon set her down on the sofa in the lobby at the entrance of the building. "I'll go get your things," he said as soon as she un-wrapped her arms from around his neck.

Gulping hard, he walked away before he could get caught up in the eyes he *needed* to stop thinking about, even when they weren't in front of him.

As he reached the stairs where she'd fallen, he picked up her purse and began putting the spilled contents into it. After picking up several makeup items, he noticed her open wallet at the bottom of the staircase. He didn't mean to be nosey, but it was open to a photo of her and two other women standing around an older guy. The other women looked about her age. Going by the resemblances they all shared, he presumed these were her sisters, and the way they all touched the man's shoulders so endearingly, he assumed this was *Daddy*. If it was, this blew his theory about her dad possibly being Irish—a Brady. The man in the photo looked every bit as Hispanic as she did.

Why was he even going there?

Holding the photo still in front of him, he couldn't stop looking at it. He focused on something else now. They all looked so happy. He stared at that smile and her sparkling eyes. It was almost maddening. All these years, he'd managed to remain immune to and kept that part of him—the part that might actually feel emotions—completely sedated. He couldn't allow a sweet smile and a pair of dark captivating eyes to wake that part of him. He'd so effortlessly managed to snuff it to its death, or so he thought, for so long he didn't think he'd ever have to worry about it.

Clenching his jaw, he lifted the photo only to see another one of Ms. Brady behind it. Once again, Brandon felt drawn to her eyes. In the second photo, she was alone, her face very fresh as if she'd just gotten out of the shower. Even with no makeup, she was stunning. It was such a simple photo of her, sitting cross-legged in the middle of a bed, wearing an oversized white T-shirt, but unlike the other smiling photo, in this one she wasn't smiling at all. She was staring at the camera with her head tilted, looking almost angry.

Brandon smiled, remembering the fuming yet adorable glare he'd been indulged with when he'd asked her for her name earlier. He still didn't understand why seeing that glint of fire in her eyes, especially when directed at him, amused him so. Even this less-enchanting portrait did just that: enchant him in a way that scared him. He shouldn't be feeling anything for her. He didn't know her, and he didn't want to get to know her—he shouldn't.

A buzzing sound pulled him out of his thoughts, and he turned around to search for the source of the noise. The screen on a cell phone at the bottom of the staircase lit up. He walked over to pick it up and read the screen: *Incoming call—Antonio.*

Remembering her sweet conversation in the elevator with someone named Antonio, who she apparently worked with in this same building, another alarm went off. He'd chalked up the irritation he'd felt that day when he listened to her on the phone to his irritation with her in general. The fact that Antonio had done something for her that warranted a very grateful thank you from her was only further proof of the kind of princess she was. It reminded him of how irritated he'd been just the other day when he'd seen her talking and laughing with one of her co-workers. She'd only been working at this place for a little over a week, and already she'd had these guys seemingly smitten.

Ignoring what seeing Antonio's name on her phone screen did to him, he tossed the phone into her purse and gathered the rest of her stuff. It took him a few minutes to find her second shoe, because it was way up on the upper steps, not at the bottom like everything else. He walked up and shoved it in her purse, glad it was big enough to hold both shoes, and started back down.

She was holding her leg out in front of her with a grimace, trying to move the ankle as he approached her.

"Don't do that."

Even her startled expression was enough to make him want to smile—something that up until lately he didn't do often. Being a drill instructor for so many years, he'd just fallen into the habit of hiding any kind of amusing emotions. Good and bad, Ms. Brady was bringing them all out of him. He remembered how impossible it'd been to hide the annoyance he'd felt that he hadn't been able to keep his eyes off her Friday night at the restaurant. Her continued staring at him the way she had with such interest and more, had him questioning if maybe getting to know her better might not be such a bad idea. That *could not* happen. He'd been so desperate to end what he was feeling—what *she* might be feeling—he did something he so rarely did and engaged in a public display of affection by kissing the girl he'd met only an hour earlier.

"It might be broken," she said almost through her teeth. "It's really hurting bad now."

Brandon put her purse down next to her. "I think I got it all." He knelt down in front of her then lifted her injured ankle gently. She immediately gasped at his touch. "Sorry."

"No, you didn't hurt me." She laughed softly. "I was just bracing myself."

Like earlier, he lost the battle and smiled. Looking up at her pained but laughing mood despite her injury, he just couldn't help himself. As soon as he smiled, he saw the same thing in her eyes he'd seen earlier—an almost bewildered gaze—and there was something so sweet about it he had to look away.

He focused on her ankle instead. Trying to ignore her dainty, painted-pink toes, his eyes traveled to the upper right hand side of the top of her foot and the small heart tattoo. A picture of an open book with the words Uni & Boot was inside of the heart. Draped around the heart so it looked almost like a vine hanging off the heart were the words: Together forever.

Brandon had no idea what Uni and Boot stood for, but obviously it had to be meaningful to her or she wouldn't have something so permanent on her body. Regardless of the meaning, it was none of his business, and while the curiosity to know was already beginning to fester, he refused to get personal with her about *anything*.

Touching the swollen area around her ankle very carefully, he saw that no bones seemed to be protruding like some of the uglier ankle injuries he'd witnessed out in the field. "It might just be sprained. Did you hear anything crack when you twisted it?" He looked up at her. That bewilderment was still in her eyes, and he swallowed hard trying his damnedest not to react inappropriately to it.

She shook her head. "I don't think so, but it happened so fast."

He brought his eyes back to her foot. He had to. Looking into those big innocent eyes was breaking his will to fight the urge to speak more freely to her. Lowering her foot gently, he stood up.

"There's no way you'll be driving tonight. And you really need to get this X-rayed to know for sure. Stay here." He started towards the door, but he saw the look of apprehension on her face, so he turned back to her and for some reason was compelled to smile. "I'll be right back."

He knew that bewildered expression would make an appearance, and as pissed at he was at himself for weakening so fast and giving in just to see it, it had been totally worth it.

Shaking off the alarming thoughts, he hurried toward the golf cart still parked on the side of the building. Technically, he had to check it out if he ever needed to use one, but he hadn't checked it back in today after using it all day. Since he'd gotten back so late today, he planned on doing so in the morning.

In less than a couple of minutes, he had it parked at the building's front door. He jumped out and hurried through it, already looking forward to having her in his arms again.

This was not good.

He found her squeezing her eyes shut, her face scrunched in agony.

"It's hurts that bad?"

She nodded but said nothing as he knelt down to look at her ankle again. The swelling was getting worse. He grabbed her bag with one hand.

"Okay, let me help you stand on your good foot," he said, holding her elbow. She rose from her seat slowly, wobbling as she leaned into him. "I got you," he assured her as he brought his arm around her small waist, holding her firmly.

Once she was all the way up, he bent down to bring his arm under her knees again as he had earlier. "Put your arms around my neck."

She did, and just like earlier, he inhaled her blissful scent. He knew with her foot dangling it had to make the pain worse, and she buried her face in his neck, gasping. He held her tighter in hopes of keeping her foot from moving too much. Walking backwards, he pushed the glass door open with his back, careful not to hit her foot against it as he swung her around and walked through it.

He'd never actually been in combat, but in his day, he'd been through plenty of drills where he had to carry a fellow soldier in full combat gear for long grueling sessions. Ms. Brady felt so tiny and delicate he could hold her like this forever, as small as she was in comparison. The scent of her hair alone and the feel of her soft but firm body pressed against his was incentive enough to hold her as long as he could. It was actually a disappointment to have to set her down in the golf cart, but he did so gently and slowly.

"Are you okay?" he asked as he watched her slowly and apparently very painfully lower her foot to the floor of the cart.

Again she nodded without saying a word as if words alone might make it hurt more. "We'll get you some pain killers in a little bit. The base hospital isn't too far."

Setting her purse down in the back of the cart, he rushed around to the driver's side and jumped in. Brandon was almost glad she didn't seem to be in a mood to talk. He already felt too close to giving into what he'd previously said was out of the question, getting to know her a little more by asking generic questions that could be construed as perfectly innocent inquiries in a situation like this. Asking her if she had anyone that could come pick her up for example would be entirely acceptable. Knowing there were other reasons he wanted to know and that there shouldn't be, he refrained from asking.

"I'm sorry for taking up so much of your time, Sergeant Billings," she said softly. "Once you get me to the hospital, I can call someone so you can leave."

Someone? Like Antonio? "I had no further plans for the rest of this evening, Ms. Brady," he said, looking straight ahead. "I can take you home. You won't be able to drive tonight. That's for sure, maybe not even for a few days."

She groaned, shaking her head and squeezing her eyes closed again.

"Is the pain getting worse?" he asked, looking down at her swollen ankle.

"No." She sighed. "It's not that. I mean, yeah, it still hurts, but not any worse. It just hadn't even dawned on me that I might not be able to drive for days. I had a major breakthrough today at work and planned on being very busy the next few days."

Brandon glanced over just in time to catch her frowning face. It was so sweet he had to look away. He might've smiled again if what that adorable expression did to him didn't scare the hell out. "Well, maybe they'll tell you otherwise," he offered as solace, staring straight ahead. "If it's not broken and you ice it enough tonight, you might be able to put a little pressure on it by tomorrow."

She sighed heavily, and he dared not look her way for fear she might be making another expression that might have him sighing too. This was getting ridiculous. Already, he was having unacceptable thoughts and visions of things that were completely inappropriate.

They reached the emergency room, and he drove right up to the entrance. "Stay here," he said as he rushed in.

He was able to quickly acquire a wheelchair and brought it out then helped her out of the cart. Trying not to put too much thought on how tightly she wrapped her arms around his neck, he abstained from holding her just as tightly. He did, however, allow himself to indulge in her scent again. As he lowered her onto the seat, he glanced up just as she loosened her hold on him and froze when he realized he was close enough to taste those lips. She stared at him for a moment as he stood there bent over, unbelievably tempted at that most inopportune moment to kiss her.

"You okay?" he asked, still not moving away.

She nodded, continuing to hold his gaze.

He swallowed hard because this was so unlike him and because he knew once this night was over he'd be regretting this. Finally he moved away. Handing her the purse from the back seat of the golf cart, he came around the back of the chair and began pushing her inside the emergency room. As much as he knew he should take her up on her offer to call someone else, he wasn't ready to leave her side just yet. Damn, he was going to regret this tomorrow.

Already, he regretted having met with his original drill instructor last weekend. Brandon hated to admit it, but unlike *anyone*, Sergeant Taft held a special place in his heart. Taft had been the one who straightened Brandon's ass out in the first place. As far as Brandon was concerned, Taft was the reason why he hadn't dropped out those first few punishing weeks of boot camp when he'd considered doing so on more than one occasion. He was also Brandon's inspiration and why he'd become a drill instructor in the first place. For those reasons, he kept the man at bay. It'd be too easy to start to feel an emotional attachment to this friend. Brandon didn't make emotional attachments. He made no exceptions. But when Taft heard Brandon would be in California, he invited him to his home for dinner with his wife.

Feeling too duty-bound to a man he held in such high esteem, he'd accepted, but the thought of getting too close scared the hell out of him. The now semi-retired Sergeant and his wife had been so pleasant and welcoming. They even insisted now that Brandon was based in California he visit more often and said they'd be visiting him too. Brandon had regretted the visit the moment he'd walked out of their home. Just like then, he knew he'd be regretting this entire night by tomorrow morning, possibly even sooner. So why the hell wasn't he walking away yet?

The emergency room was busy, but they still got in fast.

"Just wheel her over behind that second curtain on your right." The nurse pointed as Brandon started wheeling her in that direction. "There'll be someone in there to take all her information in a few minutes. You can help your wife onto the bed. The doctor will be with her shortly after they've taken her vitals."

She walked away before either of them could explain the misunderstanding. Brandon and Ms. Brady exchanged glances as her cheeks shaded with slight color.

Without a word, Brandon continued to wheel her over to the bed the nurse had pointed to. When they reached it, Ms. Brady attempted to stand on her own, holding the end of the bed and the arm of the chair. "Let me help you," he quickly offered, pulling her arm around his neck.

Grabbing on to him, she hopped toward the bed that was a bit high for her, so he lifted her by the waist. Again their faces came just inches from each other. Thankfully, just as they'd been caught in another staring contest, someone cleared his throat loudly just behind Brandon, snapping them out of it.

A young man held a clipboard and smiled broadly then pulled a pen out of his front pocket. "Good evening." He spoke quickly, holding the clipboard in front of him. "I'm Rob, and you are Mrs. Brady, right?"

"It's *Ms*." She corrected him politely. "I'm not married, and you can call me Regina."

Rob looked up at her then at Brandon, his eyebrows furrowing. "Oh, I'm sorry, Regina." He looked back down on his clipboard and wrote something. "The nurse out front said you were here with your husband."

Ms. Brady glanced at Brandon, her poignant eyes looking even more innocent as he saw how she tried to hide the pain she was feeling. She quickly brought her attention back to Rob. "No, um." She winced now, unable to hide it anymore. Brandon had had his share of sprained ankles and ligament injuries, and he knew how painful they could be. "I guess she just assumed," she continued, pressing her lips together for a moment. "This is Sergeant Billings. We work in the same building where I fell. He was there when it happened and was kind enough to help get me here."

Rob and Brandon's eyes met for a second before Rob turned back to Ms. Brady. "Ah, I see. Okay, well, now that we got that straight, I need to get a little more information from you before we start with your vitals." He looked down at her ankle. "Yep, that's pretty swollen. It might even be broken."

"Can you get her some painkillers first?" Brandon spoke up, knowing firsthand how long this could take.

"I *can*," Rob said, his brow lifting without looking up, "but I need to get some info from her first."

Brandon looked down at Rob's ID. Corporal Robert Lansing—ER. The fact that this young *corporal* hadn't referred to him as sir was enough to piss Brandon off. He'd never tolerated that kind of disrespect, but the fact that the asshole didn't even bother to look at him when he addressed him and that he'd used a condescending tone was more than Brandon would tolerate.

"Do you have a supervisor, Corporal Lansing?"

Immediately, he had both Ms. Brady's and Lansing's attention.

CHAPTER NINE

Lansing stared at Brandon wide-eyed. "Yes, I do."

"Yes, I do, *what?*" Brandon raised his voice just slightly, but there was no masking his signature drill instructor demanding tone.

Lansing stood up a little straighter, blinking a little faster. "Yes, I do, *sir.*"

"Then I suggest you go get him or her in here now."

"He, uh, he's not here tonight, sir." Lansing glanced back at Ms. Brady and down at her ankle again. "But, uh, I apologize for any disrespect. I assure you there was none intended, and, uh, I can get her those painkillers no problem. I just—"

"No excuses, Lansing. Ms. Brady is in a lot of pain. Go get them now."

"Yes, sir," Lansing said, nodding at Brandon and then at Ms. Brady.

"I still want your supervisor's name," Brandon informed him coldly.

"Yes, sir," the corporal said again before walking away in a hurry.

The only reason he let him off the hook and didn't demand he get *one* of his higher ups, *anyone*, was because getting Ms. Brady her pain medicine took precedence at that moment. But he had every intention of speaking with Lansing's supervisor.

Brandon turned back to Ms. Brady. She was staring him wide-eyed.

"Are you really gonna get him in trouble?" she asked, her brows coming together suddenly. "For not moving fast enough?"

This time the little princess's glare was not quite as amusing. He didn't expect her to understand, and he wouldn't bother to explain himself, but it was still annoying as shit that she'd question him. The Marine code of honor and respect was not something you explained. It was something instilled in you by living it. "I said I'd be speaking with his supervisor. It's up to his supervisor to decide whether or not he'll be in trouble, but if he were my subordinate, there certainly would be repercussions."

"Repercussions for *what*? He did nothing wrong."

Lansing walked to Ms. Brady's side swiftly. "I'll attach a saline lock to your hand in case you need more pain medicine again. That way I won't have to keep poking you, and the relief will be instantaneous."

Ms. Brady smiled at Lansing and thanked him profusely for doing what he should've done the moment he'd seen the size of her swollen ankle and how much pain she was in. As he worked on getting the saline lock taped to her hand, he asked her quickly about any allergies or reactions to morphine and if she was by any chance pregnant to which she interestingly answered, "Absolutely *not*." These were the questions Lansing indicated earlier that would take far more time to get to. "Now you're going to feel a little woozy, Ms. Brady, maybe even a little like you're drunk or high. Morphine is, after all, a narcotic, so expect some dizziness and even confusion, but don't worry. It's all normal."

Nodding, Ms. Brady closed her eyes as he inserted the needle in the vein on the top of her hand. Brandon watched her strained expression as Lansing began administering the medicine through the saline lock. Slowly the still-pained expression began to ease as the morphine began to take effect.

"The relief will be almost immediate," Lansing reminded her cautiously.

Yeah, no shit. That's why he should've given it to her a long time ago.

"Be careful not to move your ankle, though." Lansing warned. "Just because it won't hurt to do so anymore, doesn't mean you should. It's still injured, and moving it might make it worse."

After a few moments, she glanced over at Brandon, a silly smile spreading across her face and her eyes already drooping a little. "I feel better already," she said with a slight slur.

Brandon nodded at her but said nothing and certainly didn't offer any smiles. He knew all too well from his own past injuries and those of many of his recruits what morphine could do to you—make you feel. He didn't want to encourage any such behavior from her now that, given the circumstances, Lansing had probably given her a big fat dose of the stuff.

Lansing went back to what he'd begun to do before Brandon had demanded the pain medicine for Ms. Brady. In hindsight, Brandon understood a little now why Lansing had wanted to get all the information he collected now from her before shooting her up with the pain meds. Getting straight and coherent answers from Ms. Brady in this inebriated and confused state of mind took a lot longer than it would have if he'd done so before. Still she was out of pain now, and that's all that mattered.

Listening quietly as she answered all the pertinent questions, Brandon took note of some of the answers that shouldn't interest him but annoyingly did. She wasn't married or living with anyone. Her emergency contacts were her parents, who lived more than an hour away in one direction, and her sister, who lived a half hour in the opposite direction. She was twenty-seven, and the only medication she was on was one she said was for anxiety, but she hadn't taken it in weeks. He noticed how she lowered her voice when answering that and a few other more personal questions, such as she just finished her menstrual cycle and she had been pregnant once but never full term. She'd lost the baby at six weeks a little over a year ago.

Brandon took a few steps away. "I can wait for you in the waiting room," he offered, feeling as if he were intruding on her privacy now.

To his surprise, she shook her head quickly, holding her hand up to him. "No, please stay here."

Seeing her sitting there looking so vulnerable and those big eyes practically pleading, he reminded himself she was on a strong narcotic. Just because her family wasn't nearby and she was asking him to stay close wasn't an invitation to take care of her. So why did it feel like it, but most alarmingly, why the hell was he hoping it was?

Already, he'd had every intention of getting her the care she needed and of making sure she got home okay. Hearing she lived alone with no close family made him wonder how she'd manage if her foot *was* broken.

This had to stop.

He walked back slowly to where he'd been standing previously but said nothing. The doctor finally came in after Lansing finished with all his questions, taking her vitals, and icing her foot.

A couple of hours later, after a thorough examination then waiting for an X-ray to be taken then more waiting, the morphine had worn off, and Ms. Brady was no longer woozy and smiling silly. But she did have one request that made Brandon wonder if it was still the morphine talking. "Will you call me Regina, please? Ms. Brady sounds so formal." He nodded, but he refused to say it until he had to. "What's *your* first name?"

He stared at her for a moment, taking a long slow breath. He should've left when she offered him the opportunity. He knew he'd regret this and already was. "Brandon," he said finally.

She smiled, taking in his name. "May I call you that?"

"No" was his immediate response.

Her expression should've had him suppressing a smile; instead, he swallowed hard, feeling a bit panicked. He'd seriously fucked up by still being here with her.

"Okay, Regina," the doctor said, pulling the curtain aside.

That curtain was the only thing that separated Ms. Brady's bed from the one next to her in the emergency room, and it still felt too intimate for Brandon. She'd told him it was okay if he wanted to sit on the bed next to her, but he'd passed. Just being here with her this long was a mistake. Sitting next to her on her bed would be too damn cozy.

"Well, the good news is it looks as if there are no broken bones," the doctor informed them as she placed the X-ray up on the lighted board. "But your ankle *is* badly sprained with a few stretched ligaments. So you'll have to wear an air splint for a week, maybe two, to keep the ankle immobile and make sure you don't further stretch those ligaments."

"Immobile?" Ms. Brady asked, sitting up straighter. "Does that mean I can't go to work? I really need to be there."

"It means you really should stay off your ankle as much as possible." The doctor turned back to look at Ms. Brady. "What kind of work do you do?"

"Office work," Ms. Brady said quickly. "I'm a structural engineer, and we're in a middle of a big project, but I'd be mostly sitting all day in front of the computer, on the phone, in meetings—that kind of stuff—*all* off my feet."

The doctor gave Ms. Brady a knowing look, picking up on the fact that she seemed to be trying to convince her. Then she brought her attention back to the lighted board with the X-ray on it and pointed at the area in question. "See that?" She turned back and winced at Ms. Brady. "Those stretched ligaments are causing all the pain. You don't wanna mess with those. If you rupture or tear one completely, that pain will be so much worse, and it'll take a lot longer to heal. You really shouldn't be putting any pressure on it, and driving alone will do that. But," she shrugged, "I know what it's like to *have* to be at work. I'd suggest you at least take one full day to stay off it completely before going back. When you do, make sure that you really are mostly sitting and try to keep it elevated as much as possible."

Ms. Brady nodded, and Brandon felt something else he shouldn't be feeling—relief. He shouldn't care one way or the other if she followed her doctor's orders or not. Just because he knew the doctor was right—she should stay off her ankle and for much longer than just a day—it shouldn't be his concern.

The doctor examined her ankle again, feeling around to make sure where exactly the stretched ligaments were before adding the dressing and air splint. After all that, Ms. Brady was in pain again. They gave her another dose of the morphine, which took effect immediately.

"It's a good thing it's late because you'll go home and will sleep like a baby." The doctor smiled as she finished administering the medicine into Ms. Brady's saline lock.

The doctor left, and Lansing was back in within minutes to remove the saline lock and give Ms. Brady the prescription the doctor had written up for her pain medicine.

"These are extra," he handed her a few packets, "in case you can't get to the pharmacy until tomorrow. You'll probably be in pain in the morning when this stuff wears off."

Ms. Brady smiled goofily, taking them from him. "Thank you, Rob. That's so thoughtful of you." She reached out and squeezed Rob's forearm. "You're a very sweet guy. I meant to ask you earlier. Are you married?"

Lansing smiled, looking as surprised at her question as Brandon felt irritated by it. "No, actually I'm not."

He glanced back at Brandon, who stared him down hard. If the guy had half a brain, he'd give Ms. Brady her release papers and leave *fast*. He may know Brandon wasn't her husband and that she'd referred to him as just someone who worked in the same building, but the guy had to know there was more to Brandon's interest in being here. No guy, unless he was out of his mind, would walk into that emergency room and demand things like he had then spend all these hours waiting with a girl he barely knew. The last time Brandon had checked he was a sane man. So as much as he hated to admit it, the fact that he was still standing here already anxious to get her out of there so he could have her all to himself again, had all kinds of internal sirens going off—sirens this guy better damn well be hearing too.

Fortunately for Lansing, he did have a brain after all because he quickly changed the subject to instructions on removing and replacing Ms. Brady's ankle dressing and air splint. He gave her crutches then released her, rushing away to another patient.

Earlier while she'd been getting X-rayed, Brandon had hurried back in the golf cart, leaving it on the side of the building they worked in where it was supposed to be. He brought his Jeep back to the hospital instead.

Rolling her out to the Jeep, he was glad now that he hadn't lifted the Jeep yet as he intended to. It was already high enough that he knew she'd have trouble getting in. He threw the crutches in the back seat, opened the window, and helped Ms. Brady out of the wheelchair. "Leave everything on the chair, Ms. Brady. I—"

"You said you'd call me Regina," her voice went a little high as she wrapped an arm around his neck and wobbled onto her good foot.

He adjusted her so he could get a good hold of her to lift her into the Jeep, and their eyes met. He'd never actually said he would, but he wasn't going to argue. "Just leave your things on the chair. I'll grab them once I have you in the Jeep."

She wrapped her other arm around his neck and tilted her head to the side with a frown. "Why don't you like me, Sergeant Billings?"

He stared at her for a moment but didn't answer. Instead, he lifted her onto the passenger side of his Jeep and closed the door. He grabbed her things from the wheelchair and threw them in the backseat, walking around the Jeep in a huff.

He fucking knew this was a bad idea.

As soon as he was in the driver's seat, she was at it again. "Can you at least tell me what it is about me that you dislike so much?"

Her words were noticeably less affected than they had been when Lansing had given her the morphine. She wasn't even slurring, just speaking a little slower. The doctor must've gone a lot lighter on the dose.

He inhaled deeply as he slid the key into the ignition. "I never said I didn't like you. I just said I had no interest in getting to know you." Without turning to look at her, because he heard the gasp and he could only imagine the amusing expression on her face, he revved the Jeep up. "Fasten your seatbelt."

"But that's mean! You don't say that to someone unless you don't like them or are deliberately trying to hurt their feelings, which you did." She paused as she put her seatbelt on. "And you don't deliberately try to hurt someone's feelings unless you don't like them."

Refusing to look at her, he pulled forward to get out of the patient pick-up line. "I'm sorry I hurt your feelings. It wasn't my intention."

"Yes, it was," she insisted.

"No, it wasn't." Pulling into the exit driveway of the hospital, he finally glanced at her, instantly regretting it because she looked adorable with that little crease between her eyes and her arms mulishly crossed in front of her. Struggling not to smile, he asked, "Which way do I turn?"

"Right," she said. "And why can't I call you by your first name?"

He bit down, locking his jaw for a moment before responding. This conversation needed to be derailed and soon because he was *not* getting personal with her. "Because we know each other strictly on a professional level, and I'd like to keep it that way. Referring to each other by first names would *not* be professional." He heard her exhale a bit exasperated, but thankfully she didn't say more. "Where do you live?"

She told him where, and it should've frustrated him further; instead, he smiled inwardly that her condo was only blocks from his apartment. Of course, she lived in an oceanfront condo, and he lived in an apartment building that was a few blocks away from the beach, but it wasn't as if he couldn't afford to live more lavishly. He just chose not to.

To his relief, she was quiet the rest of the way, but he felt the tension thickening with every minute they drove in silence. He'd gladly take the tension over getting back into that risky conversation again. After spending several hours with her now, he'd be too tempted to assure her he didn't dislike her because he hated knowing he'd hurt her feelings. It was better if they left things as they were with him not exactly denying he didn't like her only clarifying what he'd actually said.

Scrutinizing the two-story building she pointed out as hers, he pulled into the security gate entrance and frowned. "I hope for your sake there's an elevator."

"I have crutches now," she said, still sounding a little irritated with him. "You won't have to carry me up."

He turned to her, suddenly overwhelmed with concern. "You're serious? You're on the second floor, and there's no elevator?"

She shook her head. "The code is 7119."

Frowning, he turned to the security pad and punched in the numbers.

"My condo is on the first floor," she clarified as they waited for the gate to open slowly.

"Then what did you mean about me not having to carry you up?"

He drove in the gate as she pointed in the direction of her condo. "It's the last one on the right. They're all on the first floor. They're just all two stories," she explained. "So my bedroom is on the second floor, and no there's no elevator in my condo. I'll be hopping upstairs or using my crutches to get up there."

"Not tonight you won't." The words shot out without even thinking. "I mean," he said, quickly backpedaling, "your ankle is still so swollen, and you're still under the influence of morphine. You could fall again."

"I'll be fine," she said as he pulled into the parking space just in front of her condo. She turned around and grabbed her crutches.

Before he could open his door, she was already opening hers. "Don't get out." His words were far more commanding than she'd obviously expected to hear from him, and she turned to look at him, her eyes confirming his tone *had* startled her. "I'll come around and help you."

He rushed around the Jeep because he was already picking up on her tenacity and decided she may very well ignore his request that she wait for him to come around and help her. He cursed under his breath. Was she really going to try to make it up to the second floor when she could barely stand without wobbling?

Sure as shit she already had the door open and her good leg hanging out, trying to place the crutches on the ground. He held his hand out for her. "Give me your hand, Ms. Brady. I'll get you down."

She'd begun to take his hand but took it back. "Oh, can we please stop with that, *Brandon*? It's so silly." Her furrowed brows were back, and Brandon stared at her, trying not to get caught up in those big dark eyes as he had too often tonight already. "We've been around each other all night. We may not know each other very well, but I'd say, after the hours we've spent together, we can at least be on a first-name basis."

Moving in closer to her, he saw her eyes widen. "Forget about giving me your hand," he said, disregarding her previous comments and took her by the waist. "Put your hands on my shoulders instead."

She didn't move right away but then huffed and complied. He lifted her off the seat, bringing her body against his as she slid down until her good foot was on the ground.

"Keep holding on to me," he said, ignoring the way she was staring at him and reached for her crutch. "Here you go." He placed the crutch under her arm but continued to hold on to her firmly, even as she put her weight down on the crutch and her good foot. "Don't let the other one touch the ground. Remember you don't want to put any pressure on it at all yet." Even after placing the other crutch under her other arm, she still swayed a little and didn't look at all as if she'd be going too far without taking a tumble. "Maybe I should just carry you. You seem a little dizzy still."

"I got it," she insisted, but he didn't let go of her, walking alongside of her as she struggled with every step.

When she nearly fell for the third time, he took the crutch from under her left arm and threw it down on the grassy area in front of her condo.

"What are you doing?" she asked.

"Keeping you from falling and breaking your other ankle."

He would've preferred throwing her stubborn ass over his shoulder, but he was afraid of hurting her ankle, so he lifted her once again, cradling her in his arms. She dropped the other crutch and wrapped her arms around his neck. Having her in his arms like this just like when she'd slid down his body getting out of the car felt too damn good. He needed to get her inside and get the hell out of there *fast*. He reached the small porch with a wooden swing bench. "You have the keys on you?"

"Oh, no." She winced. "They're in my purse in your back seat."

Brandon placed her down on the bench, careful that it didn't swing too much. He rushed back to the Jeep and grabbed her purse, determined to get this over with. Even if she did insist she was going upstairs tonight when she couldn't even make it from his Jeep to the front door, he wouldn't be arguing. She wasn't his concern. He'd get her in and wash his hands of her. He'd already gone above and beyond considering the risk he knew he'd be taking the moment he decided to stay with her the whole time tonight.

Picking up the crutches from the grass on the way back with her purse, he handed it to her, not wanting to dig through it himself. He leaned the crutches against the wall just outside her front door. Regina took the purse, and after looking through it for a few seconds, she handed him the key. He unlocked the front door and opened it. The front room was completely dark, and his hand searched the wall just inside next to the door. "Is this where . . .?" he began to ask, but then found the switch and turned the lights on. He blinked, staring into the nearly empty front room. "You don't have furniture?" he asked, not sure if maybe she'd been burglarized, because there were a few things in her front room—a couple of plants, a few boxes, and a big antique-looking trunk.

"I've only been living here a few weeks. I, uh, left most of my furniture in New York," she explained. "It would've been too much of a hassle to bring. I do have furniture coming, but the front room stuff was special order, so it's taking longer to arrive. I have appliances and a kitchen table," she offered with a smile. "Oh and the most important item I had delivered before I even arrived. My bed."

Brandon's shoulders slumped and he let his head fall back. No wonder she was insisting she could go upstairs tonight. Where the hell else would she be sleeping if she didn't? *Fuck!* As indifferent as he wanted to be about this and help her in the front door then turn around and walk away, he couldn't in clear conscience just leave her like this. "Maybe you should get a room for the night," he suggested.

It'd be a lot safer that he drop her off at one, get her in the door, and walk away rather than having to carry her up those stairs to her *bedroom*. Maybe tomorrow, once she had a clearer head, she could manage making it up these stairs without hurting herself.

"No, I'll be fine," she said, already trying to stand on her own.

Goddamn obstinate woman.

"Hold on," he said as he placed the crutches inside the condo. He hurried to help her up, and within moments, she was in his arms again as he cradled her. "Are you sure?" he asked again. "I can get you up there tonight," he said, glancing up the staircase. "But what about tomorrow? What if you're stuck up there?"

"I won't be stuck," she said, motioning with her head toward the small table with four chairs around it in the kitchen nook. "And you're not carrying me up."

"Why not?" he asked, losing his patience as he set her down on the chair. "You can't—"

"Because Sergeant—" She caught herself and lifted that stubborn but very sweet chin. "Because, Brandon, I'm starving. I'm gonna make myself something to eat before heading up, and if you plan on carrying me up, that would mean you'd have to wait. I've taken up enough of your time already. I won't take anymore. I appreciate all your help and your offer to do more, but I'll get up there on my own. It might take me a while, but I can do it. You really should get home. I've kept you up so late already."

Feeling defeated, Brandon leaned against the wall. "What if I go get you something to eat and bring it back? I'll carry you up, and you can eat it up there."

He just needed this night to be over already—needed to stop looking into those stunning eyes before she asked him anything personal again. The longer he was around her, the more his interest in getting to know her grew. He knew that the longer he stayed here the harder it would be to get her off his mind. Even before she'd fallen tonight, she'd annoyingly seeped into his thoughts too much already. The memory of having her body pressed against his, the scent of her hair, and those lips so close he could almost taste them would be impossible to forget now. But it felt equally impossible to walk away—leave her here to brave those stairs on her own. He was already too committed, and he was slowly losing the battle to fight this.

"I have leftover pizza in the fridge. It'd be faster if you could help me warm it." Her eyes opened wide suddenly, and she touched his arm. "Oh my God, you haven't eaten either. You must be just as starved as I am. You're welcome to have some of the pizza. There's plenty."

She started to stand, but he held her down. "I'll get the pizza. You stay there."

He walked into her small kitchen. Somehow he thought a fancy oceanfront place like this would be bigger, but aside from whatever was upstairs, the bottom of her condo wasn't much bigger than his apartment, and the kitchen was just as tiny as his. He opened the fridge and pulled out the large pizza box. "You ordered this big thing for yourself?"

"I always order a large," she said. "I like eating it for breakfast and lunch for the next few days."

Placing the box on the counter, he opened it and stared at the odd-looking toppings. She'd been right about one thing. He was starving, and he was hoping for meat—lots of it. Instead they'd be feasting on a pizza with broccoli, bell peppers, and red onions. At least he saw what looked like chunks of chicken. It reminded him of her pickiness at the airport with her salad.

After a few minutes of searching in her cabinets with Ms. Brady verbally walking him through where everything was and how her microwave worked, he was back in the small nook area with a tray of pizza, napkins, and two mini bottles of Coke Zero.

"I don't think I've ever had pizza with broccoli," he said as he took the seat across from her.

"No?" she asked, taking a slice and putting it on her napkin. "It's really good. Well, this place I order from is really good. All their pizzas are amazing. They have this spinach/shrimp one with goat cheese that's to die for. But I'm afraid my sister's made me a bit of a pizza snob. I don't order from anywhere else now."

Brandon stared at her as he chewed, trying not to be too obvious about watching her lick those plump lips. The pizza wasn't half bad. Maybe it was just that he'd been starving, but the more he chewed it, the more he realized that it was actually pretty damn good. He debated on whether or not to ask what he wanted to ask because it was bordering on personal, but he figured what the hell. They were just talking food. "You said you just moved here. How do you know so much about this place's pizza? You've been eating pizza this whole time?"

She smiled, holding the napkin to her mouth and shook her head. "No, this is actually the first time I've ordered from there since I got here. But I'm originally from Southern California, so I discovered this place, or rather my sister turned me on to it, years ago."

Nodding, Brandon wondered just what the doctor had shot her up with. She might've been a little wobbly on her way in, but she seemed awfully clear-headed now—nothing like how she'd been in earlier in the hospital. Except for her annoyingly friendly behavior with Lansing, asking him if he were married, the near whining she'd done just as they got in her car, and the outright questioning of why he didn't like her, she now seemed back to acting like her normal self.

"Are you seriously gonna go in tomorrow?" he asked.

She nodded immediately as if she didn't even have to think about it.

"You're not even gonna take a day off like the doc said you should?"

"I can't," she said as tenacious as ever. "I have lots of work I need to get done."

He stared at her for a moment before deciding once again she wasn't his problem. If she was going to insist she didn't need a day off, then so be it. It wasn't his concern.

They ate quietly for a few moments. Then she cleared her throat a little too loudly, so he looked up at her. "Are you really not gonna tell me what I did to make you dislike me so much? Because I don't care what you say. I know you don't."

Chewing slowly, Brandon stared at her quizzical and somewhat playful eyes without responding.

"I mean at first I thought maybe you were just like that with everyone, but then I saw you at Gaslamp, and you seemed to be really enjoying yourself until . . ." The playful expression was replaced with a wounded one, and she glanced down at her pizza. "Until you saw me."

Swallowing down his pizza, he took a sip of his soda. He should've left when she told him he should. There was no way he could now, and this was about to get personal.

CHAPTER TEN

Regina

Regina hadn't planned it this way, but she was glad now that Brandon hadn't been there when she'd discussed with the doctor the pain medicine she'd be getting before she left. Regina didn't like the way it made her feel, and she'd rather deal with a little pain than feel as high as she had after Rob had shot her up earlier. It was hard enough to play it cool around this intimidating man, even with her full cognizance. She didn't need an added handicap.

When Brandon had gone out to bring his Jeep to the patient pick up area, Regina had taken the opportunity to tell the doctor if she were going to be given more pain medicine she wanted a much lighter dose. Since he didn't know this, she could always blame the drugs tomorrow if she got too brave tonight, trying to get out of him what she was dying to know. But she needed to know now more than ever why he seemed so unrelenting about preferring to keep their relationship professional. How and why do you just make a decision like that about someone you don't even know?

She'd since stopped obsessing about what she'd thought she'd seen in his eyes the morning he stopped and asked her to finish saying what she'd begun to say, but after today, there was no question about it. She kept telling herself he couldn't be feeling anything for her good or bad. He didn't know her. But she'd picked up on something too many times tonight. Whatever he was feeling—whether it was positive or negative—one thing was clear: it was intense.

Her curiosity had reached the point of no return. She *had* to know what the hell this guy's deal was. Was it possible he was like this with everyone? One thing was for sure. She'd never met anyone quite like him. A part of her wanted to dismiss him, not care what his fickle ass thought of her. But another part of her, the part that went breathless when he got so close and stared at her with that confusing intensity as he was doing now, was utterly intrigued. He excited her when she knew he shouldn't.

"Why'd you take the stairs today?" Brandon asked.

Disappointed that he was going to ignore her inquiry once again, she looked down and stared at her pizza, frustrated for a moment. She wondered if she should just let it go. Obviously, it was not something he'd be easily talked into discussing.

"Ms. . ." Brandon cleared his throat. "Regina?"

That got her attention. She didn't think he'd ever give into calling her that, so she looked up. His expression while still intense was a bit softer. "Why didn't you take the elevator today?"

He knew or, at the very least, had an idea, or he wouldn't be asking. She was tired of the games, his being so hot and cold and her hiding from him all week like a coward.

Sitting up a little straighter, she looked him right in those deep blue eyes. "I was afraid to get caught in the elevator with you. I've been trying to avoid you all week." She saw the change in his eyes. She'd surprised him. *Good.* "I wasn't sure you were the one behind me, but just in case, I was hoping to beat you down the stairs so I wouldn't run into you at the bottom."

The surprise in his eyes was gone now, but she'd caught it before it disappeared. Now he stared at her as unreadable as usual. "Why?"

Her mouth fell open, and once again she noticed what she thought she'd imagined before: how easily he was distracted by the movement of her lips. His eyes were immediately on them. She quickly closed her mouth, pressing her lips together for a moment. "*Why?* Is that a serious question?"

His eyebrow lifted, but otherwise it was his only response to her question. He took another bite of his pizza and chewed slowly, staring at her. The intensity of his stare softened a bit, but he was still as impassive as ever. Apparently, that was answer enough. The man was inexplicable. Of course his question was a serious one.

"Well, I don't know about you, Brandon, but I don't enjoy being around people who clearly dislike me."

"I never said I didn't like you." He continued to chew, staring at her, completely unfazed while wreaking havoc on her insides.

"You may as well have," she countered, losing a little of the conviction she'd felt just moments ago as she remembered his hurtful words.

That silenced him for a moment, and she looked away, pondering why anything this man she barely knew said to her could *hurt?*

"I wouldn't have spent all this time with you and I certainly wouldn't still be here if I didn't like you. You said it yourself. I don't know anything about you, so how could I dislike you?"

She looked up at him, and unlike before, when he'd stared her so ingenuously, he was looking down at his food, noticeably avoiding any eye contact.

"Then why—"

"It's who you represented I didn't like," he said so abruptly it startled her. Regina shook her head, not understanding. "You reminded me of someone." His eyes finally looked up and met hers.

Something changed in those hardened eyes she'd become so used to, but deciphering it was impossible. He just suddenly seemed *troubled?* Then just as quickly, that steadfast gaze was back.

"But you were right. It wasn't fair and I apologize." Crumpling up the napkin in front of him, he stood up. "You ready to go up?"

She wanted to say no—wanted to ask him who she reminded of and why he said it in past tense. Did she not remind him of that person anymore? What changed? But instinct told her to be glad for what she *had* gotten out of him. And he'd apologized. She hadn't seen that coming.

Truth was she'd already kept him long enough, and getting up those stairs was not going to be easy. The staircase in her condo was much narrower than the one in their building. This would be tricky, so he may still be here a while.

Glancing down at the now empty tray on the table, she nodded, wiping her mouth with her napkin. "Yes, I'm ready."

"And you're sure you wouldn't rather get a room for tonight?" He glanced up the narrow staircase and back at her.

"Yes, I'm sure," she said. "If you'd rather not do this, I'm telling you I could make it up slowly. I'll go backwards on my butt if I have to."

He was already shaking his head before she finished. "It's not that I'd rather not. I'm just wondering how you're gonna get down tomorrow on your own."

He reached out his hand to her. She took it then grabbed hold of his shoulder with her other. As bad as she felt about being such a burden to this guy she barely knew and whose entire night had been taken up by her, she felt even guiltier that some parts about tonight had been very enjoyable, such as feeling his strong arms around her and getting to touch his big hard shoulders as she was now.

He bent over, and in an instant, she was cradled in his arms again. She wrapped her arms around his neck. "I'll get you up that first part of the staircase like this," he said as he began to walk. "But this won't work the rest of the way. It's too narrow. You won't fit sideways."

Without putting her down, Brandon stood at the bottom of the staircase. He looked to be studying the first part, the part before it turned into the narrow passageway that led up to her bedroom. Regina almost hated to look away from his intensely pensive face to look at the stairs as well. She was fighting the unbelievable urge to turn his chin to her and kiss him. The very thought warmed her face as she stared at the stairs where she should've been focusing in the first place. How could she possibly even think of such a thing at a time like this?

He started up the wider wooden part of the stairs. When he got to the top of that part, he put her down. "You'll have to get on my back for the rest of the way. It's the only way we'll fit without risking you banging your ankle against the wall."

Regina felt her eyes widen at the sight of him undoing the buttons of his shirt, but did her best to not look too alarmed. He must've caught the look on her face because his expression went even more serious. "It's getting hot, and I'm sure it'll get hotter climbing those stairs. Plus," he said as he removed the shirt, allowing for a view of the bulging chest just under the snug white T-shirt, "I'll be more flexible without this."

He hung the shirt over the railing of the staircase and crouched down in front of Regina, his back to her. "Climb on and straddle me with your good leg. Let your hurt one hang straight back so it doesn't hit the wall on the way up."

The moment she'd seen him removing his shirt, her insides had started to rumble. That rumbling was now a low roar, and climbing on his back would only intensify it, but she still played it cool and leaned onto him, bringing her good leg over the side of him as he hooked it with his arm. "I got you," he assured her as she climbed a little higher, and he gripped her leg even tighter. "Grab onto my shoulders and hold on tight."

She did, and he began straightening out slowly. "You're on, right? Do you feel like you might slip?"

"No, I'm good."

"Okay. I'm gonna pull you up just a little higher so I can get a better hold of you. You ready?"

She nodded then realized he couldn't see her. "Yes. I'm ready."

He lowered his body a little then pushed her up higher, his hand now holding her butt cheek tightly. "Sorry," he said as he started up the stairs. "It really is the securest grip."

Regina narrowed her eyes, thinking about that while his fingers dug into her spreading her cheek as he tightened his hold. Was it really the securest grip? Her sisters and Janecia would no doubt crack up when she told them. How in the world did she get herself in this predicament?

Nearly at the top, Regina began breathing easier. This would soon be over. Then his foot must've slipped because he fell forward but gripped her even tighter.

"Shit!" he muttered as they dove forward.

"Are you okay?" she asked anxiously, still holding on with all her might.

"Yeah, just hold on," he said, straightening out. "I'm gonna have to go the rest of the way on my knees. It's just two more steps, okay?"

"Okay."

When they reached the top, he made sure he was all the way down so she was literally riding him like a horse only she wasn't sitting up. He leaned over to let her off on the side of her good leg. "Put your knee down first," he instructed her. "Now slide off me, but be careful not to bring your ankle down too hard. Can you hold it in the air a bit and I'll crawl out from under you?"

"Yes, I can." She gasped as she let her body slide all the way down.

While she was lying on her side with her leg in the air, he did just as he said he would and crawled out then turned around immediately to help her bring down her leg slowly. This night could not have been any crazier. The last thing she expected to be doing tonight was lying there on her bedroom floor, looking up at this guy—the daunting sergeant she'd so desperately tried to avoid all week—on all fours looking down at her.

"You okay?" She nodded for a moment, unable to speak. He stared into her eyes for a little longer before his concerned eyes made their way down her body, seemingly to make sure she was all right, but it felt different. Having him over her like this, so close to her as she lay there helplessly, and seeing the way he took in every inch of her in, the concern in his eyes morphing into awe, made her freeze. She should say something—protest. Instead, she lay there in silence, watching as his eyes didn't just check her out for injuries. They draped over her slowly with such yearning. Was that what she was seeing? Whatever it was it literally made her shiver. Those intensely alert eyes darted back to meet hers, his brows furrowing in question. "Are you cold?"

Regina shook her head, swallowing hard and chastising herself for not being unable to put even two words together. As if he suddenly caught himself, he jerked back, straightening up on his knees and startling her in the process.

"Let's, uh," he said, sounding completely rattled now. "Let's get you up."

He reached out for her hands, and she took them. Standing to his feet, he helped her by holding her elbow with one hand while still keeping his other hand in hers.

She started to hop in the direction of her bed when he leaned over and picked her up. "Don't try and walk without your crutches," he said simply.

If he'd actually been rattled as he'd sounded just moments ago, he recovered fast enough. He was back to his no-nonsense self, and any sign of yearning was completely gone. If she had to guess what he was feeling now, it was anger. His expression was completely hard now, and his jaw was set in stone.

Regina wished she could pull that brave, playful, and outspoken girl out from deep within her. She'd never been afraid to speak her mind even at a moment like this. Her sisters both envied her growing up because, while all three of them were known as the brainy ones in their school, she was the only one of the three who fit in with the popular crowd as well. She wasn't anywhere near as shy as her sisters had been, and she'd been an insatiable flirt.

The old her would've put Brandon in his place a long time ago, instead of cowering around avoiding him. The old Regina would've looked forward to having fun making *him* uncomfortable in the elevator, not the other way around.

As he laid her down gently on the bed, his face coming so close to hers, she once again could feel his warm breath against her mouth. She thought about everything he'd made her feel tonight. The old Regina would've kissed him right about now. She knew what she'd seen when he was looking at her just minutes ago. As hard as he was trying to pretend he wasn't feeling the incredible attraction she'd been feeling for him since the moment she saw him at the airport, today he'd slipped.

Feeling the old her rise from the dead, from somewhere deep inside her, Regina lifted herself to her elbow and pecked him on the lips softly. Brandon stopped cold and stared into her eyes, his breathing immediately hitching. "Thank you," she whispered, licking her lips, and his eyes were instantly on them. "For everything you did tonight."

She actually heard him gulp, and she smiled, feeling her heart speed up. Nearly losing her courage, she fought to keep the old her around and brought her hand around his neck, kissing his lips again, only this time she kept her lips on his longer. She waited, but he didn't kiss her back, and for an instant, she felt so mortified her heart plunged. The girl with him at Gaslamp came to mind. She'd already made note of the fact earlier that he didn't wear a wedding band, but that could mean nothing. She could still be his girlfriend or fiancée.

Regina began pulling away when his arms came around her, pulling her to him, and he kissed her feverishly and so deeply like she'd *never* been kissed before. She'd been kissed plenty, and she'd felt passion, but this was an entirely different experience for her. The man was voracious the way he sucked her lips with such fervor. She *loved* it. She wanted more.

With her insides going crazy among other parts of her body, a moan nearly escaped her as he sucked her bottom lip even harder. Just like earlier, he seemed to catch himself and stopped suddenly, leaning his forehead against hers breathlessly.

"I apologize—"

"Don't you dare," she said, pulling back to look at his startled eyes. "I started that."

"You were just thanking me. I shouldn't have taken it where it went."

"If I hadn't wanted it to go there, I would've stopped you."

He stared at her, noticeably swallowing hard again, his jaw stretching. "Why didn't you?"

She shook her head and touched his face. "I didn't want to."

He closed his eyes at the touch of her hand to his face. "You don't know anything about me."

His words made her pull her hand away. "Is that your girlfriend?" she asked, dreading the answer. "The girl you left the bar with Friday night?"

Shaking his head, he opened his eyes, but he didn't look at her. "I don't have a girlfriend."

The relief was instant, but she refrained from letting out the breath she was holding in too obviously. "My not knowing anything about you is not for lack of interest on my part. You *say* you have no interest in getting to know me, but that's not what I felt with that kiss or the way you look at me."

The old Regina was alive and well, but she was scaring the hell out of the new Regina. The insecurities she'd never felt before last year, before her life had taken such a turn, were still also very much alive and well. What if she was completely off? What if he'd just gotten caught up in a moment of passion? What if what he'd been so brutally honest about before still stood—he had no interest in her.

"Trust me," he said, standing up. "You don't wanna get to know me."

"Trust *me*." She countered right back, lifting her brow as their eyes met. "I do."

At a stalemate for a moment, they were both silent until finally he spoke again. "It's late, and we've both had a long night. You should get some sleep."

He turned around and started toward the stairs. Was that it? Was he just going to dismiss her request to get to know him flat out and leave? Where the hell was the old Regina so she could tell him off? Because the new one felt like crawling under her blankets, and already her brain was scrambling for ways to get transferred so she'd never have to face him again.

"I'll be here at oh-six-hundred hours tomorrow," he said as he reached the top of the staircase but didn't turn to face her. "There's no way you're getting down these stairs on your own, and I really don't think you should try."

Regina didn't even try to hide the smile that spread across her face, but she was glad he didn't turn to look at her. "Oh six hundred it is," she said. "I'll be ready. You can leave the front door unlocked so you can just let yourself in tomorrow. This is a gated community with lots of security cameras. It should be okay. Brandon . . .?" He nodded but didn't turn to look at her. "Thank you so much. I really appreciate everything you did for me today."

Finally, he turned just slightly, indulging her once again with one of his elusive smiles. It was barely there, and like so many times tonight, she saw a tinge of unease in his eyes, but small as it was, the hint of a smile still made her insides warm. "You're welcome. I'll see you tomorrow."

Even after she'd heard him walk out and her front door close, Regina sat there with her eyes closed, reliving that incredible kiss in her head. The sweet taste of him was still very much on her lips—mouth. She had no idea what to expect tomorrow, but the fact that he hadn't just walked away leaving her hanging and that he was actually coming back despite his obvious hesitation in getting better acquainted, gave her hope. This was something that just a week ago she would've never even imagined wanting—getting to know the ominous Sergeant Billings better.

CHAPTER ELEVEN

"It's late," Brandon said, cursing himself for not being able to take his eyes off her lips. "You need your sleep and so do I. I should go."

Even as he said the words, he couldn't bring himself to pull away from her. Already, he ached to kiss her again.

"I think I figured it out," she said with a sinful smile, those full lips of hers captivating him instantly as he continued to stare at them. "You're a vampire, and you're afraid I'll out you."

If he were a vampire, she'd be dead in a few more seconds because that's about how much longer he'd be able to stand not having his lips on her again. He felt the corner of his lip lift as his eyes swallowed her up from top to bottom. "You like what you see, don't you, Brandon?"

She was as sure about herself as he'd expected her to be. Of course he liked what he saw, and of course, no matter how strong of an effort he'd put into trying to hide it, she already knew it and probably had from day one. "Ms. Brady—"

"Uh, uh, let's not go back to that," she said, tracing his lips with her fingers. "Call me Regina."

Parting her legs, she brought his hand down to her inner thigh. The warmth of the soft flesh against his hand had him straightening out. "Regina, you're under the influence of—"

The second her luscious soft lips touched his again he took her face, cradling it in his hands, and kissed her wildly, eating up every inch of her mouth, feeling on the verge of madness. She moaned in delight, spreading her thighs further, and he gave up resisting, lifting her skirt up until he realized she wore no panties. He pulled away and froze, *staring in those huge brown eyes that sparkled with anticipation.*

"You know you want me," she said with unabashed confidence as she rubbed his hand over her warm hot wetness.

He was so hard for her it pissed him off. As much as he'd like to, it was impossible to deny it. He buried a finger in her as he watched her head fall back. "You want more," she said with a moan.

"I do," he finally admitted.

"You wanna fuck me?" she purred, smiling smugly.

He stared at her as he felt her hands undo his pants' top button and begin to unzip him. Lowering his own hand, he stopped her just as her soft warm fingers had begun to pull him out of his underwear. Shuddering, he squeezed his eyes shut but held her hand firmly in his then opened his eyes slowly. Her big brown eyes stared back at him, anxiously waiting. His eyes dropped down to her lips, those lips he'd yearned to taste for too long and tasted just as divine as he'd imagined.

He licked his lips and lifted his eyes to meet hers once again. "I want more."

Sitting up in a hot sweat and with an aching erection, Brandon glanced around panicked. He wasn't still in Regina's room on her bed. He was in his own bed, and his alarm was going off. He'd slept late. He never slept late. But it was already 05:45. His alarm was set for the usual 04:45. It'd been going off for an hour, and he hadn't heard it?

Brandon jumped out of bed, still feeling the aching effects of his dream between his legs. It wasn't as if he didn't always wake with morning wood, but this was by far the most painful he could ever remember.

He tried desperately to shake the vivid visuals of last night's kiss and his dream that morning because he was in a hurry and didn't have time to relieve the ache. But just thinking about it had him throbbing and dripping already. He lathered up, stroking his massive hard-on, the kind he only ever got when he was about to do the real deed. Squeezing his eyes shut, he continued to stroke as the inevitable began to build with every visual he had of her. Those lips would be the end of him. After kissing her last night, he knew he'd be powerless to fight it if he was ever that close to her and she was once again that willing. That was exactly why he kept kissing to an absolute minimum whenever he was with a woman. It was too intimate.

He could spend hours doing other things to them—driving them nuts in other ways. To him, his sexual encounters had served one purpose and one purpose only. Like any man, he needed the release, but kissing was a no-no, especially not the way he'd kissed Regina last night. Just the thought of sucking and biting down on those delicious lips had him groaning. He leaned against the shower wall just as he burst out en masse as he only did when he was buried deep inside someone.

Even this rattled his nerves and had his heart pounding for more reasons than one. Doing this had *never* felt so damn satisfying. He stood there against the shower wall, letting the cool water immerse his still-too-warm body and took deep breaths as his body began to calm.

Suddenly realizing he hadn't taken Regina's number had him straightening out instantly. There was no way he could call or even text her to let her know he was running late. Knowing the pig-headed princess, she'd likely try to make it down those stairs on her own.

He wasn't even worried about being late to work. There was nothing official on his schedule that would have anyone notice he was late until oh nine hundred, and even that could easily be rescheduled. The only reason he'd said oh six hundred to Regina was he had a feeling getting her out of her place and into her office might take some time. He hadn't even been sure if she'd need him to help her get dressed, though secretly he hoped that might be the case.

After that dream, now he wasn't so sure if that would be a good idea. *I want more?* That went completely against his number-one rule. You never ask for more, and you never gave them time do so either. It went hand in hand with the no-attachments rule. All he'd done so far was kiss her, and already his subconscious was asking for more? He still didn't know much about her, except that she was stubborn as shit and she had one of the sweetest smiles he'd ever been caught up in, not to mention the most amazing lips he'd ever kissed. Just like in his dream, he'd felt almost crazed when he kissed her last night.

But it was what she made him feel inside that scared him. What her expressive eyes said without her saying anything at all. As he dressed hurriedly, he realized he was beginning to understand why he'd been so amused by her annoyance with him. She, too, was affected by him, even if she didn't want to be. And like him, she couldn't possibly know why since neither knew much about the other. She'd said it herself last night. As annoyed as he may've made her over the last couple of weeks, she wanted to get to know him. Unlike his dream, it wasn't just sexual tension she wanted to alleviate. She, too, wanted *more*.

Even more frightening was that, for the first time in years, Brandon was tempted to do just that, not that he'd been tempted much in the last several years. Still there had been a handful of times he'd almost been lured into getting together with someone more than once. It'd never gotten past the initial thought before he easily snuffed the idea.

Now he'd gone far beyond the initial thought. Included in those thoughts were visions and the incredible desire to kiss her again—a lot. The thought of how he might feel once he got past the kissing—if he went through with this and things got that far, especially after feeling what he had in the shower—scared the hell out of him.

Being scared out of his mind didn't stop him from rushing out of his place and into his Jeep. Glancing at the clock on his dash, he saw it was nearly oh six thirty. He muttered under his breath and was glad she was just a few blocks from him, because he reached her place in less than five minutes.

It was actually a little surprising to not see her downstairs already when he walked in her door. A part of him was certain she'd already be wobbling around in her kitchen, making breakfast or something ridiculous like that.

"I would've called you," she said in the most pained voice from upstairs, "to let you know you didn't have to pick me up after all, but I didn't have your number. I've already called in. There's no way I'm going in today."

Relieved that she'd be staying put, but at the same time instantly concerned by the pain in her voice, he started up the stairs in a hurry. "Why? Did something happen?"

Damn it. Did she try coming down on her own and injure herself further? He sprinted up the stairs now but stopped cold at the top when he saw her sitting on the edge of her bed, her half-opened short robe falling slightly off her shoulder. She quickly clasped it shut, but he'd gotten a glimpse of the top of her soft and ample milky-white bare breasts. Her clothes were all at her feet, so he imagined she'd undressed and it'd been easier to just throw a robe over.

Tying the robe around her waist and covering up completely, she cleared her throat. "Nothing happened," she informed him, wincing and rolling her neck. "I just woke up in the middle of the night, feeling like I'd been hit by a train." She winced, closing her eyes as her brows pinched together tightly in agony. "I guess the pain in my ankle yesterday mixed with the morphine really masked the pain everywhere else. I've never been so sore in my life." She groaned, trying to pull herself further back into her bed. "Every inch of my body feels bruised, and when I took a shower, I saw just how bruised and how many bumps I have all over. There is no way I'll be going in to work today. I'm just glad it's Friday and I'll have the whole weekend to try and recoup.

Brandon hadn't even thought about how sore she'd be today everywhere else after the ugly spill she took, but his thoughts were quickly disrupted. He'd been so busy trying not to focus on her appearance he just then noticed her wet hair. "You took a shower?"

She nodded, closing her eyes again as she massaged her neck with her hand. "There's a rail in there I held on to, and I had to keep my bad ankle outside. I made a pretty big mess, and it took me a while, but I managed." She looked at him, her painful expression going a bit soft. "I'm sorry I forgot to get your number last night. I would've called you and saved you the trip down here."

Brandon was already shaking his head before she was even done, his mind on other more important things. "Forget about me. I'm less than five minutes away. I'd hardly call that a trip. So what are you gonna do? Have you called your parents?"

"No," she said, pulling the blankets over herself. Her eyes were already looking a little drowsy. "I need to sleep. I've been up since three, and I just took some meds. I can already feel them kicking in. Maybe I'll call them tomorrow. I don't wanna worry them."

"Tomorrow?" Brandon asked. This girl was too much. "What about today? How are you gonna get in and out of bed or eat?" He remembered something else before she could respond. "Those meds they gave you in the ER are only a temporary batch. What are you gonna do when you run out? In as much pain as you are, you shouldn't risk running out before you can get your prescription filled."

"I'll call it in when I get up. I have enough for today. I can pick up the meds tomorrow."

Having been in a car accident a couple years back where he'd really been banged up, Brandon knew the pain was only going to get worse before it got better, and . . ."You don't even have a car," he reminded her as it suddenly came to him. "It's still at the base."

Her head fell back into the pillow in frustration then winced in pain again, squeezing her eyes shut. Her eyes suddenly opened. "When my mom was sick years ago, she had her meds delivered."

Taking a deep breath, Brandon also took a few steps closer to her bed. "How you gonna get downstairs to sign for them?"

Her lips pinched to the side, and she frowned. As if that weren't enough to have him staring at her like an idiot, her eyes suddenly widened and she smiled. "Two of the guys in my office carpool. If you could please drop off my keys, I can ask them to drop off my car here tonight. I really don't wanna get my family involved. They'll never leave." She scrunched her nose with a remorseful expression. "I love them to death, but they can be a little overbearing."

Thoughts of her overbearing *daddy* thankfully pushed away the annoying thoughts of Antonio, who she was likely talking about dropping her car off. In the process, maybe he'd hang around for a while. Without giving it another thought, Brandon pulled out his phone. He could see she was going to be difficult about this already, and her mention of the guys bringing her car home for her just convinced him to do what he'd unbelievably begun considering doing anyway.

Glad the call went to voicemail, Brandon left a quick message. "Sergeant Carter, this is Billings. I'm having a personal issue, and I need to take the day off. Please call me at your earliest convenience so that I can explain—"

"No!" Regina sat up, whispering loudly, immediately wincing in pain but held her hand out. "You can't—"

Brandon waved her protests away with his hand as he finished leaving his message and hung up.

"Oh my God, Brandon, I can't believe you're taking the day off for this. You don't have to babysit me." She reached for her phone on her nightstand. "Okay, okay, I'll call my family. It's not fair to you—"

"It's too late. You had your chance." He held his phone up. "I've already made the call."

"But you can call back and say you've changed your mind," she said, scrolling through her phone.

"Nope." He shook his head. "My superiors know me and my track record for asking for time off. I wouldn't even think of asking for it if it was something I could just change my mind about. Tell your family to come tomorrow," he said, sticking his phone back in its holster. "It'll save them having to deal with the Friday commute. I got you today."

She stopped searching her phone and looked up at him in complete astonishment. "You can't seriously be saying you're going to spend your entire day looking after me. I've already taken so much of your time."

"Well," he said, reaching for the paperwork on her nightstand that he recognized from last night. "I'm free all day now." He waved the prescription at her. "I'll go get these, and you get some sleep." She was still staring at him so wide-eyed He almost smiled until he remembered something, and he raised an eyebrow. "Your car will be just fine at the base all weekend, and I can give you a ride in Monday. No need to call anyone to bring it."

Relief washed over him when he saw her put her phone back down on the nightstand. She picked up her purse from the floor next to the bed and dug through it, finally pulling out a small white card. "This is my insurance card." She let him know what pharmacy she was already registered at. He took it from her, remembering her mention of anxiety pills in the emergency room and why she'd already be registered at a local pharmacy. "Thank you," she said softly. "This is very sweet of you."

Clenching his jaw, he nodded and began to the door. "Get some rest. I'll be back in a few hours."

Hearing her say this was very sweet of him brought a bothersome thought to mind, one he'd been trying not to think of since last night. Had he already turned into one of the pathetic chumps he'd scoffed at who barely knew her and were already doing sweet things for her?

The only time off he'd *ever* asked for was when he found out his dad was dying and then again for his services. He hadn't even done so for his mom's since there'd been no services for her. The only thing he'd done with her ashes was what she'd told him she wanted him to do when they'd discussed it just weeks earlier at his father's funeral. He'd handled that as unceremoniously as she'd requested in less than an hour on the weekend. Now he'd asked for the day to take care of a girl who, up until yesterday, he'd sworn he wouldn't so much as acknowledge if he ever ran into her again?

He shook it off as he reached the door. He wasn't a sap, and he'd never been easily taken by *anyone*. Regina didn't strike him as the kind of girl who would do what she did last night, even if she was high on her meds, with just anyone. If he'd agreed to drop off her keys with those guys at her office, she wouldn't be thanking them in the same way, especially not allowing them to follow up with the kind of kiss Brandon had last night. He wasn't sure why, but he truly believed this. Brandon was no fool, and he'd be damned if any girl would make one out of him. He'd always said as much when he was against getting attached to anyone, including his brother Marines, even if he'd gladly take a bullet for them any day. Regina may not be a fellow Marine, but she was a person in need of help just the same. Taking a day off to help her out wasn't a big deal. Her family could take over after today.

∼∼∼

Sergeant Carter, as expected, didn't even ask for details of his personal issues. He only asked if there was anything he could do and assured Brandon his taking the day off was not a problem.

The rest of the morning went by fairly quickly. After going back home to change into jeans and T-shirt, Brandon dropped off Regina's prescription at the pharmacy where she was registered. Then he stopped by an auto parts' place nearby. He went back to his place and changed the oil in his Jeep as he planned on doing this weekend anyway. By the time he was all done with that, he realized it was almost noon and he hadn't eaten anything.

Figuring Regina would likely be waking up soon if she hadn't already, he headed out to pick up her meds and grabbed some food on his way back to her place. He didn't want to chance her getting up and trying to get downstairs on her own.

Her place was quiet when he walked in, and he was relieved once again that she wasn't downstairs. It felt a little surreal that here he was making his way up to this girl's bedroom as if he knew her well enough when he hardly knew her at all.

Halfway up the stairs, he thought he heard movement, and then he heard her voice. "Brandon? Is that you?"

Her voice still sounded strained, but his thoughts went immediately somewhere else. *Who the hell else would it be? Had she called someone else while he'd been gone?*

"Yeah, it's me," he said. "Did I wake you?" he asked as he reached the top.

She was sitting up, and the phone in her hand immediately caught his attention.

"No," she smiled weakly, obviously still in pain. "I was starting to toss and turn about a half hour ago, so I checked my phone and noticed I had a few texts." Her eyes were on the bags in his hands and then back on his face. "What's all that?"

"These," he handed her the smaller of the bags, "are your pain killers. This," he shook the other bag, "is lunch."

"Ooh, whatcha get?" She reached for the bag, and he handed it to her. "I *am* hungry. Thanks. And remind me by the way," she said, pulling out the container. "I forgot to give you money for my medicine, and I'll need to pay you for this too, as well as your gas and time."

"Don't worry about it," he said, pulling the chair by her dresser closer to the bed and sat down. "Your insurance covered most of it, and I told you I'm around the corner. So no worries about my gas either. As for my time, you're nuts if you think I'm gonna let you pay me for that."

Regina was staring at the label on the container. "Grilled chicken salad, no tomatoes or eggs, with light thousand."

She looked up at him, her mouth falling slightly open, and he knew what she was thinking, so he cleared his throat. "I also got you a turkey sub and some chips in case you're hungry for more than just a salad."

"You remembered," she said, ignoring his comment about the sub and chips.

He shrugged, pulling out the Coke Zero from the last bag he'd been left holding and his iced tea. He handed her the soda. "Did I get it right?" he asked as if he didn't already know he'd been spot on.

The smile on her face now was going to make his deadpan expression crack if he didn't stop looking at her, so he reached for the bag she'd set aside. "I got a tuna melt," he said, beginning to feel like a real sap now. He hadn't even noticed the lady place the order on the container the way he very specifically had ordered her salad. "We can switch if you prefer that to turkey. I can go for either."

"I'm good with the salad," she said, still smiling when he dared glance at her. "It's *exactly* how I would've ordered it."

Great. He was definitely going to make her chump list. Desperate to change the subject now, he pointed at the top of her bad foot. "Why'd you take off the wrap? Didn't the doc at the ER say you're supposed to wear it for a few weeks?"

She frowned, opening the lid to her salad. "It got wet when I took a shower, so I tried to change it with a dry one, but it was such a pain I gave up."

Brandon stared at the tattoo curiously. He'd already appointed himself as her caregiver for the day. And since things had gotten pretty personal last night, he figured how bad could it be to ask. "What's that mean? Boot and Uni?"

Her frown softened into a small smile. "I got it years ago in honor of my late grandpa, Boot."

A bit relieved to hear the heart was for her grandpa and not some dude, he was still confused. "His name was Boot?"

"No," she laughed softly but stared down at the tattoo thoughtfully. "That's just what I called him."

Brandon un-wrapped his sandwich, even more curious now, and well aware this was personal, but talking about her dead grandpa seemed harmless. "*Okay,* why?"

"One summer when I was too young to attend summer camp with my older siblings, my grandparents decided to help out by keeping me and my younger sister, who was just a baby, during the week for the entire summer. My grandmother tended to my sister most of the time while my granddad entertained me." She smiled bigger now. "One of my favorite things to do and what we did together every morning was watch Sesame Street. My absolute favorites were Bert and Ernie only I couldn't pronounce my r's so it sounded more like Boot and Uni. By the time summer was up, I was his Uni, and my grandpa was my Boot." She waved her hands in front of her flooding eyes. "It's been years since he passed, and I can't believe I still get choked up."

She cleared her throat as the emotion seemed to pass, and she continued, "I always knew the bond between my grandpa and me was special." She laughed again, wiping what was left of a tear at the corner of her eye with her finger. "My grandma used to scold him when he'd call me his favorite, but everybody knew it. When he passed, I took it especially hard." Her lips quivered now, and she frowned. "*Jesus!*"

Swatting this time at the tears that had started up again, she looked genuinely angry all of a sudden.

"It's okay," Brandon said, wiping his mouth with a napkin.

"No, it's *not*."

She leaned over to the box of tissue on her nightstand and yanked tissue out, dabbing her eyes in an annoyed way. Even though Brandon couldn't really relate personally, he'd had enough training and experience dealing with new recruits, who could be very emotional at times, so he gave it a stab.

"It is okay to feel emotional, even after all this time. If you guys were that tight, then of course you'll always get choked up thinking of him."

She shook her head defiantly but didn't offer anything more. Brandon knew all about not wanting to talk about certain subjects. Obviously, while she started off talking about her grandpa willingly enough, she didn't want to anymore. So he figured it was best to change the subject.

"I can help you get that ankle dressed again when you're done eating."

She nodded but said nothing, and they continued eating in silence for a few minutes until she spoke up again. "I've never dealt well with loss," she whispered, staring at her salad.

"Most people don't," he said, shoving the last of his sandwich in his mouth and sat back taking a swig of his bottled iced tea.

Finally, she looked up at him, her eyes a bit weary now. They'd lost that sparkle he'd seen in them earlier when she realized he'd remembered how she ordered her salad. She started to say something but then seemed to catch herself. "I guess," she said then looked back down at her salad. "This is really good." He watched as she stabbed some lettuce and a piece of chicken. She looked up at him with a sad little smile. "Thank you for remembering how I like it."

CHAPTER TWELVE

Regina

Indebted wasn't a strong enough word to describe how Regina felt toward this man she'd referred to as a pretentious jerk just a week ago. As if last night hadn't been enough, Brandon had taken the day off work and was apparently going to wait on her hand and foot.

She watched as he undid the extra wrap they'd given her at the ER. "This is barely enough for a few days if you plan on changing it daily," he said without looking up. "I'll make another run to the drugstore and grab you some more."

"That's okay, Brandon," she said quickly, feeling like such a burden. "It should last me the weekend, and then I can get some on Monday on my way home from work."

He looked up at her. Regina was already recognizing some of his expressions. The one he wore now was the annoyed one he got every time she rejected his help.

"Okay," she conceded, preferring the smiling even serious Brandon over the annoyed one. "I guess if it's not too much trouble you can get it for me before then."

"No trouble at all," he said, lifting her ankle gently then taking a seat on her bed and lowering her ankle onto his thighs.

Regina watched how gentle he was when he removed the splint, trying to focus on that and how she would've never believed this last week. Sergeant Billings was in her bedroom, sitting on her bed with her legs technically around him. It was a silly thought, even rang a little of middle school immaturity, but she had to bite her lip to keep from smiling.

"I was gonna make a run to the drugstore anyway to get you a shower chair."

Her silly thoughts were instantly warped, and she looked up from her ankle to his very serious face. "What?"

Taking his eyes off her ankle for a moment, he glanced up at her. "Yeah, I saw the mess you made in your bathroom. Even after all these hours, the floor is still wet. It's a wonder you didn't fall trying to get out of there." He shook his head and went back to concentrating on wrapping her ankle. "A shower chair will be a lot safer."

Normally she would've said something snarky—retort sarcastically that he was taking an awful lot of liberties with decisions that should be hers. She'd never been one to need someone to take care of her, much less come in and just take over. But something about his concern for her well-being warmed her. And she had to admit there *had* been a few scary moments in the shower that morning.

"A chair in there is a good idea," she said softly. "Thanks, but I won't let you pay for it."

She saw his jaw tighten as he continued with the wrap. "All done. The swelling's gone down a bit too."

He leaned down to pick up the splint and began putting it back on her. Unable to stand it anymore, Regina inched her butt up little closer to him, hoping he wouldn't notice since he was busy with the splint. When he was done, he looked up and pulled his face back when he realized how close she was.

Smiling nervously, she licked her lips, and bingo, her lips had his undivided attention. "Can I thank you again, Brandon?"

With his eyes still on her lips, he nodded but said nothing, so she pecked him softly. "That's for taking the day off." She took his face in her hands and kissed him again this time sliding her tongue in his mouth, and he kissed her back softly, gently. It wasn't at all as ravenous as last night's kiss, but she still felt her heart speeding up. She pulled away, licking her lips, loving the taste of him still on them. "That's for bringing me my meds and fixing my wrap." Diving in again, the kiss took a turn with him leaning into her as she kissed him much deeper. He moaned and practically ate her mouth up just as he had last night, as if he couldn't get enough, and now his fingers were in her hair. It went on for what seemed like forever, but even then she didn't want it to end. The kiss alone had her so wet and aroused it was embarrassing, but she couldn't bring herself to end it. Finally, he pulled his lips away and hugged her tightly, breathing heavily against her neck.

"What was *that* for?"

Regina smiled against his shoulder. "For remembering how I ordered my chicken salad."

His body seemed to tense for just a moment, and then he relaxed and pulled away to look at her. "I have a good memory, I guess, but even I surprised myself that I remembered every detail of that," he said, indulging her with one of his almost-never-seen smiles. "I walked into the deli for sandwiches and then saw the salads on the menu, and it just came to me."

She slipped her hand in his and laced his fingers through hers. His smile instantly vanished, and she saw alarm in his eyes. They'd just shared one of the most passionate kisses she'd ever experienced, and *this* alarmed him? She started to let go of his hand, but he squeezed it and kissed her again, bringing his other hand behind her neck. This kiss was slower yet deeper somehow, their tongues dancing beautifully in perfect rhythm like a couple who'd been doing this forever.

Sucking on her bottom lip one last time, he pulled away to look at her, but his hand remained on the back of her neck. She hoped that meant he wasn't going to stop because she could kiss him all day and into the night. "You know," she swallowed, looking deep into those intense eyes of his. "For a while there, I thought my holding up the line at the airport because of my special order of that salad might've been the reason you didn't like me."

His blue eyes disappeared underneath that heavy sheath of thick lashes as he looked down for a moment. "That was really shitty of me to treat you that way. I shouldn't have. I'm real sorry about that."

"Can you tell me about her?" she said, lowering her voice a little. "The girl you said I reminded you of?"

His eyes were on her again, and she saw something different in them now, only like before, she couldn't decipher it. To her disappointment, he did pull his hand back from behind her neck. But as much as she wished she hadn't asked, a part of her really wanted to know now.

"There's not much to tell," he said, shaking his head. "She's just a girl from my past. *Way* back."

"A girlfriend?"

"Nope." He frowned. "She wasn't even a girlfriend. She was just someone I knew most my life and thought I had feelings for. It didn't end well, and I haven't spoken to or seen her in years. That's about all there is to tell."

"What about me reminded you of her? I noticed the distaste from the moment I saw you at the airport, so I take it I resemble her?"

He nodded with an apologetic smile then kissed her softly. "I saw the dark hair." He touched a strand of her hair. "The big brown eyes." He smiled then went serious again. "I heard you on the phone with your dad, and I wasn't trying to eavesdrop, but it was hard not to listen, standing right behind you. I picked up on how maybe he was going a little overboard, making sure you were okay, and that's how this girl's *entire* family was." He frowned now, the look of distaste exactly as she remembered it at the airport and those first several times she'd run into him here. "Her family was way over the top, and then you referred to your grandma in Spanish to boot. This girl was Hispanic too, so it brought back memories of someone I hadn't thought about in years. It was just a little irritating."

Without thinking, Regina's brows shot up, and Brandon kissed her again quickly. "The memories, that is, not you."

Smiling, she kissed him back and chewed her lip. "Well, you were right about my dad. He can go a little overboard. My whole family can actually. That's why I didn't wanna call them today. They'd waltz in here and just take over."

She said that as if that weren't what Brandon was slowly doing also. Somehow having Brandon pamper her, even if he had started taking liberties with what he thought was best for her, seemed a lot more fun than having her overbearing but well-meaning family doing just the same.

That last comment didn't seem to go over too well with him. Maybe she *was* a little too much like this girl he didn't like thinking of. She was about to ask exactly what he meant by "didn't end well" when his hand on her thigh distracted her.

"Are they coming tomorrow?"

"I haven't called them," she admitted, feeling bad instantly. "But I will. Don't worry. I wouldn't dream of asking you to wait on me all weekend."

Raising a brow, he stared at her for a moment. "Wouldn't dream of it?" he asked with a smirk, squeezing her thigh.

Surprised by his playfulness but even more surprised by how unnerving the very thought of what he might be implying was, she gulped. Had she given him the wrong impression? Having him around all weekend was an exciting thought, but not if he was thinking she'd be thanking him in *other* ways.

"No, I wouldn't," she reaffirmed. "You've already done so much for me. I couldn't possibly—"

His lips were on hers again, and she let herself fall into the amazing experience once again. Just when he'd begun to lean into her, the buzzing of one of their phones interrupted them. He stopped, pulling away just so, breathing heavily against her lips still.

"Is that you or me?" he asked.

Taking a deep breath, she looked around. "That's you," she said as his phone on the nightstand buzzed again. She leaned over and grabbed it, catching a part of the name as she handed it to him: Sergeant something or other.

He answered it as soon as he saw who it was. "Sergeant Billings, here." She watched as he listened intently. "Yes, sir, that's the one." He nodded a few times. "Not a problem, sir. I can do that."

All the "sirs" reminded her of the incident with Lansing at the ER. She wondered if Brandon was still planning on speaking to his supervisor. The guy *had* given Brandon his supervisor's name and number, and Brandon had been very adamant about the whole thing.

"Absolutely. Thank you, sir. You too."

He hung up and tossed the phone on the bed then leaned into Regina again. His playful expression was a new one to her. "Where were we?"

She leaned back before he could kiss her again. "That just reminded me of something, Brandon."

"What's that? he said, licking her bottom lip, making her shiver.

"Were you really going to still call the supervisor of that poor guy from the ER?"

She may as well have pulled the emergency brakes on Brandon's sudden and uncharacteristic playfulness because he pulled back sharply, his eyes zeroing in on hers.

"Why?"

"I'm just wondering." She touched his face, a part of her wanting suddenly to take the question back but another part still wanting to help out the poor guy, so she added. "I just feel bad for him. He seemed nice enough—"

"Is that why you asked him if he was married?"

He started to pull away and let her hand loose, but she held it. "*No,*" she said with the craziest feeing in her belly. "Then why did you?"

She stared at him, her heart beating a little faster. This was insane. She'd kissed the guy a few times, and yet here he was practically *demanding* an answer from her, but what was even crazier was she felt as if she absolutely owed him one.

Not liking how fast the mood had begun to take a dive, she pulled him to her and ran her fingers through his hair. The way his hardened expression softened with just that touch almost made her smile. "I just had a conversation with my sister the other day. The single one," she said, caressing his face. "She goes through phases when it comes to the guys she dates. Her latest is guys in the medical field." Regina laughed softly, feeling incredibly silly. "She told me to be on the lookout for her, and she likes them tall, so . . ." She shrugged. "I remembered, and I guess that dose of morphine made me braver than I normally would be."

Without saying anything, Brandon stared into her eyes. Then his eyes were on her lips again. She hadn't even licked them as she now knew could easily distract him. "I haven't decided."

"Can you please just let it go?" His questioning eyes were back on hers a little hardened again. "For my sister," she teased with a smile. "You never know. He may be my future brother-in-law."

"You're not going back to see him, are you?"

"No." She laughed now. "I'm kidding. But please consider giving the guy a break, yeah? I'll feel responsible if he gets in trouble. If it weren't for me, you wouldn't have ever been at his workplace last night to begin with."

His expression remained hard, and then she saw the tug on the corner of his lips. "Are you gonna have your family come down this weekend?"

They were back to this, and she still wasn't sure how she should respond. Was he saying he didn't want her to? That he'd be willing to—wanted to hang out with her all weekend? If so, was it because like her, he was enjoying the company and wanted more of it? Or was he thinking more in terms of how else she'd be showing him her gratification?

He must've read her mind because, before she could respond, he added. "I'm free all weekend if you'd rather not tell them about this until you've healed a little more." Squeezing her hand, he smiled. "I'd be a perfect gentleman. I promise."

Feeling bad that she'd even mentally questioned his motives, but at the same time completely thrilled that he was offering, she shook her head. "I don't doubt that you would be." She tilted her head. "Are you *sure?* Last night I didn't want to admit it, and I wasn't even feeling like I do today, but I feel like a total invalid now. I can barely move. I'd hate to be such an incredible weight on you all weekend."

"Nah," he leaned in and pecked her. "We'll just keep you up here all weekend. There's no need for you to go down until you have to. I can bring up anything you need. The longer you stay off that ankle, the better."

"But you *have* to let me pay you, Brandon—"

"Hell no!" he said with a furrow of his brows. Then he smiled again, and, God, she could get used to that smile. "But you can keep thanking me the way you have so far."

Cradling his face with both hands, she kissed him. "Thank you." She kissed him again a little longer. "Thank you." Then she went even deeper, making him as crazy as she was beginning to love feeling him get.

"Thank *you*," he said, this time with a groan and leaned her back into the pillows piled up behind her, making her giggle against his lips.

CHAPTER THIRTEEN

Brandon

Lying there in his bed, reflecting on the day's happenings, Brandon couldn't decide if the turn of events had been a good thing or if he'd fucked up royally. He kept asking himself the same questions: What the hell was he thinking? What was he *doing*?

This went beyond wanting to help someone in need. He couldn't hide what was happening behind that façade anymore. Taking the day off to help her out for the day was one thing, but offering to continue doing so for the rest of the weekend, especially knowing how impossible it would be to keep his lips off hers now, was a whole other monster.

He may as well toss his rulebook—the one he'd lived by for years—right out the window. So far he'd broken every last damn rule in that book. He'd gone back for more after last night's kiss. He'd practically told her she'd been under his skin since the moment he'd laid eyes on her. If memorizing the way she'd ordered her salad way back at the airport didn't say he'd been putting way too much thought into her, he didn't know what did. Hell, he even told her about Sofie, something he hadn't spoken to *anyone* about *ever*. This after spending a day and a half with her?

There was no way he could deny feeling an attachment to her already. When she'd brought up Lansing, reminding him of what she'd asked the guy at the ER, he'd been ready to spit nails. Why? Because just like seeing Rodriguez with her, the thought of her feeling anything for anyone else after just a few kisses had him burning up.

For someone who for years said he'd never show interest in anyone else's personal life, he'd been utterly immersed when she'd brought her tablet out tonight to show him photos of her Grandpa Boot. She'd then proceeded to show him all her other photos on her tablet of her family, and he'd been equally engrossed. Seeing photos of her when she was a young high school girl fascinated him. He wouldn't tell her, but she looked even more like Sofie than he first thought. That wasn't the fascinating part. While he'd felt a bit envious of her normal and happy upbringing, the only photo he'd seen her in where she wasn't smiling hugely was the one she didn't know he'd seen in her wallet. Except for when she'd gotten a little emotional about her grandpa, the girl was nonstop sunshine and happiness. It was contagious, and after just spending a day and a half with her, he'd begun to smile and even laugh a lot more.

Once again, the sirens were going off, but unlike before, he was seriously considering silencing them. He had no idea where this might be going. Nor did he know where he *wanted* it to go.

They'd talked for hours tonight. She'd offered to turn on the television, but he passed, preferring instead to talk. He wanted to *talk*—get better acquainted with someone—something that had always made him so uncomfortable before, not because he was in anyway inept at holding a conversation but because he feared enjoying such conversations. That would mean enjoying said company, which in turn would lead to wanting to spend more time with *anyone,* which ultimately meant attachment. But tonight he'd wanted it, and he'd enjoyed every minute of it. It was *insane*. Though, in hindsight, she'd done most of the talking.

At one point, he'd been lying there in her bed with her snuggled up next to him, wondering what the hell he was doing there. How the hell did he let this happen? And then she'd kiss him, and all those doubts about whether or not he should get up and run from there as fast as he could, would go away.

He could no longer say he hardly knew her anymore. Tonight they'd talked in depth about her family, her career, and her friend Janecia, the one he'd seen her having dinner with at Gaslamp. The only significant part of her life she merely brushed over was her late husband, who'd passed away suddenly last year in a motorcycle accident. Brandon picked up on the fact that she hadn't planned on talking about all that, until he asked her about the last relationship she'd been in.

Judging by how emotional she'd gotten when the subject of her grandpa was brought up and the fact that she'd admitted to not dealing well with loss, Brandon didn't push. It was one thing to see her cry over her grandpa, but he wasn't sure how he'd feel about seeing her cry over a guy she'd obviously been in love with, someone she'd likely still be with if he were still around. Brandon wasn't ready to deal with something that heavy yet—he didn't know if he ever would be. This whole attachment thing, to *anyone,* would be completely new to him. If he decided to let it happen, he wasn't sure how good or bad he'd be at it. Already, he was beginning to feel an unreasonable sense of entitlement to her. Hearing her talk about her feelings for someone else, even if in the past, was not something he'd be looking forward to. So if she chose to never talk about her late husband again, he'd be just fine with it.

He too had been pretty short on subjects he'd rather not talk about. Keeping it as simple as possible, she now knew the basics about him. He had no siblings. Both his parents had died years ago, one of cancer and one in an accident. Regina was obviously as good as he was at picking up on sore subjects, because she'd let it go, not pushing for details.

Brandon's phone buzzed, and he was almost afraid to check it. Regina had programmed her number into his phone tonight and texted herself so they'd now have each other's numbers. He'd just spent the last six or seven hours straight with her and then came home only to think of her nonstop. This could very well be her because no one else ever called or texted this late. He was as afraid as he was anxious to see if it was.

He smiled at the envelope and caption: Text from Regina. Clicking on it, he opened and read it.

> Just wondering if you're having as hard a time as I am sleeping. I CANNOT stop thinking about you! =O

Feeling that now familiar smile spread across his face—the one that hadn't made an appearance this often until Regina—he let out a small groan, closing his eyes. Okay, maybe this wasn't such a bad thing. Having someone in your life that made you feel this good couldn't be that bad, right?

He sat up and texted back.

> Thanks for this. I was beginning to think maybe I was nuts. I've been lying here since I got home, thinking about everything we talked about today.

Waiting there in the dark, knowing he was smiling like an idiot, he thought about something. He was living proof that fate could very instantly and very drastically change whatever plans you'd made for your future. Could his life be taking a turn once again—this instantly? And was he really going to let this happen?

His phone buzzed, and he clicked on the envelope.

> Well, since it is the weekend, and for the sake of us getting some rest before having to go back to work Monday, maybe tomorrow I can have a sleepover? Popcorn, movies, and junk food until we pass out? No sense in you leaving if you're just gonna be back the next morning, right? Of course, you're promise of being a complete gentleman will have to stand. You're invited to sleep in my bed, nothing else, well, except for what we've done already. ;)

Groaning even louder, he brought the pillow over his face and did something even more foreign than his constant smiling now—he laughed out loud. Once again, his subconscious was already deciding for him. Even if he wanted to stop it, which he didn't, this was *already* happening.

~~~

After Regina's late texts last night, thoughts of seeing her again today had kept him awake into the wee hours of the morning. Then later in the morning when he'd woken, the second his brain was awake enough to remember everything that had happened yesterday, he hadn't been able to go back to sleep.

Knowing the drugstore wouldn't be open that early, he headed to Walmart for that shower chair, the wrap for her ankle, and the popcorn and junk food she mentioned for their *sleepover*. Among all the things Regina had shared with him yesterday about herself, she'd mentioned some of her guilty pleasures. Chocolate was on top of her list. She said it didn't matter what shape or form. It was her ultimate weakness, so he grabbed plenty of things with chocolate as well. But there was one other very specific thing he'd immediately thought of when she told him, and with that in mind, he was now headed to the one place he'd vowed never step to foot in again—La Jolla.

It was early enough that he was fairly certain he wouldn't have any uncomfortable run-ins with anyone from his past there. Still just being in his old neighborhood brought back the bad vibes—vibes he was certain Regina would easily chase away just as soon as he saw her. But he'd rethink doing something like this next time. He was pretty sure the chocolate-chocolate-chip waffles from the waffle house he grew up having breakfast at every Sunday were not the only good ones in the area.

As he jumped on the freeway, waffles on the passenger seat, he felt an immense relief wash over him. The further he drove away from that city, the better he felt. He made the same vow he'd made long ago, only this time he was sticking to it. He'd never step foot in that neighborhood again. Nothing was worth it. He'd find another damn waffle house.

Smiling the second he walked into Regina's place, he was glad he'd been right. He hadn't even seen her yet, and already being this near to her had snapped him right out of the weird mood going into La Jolla had put him in.

He started up the stairs, wondering if she was awake yet. It was early still.

"Is that you, Brandon?"

The question puzzled him again, but he didn't respond because he was already at the top. She was just walking out of the bathroom, holding on to the wall, and the second she saw what he held, her eyes brightened. Starbucks was another of her guilty pleasures, and he'd made a stop there as well.

"Oh, yay!" she clapped her fingers together, wobbling a little, then stopped, her jaw dropping when she got a closer look at the coffee cup. "Don't tell me," she said, "you got me a Chocolate Dalmatian?"

He nodded but frowned. "You didn't tell me it wasn't on the regular menu. I froze when the guy asked how I wanted it."

She brought her hand to her mouth and laughed unapologetically as she reached her bed then sat down.

"Lucky for you, the other barista knew what was in it, or you would've ended up with a plain coffee. Since I hate coffee, I wouldn't have had any idea what to order you."

He leaned over and kissed her softly before handing the cup to her then put the rest of the stuff down on the bed. Regina scooted back onto her stack of pillows, savoring the coffee, and Brandon sat down on the edge of the bed next to her. "How you feeling today?"

"Still sore but a little better than yesterday morning."

He leaned into her and kissed her again a little deeper than he had the first time. He'd been right that first time back on the base when he'd guessed that tasting the coffee on her lips would be delicious. Her mouth tasted damn good. "I'm glad," he said then bit her bottom lip before asking what he'd wanted to ask yesterday morning and now, only a day later, felt more entitled to. "You wanna tell me why you've asked if it's me walking in here the past two mornings?" He pulled back and peered at her. "Who else would it be?"

She stared at him seriously for a moment then smirked and lifted a shoulder. "Oh, I don't know. One of my other very sexy caretakers maybe."

He knew she was kidding. Still he went serious, raising an eyebrow, because this was a good lead into something he'd begun to wonder yesterday and even more so after her late night text.

"I'm kidding!" she said suddenly with a laugh. "I don't know. I guess because I know the door isn't locked. I just want to make sure no one else has walked in."

"I thought you said because this is a gated community you didn't have to worry about that?"

"I don't." She shrugged, taking another sip of her coffee. "But sometimes I hear other things like the ice machine going off in the kitchen. Makes me wonder if maybe you're already here and I didn't hear you come in. So I call out for you."

He stared at her with a suspicious but playful smirk. "So last night you said you haven't been in a relationship in over a year." The playfulness in her eyes seemed to wane a bit, so he hurried his point along and got past that part. "But are you seeing anyone else? Or is there anyone you go out with even casually?"

Lifting that cute little brow, her eyes challenged him now, confusing him. "You mean like you casually left the bar with that blonde?"

Okay, he walked right into that one. Damn it. "Well, yeah, something like that, only I'm not seeing her in *any* way." He paused before saying what he wanted to say next, because it was a risk, but then just being here was a risk, so what the hell? He may as well get this straight now. "Until you, I didn't do repeat visits, no matter what the circumstances. And I can't even remember when the last time was that I spent the night with someone or had someone stay overnight at my place. Now I have an overnight bag in my Jeep outside."

Her eyes widened a bit alarmed. "You do understand that tonight—"

"I got it," he said with a smile. "I'm invited to sleep in your bed, nothing else, and *that* is definitively a first for me too, but I'm still looking forward to it."

Her eyes went playful again, and she chewed her bottom lip. He did what he always wanted to do when he was distracted by her lips. He kissed her. Somehow, one day had changed everything, and he wasn't holding back anymore.

The doorbell rang, and Brandon pulled away slowly. "You expecting someone else?"

From the puzzled look on her face, he already had his answer. "No."

He got up then thought of his hermit parents and how they almost never got the door when someone knocked. He turned back to her. "You *do* want me to get it, right?"

"Yeah." She nodded, the expression on her face as curious as he felt.

His insides tightened a little as he made it down the stairs. They definitely would be getting back to that conversation they'd started upstairs. Just the thought that he might be opening the door to a male friend of hers had him working his jaw already.

It *was* a dude at the door, but thankfully he was in an UPS uniform, holding a large square envelope with what felt like a book or something inside. Brandon took it from him, signing for it, and read who it was from: Chris Devereux MD. The originating address was from New York. He remembered her saying her mom used to have her meds delivered. Though he thought if that's what this was it'd be coming from a pharmacy, not from what appeared to be a private address. He highly doubted any doctor's office would be on Cherry Lane. Typically, it would have a suite or office number; this had neither. He shook it very subtly anyway as he walked up the stairs, but there was no noise.

Regina's expression went as curious as he felt as soon as she saw him walk into the room with the package in his hand. "Hmm, I wasn't expecting anything."

"It's from New York," he said, handing it to her.

She read the return label, and the change in her demeanor was unmistakable. She even lost some color in her face.

"Your doctor?"

He pulled the tray with her waffles out of one of the bags on the bed, pretending not to notice her obvious sudden unease.

"No, um." She glanced at him then put the package down next to her. "An old friend." Bringing her attention to the tray he was now holding, with the see-through plastic cover, she smiled. "Are those chocolate waffles?"

"Chocolate chocolate chip, actually," he said, pulling the lid off and handing them to her.

Her lips parted slightly in surprise as he sat down next to her and kissed her. She brought her hand to his face and kissed him deeper. "Thank you. These look delicious!"

Her reaction was pretty much what he'd expected, but something about it felt a bit forced. The package, or rather who it was from, had rattled her, and for as much as she tried bringing the focus onto her waffles and away from the package, he caught the struggle.

"Aren't you curious?" he asked as she dug into the waffles.

She looked at him while chewing, her eyes nearly rolling back in ecstasy. "God, these are good," she said, covering her mouth with her fingers.

Deciding to let it go—for now—Brandon pulled his steak and egg sandwich and orange juice out of the bag and joined her in eating breakfast. He told her about the shower chair he'd gotten from Walmart that morning and his history with the place he got the waffles from.

"Oh, one of my sisters lives near there. Wait." She covered her mouth again as she finished chewing and thought about that. "Is Pacific Beach near La Jolla?"

"Yeah, that's nearby there," he said, crumpling up the wrap his sandwich had come in and throwing it in the bag.

"I thought so. I'll have to tell her about this place. These waffles are to die for."

Regina finished with her waffles, and Brandon gathered up the garbage in the bag.

"That was so good," Regina said, tapping her belly. "And it was the perfect size, because I'm not overstuffed."

"I thought you'd like them." He smiled.

Seeing how content the waffles made her, Brandon was beginning to think maybe a drive out to La Jolla once in a while wouldn't be so bad. *Geez.* Here he'd had the nerve to make fun of the other guys she very possibly had wrapped already. At least those guys had been around her for a few weeks.

Shaking his head, he stood. "I'll go get the chair from my car."

"Oh, yes!" she said with a big smile. "That's gonna make showering so much easier. Thank you."

He turned to her with a smirk, and she held her hands out. "Yes, I wanna thank you for it. Come here."

She wiggled her fingers in front of her, and he was there in an instant, leaning over. Pulling him gently by his shirt, she gave him one of the deepest kisses yet, one that had parts of him shifting. He had to pull away before things got embarrassing. She'd already made it clear there'd be nothing more going on than what they'd already done, but if she kept this up, he may be tempted to try and change her mind.

"You're welcome," he said, pecking her one last time. "I'll be back."

The moment he was out of sight, he adjusted himself. As much as he avoided kissing in the past, he'd never let them get this frenzied, so while he had felt aroused by a single kiss before, he'd only felt the *beginning* of arousal. Never before had he gotten a full-blown erection from one kiss as he had now. This wasn't just embarrassing. It was ridiculous.

CHAPTER FOURTEEN

Regina

Waiting until she heard the door open downstairs, Regina chewed her lip before ripping the package open from Dr. Devereux. First, she pulled out the card. She ripped the envelope it was in, saw it was an anniversary card, and read it quickly.

Regina,

I hope this finds you well. I was in the bookstore the other day and saw a sign announcing that E.R.Rico would be doing a book signing there in a few days and immediately thought of you. I remembered how books were your escape, even during your darkest hours, and that she was one of your favorites. So I decided to come back and get you a signed copy of her latest. In revisiting your file for your forwarding address, I noticed it's been almost eighteen months since your very first therapy session. So I thought this would make a nice little anniversary gift.

Warm regards,

Chris

Regina put the card back in the bigger envelope as she heard the door downstairs open. Unable to resist, she pulled out the book to see which one it was: *Endless*. She smiled. It was one she hadn't read yet. She flipped it open to get a sneak peek of the inscription and was startled by how fast Brandon had made it to the top of the stairs.

Catching herself, she slowed down after instinctively shoving the book back in the envelope in reaction. She could've kicked herself for being so stupidly obvious about it.

"Is it a secret?" Brandon asked, peering at the envelope as he walked toward the bed.

He placed the box with the chair on the end of her bed, but his eyes were still on the envelope.

"No," she said, clearing her throat a little. "It's just a book—a romance novel by one of my favorite authors. My friend had it signed by the author and sent it to me."

She smiled, trying to make light of it. As surprisingly comfortable as it was to talk to Brandon, this was *not* a topic she was ready to talk about. Telling him about her former therapist was something she hadn't even decided if he needed to know at all. She pulled her legs off the side of the bed and pointed at the box he was now working on getting open. "That's a good size. I didn't know they made them that small."

Brandon eyes went from her to the envelope then back to her. She knew he must be wondering about it still. She'd already bypassed his question earlier about not being curious about the package. Then she'd obviously waited for him to leave to open it, only to practically gasp when he'd walked back in the room so quickly.

To her surprise, he didn't press further. But the raised eyebrow remained up even as he spoke of the chair. "I noticed your shower is on the small side, so I got the smallest one they had."

He pulled the chair out, made some adjustments, and then walked over to the bathroom. "Yep," he said. "Perfect fit." She smiled as he walked out. "Did you want to take a shower now or later?"

"Now is good."

He walked over and helped her up. She was getting better about walking on just one crutch. Her ankle was still very sore, but at least, the throbbing had subsided, so she didn't need such a big dose of her painkillers. They made her feel sluggish, and today she hadn't even taken them. Regina wasn't sure if it was the distraction of having Brandon around or if her ankle was healing a lot faster than she was expecting. But if the pain didn't get any worse than it was now, she probably wouldn't be taking any more meds from here on.

Brandon helped her all the way into the bathroom. Then she waved at him with a smirk. "I got the rest from here."

"You sure?"

Regina laughed. She was beginning to love seeing his playful side. The fact that not too long ago she'd actually wondered if he ever smiled made the silly grin on his face now feel like that much more of a treat.

"Yes, I'm sure," she said, leaning in and kissing him.

He brought his hand around her waist and kissed her a little deeper before pulling his face away. "I'm serious. You sure you're gonna be okay on your own?"

"Absolutely," she assured him. "But I'll probably be in here a while, so if you have anywhere else you need to be or any errands to run, by all means, go."

Frowning as she once again rejected his help, he exhaled. "I have a few phone calls I need to make, and there's something I needed to do at the base but was going to wait until Monday. Maybe I can knock it out today. You sure you're gonna be a while and you don't need me here?"

"Positive, and even after I'm done, I'm sure I'll find a way to keep myself busy." She squeezed him. "Just get back in time for our movie night."

"Oh, I'll be back way before that."

After a few more kisses that had her wondering if maybe she should've taken him up on his offer to help her in the shower, he was gone.

Just as she anticipated, the shower took *forever*. Moving around with that damn splint and trying not to put weight on her ankle slowed everything down. She had plenty of time in there to think about what was happening between her and Brandon.

The untimely delivery had interrupted a conversation that had begun to make her insides wild. Was he really going to suggest a relationship? Or was it his way of trying to warn her he didn't do them and this weekend was just an exception? On the other hand, he'd been pretty aggressive about getting down to the business of whether or not she was single.

Was *she* ready to move on as Dr. Devereux had insisted she needed to? As much as she'd enjoyed her single status in college before settling down—which had given her the opportunity to deal with a lot of different personalities—she'd never met someone quite like Brandon. He'd proven he could be such a sweetheart already, but there was something deep in those eyes that could go hard in an instant. She'd seen it happen several times now.

He admitted to never wanting to make attachments and that he had no family, nor did he mention any friends or acquaintances. That was a little alarming as well. Was it really a good idea to finally start to move on with someone like Brandon, so intense and atypical, which most likely translated to difficult?

Sure he'd been easy enough to get along with now that he'd finally come around. He'd been wonderful actually, and while he had his intense moments, he could be so down to earth. Even their kisses felt like something they'd been doing forever. But they hadn't gotten into any heavy subjects yet. Everything so far had been light and fluffy. There was no hiding the fact that they were both skimming the heavier stuff and allowing each other to do so. Avoiding the tougher subjects was not the smartest way to start a relationship, but she'd tread cautiously for now.

Deciding she wasn't even sure where this could go and that could very well mean nowhere, Regina wasn't going to worry about all that yet. She'd take her weekend with him for what it was worth and enjoy it. At least, she didn't have to worry about feeling dirty or used afterwards because she'd already set that boundary, and he'd assured her today he would be respecting it.

~~~

"I can't believe that's the first time you've ever seen *When Harry Met Sally!*" Regina said, shaking her head as she clicked the remote, turning the television off.

Smiling, Brandon shrugged. "It just never seemed like something I could get into."

Brandon slid down from his sitting position on her bed and lay back all the way. Regina did the same, turning to her side and resting her head on her fist. "So what's your take on it? Do you agree men and women can't be friends?"

"Yep, absolutely."

This surprised her. "Really? They absolutely can be friends?"

"No, I agree that they *can't,* and I think Harry nailed the reason why perfectly. Men and women can't be friends because the sex part always gets in the way."

"Wow, you really do have a good memory."

"Not *that* good," he said, smiling and playing with her hand. "I said I've never seen the movie, but I've seen plenty of parts, like that one and the part where she fakes the orgasm in the diner. Actually, I've seen most of the more famous parts. I just never sat through the whole thing from beginning to end before."

"Well, this will probably get my woman card taken away, but I'm gonna have to agree too." This seemed to surprise him. "But not exactly for the reason you or Harry think. I think it comes down to feelings, not just sex. I think, even if you don't have sex, the relationship can be ruined because one side starts developing feelings and the other side might not."

He shook his head. "Maybe for you that's the case because you've probably never met a man who hasn't fallen in love with you immediately. So you've never been able to keep friendships with men. But most of the time it's about the sex, especially if, say, the woman you had sex with—and *didn't* fall in love with, so you remained friends—gets an actual boyfriend or even husband. There's no way that friend is gonna stay a friend without her man having issues with it, unless, of course, she lies about never having slept with her *friend*." He frowned, glancing at her, his expression going grim. "In that case, if they're starting off with lies or cover ups, the relationship with her new man is probably doomed to begin with."

With her heart beating a little faster, Regina tried not to put too much weight on his statement about her not having met a man who didn't fall in love with her immediately. He was just being sweet. She'd already established that he could be sweet—very.

Caught in his eyes for moment, her heart pounded even harder before she managed to counter. "But that's not exactly what Harry argued in the movie. He said that men and women can't be friends because attracted to them or not," she laughed nervously, "you pretty much want to nail them all anyway. *You* seem to be saying that *only* if you have sex with them you can't be friends but if you *don't* you can?"

"I'm probably the wrong person to be arguing this point to begin with, because I've never had many *friends,* period." He reached out and ran his fingers through a few strands of her hair that fell to the side of her face, making her shiver. "So I can't say for certain if I would or wouldn't want to nail every one of my female friends if I *had* any. All I know is that's my reason for no return visits with them whether we've had sex or *not*." He paused, and it almost seemed to Regina as if he wanted that part emphasized. Then he went on. "Return visits with anyone form attachments. So maybe your reasoning is more correct than mine. Those attachments could lead to wanting sex, and, therefore, unless that turns into a relationship, the friendship is ruined."

Regina tilted her head, staring at him curiously. "Why is that?"

He seemed confused. "Why is what?"

"Why is it that you don't form attachments with *anyone*? You mentioned that before. You really don't have *any* friends?"

He brought his hands behind his head and stared at the ceiling, his features going a bit stiff. "I really don't."

"But why? It's obviously not for lack of personality or ability to hold a conversation. I'll admit after the start we had I'm a little surprised, but never in my life have I felt as comfortable being around someone as quickly as I have with you."

His smile surprised and relieved her a little bit, but he continued to stare up at the ceiling. "It's never been because I can't make friends or keep them, Regina. I *choose* not to make attachments that might lead to friendships." He turned to her now, his expression much softer than when she'd first posed the question. "At least I had until now."

Feeling her heart flutter, she couldn't help smile. "So what changed your mind?"

He slid over and lifted himself onto his elbow to face her. With his hard body up against hers, he looked deep in her eyes. "You did." Bringing his hand behind her neck, he pulled her gently to him and kissed her softly, stopping to suck her bottom lip for a moment. "Though I didn't admit it then, you sucked me in from the moment I first laid eyes on you. Your lips alone are enough to drive me insane." He ran his tongue across her bottom lip slowly. Then those intense eyes of his were on hers again. "I thought it was just a physical thing, something I could easily ignore like I always do when I meet attractive women, but little by little," he said, leaning in and kissing her very slowly—very deeply—before pulling away, "I could tell there was more to you. After spending just a few hours with you, I knew I'd be in danger of wanting to come back for more of you." He smiled. "Then you kissed me. Just one taste of this mouth," his eyes dropped down to her lips, "and I was a goner."

He took her mouth again and kissed harder now. With the excitement of knowing how crazed he could get from just kissing her and after what he'd just told her, she was hot and tingly all over. She brought her hand around his strong back, running it up and down and beginning to feel a little crazed herself.

Feeling his heartbeat thunder against her chest as he held her tighter had her having second thoughts about the nothing-more rule she'd set for tonight. But she had to keep a straight head. Her insides were a burning mixture of desire and excitement but at the same time fear. A part of her was completely intrigued by him, this incredibly complex man who was telling her he wanted *more*. Another part of her was afraid of what she was getting into. No attachments ever? No friends? Was she ready for someone so complicated in her life?

Falling deep into his amazing kisses and his gentle yet possessive embrace as he continued to kiss her endlessly, she could already feel herself giving into the idea.

He finally pulled away to catch his breath and stared deep in her eyes. "Brandon?" she asked, breathlessly.

"Hm?" he said, kissing her lips again softly then her chin and working his way down her neck.

"Are we friends now?"

His kisses ceased for a moment before he kissed then sucked on her neck softly. "Nope," he said before sucking her neck a little harder, every part of her body trembling in response.

Confused because he'd just given her this speech about how he was making an exception for her, she had to ask. "Why not? I thought—"

He lifted his head and latched his teeth onto her bottom lip before she could finish, then bit down just enough to make it hurt so good—a sensation she'd never felt before. Sucking it one last time before pulling away, he stared at her very seriously, and his expression went soft again. "Silly girl," he said with a peck. "I already told you my stand on men and women being friends."

"But—"

His mouth was on hers again, kissing her in that crazed way he had the first day, the way that made her wild with desire, and she moaned in reaction to it. She wrapped her arms around him as he lifted himself onto her, obviously being careful that he didn't touch her bad ankle. Pressed against her like this, there was no denying he was as aroused as she felt, and he continued to devour her mouth, her lips, and her tongue, like a man on a mission to make her come by just kissing her.

Just when she thought she couldn't take it anymore, that she might shamelessly moan, he pulled away and stared into her eyes very seriously, his hands cradling her face as he tried to calm his own labored breathing. "We're not friends. We never will be, okay?" She nodded, not sure if she should be hurt or not. "I'm just gonna be upfront about this now so there is no doubt. I don't mean this sexually, Regina. In *that* sense, we can go as slow as you want, but if, after this weekend, we're not *more* than friends, then things go back to the way they were before Friday. If I'm gonna make this exception, then it's either all or nothing. Anything in between is unacceptable."

He stared at her for a moment, no doubt waiting for a reaction from her. She tried not to look as alarmed as she felt about the loaded statement he'd just dropped on her.

"All?" she asked cautiously. "What exactly do you mean by all?"

His brow lifted, and he continued to look at her very intensely. "I mean I'm not breaking my rule of no attachments to become *friends* with a woman who fascinates me and I can't get enough of kissing. It would never work. Since I did offer my assistance for the entire weekend, you have it until then, but if you're not looking for more than just a friend you enjoy kissing, then I'm out after tomorrow."

At the risk of sounding dense, because she wanted to make sure she was absolutely clear on what he was saying, she had to ask. Her insides were already going nuts, and she didn't want him to notice. Was he really saying what she thought he was saying?

No longer able to remain composed and hold back how secretly thrilled this made her, she smirked. Already lying here in bed with Brandon was something she *never* would've believed she'd be doing just a few days ago. So asking what she was about to ask after spending just two days with him seemed even more absurd. Still, before she agreed to anything, she wanted it unmistakably clear. "Are you asking me to be your girl, Sergeant Billings?"

Finally, a smile softened what had now turned into an unyielding near glare after she'd apparently taken a bit long to respond for his liking. He nodded, but like so often when he responded to her before, he said nothing more.

As absurd as it seemed, she did feel as if she were his girl already. Not since college had she done the casual thing, and she certainly didn't plan on moving on by starting off with just a casual thing now. Although ever since last year, she hadn't considered doing *anything.* She still wasn't sure she was ready, but he was being so all or nothing about it, and she didn't want to risk him going back to the guy she once thought him to be now that she knew how amazingly sweet he could really be. She smiled. "I'd ask you to let me sleep on it, but I get the feeling I won't be getting any sleep now. I know myself. I'd toss and turn over this all night."

"What's there to toss and turn about?" he asked. "I'm not asking you to marry me, *Ms. Brady*." He leaned in and kissed her softly. "Not yet anyway. I just need you to understand this now." He looked into her eyes, suddenly going very serious again. "I don't do the friends' thing. So if you decide it's all you wanna do, I don't want you to be upset later because it's not gonna happen. If you prefer we don't take this any further, Monday things go back to the way they were before."

Regina stared at him for moment. She would've liked to have tried the friends' thing first before getting into anything too intense with him. But admittedly she'd never had a *friend* she kissed the way she and Brandon had already. So what difference did it make if they made this official? It was better than doing this and then wondering what *this* was. She'd already begun to wonder. Like he'd said, "At least this way there were no doubts."

Smiling big, she could hardly believe she was about to agree to this. She nodded very softly at first and then with a lot more enthusiasm as she saw that *beautiful* smile spread across his face. "Okay," she whispered.

"Okay, what?" he asked.

"I *am not* calling you sir!"

Brandon laughed heartedly and kissed her. "That's not what I meant. I mean I wanna know exactly what you *think* you're agreeing to."

She looked at him, confused and a little embarrassed. "Being your girl, right?"

He leaned in and kissed her so deeply she began to squirm, but she wrapped her arms around him tightly, relieved she'd clearly gotten it right.

Pulling away just slightly, he looked deep into her eyes. "My princess," he whispered.

The term of endearment and how sweetly he said it took her by surprise, but she immediately loved it, so she smiled big. "I like that," she whispered back.

As unexpected as this sudden change in her life was, Regina's heart pounded with the eager anticipation of what was to come.

~~~

The next day had been as wonderful as the rest of the weekend. She'd been able to keep her family at bay by telling them a little white lie. She knew her mother would want her there again for their Sunday family brunch. But there was no way she could go with her ankle like this. And Brandon had been right. It was better that she not tell them about her injury just yet. They'd make a big deal out of it, so she told them she was still having some things delivered and while they'd told her they'd deliver on Sunday they didn't give her a time. She also mentioned having a major breakthrough at work and had some things she really wanted to work on ASAP. That wasn't entirely a lie, so she felt less guilty about the first lie.

Brandon had been as sweet and attentive as he'd been from the first day. Then things took an unexpected change. After the struggle of getting Regina down the stairs Monday morning, he insisted they stay at his single-story place at least for that week.

"No sense in having to deal with those stairs all week," he'd said. "We'll take whatever you need to my place for the week, and maybe by the weekend your ankle will be strong enough for you to climb up on your own."

At first, Regina tried to protest she couldn't do that—just move into his place for the week and intrude on his life that way. But after getting that scolding look because she was apparently being difficult and he was only trying to make life easier not just on her but himself, she gave in.

Monday she'd given Brandon a tour of her small office space at work when he walked her there in the morning. They'd arrived early before anyone else was there because they'd made sure to allow enough time for her to walk as slowly as she needed from the parking lot to the building. Then, just as she'd finished the tour, Antonio and a couple of the other guys she worked with arrived. Regina made sure she introduced Brandon as her boyfriend since he'd been so adamant that he didn't do the friend thing. She'd gotten the distinct feeling from the way Brandon eyed them the moment they walked into the office Brandon might be ticked if she hadn't introduced him that way.

He appeared pleased enough but still planted a long deep one on her just before he walked out of her office. He finished it off by telling her to have a good day and that he'd be back at the end of the day to help her to her car. Then he gave the guys, but especially Antonio, one last very significant look.

Monday night they'd gone back to her place as she gathered everything she'd need at his place for the week. Or rather she told Brandon where he could find everything, and he'd fetched it all, including her fancy single-cup coffee maker. She'd already begun to notice what a control freak Brandon was, so it didn't even surprise her when he'd wanted to know how to work it even though he hated coffee. He told her he wanted to make it for her in the mornings so she could concentrate on taking her time getting ready.

"Rushing could lead to injuries," he'd said as she showed him how easy her coffee machine was—fill with water, drop the pod in and hit start.

That night, he also surprised her with another question as they lay there in bed, enjoying their now usual goodnight kissing. He'd been lying over her, his body half on hers when he pulled away and stared at her very seriously for good long moment. "The morning we got stuck in the elevator, two Fridays ago," he said, and she stared at him, the memory of that morning coming back to her.

It was hard to believe how drastically things had changed between them since that morning. She nodded running her fingers through his hair. "Yeah?"

"Your co-worker Antonio, the one you called to get the power back on?" Again she nodded, curious now where he was going with this. "You thanked him for doing something for you. You called him sweetie."

"You remember that?"

This time he nodded, still staring at her a little too seriously. "What did he do that had you smiling so big and made you even more anxious to get to your office?"

Regina's lips parted, still stunned that he remembered these things with such detail. Even she'd forgotten about that conversation until just a few days ago.

Brandon's eyes moved down to her lips, and he pecked them softly. "Tell me," he whispered.

"He bought bagels for everyone, and he brought me my favorite."

"Which is?"

She smiled, knowing once she told him he'd likely never forget. "Blueberry."

He nodded again, and she was certain that confirmed that the fact had been locked away in his memory vault, which apparently held on to even the most insignificant of things. "You'd only been there a week. How'd he know it was your favorite?"

Regina tilted her head with a smirk. Would he always pay attention to the smallest of details? "The very first day, when I was introduced to the whole office, they had a list of *very* important questions for me. How do I take my coffee and was I a donut or bagel girl were among them. When I said, "Bagel," he immediately asked what my favorite was."

Brandon's eyebrow went up, but not in a playful way. "Immediately, huh? You and he talk on the phone outside of work?"

Uh oh, now she knew exactly where this was going. "Not really."

"Yes or no, Regina. Not really isn't gonna fly."

Just like when he'd made it clear that it was all or nothing, as nervous as he could make her, being so upfront, Regina had to admit she appreciated his not beating around the bush. She hadn't even noticed she had a missed call from Antonio Thursday night until the Friday morning when she got a text from Antonio asking if she was okay. After their post-*When Harry Met Sally* conversation and especially after his all or nothing proposal, the thought *had* crossed her mind that any relationship with Antonio outside of work might be an issue. But just like everything else when it came to Brandon, she never imagined they'd be addressing this so soon.

"I exchanged numbers with everyone in the firm. Things do come up after hours, so occasionally, we may need to speak outside of work."

"But he's not your *friend*?"

The caveat in his tone was undeniable. Brandon wasn't just asking a question. He was making a statement. He'd certainly made himself clear last night, and he was doing it again now.

"He's my co-worker," she said, feeling a little stupid now that she'd actually laid the syrup on when talking to Antonio that morning on purpose. The last thing she would've imagined then was that it would come back and bite her in the ass in this way. "Subordinate actually, but I prefer to see them all as co-workers."

"You call all of your subordinates sweetie?"

"Okay," she said, straightening out a little. For someone who liked cutting right down to the chase, he sure was dragging this one out and painfully so, since they both knew what he was trying to insinuate. "First of all, no, I don't. Second, I'll just admit it because I don't want this to become an issue moving forward. That morning I was extra nice to him *because* you were standing right there listening. You'd been pretty curt with me up until then, and I just wanted to make a point that I wasn't the anti-social one. I can be very nice when people are nice to me. But no, that was the first and last time I ever called him that."

His continued heavy stare dug into her. Now that she knew how closely he was paying attention to even the smallest of things, she wondered what was going through his mind. To her surprise, his stern expression softened. "You are very nice," he said, kissing her softly, "and very beautiful." He kissed her chin then moved down to her neck and sucked, making her squirm in response. Kissing his way back up to her lips, he stopped, and their eyes met again. "He shouldn't be an issue. I was gonna let it go actually. I didn't wanna make a big deal out of something so trivial, but after seeing the surprised look on his face today, it made me wonder just why the fuck he'd be so surprised that you were with someone, so I had to ask." He smirked, though it wasn't as playful as his usual smirks. "As of right now, I'm not fond of any guy so willing to go out of his way for *my* princess, but I'll take your word that he's nothing more than your eager-to-please subordinate. Just be warned. Unless you want me to really hate the guy, please never let me hear you call him sweetie again."

"I won't," she whispered with a smile, and Brandon took her mouth in his again.

Her insides churned with a mix of excitement and nerves as he kissed her slowly but incredibly meticulously, not missing a single spot of her hungry mouth. She wondered even through her suddenly aroused state how long it would take for her to get used to Brandon's emphatic way of getting straight to the point when it came to certain things. There'd be no guessing games in this relationship about things of this nature. That was for sure.

~~~

By Thursday, they had their routine down. That evening, Brandon had to make a run because she was getting low on the wrap for her ankle, even though it wasn't nearly as sore as it had been days ago. He still insisted she continue to wear the wrap. He also said he'd be stopping to pick up dinner and a few other things he was getting low on from the market. As usual, he refused to take any money from her.

From the first day Regina had stepped foot into Brandon's meticulously organized apartment, she'd been even more overwhelmed with concern over what she'd gotten herself into. She was almost embarrassed now that he'd been witness to her less-than-organized place. She wasn't a slob or anything, but Brandon's apartment was a perfect exhibit of a neat freak bordering on OCD.

Regina had teased him about it, and he shrugged it off, explaining he hadn't always been this way. Being a Marine had a lot to do with it, and then becoming a drill instructor had made him even worse. Only Regina was the one using the word worse. He'd used the phrase "helped me become even better organized, not just at work but in my personal life."

This was the first time she'd been left alone in his place all week. Trying not to be nosey but incredibly curious, she peeked into his closet. Already she'd walked around his front room, looking through his neat but sparsely decorated shelves a little closer than she had all week. Most of the week she'd had glimpses of his well-organized closet from when she'd seen him go in and fetch something, but he'd always quickly closed the door.

She took in his clothes first. They were perfectly hung and separated by color with his uniforms off to one side. Many were still in their plastic coverings from the cleaners, and his shoes were neatly lined on the floor. The see-through totes in the above shelves were all the exact same size and stacked just so. Something in one of the totes caught her eye. It looked too much like a pair of handcuffs.

Tilting her head, she tried to make out the other things in the tote, but it was hard to tell from where she was standing. She saw what looked like rope and some kind of harness with buckles.

Glancing back at the open bedroom door, she wondered if she dared take it down and peek in. Indulging her curiosity by being nosey and looking into his closet was one thing. Digging into his drawers or even totes was pushing it. She decided she wouldn't go there but did continue to look through his clothes. She'd seen him in uniform many times and seen his laid-back jeans and T-shirt look on the weekend and evenings, but the only time she'd been witness to him all dressed up was the night at Gaslamp. Yet he had many civilian dress shirts hanging in his closet. Really nice ones too. For someone who kept to himself and made no attachments, he had an awful lot of socializing clothes.

She moved one particular shirt aside because the color, a deep royal blue, was eye catching, and she could only imagine how incredible the blue in his eyes would stand out when he wore this. Then her hand hit something hard, hanging against the wall. It caught her attention because it was long cold and slender like a weapon maybe? But it wasn't. It was a metal stick? She spread the shirts apart to get a better look, and her jaw dropped. There wasn't one stick but two, only they weren't sticks. They were riding crops, and hanging right next them on its own individual hook as well was a long black wooden paddle with a red heart painted in the middle.

Her head jerked up to the tote on top. Those *were* handcuffs. Holy crap! Was he really into this stuff? As much fun as she'd had in college, there had been several things she'd never tried. This was one of them. As nervous as it made her, there was a slow bubbling inside her. She'd never trusted anyone to tie her up, and she hated to admit it, but her sexual life with Ryan while sweet, safe, and very loving had also been very vanilla. It never even crossed her mind to ask him to do anything kinky to her.

Pushing away painful thoughts of Ryan, she wondered instead if Brandon would be bringing this up once she was ready and *how* he'd bring it up. Would he just spring it on her? The way he'd closed his closet so quickly all week made her wonder if he'd bring it up at all or if that was another of the few topics he seemed to skirt and she wouldn't get to explore.

Forcing herself to stop thinking about it, she moved into his kitchen. She'd been in there for a few minutes, looking through the neatly lined cans of food in his small pantry and noticing how orderly everything his fridge was. He must really think her a slob. Since she'd only been here a few weeks, she hadn't bothered to clean out her fridge even once yet. She didn't have a whole lot in it, but it definitely didn't look as if it could pass the white glove test as Brandon's did.

She heard the front door open and smiled. He'd been gone just over an hour, and she was already excited to see him again. Only he didn't come into the kitchen, so she walked out to meet him. He'd dropped off some bags and a box of food on the table, but he was gone. Worried that somehow he'd gotten wind of what she'd been doing while he was gone, she actually glanced around, expecting to see cameras she'd missed all week, but there were none. What if he'd had some kind of sensor on his closet door that went off, alerting him she'd been snooping? There was a phone app for just about everything these days, and, of course, that would be just her luck.

She walked slowly into the bedroom and froze when she saw him standing in front of his open closet, shirtless. He turned to her, his jeans hanging just off his waist and frowned. Did he know? Would he be kicking her out now?

CHAPTER FIFTEEN

Regina held her breath, her eyes on Brandon's clenching fist. He turned to her with a frown. "Damn bird shit on my shirt outside the drugstore." He pulled a shirt out from the closet. "I wanted to soak it first thing." He motioned toward the bathroom with his chin. "Since it's white, I don't want it to stain."

Relieved, but now completely distracted by his bare chest and shoulders, she stared at them with a sinful grin. This entire week his shirtless chest managed to elude her, despite all the showers he'd taken and times he'd changed. "Wait," she said, before he could put his shirt back on. Her eyes dropped to the lower right side of his abdominal muscles. "Can I . . .?"

She pointed at the string of words tattooed as she got closer. For a moment, she was almost afraid to finish her question. What if the words were for another girl? Someone in his past. The girl she reminded him of maybe? He'd gladly and proudly explained all his other tattoos. The ones on his arms were all tributes to the Marines. He'd even lifted his sleeve a couple of the times to show her a few a little higher on his arm she might've missed, but he hadn't mentioned this one. If they ever made love, could she stand staring at something so profound he felt for someone else he decided to have it tattooed on his body forever?

Staring at it now, she was close enough to make out the words written in script, and read downwards. The sentence ended with a small heart woven into the script itself. She didn't understand it, but it *was* about his past. "What does it mean?" she asked.

"What's past is prologue," he whispered, before lifting the shirt over his head and bringing it all the way down to cover the tattoo. "Technically, it means history repeats itself, but I like to think of it how my mother explained it. While our past does set the stage for what's to come in the future, ultimately it's *your* decisions based on what's happened in that past—good or bad–that determine your future."

The way he looked at her when he said that last part was so piercing it almost felt personal, not as if he were explaining but rather telling her. Did he know something about her past already? Could he possibly know about what she'd almost done? Or was there something else he was trying to tell her?

She cleared her voice, trying not to sound as nervous as those last words made her. "That's very profound. But do you really believe you can dictate the future? There are some things you have no control over. Sometimes things just happen."

Taking a few steps toward her, he looked at her with a vacant expression. "But they happen for a reason, like you falling down those stairs and me being there to help you." He slipped his hand in hers as he reached her. "If I had let past experiences interfere with the decisions I made after that night, you might not be here with me right now."

He slipped his arm around her waist, pulling her against his hard body. Gulping, because her heart was already doing that thing it always did when she was in his arms, she searched his eyes. As risky as her next question was—because he might turn it around on her—she had to know. "Is there something in your past I should know about?"

Slipping his hand out of hers and bringing it behind her neck, he smiled softly, shaking his head and mouthing the word "no." His eyes were immediately on her lips, and he licked his own. "I can hardly stand to look at you for very long without kissing you."

Then his lips were on hers, and she sighed against his. Regina had come to the conclusion earlier that week that nobody had ever kissed her the way Brandon did. From the very first time, he'd done so with that unabashed craze, and she'd felt it. But since then, even though the craze had calmed a bit, the passion hadn't. Even when he kissed her softly and gently, as he did now, there was so much in those kisses. They reached a place in her she didn't think had ever been touched. *Kisses.* These were just his kisses!

But they were so much more than just kisses. She wished she could explain it—understand it—because if she ever said it out loud, it would sound preposterous. They'd been together for less than a week, and already his kisses held so much emotion. Emotion he was yet to express verbally. He'd told her she fascinated him and that after she'd kissed him he was a goner—he wanted more of *her,* but why? Even with as much passion as he'd kissed her all week, he hadn't so much as attempted to take it any further. It was almost as if kissing her as he did satisfied something much deeper than sex would for him. Regina felt it too, but even as satisfying as his kisses were, she was ready for more. She was more than ready.

Moaning as they moved closer to the bed, she pulled him along, tugging on his shirt. She wanted him to see—*feel* how ready she was to take this further. Even as they sat on his bed, he never took his lips away from her, immediately pulling her to him as they lay back. His hand moved up from her neck, and his fingers massaged her head as he continued to kiss, sucking her tongue a bit harder as the kiss went on.

Finally, he pulled away, only to breathlessly admit, "I'll never get enough of your mouth."

Before she could beg him to make love to her, his lips were on hers, and she was helpless to pull away. She too was beginning to feel addicted to his tongue in her mouth. What was he doing to her? She felt completely spellbound by his mouth—his tongue. So much so she was beginning to think if he did this much longer she might come undone and cry out in pleasure from just kissing him. Was that even possible?

If his mouth on hers alone could do this to her, she could only imagine if . . . The moment he took to catch his breath, she gasped. "Make love to me, Brandon. I wanna feel you inside me *so* bad."

He stopped and stared at her. "Are you sure?"

She nodded eagerly then wrapped her arms around his neck. "Yes, I'm sure."

Without saying another word, Brandon pulled away and began undressing her slowly. Luckily, there was not much to remove. When he'd left earlier, the first thing she'd done was shed her work clothes for a San Diego Padres T-shirt of his that she'd come to love in the short time she'd been staying with him. It smelled like him, so fresh and clean and perfect but with that hint of his personal scent. That first night when she'd spent the night at his house, she realized in her haste to make sure she brought everything she needed for work and all her toiletries, she'd forgotten any pajamas. He'd offered her the shirt, saying he often changed into it in the evenings after taking a shower to relax in. When she'd gone into his bathroom to change into it, the smell of it as she brought it over her head combined with the perfectly worn soft cotton fabric had been almost orgasmic. If she had it her way, she'd live in his shirt.

Brandon kissed her naked shoulders after pulling the shirt off of her. Sprinkling more kisses down her collar bone, his touch was so incredibly gentle she could hardly believe he was into the stuff in his closet. Maybe those things weren't his, but they had to be.

Continuing to make his way down under her neck, he pulled her panties off without ever stopping the rain of soft kisses all around her neck and just under her ears.

Lifting his body away from her for a moment, he pulled his own shirt off, and it was her turn to kiss his shoulders as he leaned back onto her. She ran her fingers over his hard chest and perfect abs. This whole week he'd hardly left her side, except for when they'd been at work, so he hadn't mentioned working out, but judging from his perfectly sculpted hard body, obviously he did—a lot.

He kissed her, and once again, she fell into that place only his kisses ever took her. She closed her eyes, and her mouth soaked his up. Even though she was lying there completely nude under a man, something she hadn't done in over eighteen months, she couldn't think of anything more than giving into his masterful kisses. She felt him move around doing things as he occasionally ran his hands over her naked body.

She'd been so lost in the magic of his kisses she didn't even notice he'd stripped down to nothing until he stopped to place the condom on. She stared breathlessly, knowing he'd soon be inside her, something she'd practically begged for, and now the reality of it really sunk in.

Before she could give it another thought, Brandon positioned himself between her legs. "You ready, princess?" he whispered with a smile almost as nervous as she felt.

Somehow, she thought there'd be more foreplay, that he'd do a lot more to her before they got to this part. Maybe he'd bring out his tote of naughty treasures. She'd imagined him taking her roughly, spreading her wide then plunging in her with force. Instead, he lay down gently over her, bringing those lips that would be the death of her and began kissing her just as gently as he slipped into her. The one thing he did that was different from anything she'd ever experienced was he brought her hands over her head and held them there with both his hands.

The only time their lips parted from that moment on was when he was inside her completely, and she gasped at the incredible feeling of fullness it gave her. She'd been right. Having him inside her was amazing. He slid in and out in the same rhythm as his kisses for a very long time. Even as he began to rock into her harder and faster, holding on tighter to her hands still above her head, she got the distinct feeling that he was getting just as much arousal from kissing her as he was from fucking her.

Shifting his body ever so slightly, she felt him smile against her lips as his erection began to slide over that perfect spot, making her entire body quiver in reaction. Regina moaned as each time he slid in and out, and her body trembled uncontrollably. She cried out as the sensation began to peak, but even that didn't make him release her mouth. He slammed into her harder—faster—and she lifted her hips up to take him as deep as possible. Regina didn't just climax; she erupted. Even as the explosions of pleasure went off again and again, she felt him bury himself in her, and not once did his tongue ever stop.

She closed her eyes tightly, and the mixture of her continued throbbing climax and his enthralling *deep* kisses had her climaxing for so much longer than she ever had. Long after they'd both come, he continued to kiss her and slide in and out of her until she felt him harden again. Feeling him slowly fill her again as he slid in and out, she lifted her good leg around him, suddenly wanting to—*needing* to—relive the best sex she'd ever experienced. There'd been nothing out of the ordinary about it. She and Ryan had done it almost just like that every time, minus the amazing marathon-long kissing. Something as simple as her hands being held her over her head coupled with the *perfect* positioning and timing when he'd driven into her near the end, had made for such a profound climax. Or maybe it was just him. He was so different from anyone she'd ever been with this felt so different—so incredible.

To her disappointment, Brandon pulled away, moving her leg down. "I'd go on, but this condom's had it." He chuckled as he pulled out of her, leaving her feeling incredibly empty and yearning to have him inside her again. "Damn, this thing is *done*."

Climbing off the bed, she watched as he walked off into the bathroom then came back with a towel. Almost ashamed that her eyes had gone directly *there*, she smiled when she saw he was still as ready as she was to go at it again. The moment he was done cleaning her up so gently it drove her nuts, she wrapped her arms around his neck.

"Again," she whispered in his ear, and in the next second, she was flat on her back again, giggling in delight as Brandon pulled out another condom.

~*~

Brandon

No way would Brandon have believed it if anyone had told him this would happen just a week ago. The little princess from the airport was his girl now, and they were making incredible love day and night. For years, Brandon hadn't allowed himself so much as a distant acquaintance with any girl. He'd gone to great lengths to make sure any interaction he had with women remained safely unemotional. Now just like that he was in a formal relationship with a girl he already felt crazy about. He was completely helpless to remain unemotional. Everything he said or did to her overflowed with emotion, an emotion he'd been afraid to give into for years. Now he couldn't imagine going even a day without hugging her, kissing her, and making love to her the way he'd been doing for such a short time. He had a girlfriend now, and *he'd* been the one to suggest it.

As scary as the thought was when he'd decided to put it out there, Brandon knew he'd made the right decision. There was no way he would've been able to remain just friends with her, no way he would've ever agreed to the idea of not having the right to protest the other men in her life. That was one of the most pressing reasons why he needed things this way. And now that he'd felt what it was like to make *love* to a woman—felt what had been written about in poems and songs for centuries—he was damn sure he'd made the right decision demanding exclusivity so early on.

Over the course of the past week, they'd talked about a few things, and one of them was how they'd be introducing each other to friends and family.

"Are you really going to introduce me as your girlfriend?" she'd asked a bit skeptically.

"Of course," he'd answered, trying not to sound as terrified as the thought had made him.

He hadn't even thought that far ahead when he'd made his all-or-nothing declaration last Saturday night. Being holed up in her apartment that whole weekend then having her in his bed all week, the entire thing felt a bit surreal still. But it didn't get more real than going out and introducing her to his colleagues as his girlfriend and meeting her friends and *family*.

At first, he'd wondered if he was going to regret this. But once he heard her introduce him to Antonio and the other guys as her boyfriend, as weird as it felt, he was glad they'd had that conversation.

Fortunately, Brandon had one less thing to worry about when it came to this sudden enormous change in his life. Rodriguez had been sent out of state to cover for another sergeant. He'd be gone at least a month. He knew how hypocritical that would look. Although Brandon was very hard-nosed about the rules being followed at work and Rodriguez's comments about being willing to risk his job were off the charts stupid, Brandon's reaction had been a bit over the top. So while he'd had no intention of keeping his relationship with Regina a secret from anyone, he certainly wasn't looking forward to that conversation with Rodriguez.

To his relief, Regina had been right about one thing. His not having friends in his life was not for lack of personality and being able to hold a conversation with someone. He was way more comfortable having her in his life and even staying in his place than he'd ever imagined he would be.

Saturday morning, Brandon started to slip out of bed to go make her coffee. As much as he hated the stuff, he loved seeing that smile on her face when he brought it to her. Since being on the receiving end of Regina's grateful and breathtaking smiles, he was beginning to understand what the allure was for her *daddy* and possibly most of the men she'd ever met to want to spoil her. Making her happy and taking care of her had quickly become his first priority. It was the weirdest phenomenon. He'd always heard that giving was so much more satisfying than receiving, and this entire past week had been proof of that. He'd never felt as satisfied as when he saw that content smile on her.

Just as he got up, her phone rang by the chair where she'd left it, and it woke her. Frowning, he walked over to pick it up and bring it to her. He glanced at the name on the screen. C. Devereux.

"Your friend Chris from New York," he said, making sure she knew he remembered what the "C" stood for.

Her eyes widened, and she took the phone but didn't answer him. Brandon waited for her to comment, say something, *anything* that might explain her strange reaction to this guy. But she offered nothing, so he had to ask. "Aren't you gonna answer?"

Looking up at him, she started to say something then seemed to change her mind and answered the phone instead. "Hey, Chris." She smiled, pulling a strand of hair behind her ear. "Yes, I got it. Thank you so much. That was very sweet of you. No, no, everything is fine. I meant to call and thank you, but this week has been so crazy it totally slipped my mind."

Brandon stood there, watching her, his jaw tensing at her telling this guy how sweet it was of him. Did *all* her guy friends go out of their way to do sweet things for her? This was exactly why he didn't believe for a second that men and women could be friends. So this guy sends her a book, and she never responds. Can't he take a hint? He has to follow up and call her and pretend he was worried because she hadn't bothered to call him and thank him? Brandon could already tell he wasn't going to like this old friend of hers, if, in fact, that's all they'd ever been.

"In a few weeks? Yes, I'd like that. We can do coffee or dinner or something."

Oh, *hell* no. She wasn't going to start this shit. She *had* to know that unless she was planning on bringing Brandon along for that coffee or dinner with this guy this would never work. Panic crept in him slowly because things had been so perfect all week. Even when he'd brought up Antonio and her relationship with him, it had gone smoothly. He didn't want to ruin things by getting into an argument now, but there was no way he could begin to hide what he was feeling.

"No," she said, her voice going a little strange. "I have had my moments when I've been very tempted to call you."

She glanced up at Brandon and cleared her throat, sitting up a little as he struggled to remain calm and not glare at her. *Very tempted* to call him?

"Listen, I gotta go, but it was really good to hear from you, and, again, thank you so much for the book. Call me when you're in town."

She hung up and smiled at him. "Were you going somewhere before the phone rang?"

"To get you coffee," Brandon said with no intention of letting her brush the subject of her *friend* away again as she'd done before. "Your friend's gonna be in town?"

She nodded, bringing her legs to the side of the bed. "In a few weeks."

"And you two are getting together?"

"Most likely," she said, getting up. He reached his arm out to help, but she motioned that she had it.

She hadn't worn the splint all day yesterday, and she was actually walking on her ankle now. She said it didn't hurt to step on it anymore, but Brandon had still warned her to take it easy.

"You said this was an old friend. How long have you two been friends?"

Without looking at him, Regina reached the bathroom. "Did I say old really? Not too long. We met last year. I'll be right out."

Last year? After her husband passed? A part of Brandon wanted to just let it go—not stir the waters. But he'd picked up on something ever since her reaction to the book this guy sent her. There was something about this subject—this guy. Something made her nervous to talk to Brandon about this *friend*. He'd since decided he wouldn't push it, that it wasn't a big deal. The guy didn't even live in California. How much trouble could he be? But now he was calling her, and she was talking about meeting up with him? A guy she'd been *very* tempted to call?

Brandon was determined not to make a big deal of this, but he was absolutely getting to the bottom of this *today*.

A few minutes later, he heard the toilet flush then the water running. More minutes passed. Then she opened the door, her toothbrush still in her mouth, and she smiled. Even with a mouthful of toothpaste, bed head, and no makeup on, she was adorable. He couldn't help smiling, but it only made him more anxious about this guy she *thought* she'd be getting together with.

After rinsing and wiping her mouth with a towel, she walked out. "You know what I'm craving?" she said, all bright-eyed. "Chocolate-chocolate-chip waffles."

He hated to put a damper on her cheery mood, but he had to know. "We can go get some if you want. But you wanna tell me about this friend of yours from New York first?"

Her smile instantly vanished, and she started toward the bed. "No, not really," she said, surprising him.

Brandon thought for sure she'd try to make light of it and change the subject. This just turned up the need to know more about this guy a few hundred notches. "Why?"

"Because it's not something I feel like talking about." Her response was abrupt—terse—not at all what he was expecting.

Taking a few steps toward her, he chose his words wisely because he could feel this getting tense already. There was *no way* he was letting this go now. "Why do I get the feeling there's more to this *friend* that you're not telling me?"

She turned to him with a look he hadn't seen on her since the day she confronted him at the base, the glare that had him holding back a smile then. Only now he was in anything but a smiling mood. "We've been together for all of one week, Brandon. You really think I've told you everything about my life? I agreed to do this with you because I didn't want things to go back to the way they were. I like having you in my life, but, Jesus, give me some time. There are some things I'd rather not talk about just yet."

Brandon didn't want to regret having done this with her. He didn't want to regret that they were just into this one week and already the thought of her having a guy friend she didn't want to tell him about had him wanting to punch a hole through a fucking wall. "Like ex-boyfriends or male friends you plan on getting together with?" he asked, every word louder than the last. "Because I'll be damned if—"

"Chris is a *she*," Regina said sharply, but then the severity in her own expression lessened, and the corner of her lip rose. She reached out and touched his face with her hand, relieving some of the enormous pressure already brimming in every one of his muscles. "If that's what you're worried about, don't. You've made it very clear how you feel about men and women being friends, and if you recall, I agreed with you."

He reached for her, pulling her into his arms, and buried his face in her neck. The relief was replaced by instant fear—

fear that he was going to blow this. Even he hadn't anticipated his reaction to be so heated. "I'm sorry." He kissed her neck twice before pulling away. "I had a feeling I might suck at this, but I promise I won't always be like this. I just . . ." He shook his head. "I'll give you all the time you need. If you'd rather not talk about her yet, I'll wait. I won't be so—"

She kissed him, not letting him go on, and that was a damn good thing because, unbelievably, another thought he never expected to be thinking had begun to cloud his mind. For a moment of insane desperation, he actually considered doing something he long ago vowed he'd never do for *anyone*—beg. As much he felt for Regina, even she wouldn't make him break that vow.

He had to get it together. His insecure ass was going to destroy this—this thing that after only a week he could already tell was the best thing that'd ever happened to him. Still, his reaction to thinking she didn't want to tell him about another guy in her life hadn't been unfounded. "I'm sorry I misunderstood," he explained. "I really thought it was a guy you were on the phone with and sent you that romance novel."

He kissed her deeply, wanting that last comment to register loud and clear. He wasn't apologizing for nearly losing it because of *that*. If that were ever the case, she should expect nothing less. In fact, it'd probably be even more severe. The longer he was around her—spoiling her—claiming her with every kiss every time they made love, the likelier it'd be that he'd have less control over his emotions over *anyone* coming between them.

She ran her fingers through his hair as their kissing began going into that familiar, wild, uncontrolled place. Just like that, as always when he kissed her, he was instantly aroused, and his throbbing erection was already impossible to conceal through his thin boxer briefs. Remembering she was hungry and this was his chance to appease her with what she was craving, he pulled away gently, but she pulled him back, holding his shoulders tight.

Taking that as an invitation to dive in, he did so as wildly as only she could make him, as he had that very first time he kissed her madly. He picked her up, and she wrapped her legs around him instantly. "Careful," he reminded her, mindful to not hurt her ankle.

He may never beg, but spoiling and appeasing his girl he could do. In fact, he couldn't think of anything that felt better than seeing that beautiful smiling face or, in this case, her crying out in pleasure. Just like the spoiling, he wanted to make something perfectly clear: she didn't need anyone else spoiling her or making her cry out in pleasure ever again.

Laying her down on the bed, he pulled her panties off and spread her wide. Her eyes went equally as wide. Since the first time they'd made love, while he'd made sure she was satisfied to near exhaustion, they'd done it his new favorite way *every* time—feeling her come while he kissed her insatiably, something completely and utterly new to him. He knew if things didn't work out between them it would never happen again. That was something reserved exclusively for Regina, and he would *never* even try it with anyone else. So he could not get enough of it.

But right now was all about spoiling his little princess. Getting comfortable between her legs, he smiled because he hadn't done a thing yet, and already she was trembling. The whole giving-feeling-so-much-better-than-receiving theory certainly applied here. The moment his mouth and tongue began greedily sucking up every ounce of her sweetness and he heard her moan in pleasure, he knew it. Just like kissing her, this was just another thing he'd never get enough of.

CHAPTER SIXTEEN

Regina

That Sunday was the first time since Regina's fall that she felt ready to get back in the driver's seat. She didn't think her family would fall for another excuse not to make it for their Sunday brunch, and she had to admit she missed them and was looking forward to seeing them again.

Fortunately, Brandon immediately mentioned that her visit to her parents would work out perfectly since he had errands to run and wanted to get back in the gym. Feeling guilty that it was her fault he'd neglected working out and possibly doing other things he normally did, she didn't dare ask him to come with her. Secretly, she'd been relieved. She knew she was a grown-ass woman, and if she chose to all but move in with her boyfriend of just over a week, it was her business, and her family had no say in it. Still, she preferred to wean them to this unexpected change in her life. It was better to tell them about him first rather than just showing up with him.

Seeing her family once again had been great. As expected, they grilled her about Brandon the moment she'd mentioned meeting someone. They still didn't know the half of it, but she did tell them she was very serious about him and told her sisters that he was possibly the most amazing kisser *ever*. Of course, they all asked when they could meet him, but she made no promises. She only assured them that it would be soon.

On her way back from her family's brunch, Regina smiled, feeling her insides simmer with the excitement of simply knowing she'd soon be indulging in those amazing kisses again. To her surprise, Brandon walked out the door of his apartment as soon as she pulled in.

"Feel like Tiramisu?" He asked with a breathtaking smile.

Her brunch with her parents had been hours ago. Most of the last couple of hours she'd spent being the center of attention as they all continued to interrogate her about her new man. Tiramisu right then sounded perfect.

Nodding, she walked toward him. "You bought some?"

"No." He held his keys up. "We can go knock another Gaslamp restaurant off your list."

Regina had told him about her and Janecia's quest to try every restaurant on that strip. She'd also told him about how weak-minded she was when it came to cravings setting in. Advertisers loved simpletons like her because the moment she saw anything tantalizing on TV or anywhere she'd have a craving for it until she got it. Last night they'd been lying in bed with the television on when Brandon clicked on a cooking reality show where the contestants were asked to make Tiramisu, one of her all-time favorite desserts. Brandon had laughed at the way her eyes sparkled as she watched the judges tasting the dessert. He'd even offered to go out and buy her some, but she declined, feeling like a spoiled brat. At the same time, she'd felt like the luckiest girl in the world to have found such an amazing guy, who'd be willing to run out and buy her cake just because he thought it would make her happy. Now he was offering to take her to get some.

"Yes!" She smiled brightly before kissing him as she reached him. "I don't deserve you," she said as she pulled away.

"Because I'm taking you to get Tiramisu?" He grinned playfully, already tugging her along toward his Jeep.

"No, because you remember everything, Brandon, even the silly things I tell you, and then you turn it around and do something so sweet. Do you even like tiramisu? Its main ingredient is coffee or espresso, and I know you don't care for either."

"I've had it before and it's okay. I can always order something else." They reached the passenger side of his Jeep, and he pulled her to him then leaned against the door, kissing her, her insides melting instantly. Pulling away, he stared in her eyes. "If I tell you something, you promise you won't laugh?"

She stared at him curiously, and already she was smiling silly. "What?"

"I missed you like crazy today. You talk about having your woman card being taken away once. I should have my man card pulled and burned." He chuckled now, making her laugh nervously as her insides went wild. "Once I was done with my errands and my workout, I didn't even know what to do with myself." He lowered his voice, leaning his forehead against hers. "I shouldn't even be telling you this, but for the past hour, I've been looking out the window every five to ten minutes."

Regina giggled, relieved that she wasn't alone in how terrifyingly fast she'd fallen for him, so she admitted, "Okay, maybe I drove home a little faster than I should have. The closer I got, the heavier my foot got."

He lifted a brow, feigning anger about her speeding but didn't quite pull it off. Then he kissed her, squeezing her even tighter than before. "Let's go get you dessert, princess," he whispered in her ear.

As they drove down the busy strip, Regina was still feeling a little dazed by his thrilling admission, when her eyes narrowed in on something, making her sit up a little straighter. They were passing by the very bar she'd spotted him with that blonde the last time she was here. Her joyful splendor was quickly jolted by the irrepressible jealousy at the thought of Brandon kissing that woman and how he'd done it so blithely in front of everyone watching.

They drove into a parking structure as Regina struggled to conceal her sudden unreasonable anger. He'd just admitted to her he was as crazy about her as she felt for him. Still, the visual of his lips on that woman, especially now knowing firsthand the power behind those kisses, had the demanding question spilling out before she could think straight. "What was her name?"

Brandon turned to her, brows furrowed as he pulled into the parking space. "Who?"

"The blonde," she asked, swallowing hard. "The one you left with that night I saw you here."

Frowning, he pulled the keys from the ignition. "Why?"

Why? Good question. She was an idiot. Was she really going to pick a fight with him now after he'd been so wonderful to her all week over someone in his past? But the visual assaulted her again, and she thought of how he probably took the girl back to his place and made love to her the incredible way he always did to Regina, kissing her the entire time, until the two-bit whore was screaming his name.

"Because I wanna know," she said, her words even more demanding.

Apparently not only was she going to do this she felt ready to ruin their entire evening. She was this close to telling him to take her home and fuck the tiramisu. Could she be any more ridiculous?

"Serenity," he said, opening his door.

"What?"

"Serenity," he said again, stepping out of the Jeep. "That was her name." He leaned in before opening the door. "Don't get out yet. I wanna help you."

Regina opened the door and started getting out as he came around with a frown. "Serenity?" she asked, her words dripping with disgust. "What is she a stripper?"

Holding on to her elbow so she wouldn't come down too hard on her ankle as she stepped out of the Jeep, Brandon seemed more concerned with her ankle than he did her line of questioning.

"I don't know," he said simply.

Stupidly, Regina refused to let it go. "What do you mean you don't know? She went home with you, didn't she? Did you not—" She stopped cold, knowing what a no to her next question would confirm, and even though she'd automatically assumed so that night, the thought now sickened her. Still she had to ask. "Did you not talk *at all* that night?"

"Nope."

They'd started walking. Brandon had slipped his hand in hers, and Regina stopped suddenly, attempting to take her hand back, but he held it tight. Was she really going to get this upset over that *now?* Yes! He'd harped so much about his no-attachment rules, yet he kissed that bitch the way he had in front of the entire world. Did he expect her to believe now that he hadn't even talked to her? He'd been chatty and all smiles with the girl that night. That is until he'd seen Regina.

"Do you always kiss these girls you want *no attachments* with the way you kissed her that night?"

Another couple walked by them, noticeably avoiding eye contact with them. Only then did Regina realize she'd gotten loud, so she started walking again. But she wasn't letting him off with his short answers. Brandon had asked about Antonio, someone she merely worked with and happened to speak to a little too sweetly for his liking. He, on the other hand, had slept with this girl not more than a few weeks ago.

"No, I don't," he said, looking straight ahead. "But why does that even matter now?"

Regina wasn't sure why it mattered, but it did. It hadn't dawned on her until today, when seeing the restaurant brought back the blinding reminder of how recently he'd been with someone else. Suddenly, she needed to know more about Serenity. They'd both looked a little too smitten with each other that night. Given that one kiss Regina had been witness to, it turned her stomach to think of the night they must've had. She wasn't so sure anymore if she'd been stupidly naïve or not to buy into his no-return-visits' rule. Who behaved that way in public the very first time they met? Neither of them appeared to be drunk. And who did Regina think she was to believe she was so damn special she'd been the only one he'd ever *returned* to?

"No?" She glared at him. "So she was special, then?"

If they weren't already on the crowded sidewalk of the strip, she might yank her hand away from him like a child having a fit. She felt completely duped. Had he made that girl with the stripper name feel as special as he had Regina all week?

They walked up to the young lady standing at the hostess bar just outside the Italian restaurant. Still seething, Regina hadn't even heard what the hostess asked them until Brandon tugged at her hand gently.

"You like to people watch, right?" he asked. "So outside?"

Regina barely acknowledged him. She was in no mood to do any people watching or even be there anymore. A part of her told her she was being ridiculous getting so worked up over something like this, but then clarity kept winning out. The little naïve bubble she'd lived in so blissfully this entire last week had just burst. She should've known this was too good to be true. *He* was too good to be true.

The moment the hostess took their drink orders and walked away Brandon reached across the table and took her hand before she could pull it away.

"That kiss you saw . . ."

He squeezed her hand when she tried to pull it away. Okay, maybe she didn't want to know more about that damn kiss anymore. Hearing him address it made her sick to her stomach, and a knot was already beginning to form at her throat. Why hadn't she just let it go?

"It was the only time I kissed her that entire night."

Regina laughed; although, she felt more like crying now than laughing. Had she really been so blinded by his charm and trying to figure out his inscrutable personality all week that he now thought he could pull this bullshit on her too? She was only glad they were outside and the buzz of the people and cars going up and down the strip was so loud because her exaggerated scoff had been pretty loud.

"Really?" she asked, lowering her voice. Her heart felt completely smothered now because she knew how much kissing went hand in hand with his lovemaking. "So when you took her home and fucked her, you never once kissed her?"

That did it. She'd officially ruined their evening. She'd taken this from a fairly calm and still-salvageable argument and made it nasty. They could've been sitting there enjoying a delectable dessert and then gone home to make beautiful love again. Instead, she wouldn't even be able to eat now, and she'd probably be spending the night alone for the first time since he'd first spent the night at her place. Worse yet, she felt on the verge of crossing over to that other side, that side she'd crossed over one too many times and was the reason why she'd been on meds for months. She picked up her glass of water, hoping Brandon didn't notice her shaking hand.

Brandon squeezed her other hand a little harder, closing his eyes for a moment before taking a deep breath. "This really is not the time or place for this, baby—"

"Don't call me that," she snapped, tugging her hand out of his grip. "But you're right. I don't think I wanna be here anymore."

"That kiss was for you, Regina," he said, very determined. "I kissed her out of desperation. I panicked, okay?"

"What?" Regina peered at him.

Desperation? He looked anything but desperate that night. Regina crossed her arms in front of her, not sure if she was more annoyed or curious now.

"I supposed you took her home out of desperation too?"

"Look," he said, glancing around, and lowered his voice a bit. "You said it yourself the other day." He glanced down at her still noticeably unstable hand. "Obviously, there is still a lot that you and I don't know about each other. But trust me on this one. *Please.* That girl that night meant as much to me as any of the other girls I've *never* seen again."

Sitting up a little straighter, Regina tried desperately to regain some of the composure she felt slipping away so quickly. "What exactly did you panic about, Brandon?"

This time Brandon took a sip of his own water, and that made her nervous. Her heart ached to think maybe she really was on to him and he knew it.

"Give me your hand," he said, gently but firmly reaching his out for her.

If she weren't in such need to feel instant comfort, she might've protested. Instead, she glanced down at his hand, tempted to give in.

"Please," he added.

She did, trying her damnedest to keep it from shaking, and prayed whatever he said next would make everything better. She wasn't ready to give this up just yet.

"I told you," he began as reached for her other hand and squeezed both in his. "I fought my attraction to you from the very beginning. That morning when you confronted me, I already knew I was losing that battle. As much as I was still determined to continue fighting it, I knew the one thing that would make it impossible was the remote possibility that you were attracted to me too. Because of the way I had treated you up until then, I didn't think you could be. Yet I saw something in your eyes, even through your anger, that morning. Then, when you showed up at that restaurant looking at me like you did, I panicked." He shook his head with a frown. "It was a last-ditch effort to walk away with my rules still safely intact and my world not being turned upside down."

Regina stared at him, relieved by everything he'd just told her, except that last part. Before she could ask, the waitress dropped off their coffee and tea, and Brandon put in the order for her slice of tiramisu and a crème brûlée.

Hating that she couldn't bring herself to even look away from him for even a moment, she chastised herself for the instant heat she felt as he smiled at the waitress sweetly. She'd never been this insecure. Ryan used to flirt with their waitresses openly, and she'd laugh. Brandon was just being polite here. As serious as he was, until that night she saw him with that girl, she'd been certain he never smiled, much less had a flirtatious side.

The waitress had just walked away when Regina asked, "I turned your life upside down?"

To her surprise, he nodded, still very serious. "Yes. Yes, you did." He lifted one of her hands to his mouth and kissed it. "But in a good way. As fast as this happened, I already can't imagine my life without you. I just wish I could make you understand the reasons behind my rules. Kissing like I love kissing you was another major no-no. It's why that kiss you saw me give Serenity was the only time I kissed her that entire night. And it was only because I panicked."

Regina peered at him, still finding that hard to believe.

Taking a deep breath, he suddenly looked very determined. "I've always been a loner, Regina, my whole life. My home life wasn't anything I wanted to share with anyone. It wasn't pretty." His jaw went taut as she'd seen it before when his expressions would go so icy all of a sudden, so she squeezed his hand. "My father was abusive, mostly to my mom but also with me sometimes if I ever tried to defend her, which happened more and more as I go older. Then, the only time I ever allowed myself to get close to anyone and open up even just a little bit was with the girl I told you about." He shook his head. "It's a long story, babe."

"You said she wasn't a girlfriend."

"She wasn't, and she's not the whole reason for my fear of attachments."

Fear? He'd called it a rule. Never once had he mentioned a fear, and this girl was *part* of the reason? Swallowing back her sudden anxiety, Regina reminded herself this was a long time ago. Obviously, he'd seen the unease on her face because he reached for her other hand.

"It's complicated, Regina, not the part about her but—"

"Then tell me the part about her. You said she wasn't your girlfriend but it's a long story. I'm curious now."

Brandon's head fell back for a moment; then he inhaled deeply and began. He went all the way back to when he was a kid. Her name was Sofie. He'd grown up down the street from her and what he referred to her junkyard dog brothers. No one dared mess with her unless they had a death wish.

"I lived in that house in the neighborhood," he said then took a bitter drink of his tea. "You know the one. There's one in every neighborhood—the one where the cops have to be called out at least once a week because of some domestic disturbance. My family was the only trouble in the otherwise peaceful upscale neighborhood. I was known as a loner and a loser, and, yeah, when I was a lot younger, my way of dealing with being called a loser or looked down on was to act out. So I pissed her brothers off a lot. Even got my ass kicked a few times, so, of course, there was no way I was allowed anywhere near her where her brothers were concerned."

Regina listened intently as he fast forwarded to his senior year in high school. Sofie was all grown up and really turning heads, including Brandon's. He said he really thought he'd made a connection with her because she was in his Geometry class and they sat together. Sofie had told him she'd come to realize over the years he was misunderstood, not bad like everyone made him out to be.

"We talked a lot, and I thought we'd gotten pretty close." He shrugged. "Closer than I'd ever been to anyone in my life. And then I left to join the Marines. Long story short is during a leave when I came back she was all grown up and in a relationship. But that didn't stop us from having a moment." For the first time since he'd begun talking, he broke their eye contact, looking down at his glass. "I kissed her, and not only did she let me but she kissed me back. Up until then, it was the only time I'd kissed someone, and it didn't feel meaningless. I thought she felt it too." Finally, he looked up and met Regina's eyes again. "I was wrong. End of story."

"What do you mean you were wrong? Did she tell you or you just assumed?"

"Nope, she told me." He shook his head. "I was nothing more than a curiosity to her, a chance to be with the forbidden bad boy, to kiss someone other than the only other guy she'd ever kissed—her boyfriend. But she called it a mistake. *I* was probably the biggest mistake a good girl like her ever made."

"How good could she be?" Regina asked, trying not to sound as bitchy as thinking about this girl made her feel. "She let you kiss her when she had a boyfriend."

"Yeah, well, like I said, she took it back real fast and sent me packing. She didn't want anything to do with me after that. Of course, when her brothers found out about our moment, they made me out to be the villain who'd taken advantage of their innocent little sister. One of them even made it a point to come down to my place and warn me of what would happen if I ever came around her again. So that was that." He squeezed her hand but sat back when the waitress arrived with their desserts.

Regina had just about lost her appetite. Brandon thanked the waitress and motioned for her to eat as the waitress walked away.

"She's not the reason I swore off attachments of any kind, okay? She's just been the closest thing I ever had to one. I'd been so far off the mark it confirmed I didn't do them—I was no good at them. My dad was cold and heartless with no desire to connect with anyone. It wasn't a surprise. I didn't even cry at his funeral, but then when my mom was killed less than two weeks later, I went completely numb. I didn't feel anything. I never cried. I didn't take time off work. Hell, I didn't even give her a proper good-bye. No services, no nothing. Just took her ashes and dumped them out in the lake the way we discussed at my father's funeral just weeks earlier. She didn't want services, but as her only son, I should've given her a proper good-bye. That's when I became convinced that I'd turned into my dad, and I wasn't about to put another woman through the hell he put my mom through."

Regina had only taken a few bites of her cake, but now she was sick to her stomach. She stared at him, speechless.

"*That's* why I swore off attachments of any kind."

"You said you feared them," Regina reminded him, but he said nothing. "Do you still?"

To her relief, he shook his head. "I know now that, unlike my dad, I *am* capable of feeling very deeply for someone, but I'm not gonna lie. It makes me nervous to think maybe this won't work out. I made the exception to take a chance this *one* time. If something goes wrong, I know I never will again."

Suddenly, that knot she'd felt earlier was back, but this time it was for a different reason. She reached for his hand and kissed it as he so often did to her. "Nothing's gonna go wrong," she assured him. "As long you promise me you'll always be this honest with me, we'll make this work."

Regina had thought it before, but now she was sure of it. Brandon *was* different from any guy she'd ever met. Now that she had a better understanding of his heartbreaking past, she understood why. They weren't so different from each other. She too had gone through some very dark times. Now she and Brandon could look forward to the brighter times ahead of them. Together.

And those kisses. Dear God those kisses that melted her into a puddle were something he'd saved exclusively for her—the only girl he'd made an exception for. Her heart felt swollen to twice its size.

"What's past is prologue," she whispered.

His eyes brightened, making her smile. "That's right," he said. "That's why I'm here with you now."

CHAPTER SEVENTEEN

Brandon

The following two Sundays, Brandon had made sure to mention before Regina even brought up the brunches that he had plans. She had already told him these brunches would be a weekly thing and unless she had good reason to not make them she'd likely be there every time.

Brandon knew it was just a matter of time before he'd have to suck it up and meet her family. He just needed a little more time. This whole relationship thing was a huge change for him. While everything seemed to be going smoothly and telling her about his past and his dad had been less painless than he'd anticipated, he was still trying to get it right. What he *had* agreed to was to meet her friend Janecia for what had started out as their girls' night out on Fridays but had now turned into date night.

This, of course, was another first for him. Fortunately, Janecia's boyfriend, Clay, was a cool dude. He was a little on the foul-mouthed side but otherwise easy to hang with and talk to while the girls caught up on their girl talk. It helped that he seemed just as crazy about Janecia as Brandon was about Regina, because at this point, there was no hiding how he could barely keep his hands and lips off her. It should have been embarrassing, but Clay's behaving pretty much the same way with Janecia made Brandon's behavior seem less offensive.

This was the third Friday they'd done this, and Brandon was feeling way better about it than the first time. Just like the first two times, the girls laughed a lot, but this time there was a lot more talking between the couples, not just the girls having their own girl conversation while Brandon and Clay talked motorcycles, their careers, and sports.

Everything had been going fine until the girls came back from their third trip to the restroom. They were both very quiet compared to how they'd been before they left, and Regina was noticeably upset. Brandon had noticed they were gone a bit longer this time, and he wondered if something may've happened to them on their way back.

"What's wrong?" he asked, leaning in and clenching the arm of her chair as soon she sat down.

Regina shook her head, and Brandon stared at her for a moment then looked up at Janecia. "Did something happen?"

Clay's concerned expression went hard as he too noticed the change in the girls' demeanor. Janecia quickly took Clay's hand with both of hers. "Nothing happened, but Regina . . ." She gave Clay a strange look Brandon didn't understand. "She's not feeling too hot all of a sudden."

Brandon turned back to Regina, feeling more than alarmed and rubbed her back. "What is it, babe?"

All Regina would do was shake her head, until she finally admitted it might have been something she'd eaten. "Maybe we should just call it a night?"

Her words were barely audible, spiking Brandon's concern into overdrive.

"Yeah," he said, immediately holding his hand up to the passing waitress. "Whatever you want." Both he and Clay pulled out their wallets, but Brandon told Clay he had it then turned back to Regina. "Should we go to urgent care?"

She assured him she just needed to get home and lie down. They paid and said their good-byes to Clay and Janecia. Brandon didn't miss how Janecia's and Regina's words to one another seemed strained.

By the time they reached his Jeep, Regina was in tears. Brandon held her against the door, his heart speeding up as he searched her eyes. "What is it, baby? Something hurt? Are you sure we shouldn't stop at the ER?"

She shook her head again. This time she seemed angry. "Let's just get out of here, please. Take me home."

Things only got worse on the ride home. Brandon couldn't get a thing out of her, but by the time they made it back to his place, she was *really* crying. He started to pull out of the driveway. "We're going to the hospital," he said as he turned to look back.

"No!" she finally said, reaching out for his arm and holding it. "I don't need to go the hospital. I just need to get inside, *please*?"

She looked so broken up it he could hardly stand it. Parking the Jeep again, he jumped out and practically sprinted around to help her out. He had no idea if whatever she was feeling might have her lightheaded, and he didn't want to chance her falling.

Holding her close, he walked her into his apartment's front room. As soon as she sat on his sofa, she buried her face in her hands and sobbed. Feeling completely helpless, Brandon sat down next to her and held her. She continued to sob against his shirt. He racked his brain, wondering what could have her so upset as he smoothed her hair and kissed her head. A couple things came to him: the strange look he'd seen Janecia give Clay that calmed him immediately and Regina and Janecia's strained good-bye.

"Did . . ." He stopped to kiss her head again as she struggled to catch her breath between sobs. "Did something happen between you and Janecia? You two argue?"

To his enormous relief, she nodded against his chest but clenched her hands on his shirt a little tighter. Whatever they argued about was obviously upsetting, but at least she wasn't sick.

He pulled away from her, gently wiping a few of her tears as they continued to flow without slowing. He kissed her wet cheek then got up. "I'll be right back."

Rushing into his bedroom, he grabbed the box of tissues and brought it out to her, taking a seat next to her again and wrapping his arm around her. He couldn't imagine what she could be so upset about. Whatever it was, it wasn't something she'd be getting over anytime soon. Kissing the top of her head as he continued to run his hand up and down her back, he whispered, "You wanna talk about it?"

"She promised me!" Regina said, startling him as she pulled away to look at him. "She promised me she'd never get on Clay's motorcycle, and now she's gonna do a run to Puerto Nuevo with him." She sobbed. "A whole weekend to and from Puerto Nuevo on that death trap!"

Brandon stared at her, not sure how to respond to this. He knew Regina's late husband had been killed on a motorcycle, but they'd yet to discuss the details.

"Babe," he said cautiously as he rubbed her thigh gently. "Not everyone who gets on a bike gets hurt."

She stood suddenly. "Yes, they do!" It took him a moment to recover from her sudden jump, but he was up with her now too. "When I was in grade school, my friend's dad was killed on one. In middle school, my little league softball coach was killed on the way to one of my games. Then in high school, two different boys I knew were in accidents on them. One was killed instantly. The other one was a vegetable for years before he died. Everyone I've ever known who'd come in contact with one of those things has died or has been very seriously injured." She looked around desperately. "I have to call her!"

She grabbed her purse and started rummaging through it. Brandon took her by her hands and realized she was trembling. "Calm down, Regina," he urged as she fought with him to grab her phone.

"Let go of me! I have to call her and beg her not to." She was beyond crying now. She was hysterical, but most alarming was how her eyes bugged out and her hands flayed and trembled uncontrollably.

Brandon had no choice but the bear hug her and bring her down to the sofa over him, risking a knee to the groin if she didn't calm down. "Regina," he said loudly and firmly as she squirmed to get loose. "Stop this and look at me, baby."

Breathing very heavily, she stopped for a second to look at him then collapsed against him, crying again. "I can't let her go, Brandon. She's gonna die. I know she is."

"Sweetheart," he said a lot gentler this time. "When you hurt your ankle, you told the guy at the ER you were on anxiety pills before but didn't take them anymore."

Regina pulled away from him and looked at him wide-eyed. Like all the other times he'd sprung something on her, she'd obviously expected him to have forgotten, and he'd stunned her again. "I don't need them anymore."

Brandon remembered the other time he'd seen her hand tremble out of control: the day she'd been upset and confronted him about the girl she'd seen him with at Gaslamp. He'd let it go then without mentioning it, but there was no way he was letting it go this time. "I think you do."

She continued to shake her head. "No."

"Yes, baby." Sitting up, they both straightened out, and he took her trembling hand in his, showing her how it shook. "Look at you."

Pulling her hand away, she continued to disagree. "That's not why I was on them."

"Then why were you?"

She still sniffled, but at least she wasn't hysterical anymore. His bringing up her anxiety pills seemed to have done the trick. He'd stunned her into calming.

"It was for something much worse," she whispered then looked up at him with those big beautiful but worried eyes. "But I'm better now. I don't need to be on those pills anymore."

"Okay," he said simply with a reassuring smile. "Maybe not the pills you were on but," he touched her still trembling hands, "maybe a lower dose?"

She stared at her hand for a moment without saying anything, and he hoped to God she wasn't going to get upset again. Then she took a very deep breath. "I'm a fraud, Brandon."

"What?"

She nodded, continuing to stare at her hand. "My family all thinks I'm the headstrong, independent, always happy one of all of us. My parents and siblings are in awe of my *strength,*" she said sarcastically. "But look at me. I'm a mess. None of them know the real truth. They don't even know I had to be on medication." She looked up at him a bit hesitantly then continued. "Chris, my friend from New York? She's actually my ex-therapist. Nobody except Janecia knows I was even in therapy or that I needed to be on anxiety pills for as long as I was."

"That doesn't make you a fraud."

"Yes, it does. I lost it." She stopped and seemed to think over what she was going to say next. "I held it together after Ryan's death. My family came out to the services, and my mom even stayed with me for a week. I assured them I was fine but then weeks later I completely lost it."

Brandon had no idea what she meant by lost it, but if it was much worse than tonight, he was almost afraid to ask. So he offered something else. "You lost your husband suddenly and very tragically. Maybe it took some time to sink in, but it's normal to grieve and feel inconsolable over something like that." She shook her head. "It is, babe, and if—"

"I bought a gun, Brandon. At first, I was just really lonely and depressed and missed him terribly. Then I found out I was pregnant."

The pregnancy she mentioned in the ER was another thing he hadn't forgotten, but he'd had no intention of asking her about it. It was just another thing he wasn't sure he could stomach hearing about.

"The baby gave me hope that at least I'd have a part of Ryan with me for the rest of my life. It was bittersweet, but I was happy, and then I miscarried. I hadn't even had a chance to tell my family about it. I was waiting for the perfect moment." Brandon wrapped his arms around her as the tears began to slide down her face again. He was determined to not let her lose it again. "As sad as I was, I was also angry. I hated him for having gotten on that motorcycle when he'd promised me he never would. He did it behind my back. He used to ride back home before moving out to New York, and he'd told me about it when we first started dating, but I told him I didn't date guys who rode motorcycles, so he assured me he never would." She stopped suddenly and looked at Brandon wide-eyed. "You don't ever ride motorcycles, do you?"

Brandon had, but he'd never had any desire to own one. At this point, if he planned on keeping Regina in his life, and he had every intention to, he certainly wasn't going to ride one now. "No," he said, wiping away a tear from her cheek. "I don't. And I won't ever. I promise."

Her eyes searched his trying to find any trace of dishonesty. Brandon felt for her since obviously both Ryan and Janecia had made the same promise and broken it. He kissed her on the forehead. "I'm into Jeeps and off-roading. I've never even been into dirt bikes. I swear to you I'll never ride a motorcycle."

That seemed to calm her worried eyes a bit, and she went on. "The day I miscarried I drank an entire bottle of wine, and I trashed my apartment." They were both silent as she stared at her still-trembling hands, and Brandon held his breath. "I had every intention of taking my life. I even bought the gun off the street because I didn't want to go through the waiting period and all the red tape of getting it registered. I was too much of a coward to take pills and try to overdose." She looked up at him her, pained eyes once again swimming in tears. "I have the worst luck in the world, and I figured I may as well do it the sure way. Knowing me, I'd make it through an overdose and would have to face my family, who would then know what I coward and a fraud I really am. I bought the biggest gun I could find to make sure it did the job."

"Why does that make you a coward or even a fraud, Regina? You had two terrible losses back to back, and you snapped. It's not unheard of."

"I'm not the first person to lose someone," she said, raising her voice. "People lose loved ones all the time, and they get through it. I never even got rid of the gun" She frowned, motioning to the wooden chest." It's buried in there somewhere. I made the mental argument with myself that I should keep it since I was a single woman living alone, but deep inside, I knew it was really for fear that I might need it again someday." She pointed at him with that feral look in her eyes she had earlier when she'd told him about Janecia, so Brandon held her tight. "You lost both your parents, one of them just as suddenly and tragically as I lost Ryan, and I bet you never considered taking your life." Shaking her head, she stared out at nothing in particular. "I can't even imagine," she whispered. "You're so much stronger than I am. I'm so weak. After everything you've been through and all by yourself, you didn't fall apart like I did. I had my entire family and friends, and still, if it hadn't been for my neighbors, I wouldn't be here right now."

Brandon lowered his face to try to get her attention. He waited until he had it and she was looking right at him. "People handle things differently, and everybody grieves differently, okay? No, I never considered taking my life, but think about it. What *did* I do? I did the very same thing you almost did. Maybe not literally but I made the decision to stop living. I went through the motions of waking and working and continuing with my life, but I wasn't living. I didn't even realize it until you came along. *This* is living." He kissed her softly because he'd just had a huge revelation. "What I was doing before you . . . Baby, I may as well have been dead. My life now with you compared to what it was then . . . I *was* dead."

The corner of her lip lifted, and her eyes were flooded once again, but this time there was a smile behind them, and she wrapped her arms around him tightly.

"I was so afraid to tell you about what I'd done," she said against his neck. "The only people who know are my therapist and the neighbors who broke down my apartment door after hearing me trash the place and screaming like a crazy person. Janecia doesn't even know. All she knows is I had a breakdown and had to start seeing a therapist. I was afraid you'd see me differently—lose respect for me—but as usual, you're amazing, Brandon." She pulled away and their eyes locked. That gentle innocence he'd been drawn to way back when, reflected in the way she looked into his eyes now. "I love you," she whispered.

For a moment, he froze. Aside from his mother, no one else had ever said these words to him, and it nearly suffocated him. It was subtle, but there was no hiding the disappointment in her eyes when he didn't immediately respond.

"You do?"

She nodded nervously. "I do."

This was the last thing he expected to hear tonight, especially after everything they'd just discussed. As terrified as he was to admit it—say it out loud—he had to.

"I love you too."

He got that look from her, that same one she'd given him when he promised he'd never ride a motorcycle. It was suspicious, and he knew why. "I do." He laughed, hugging her tightly then kissing the top of her head. "You just caught me off guard, but I do." He leaned his forehead against hers. "I love you, Ms. Brady."

She laughed, and it was a beautiful sound—beautiful and satisfying—considering she'd been so miserable just minutes ago.

"Make love to me, Sergeant Billings," she whispered against his lips.

"Yes, ma'am," he said with a growl as he stood up and lifted her in his arms. "Your wish is my command, princess."

Feeling like the luckiest man in the world, he rushed off with her.

CHAPTER EIGHTEEN

The following Friday Regina walked out of his bedroom after changing into nothing more than Brandon's Padres T-shirt and panties as she often did after work during the week. She informed Brandon they wouldn't be meeting Janecia and Clay for appetizers and drinks like they had the past few Friday nights.

Brandon chose his words carefully because he didn't want to ignite anything, but he had a feeling she'd be regretting this later. "Babe, you can't just stop talking to your best friend over this. I know how strongly you feel about it, but do you really want such a long friendship with someone you care so much about to end like this?"

Regina opened up the box of pizza she'd ordered in lieu of their date night out. "It's not ending," she said, pulling a slice out of the box and setting it onto a paper plate but didn't look at him. "They left this morning for Puerto Nuevo."

"Oh," Brandon said, feeling like a complete ass now.

The last thing he wanted was to have her thinking about this all night. Mercifully, before he could come up with a way to change the subject, her phone rang. She walked away from the pizza on the table and into the kitchen where she'd left her phone.

Brandon walked over to the pizza box and opened it, examining the gourmet pizza she'd ordered from her favorite place. Unlike the pizzas he was used to with lots of red sauce, she'd mentioned this was made with white garlic sauce, so the whole thing was mostly white, but it at least it had sausage.

He'd just taken a bite of the pizza and the flavors had exploded in his mouth when he heard the tail end of Regina's conversation and froze.

"She's dating *my* Ricardo? Are you sure it's the same one?"

Chewing slowly, he waited as Regina paused and he heard the refrigerator door open. "Get out!" she said, suddenly sounding a little too giddy for someone who'd just walked away in such a somber mood. "She's bringing him Sunday? Does she know he's my ex?"

She paused again while Brandon swallowed down his pizza. It went down a little harder than he'd expected.

"Oh, wow. Did she say if he's still surfing? I wonder if he still looks the same."

After hearing that, Brandon started toward the kitchen. He didn't want to be petty, but Regina's interest in *her* Ricardo was irritating as shit, so he figured he may as well get close enough to hear every word. It wasn't like she'd hushed her voice or was trying to keep this conversation private, so he leaned against the kitchen entryway and took another bite, looking straight at her. Suddenly, she seemed uncomfortable. It was almost as if it'd just hit her that Brandon could hear what she'd been talking about.

Clearing her throat, she turned away and reached into the fridge. "No, don't be silly." *Now* she lowered her voice, making Brandon chew slower in an effort to remain calm. "I know she's annoying, but I'm seeing someone now, remember? Besides, I wouldn't play those immature games. Listen," she said, abruptly turning back to Brandon with a smile. "We were about to eat. I'll call you later. Let me know if there is anything you need me to bring."

She hung up and put the phone down on the counter. "You want a soda?" she asked, reaching back for the refrigerator handle.

Brandon shook his head, staring at her as he stuck the last piece of pizza in his mouth and continued to chew.

"Did you like it?" she asked, smiling brightly.

Again his response was nonverbal; he simply nodded but continued to stare at her. She tried walking past him, but he didn't move. His body took up most of the door frame, so she stopped, placing her hand over his chest. The tiny smirk on her face relieved him slightly. Obviously, she wasn't too worried about this.

"My sister was just telling me about my cousin's new boyfriend."

"I heard." He finally spoke up. "*Your* Ricardo?"

She brought her fingers over her mouth in an attempt to hide a bigger smile. "I just meant my ex."

Brandon brought his hand around her and squeezed her ass, making her yelp then laugh nervously. "Your ex who you're still curious about?"

"No," she said, caressing his face as she pressed her body against his. "Not curious." She pecked him softly. "I just haven't seen him in *years*."

She tried to kiss him again, but he pulled back. "Curious," he restated then nipped her bottom lip as he brought his other arm around her and squeezed her other ass cheek even harder. "What kind of immature games was your sister asking you to play?"

That surprised her though she quickly recovered and kissed him a little more aggressively, but he pulled away again.

"Answer the question, Regina," he said, spreading her ass cheeks and sliding his fingers upwards.

He almost smiled at her gasping, but he continued to stare in her suddenly aroused eyes.

"Our cousin can be annoying, so my sister thought it'd be fun if I flirted with him Sunday."

He spun her around and pinned her against the kitchen wall. "And that's how you refer to me to your family? Someone you're *seeing*?" Before she could respond, he ripped her panties off. "Is it? Not your boyfriend? I thought we discussed this?"

Sliding two fingers into her, he loved that she couldn't even respond since she was so hot she was almost moaning. He dove into her neck, sucking harder than he normally did. *His* immature side was tempted to leave a mark so *her* fucking Ricardo could see it Sunday, but then he thought better of it. This was not the impression he wanted to make on her family before they even met him, so he spun her around again and lifted her up, setting her down on the counter. Spreading her wide, he fucked her with his fingers while he dug for his wallet with his other hand.

"They know," she said breathlessly as she ran her fingers frantically through his hair, "that you're my boyfriend."

He unzipped his pants and pulled out his aching erection, all the while kissing her madly. He pulled away just long enough to slip the condom on.

"They know we're living together," she said, making him stop for a moment and look up at her. Her eyes widened, looking a little alarmed. "Because we are, right?"

He hadn't even thought about it, but it made sense. They'd been inseparable since that first night. Whether it was here or her place, they hadn't slept apart once. "Yeah," he said, slipping his hand behind her neck and kissing her then slamming into her.

Regina cried out and slid closer to the edge of the counter, spreading wider, and he went in deeper—harder—kissing her just as hard the whole time. He pounded away again and again, trying to push aside the unreasonable jealousy he felt over her and an ex she hadn't seen in years. Then he remembered her curiosity about the guy and pounded into her even harder, making her cry out even louder, until she was trembling all over.

"I'm . . ." he said as he slammed in as deep as he could.

She moaned, squeezing her legs around him at the same time lifting up to him. "What?" She gasped.

"I'm coming . . ." he said as he exploded into her, and her thighs clung on to him for dear life.

Her arms squeezed around his neck as both of them gasped and struggled to catch up with their pounding hearts and breathing.

"I'm coming with you Sunday." He was finally able to say it as his lungs struggled to gasp in chunks of air.

She didn't say anything, and he helped her off the counter. They walked over her ripped panties on the floor as he led her out of the kitchen and into his bedroom where they could collapse. "You ripped my good *chonie*s," she said.

"I'll buy you more," he said, smiling and hugging her to him. "So your ex is a surfer, huh?"

Regina groaned bringing her arms around him and hugging his waist as they continued to walk. "It's been over seven years since I last saw him, Brandon. That was girl talk you weren't supposed to hear. I didn't realize I was speaking so loudly. Even my married sister says things her husband would seriously have a fit about when he's not around. But it's just how we girls talk. It's harmless."

Brandon brought his hand down and squeezed her naked ass. "You're not still gonna call him *your* Ricardo when I'm not around, are you?"

Regina giggled, pulling away from him quickly, but he caught her just as they made it to his bed, and they fell onto it. "Maybe I didn't fuck you hard enough," he said, pinning her down, and she laughed even louder. "I was trying to send a message." He struggled to keep a straight face as he stared down at her. "I don't think you got it."

Barely able to speak from all the laughing, Regina squirmed under him, spreading her legs. "Clearly, I was too caught up in the moment," she teased with a murmur. "Maybe you need to send that message again." She bit her bottom lip. "Even harder this time."

Instantly, Brandon was on his knees reaching over to his nightstand for another condom.

~*~

Regina

The outcome of Brandon overhearing Regina's conversation with her sister Friday night couldn't have gone better if she'd planned it that way. In fact, with her rotten luck, if she had actually done that on purpose, she was certain it would've backfired on her and ended with an ugly fight instead of ending the somewhat unnerving yet thrilling way it had.

Over the past several weeks, Regina had been privy to that softer, sweeter side of Brandon. But what secretly thrilled her was that, as sweet as she knew he could be now, he still hadn't lost that dark bewildering side. That side was still there when he was on duty at the base and resurfaced every now and again even around just her, though she could tell he did his best to conceal it. As nervous as it made her, there was something so incredibly sexy about it. She especially loved the power she had to lessen his tension with just a few kisses.

Today's visit with her family wasn't the usual Sunday brunch. She'd casually mentioned her nephew's baptism to Brandon weeks ago. The way the guy remembered even the smallest details of things she'd told him so long ago she'd been certain he hadn't forgotten. Yet, up until Friday's incident he hadn't mentioned anything about going with her. She knew him well enough to have picked up on one thing. He wasn't anxious to meet her family. Regina knew this was all new to him. Just making an attachment was a huge step for him, so she knew meeting her family would only reaffirm just how attached they were becoming. When she mentioned her nephew's baptism, she hadn't wanted to make him feel obligated or forced to go, so she left it on the table but didn't so much insinuate that she wanted him there.

He already knew that her family Sunday brunches meant just that. Her whole family would be there. This was a little different, and she hoped it would make it a little less intimate so he wouldn't feel so overwhelmed on his first meeting with them. Since it was her nephew's baptism, it would be at her sister's, not her parents' place like the usual brunches. There would also be other people there besides her immediate family: extended family, friends, and her brother-in-law's family. Brandon wouldn't be the center of attention as she knew he'd be had his first visit with them been at one of their brunches.

Running her fingers through his hair, she stared at her new love as he slept soundly. He shifted at the touch of her fingers and wrapped his arms around her even tighter. A soft moan escaped him, but he didn't open his eyes. "How much time do we have?" he murmured.

She smiled, continuing to run her fingers through his hair. "A few hours. I'm gonna get in the shower, but you can sleep longer if you want. We have time. I just take long getting ready."

Fortunately, since her sister had chosen a Sunday to have her nephew baptized, those Masses were held in the wee hours of the morning at their church before all the other Sunday Masses began. Her sister had told everyone who wasn't an actual mandatory part of the ceremony they needn't be there at the early Mass and the family gathering at her home wouldn't be until noon. They were having the ceremony professionally taped anyway, and no doubt Regina would be watching it over and over as she did the other videos of her niece and nephew.

Brandon ran his hands up and down Regina's naked body as he squeezed one eye open. "I could join you in the shower if you want." The corner of his lip tugged as he nudged her thigh with the erection she'd already felt earlier. "It's not like I'll be able to go back to sleep now anyhow."

Un-wrapping his arms from around her, Brandon jumped out of bed suddenly and headed to the bathroom. She knew what he was in a hurry to do more than actually use the bathroom—brush his teeth. She'd already brushed hers and knew it was just one of the things he was obsessive about. Within minutes, he was back and crawled in next to her again with a very mischievous smile. His hands were already roaming her body.

Staring at him with a smirk, she knew it was a risk but one she'd chickened out of too many times already. She'd waited so long for him to bring it up on his own. A few weeks ago she noticed that the tote with the handcuffs, the riding crops, and the paddle was gone. As exciting as their sex life was, this past Friday was one of the few times they'd done anything out of the ordinary in bed or in the shower. He was as meticulous about making sure she was absolutely satisfied each and every time as he was about everything else he did, so she had no complaints there. Still, a part of her was very curious about his naughty tote and especially why he hadn't introduced her to it. Now with it gone, she was fairly certain and slightly disappointed that he wasn't going to ever.

"I have a confession to make," she whispered.

His roaming hands stopped midway down her back. The mischievous smile flattened, and both his eyes were on hers now. "What's that?"

Suddenly a little nervous and tempted to take it back, Regina felt her heart speed up. Biting her lip, she tried to continue smirking playfully, but the way he was staring at her now made it tough to do. "You have to promise you won't get mad."

Brandon's brow creased as he adjusted himself and sat up a little. "Is it about Ricardo?"

"*No*," she said, surprised he'd even go there. "I told you I haven't seen or heard from him in over seven years."

He didn't appear at all remorseful to have jumped to that conclusion. His expression remained vacant, but his eyes searched hers still. "Then what?"

"I . . ." She glanced at his closet. "I saw what was in that tote on the top shelf of your closet. I wasn't snooping," she added quickly, knowing that was a bald-faced lie. "I just happened to glance up when the door was open one day weeks ago. There were some things in there . . ."

She waited, but he said nothing. His expression was still the same—unreadable—and the stirring in her belly started up, the kind that always did when he turned back into Sergeant Billings. It was usually a mixture of nervous but exciting anticipation. Right then it was mostly unnerving. "I was waiting for you to maybe share with me about them—"

"No," he finally said, still staring at her very seriously. "I got rid of all those things."

"But why?" As tense as the conversation was beginning to feel, she wasn't backing down. "Obviously you had them for a reason. I'm not judging you or anything. I'm just curious."

"Judging?" Now his expression was readable, but that wasn't a good thing. She'd struck a nerve. "Is that why you think I didn't tell you? Because I was afraid you'd judge me on something you knew nothing about?"

"No," she shook her head, reaching for his hair again, but he sat up quickly. "I just wanna make it clear that I'm not asking because I had a problem with it. I was curious about it actually. I uh . . ." She swallowed hard, the unyielding hardened expression he now wore almost making her regret bringing it up. But she didn't want to regret it. She wanted to be able to talk to him about anything. "I thought maybe you'd use some of those things on me."

Finally his hardened featured gave way to a softer stare, but he shook his head. "Never," he said with such finality it felt almost like a slap. "I'd never use those things on you."

Just like that, he brought his legs over the side of the bed as if the conversation were over. "Wait," she said before he stood up. "Why not? You don't think I'm up for that kind of stuff?"

The unexpected smirk was even more insulting. Then he topped it off with small smile, shaking his head and mouthing, "No."

He stood up, his hard body completely naked, making Regina lose her train of thought for a moment. This wasn't the first time she'd seen him like this, but it took her breath away every single time.

"Ready for that shower?" he asked as if they weren't in the middle of discussing this.

"No," she said, completely irritated now. "You really think I don't have it in me to do those things? I suppose you think only skanks like Serenity can think outside the box?"

His shoulders dropped dramatically. "Let's not start with that, okay?" He walked around the bed, so she stood up, holding the sheet in front of her. "What are you doing?" he asked, looking down at her covered body as he approached her.

"It's too bright in here," she said sarcastically. "I'm not comfortable unless the lights are off."

Unbelievably, he smirked again. "Since when?" he asked, tugging at the sheet, but she held it tight.

"Oh, don't you know?" She took a step back. "I'm a prude. At least that's what you seem to think."

"I never said that."

The continued smirk on his face was beginning to infuriate her. "Yes, you did. You'd *never* use those things with me, yet you had an assortment of them." She backed up with every step he took forward until she was backed up to his bed. "Things you used with all those other women but with me—"

He lifted his fingers to her lips. "Shh," he said gently.

She tried to move away from him, but there was nowhere to move. He had her backed up to his bed, and he pressed his body against hers. The sheet she held in front of herself did nothing to block what he so boldly and shamelessly pressed against her, considering the circumstances. "I never said I didn't think you could handle it."

"Yes, you did. I asked you if you thought I couldn't and you said—"

"I meant, no, I don't think that you *can't* handle it." He tugged on the sheet a little harder until it came undone and fell, leaving her naked and feeling completely vulnerable, not to mention confused over what he was saying. "That's not why I'd never use those things with you."

"Then why?" she asked, staring at his lips now, struggling to regain the conviction she felt just minutes ago.

"Because," he brought his strong hands around her naked back and pulled her against him, kissing her softly, "I like how we do things now."

She began falling into his amazing kiss like she always did but pulled away. "But what if *I* wanna try it."

This close to him she saw the flicker in his eyes, but he managed to recover and took a deep breath. "It's not anything I want to associate with you, babe."

He started for her lips again, but she pulled away unconvinced there wasn't more to it, that he really didn't just think of her as the vanilla type only. If he'd been into that stuff enough to have a collection of things, how long would it be before he craved it again and became bored with the way they did things now?

Closing his eyes momentarily, he took another deep breath like the one he'd taken when she brought up Serenity. Once his eyes were open, he brought his face next to hers and whispered in her ear. "Close your eyes."

"No," she said defiantly.

He was going to try to avoid finishing this by seducing her. It would probably work, but she was determined to at least put up a fight.

"Please?" he said so nicely she frowned but closed her eyes.

"Okay," she whispered, angry that she was so completely helpless to resist him.

Feeling him pull away, she felt his warm breath against her lips, and then he kissed her softly again. Her insides tingled in anticipation for his crazed but knee-weakening kisses to begin. "Think about it, princess," he whispered against her lips. "Before you, I never wanted attachments. Even kissing was too intimate, too risky." He kissed her deeply, sucking her tongue the way that made every part of her body yearn for more. Then he pulled away. "Before you, the first order from me after covering their eyes was no talking."

The visual of him covering her eyes made her heart beat faster, and she focused on that instead of visualizing him with someone else. His lips moved down her chin and onto her neck as his hands slid over her bare ass squeezing softly and making her tremble.

"Before you," he whispered against her neck then licked it. "Sex was nothing more than a release. If I'd had it my way, names would never have been exchanged. In fact, many times they weren't." He sucked her neck a little harder as a soft moan escaped her. Kissing his way up to her lips, he licked her bottom lip. "Open your eyes, baby," he whispered. She did and he smiled. "Before you, I had no idea what it felt like to make love. Now I do." He pecked her softly, staring into her eyes. "I don't ever wanna go back to that."

He pulled her down with him onto the bed, kissing her the whole time. He did nothing but kiss her, and it drove her so crazy she couldn't help moaning against his mouth. What he did to her mouth alone was pure insanity.

She felt him reach for the drawer on the nightstand, and she knew what he was reaching for, but she held his face with both hands, not wanting his lips off of hers even for a second.

Obsessed—obsessed is what he made her feel like. She was completely obsessed with his lips, his tongue, and his mouth on her body. She understood now what he meant about before her, because before him she'd never felt *anything* like this.

He managed to get the condom on by moving away from her lips just a few times. He brought her hands over her head and laced his fingers through hers then stopped kissing her for a moment to look in her eyes so profoundly it made her breathless.

"I love you," he whispered.

"I love you too" she whispered back, the emotion so much that she felt her eyes well as he slid into her slowly, gently, and, oh, so deeply.

How was it possible for someone to make her feel so incredibly special? "*God*, I love you" were the last words she said before their mouths became one and he kissed her as she knew he would until they both came in explosive climaxes.

CHAPTER NINETEEN

As if there weren't already enough wonderful things about Brandon to love, another luxury about being the girlfriend of a drill sergeant was that he was so anal about ironing. He'd taken to ironing even *her* clothes now. He said he didn't mind, and he did a much better job than she did, so she gladly let him.

Since he'd ironed her outfit for today as perfectly as he always did, Regina had been walking around in nothing more than his Padres T-shirt and a pair of panties again as she got ready. Whenever he ironed for her, she waited until they were ready to walk out to put her clothes on.

Brandon had walked in and out of the bedroom as she got ready, stopping to kiss her and telling her how beautiful she was more than once. A few times he'd stopped and sat on the bed to watch her apply her makeup. The way he stared at her was so intense it made her insides a little crazy. They'd just made love that morning, but something about the way he was looking at her had her thinking it may just happen again. They had plenty of time before they had to leave. If he didn't stop looking at her like that, she just may have to attack him.

She did think it was kind of weird that he hadn't tried anything in the shower aside from running his hands up and down her body, but then they'd just made love before they got in. Still, it wasn't unheard of for them to go at it again so soon after having gone a round—or two.

A few of the times he sat on the bed, it almost felt as if he wanted to say more but held back. He was leaning back on an elbow on the bed, watching her again, and she eyed him through the mirror, smirking when she noticed the subtle swell in his crotch.

"Something on your mind, Brandon?"

The corner of his lip lifted. "I'm just wondering when the hell I became such a push over."

She lifted a brow curious now and continued peering at him through the mirror. "What do you mean?"

"Why can't I ever just say no to you?"

Now she had a feeling what was going on in his mind all this time, and it excited her. That swell in his pants meant he wasn't just thinking about giving in to her earlier request; the thought was turning him on.

She watched as he stood up and walked toward her. "You've said no to me," she reminded him with an evil smile as he reached her from behind.

The flutters in her stomach doubled at his touch. Kissing the side of her neck, he brought his hand around her waist, slipping it into the front of her panties. Gasping, she let her head fall back against him, tracing his hard forearm with her fingers.

"You really wanna give me complete control?" he whispered in her ear then nipped at it, making her shiver as she breathed in deeply.

"I trust you," she whispered, her heart already speeding up.

"I'd never hurt you."

"I know you wouldn't."

His hand slipped into her panties further down, and he caressed her softly. "I'd be different with you, princess." He kissed her temple softly. "Gentler." He lowered his voice. "It may not be what you're expecting."

She loved when he called her that now. Licking her lips, she turned her face to his, and she kissed him. "I don't know what to expect. I just know I'm very curious."

Pulling his hand out of her panties, he turned her around to face him. "Curiosity can be a dangerous thing." He stared into her eyes. "I'd never hurt you, but you may not like the denial."

Tilting her head to the side, she asked, "Denial?"

He nodded, looking deeply in her eyes. "It's the only way I'd ever torture you." Her eyes flew open, and he smiled wickedly. "There's still time to back out."

Torture?

"But you said you'd never hurt me."

"I won't *ever*." He hadn't done a thing to her yet except touch for a few moments, and already she had the strangest sensation all over. He tugged her hand and lifted a brow then leaned in and rubbed himself against her leg. "You sure you want to? This may be your only chance before I change my mind."

She nodded, remembering what her sister always said to her. *Be careful what you wish for.* But at the moment, she was really wishing he'd do this.

What in the world could he mean by torture? He walked her toward the bed. "I did get rid of everything, so we'll have to improvise, okay?"

She nodded as she watched him take one of the king-sized pillows from under the comforter on the neatly made bed he'd fixed earlier. "First rule," he said. "If we do this, we do it my way."

She nodded again, beginning to feel nervous, but she did trust him. He wouldn't do anything to her that would make her uncomfortable.

"Second rule." He turned back to her. "You do everything I say."

The thunderous gulp made her face warm. She hoped he hadn't heard, but she nodded again obediently. He'd slipped into his Sergeant Billings role, and it excited her so.

"Good girl," he whispered, kissing her forehead. "Now take everything off."

He dropped the pillow case on the bed, staring at her hard as Regina stared back, pulling off her T-shirt. Glancing down at her panties, he nodded, so she removed them too. Now she stood there completely naked before him, wondering what he'd ask her to do next.

"Lie down," he said but slipped out of character when he smiled and kissed her sweetly. "You still okay?"

"Yes," she whispered, already breathless and embarrassed by that, but she didn't want him to change his mind, so she got on the bed and lay back.

Brandon climbed over her and brought her hands over her head. "Leave them there," he said.

Doing as she was told, she lay there, taking deep breaths, her heart going a mile a minute as he took the pillow case and brought it above her head. Her insides went nuts when he used it to tie her hands together, then he lowered his face to kiss her softly. Moving down a little lower, he tugged at her nipple with his teeth, making her squirm, and then let go suddenly.

"Don't move," he ordered again and got off the bed.

She watched him, her eyes widening as he walked over to the closet. He told her he'd gotten rid of everything. With her eyes glued to him, she watched as he pulled at something then turned around with one of his ties and sheets?

He walked over to the bed and unfolded the sheets he'd brought out of the closet. "Another rule," he said, looking up at her very seriously. "And this one is a big one." He paused as if waiting for her to acknowledge that, so she nodded. "The moment you feel the slightest discomfort you let me know. Understood?"

She nodded a bit more animated this time, and she saw the humor dance in his eyes. She wondered if that humor in his eyes was supposed to calm her nerves—it didn't. *Discomfort?*

She watched as he tied one end of the sheet to the bed post then grabbed her right leg and tied the other end of the sheet to her ankle—tightly. "Is that too tight?"

Thinking about it for a moment, she shook her head. She tugged at it gently, hoping he wouldn't notice, but she wondered how much slack he'd given her. None.

He did the same thing with the sheet to the bed post on the other side. What he did next she knew was coming, but she still wasn't ready for the eroticism of it. He pulled her other leg toward the other bedpost, spreading her wide open. She'd never felt so incredibly exposed or vulnerable, but at the same time, there was something so arousing about it. He tied the other sheet to her ankle so all her limbs were bound and she was completely vulnerable to him. He could do to her whatever he wanted, and she was helpless to stop him.

Suddenly, she was dying for him to start. He walked around the bed slowly, looking her up and down, his smoldering eyes coming to rest on hers. "That's enough watching for you." He picked up the tie and dangled it in front of her. "Do you know why I'm gonna blindfold you?"

Regina swallowed hard, shaking her head. She still couldn't believe she was really lying there naked and spread eagle and he was about to blindfold her too.

He leaned in and lifted her head, bringing the tie over her eyes and tying it loosely around her head. Everything went dark except for a tiny bit of light that seeped in from the bottom near her nose. "Is that good?" She nodded and felt the warmth of his face come close to hers. Then he spoke into her ear. "You'd be amazed," he whispered, "just how much more heightened all your other senses are when you take away your ability to see."

As if to demonstrate, he kissed her just under her ear then sucked softly. Yes, she was amazed. He brought his mouth down on her chin, and when he reached her mouth, he stopped. "Oh," he said, and she felt him chuckle. "Your *needing* me to stop torturing you doesn't count as discomfort, so don't even think about asking me to stop."

His mouth devoured hers. It was the weirdest thing to want to kiss him so deeply but not be able to move any other part of her body. Before their kissing could get too crazed, he pulled away, leaving her breathless.

For the first time in all the times she'd been aroused with him, she prayed he wouldn't touch her down there because he'd see just how wet she was from just this already. She wasn't sure how much more she could take, and he hadn't done anything but kiss her yet.

She felt him leave the bed, and she bit her bottom lip in anticipation. The sound of a drawer opening near the bed had her wondering if he was already looking for a condom because she was so ready for him. Trying to calm her breathing so she could hear better, she listened, but she didn't hear the crackling or ripping of any plastic.

The bed moved with the weight of him, and she braced herself. "I did hold on to a couple of things I thought you might enjoy eventually. She flinched, gasping when she felt something soft tickle her nipple then his mouth on her other one. His mouth pulled away for a moment. "Relax," he whispered. "You're gonna like this."

Doing her best to relax her tensed body, she took a deep trembling breath and concentrated on trying to figure out what that soft frilly thing was he was tickling her nipple with. It was suddenly on her arm, and he swiped it down slowly giving her goose bumps all over. She hadn't decided if she really liked it or not when it lifted away. The next place she felt it was between her legs and her entire body flinched again.

"Relax," he whispered, and she tried desperately to, biting her lower lip.

The tickling sensation down there was incredible—like nothing she'd ever felt. But it was only for a moment and then she felt it on her inner thighs. Up and down.

Slowly.

Teasing.

First one inner thigh then the other. It was between her legs again just long enough to make her squirm, and then he pulled it away again.

Next she felt it over and around her belly button. Again slowly. Sometimes with more strength and then softer. Then it was on her other nipple. His mouth latched onto the other one. Her body quivered in reaction. He'd been right. The sensation was heightened so much more than when he usually sucked her, and she could hardly stand it.

He moved away from her nipple and slid down. Feeling his fingers massage her between her legs made her arch her back. Then he kissed her there. She squirmed in anticipation of feeling him suck her because he spread her with his fingers as he always did when he pleasured her that way. Instead, she felt that thing tickle her again as he spread her wide with his fingers, so wide it tickled her most sensitive of spots. She moaned loudly, feeling the beginning of an orgasm just from that touch alone.

Just then he stopped, and the buildup subsided, leaving her agonized and wanting more. She felt it again a little softer, so the tickle wasn't quite as strong as the first time, but the throbbing started up again. If he tickled just a tiny bit harder—just a little bit more—she'd feel the beginning start up again. She was so close.

She tried lifting her hips to catch more of it, but with her legs tied, she could only move so far. Thankfully, he gave her a little more, and that amazing sensation started up again. Then he stopped again. "You're pulsating, baby. And it's beautiful."

Letting out an agonized moan, she gasped. "Please," she said, wanting so badly to feel it again. It felt so damn good.

His fingers spread her even wider, and she felt his tongue on the very spot that was yearning to explode. She lifted her waist again as far as she could with an even louder moan, and then he pulled away again, leaving her breathless, her body pleading for him to finish her. "I've never felt it throb that much before." He nearly growled. "Maybe we will do this more often."

"Please!" she begged shamelessly.

"No," he said simply. "Not yet." The tickling moved down her thigh again.

"You're lucky my legs are tied, Brandon Billings!" she said through her teeth as the yearning between her legs begged to be tended to.

She heard his soft laugh. "I didn't think you'd like the torture."

It hadn't even dawned on her, but that was exactly what this was.

Denial.

Unbelievably, she felt him get off the bed. No, he didn't!

Luckily for him, she heard what sounded like a condom package and then what sounded like him taking off his clothes. "Yes!" she said. "I need you inside me, baby."

This time she felt him climb the bed a bit more aggressively than he had before. What felt like his knees pressed against her ass. He spread her wide with his fingers again, and that magical tickle began again, igniting once again the beginning of what now felt would be one of the most explosive orgasms she'd ever felt. Then he slipped into her. The combination of him thrusting into her and filling her so suddenly along with the unrelenting tickling made her cry out in ecstasy as he finally allowed the *glorious* release.

She continued crying out loudly, swaying her hips as he thrust harder and harder again and again. The sensation mounted as he rocked into her on and on until she thought she might scream. With one last hard drive into her, he, too, grunted in satisfaction. He stayed there buried deep in her for a few moments then pulled away, and she felt the sheet on one of her ankles come loose and then the other. She brought her legs together, still tingling all over as she felt him slide up next to her. He pulled the tie off her then proceeded to untie her hands.

"I wanted to watch you come." He kissed her. "It's such a turn-on to watch it up close, but damn it, I could hardly stand it."

She wrapped her eyes around his neck. "That was amazing," she said then pulled away to look at him. "A little agonizing but amazing. What was that you were using?"

He looked around then reached down and lifted his hand to show her what looked like a miniature feather duster. "It's one of the few things I'll allow with you. I was thinking maybe something that buzzes would be fun too, but this was way too fun. I don't know that we need anything else."

Smiling big, Regina threw her arms around him again. "Well, thank you for *allowing* this. I know you said you didn't want to ever go there again." She smirked. "Something tells me that wasn't too painful for you."

Brandon laughed. "Not at all. But it won't get much more tortuous than that *ever*."

Glad to hear him speaking in terms of this happening again, because she enjoyed that much more than she expected to, she grinned. "I love you, baby.

"I love you more," he said, cradling her face in his hand and kissing her so sweetly she sighed.

~*~

Brandon

Regina had told Brandon it would likely be a full house at her sisters, so Brandon was surprised to see so few cars out front of the house when they arrived. This was the sister she'd mentioned lived in Pacific Beach. They'd driven by La Jolla to get there, and Brandon had gotten that uneasy feeling again, the same one he'd felt the morning he'd driven into La Jolla to get Regina waffles.

Even as they got out of his Jeep, Brandon was beginning to have second thoughts about jumping the gun when he decided on a whim that he wanted to be here with her today. Was he really ready to meet her family? *Daddy?*

They walked in through the side gate. The party or gathering as Regina referred to it was being held in the backyard. This area was just as ritzy as La Jolla, and her sister's house was impressive. One of the women standing by the table where a buffet was set up turned and smiled big when she saw Regina. Brandon recognized her from one of the many photos Regina had showed him as her younger sister.

"Here she is," her sister said, turning back to a table where a few other women and men sat. "Mom was just asking when you were getting here."

Regina hugged her then turned to Brandon. "Brandon this is my sister Bell. Bell, this is my boyfriend, Brandon."

Bell who was a slightly taller version of Regina smiled just as sweetly as Regina did and held out her hand. "Nice to meet you, Brandon. Gina's told us so much about you."

"Likewise," Brandon said, surprised Regina had never mentioned she went by Gina. "Regina's told me a lot about all of you."

He looked up at the other woman walking up behind Bell. He recognized her as Regina's mom.

"I'm Gloria," she said, holding out her hand and smiling just as big as Bell had. "Finally, we get to meet you. We were beginning to wonder if you actually existed."

Regina gave her a look but chuckled. They moved on as Regina introduced her one by one to the rest of the family members who were there: her other sister, a few cousins, and some of her brother-in-law's relatives.

"Speaking of," Regina said, bending over to kiss her niece after introducing Brandon to her brother-in-law's uncles, "where's your daddy?"

"He went to get more ice," her sister Bell explained, saying he should be back soon.

They sat down under a canopy where her mom and some other relatives were sitting." Honey, how's your ankle doing?" her mother asked, looking down at it.

Regina wiggled her foot in the air. "*All* better," she said with a big smile.

Brandon couldn't help but frown at the very high heels she'd insisted on wearing. They were sexier than hell, but he'd warned her it might be too soon for such high heels. The past few weeks he was able to talk her out of wearing the higher ones to work, and he was still reminding her to do her ankle-strengthening exercises.

One of her aunts asked her how she'd hurt it, and she explained. Her mom then went on to tell them about Regina's bad luck.

"My poor baby," she said with a pout. "We've always called her Charlie Brown because it never fails that if something is going to go wrong she always seems to take the brunt of it." Her mom reached out for Regina's hand and took it in hers. "But like I always say," she said, rubbing Regina's hand in between hers, "God doesn't give anyone everything. She may have the worst luck, but she has the best spirit of anyone I know. Nothing brings this kid down."

Regina and Brandon exchanged glances as her smile began to wane, and he squeezed her hand.

"Ha!" One of her brother-in-law's uncles suddenly laughed. "Charlie Brown. That's what we should've called that nephew of mine growing up. Talk about bad luck." He laughed. "That kid had a fucking rain cloud over his head all through middle school and high school. Am I right?" He nudged the guy next to him, and they both laughed. "I could tell you stories."

Her sister Bell brought over a bowl of nuts, placing them on the table where Brandon and Regina sat and rolled her eyes, smiling at Brandon. "Something tells me you're gonna hear a few stories now."

As if on cue, his uncle started up loudly. "Remember that time we were in Maui?" He nudged the guy next to him again, who also started laughing. "We're on this *beeeautiful* beach. All blue for miles. Totally clean, right? 'Cept there's a couple over down that way with a dog. Tell me why out of all of us my knucklehead nephew takes a swim and comes up with a turd mustache?" He wheezed so loud and long, even Brandon couldn't help laughing, especially when he put his finger over his lip to demonstrate all animated. "Everyone's having a good ole time on this beautiful beach," he said barely able to get the words out he was laughing so much. "And son of a bitch if that kid is the only one who pops out of the water like this."

He demonstrated some more.

"All right, all right," A guy walked out the back door of the house, frowning and holding a very bald baby. "This guy." He shook his head but smirked. "Now it's a turd mustache?" He rolled his eyes. "I told him I saw one floating around in the water, and after all these years, it turned into me walking around with turd mustache in Maui." Then he turned back to his uncle. "You never even saw it!"

They were all laughing now, including the lady who kept snorting on the other side of the wheezing fat man. Brandon was only glad Regina had snapped out of what might've turned into a sour mood after her mom's mention of her good spirit.

"Hey, look who's up?" Regina's mom said, smiling at the baby in the guy's arms. "It's the little prince of the hour."

Glancing back, Brandon peered at the guy who'd walked out with the baby. This was the fat man's knucklehead nephew, who looked disturbingly familiar. Obviously, he was Regina's brother-in-law because he walked over and kissed Bell before handing the baby to her. Regina's niece Mandy tugged at the guy's pants, and he picked her up. It wasn't until Bell pointed in Brandon and Regina's direction and said something to her husband that Brandon made the connection.

Shit.

The guy smiled then it seemed to hit him, too, as his face suddenly brightened. He laughed, walking over to them "No fucking way," the guy said then turned to his daughter who tapped his lips with her little fingers. "I'm sorry, baby," he said, kissing her fingertips. "Bad daddy." He turned back to Brandon with a wide smile. "That you, Billings?"

Doing his best to hide how incredibly uncomfortable he suddenly felt, Brandon forced a smile. Regina was already smiling at him quizzically. "You know each other?" she asked.

"Yeah." Brandon stood up, reaching to meet her brother-in-law's already outstretched hand. "That would be me," he confirmed. "Romero, right?"

"Well, I'll be damned," Romero laughed, nodding. "You and Gina? Holy shit what a small world." His expression went a bit serious, but there was no hiding the continued smirk, the one Brandon remembered his smartass wearing all the way from grade school through high school. "She's my baby sis now. You better be treating her right."

Regina laughed. "I'm older than you, Romero."

"Yeah, but much smaller." He winked.

Just then Mandy squealed loudly and nearly jumped out of Romero's arms, reaching her hands over his shoulder. "S and S!" she screeched, squirming for Romero to put her down.

All three of them turned as two little girls in frilly dresses, who looked to be a few years older than Mandy, walked into the backyard from the driveway, each holding onto an even younger boy's hand. Romero lowered Mandy down to the ground, and she ran to them. As they got closer, Brandon could see the two girls Mandy now hugged were identical.

"Oh my God, is that the twins?" Regina asked.

"Yep," Romero said, looking back at them with a smile. "Sienna and Savannah."

"They're so big!" Regina gasped. "Jesus, the last time I saw them they were babies."

Brandon was still trying to make sense of what this all meant. Just because Romero had been good friends with Sofie's brothers growing up didn't mean he kept in touch with them still. Most people lost touch with their childhood friends. He stared at the two little girls, pretending to be as interested as Regina and trying to keep his cool. This was not so bad, he tried convincing himself. It could be worse.

"Yeah, well, that little dude with them is little Alex a.k.a. The Taz." Romero laughed. "As in Tasmanian Devil. He's nonstop trouble. And now he has two of them little devils," Romero shook his head. "Alex has his hands full lemme tell you."

What Romero had just said didn't even register until Brandon's eyes moved up from the kids to the guy standing behind them now, holding a baby carrier in his left hand and a tray of some kind in the other—Alex Moreno—and he was as big as ever.

Brandon watched, frozen to that spot as the petite blond woman walking in behind him in heels as big as Regina's and carrying a baby bag asked Alex to take the baby inside. Bell walked over to greet them as everyone's talking began to buzz in Brandon's ears: Regina and Romero talking about Alex and his siblings and their kids, Romero's uncles talking loudly and laughing even louder, the kids laughing and squealing, chasing each other around his and Romero's legs, and then Regina's words that brought everything to a screeching halt.

"Oh, good, they're all gonna be here today? I need to catch up with them. I haven't seen any of them in years."

Well. Fuck. Me.

"So how do you two know each other?" Regina asked, smiling as she leaned into Brandon.

"We grew up in the same neighborhood," Romero answered first. "Izzy told me you were seeing a marine." He turned to Brandon, his eyes still big with enthusiasm. "I knew you were in the Marines, but even when she told me Gina's new boyfriend's name was Brandon, I never would've imagined it was the same one. This is some crazy shit." Romero turned toward the back door then back to Brandon and pointed with his thumb. "You remember the Morenos, right? That's Alex and his brood there. Remember Valerie from high school? After all their drama . . ." He laughed. "Those two are married now. They all are, and . . ." He stopped and seemed to ponder something for a second, bringing his fist to his mouth." *Er,* you guys didn't get along the greatest back then, huh?"

Regina and Brandon exchanged glances; then Romero tapped his arm and laughed. "That was a long time ago. Some people may disagree, but I think we've all matured since then."

Romero puffed his chest, making Regina laugh. "Yeah my sister would definitely disagree."

Just as Romero began to protest, there was an outbreak of laughter, wheezing, and snorting coming from the table behind him. "No fucking lie!" His uncle was saying to Regina's sister Patricia, pointing at the other guy at the table. "Just ask him. Tell 'er, Max. And don't leave shit out."

"Hey!" Romero called out loudly with a frown. His uncles both looked up at him, still laughing. "Watch the language. There's a bunch of kids around!"

"Not to mention ladies," her sister Patricia added with a raised brow and a smirk."

"Where?" his uncle asked, looking around as animated as ever, and the laughter erupted once again.

Romero rolled his eyes, turning back to Regina. "Okay, maybe not everyone's matured."

Regina laughed, but something distracted her. "I still mix them up," she said, looking in the direction of the driveway with the smile. "They all look so much alike. Which one is that one?"

Both Brandon and Romero turned at the same time. "That's Angel," Romero said, waving him over.

Again as if frozen in time, Brandon watched as Angel waved but motioned he'd be over in a bit. Both he and his wife, who Brandon remembered as Sarah, his girl from way back, were surrounded by Regina's mom and some of her other relatives greeting them, including Valerie who'd resurfaced from within that back sliding door. This was a fucking nightmare—Brandon's *worst* nightmare. For a moment, he actually considered that he might be getting punked.

"They're gonna trip out when they find out you're Gina's new man."

"Why?" Regina asked smiling—obviously oblivious as to what was unfolding before her eyes.

Brandon turned in time to catch Romero wink at her. "You gotta know the history. We all go way back."

It had just dawned on Brandon that since he realized who Regina's brother-in-law was and that he'd shortly be reunited with the *last* family on earth he ever wanted to be reunited with he hadn't uttered a single word—he'd gone mute.

"I know *that* one," Regina said. "That's their sister, right?"

Swallowing hard, Brandon didn't even want to look. He kept his eyes on Romero, who glanced in the same direction Regina was focused on—the driveway. "Yep, that's Sof." He turned back to Brandon with an evil grin. "Betcha remember her, huh, Brandon?"

Feeling his insides warm by the second, Brandon knew there was a choice to be made here. Either he turned to look at Regina, who he could feel staring at him or turn in the direction of the driveway. Still hoping this day—this whole fucking situation—could be salvaged somehow, he chose the latter and turned in the direction of the driveway.

Sofie was addressing the little girl whose hand she was holding. Eric walked up next to her, holding a sleeping baby against his shoulder and was quickly mobbed by a few women wanting a better look at the baby. The little girl had the same huge brown eyes as Sofie. Then Sofie glanced up, meeting Brandon's eyes for a second before looking down at the little girl again. Not a second later, her head jerked up, and their eyes locked.

CHAPTER TWENTY

Regina

Betcha remember her, huh, Brandon?

It wasn't so much Romero's question as it was Brandon's reaction to it that had Regina slowly coming unglued. As if watching the uncomfortably long moment he and Sofia shared when they first saw each other hadn't been enough to make Regina's skin crawl, what Romero had said suddenly sunk in. Brandon grew up with these people, *the junkyard dog brothers who didn't like him around their sister.* Brandon had practically frozen at the sight of her then was in no way able to recover casually from what seeing her had done to him.

Sofie.

This was the girl from Brandon's past—the *only* girl he'd had such heavy feelings for before Regina—the girl who'd started off the chain of events that ultimately led him to give up attachments of any sort, to stop living.

Regina wanted to think rationally. That was a long time ago. Sofia was happily married now and had been for years. Brandon was in love with Regina now, and she absolutely believed that—his feelings for her were practically tangible. But that moment he and Sofia shared had spoken volumes. There was still something there, and Regina, who'd never once been insecure, was now drowning in utter jealousy. As special as Brandon made her feel, Sofia was even more special to him. She'd been his very first *real* experience—the only girl to have touched him in such a way he'd never forgotten her. Evidently, no matter how many years had gone by, he was still feeling something.

Regina had always liked Sofia. She'd always liked the entire family. They were beyond pleasant to be around, and she'd even had some great conversations and good times with Sofia and her sisters-in-law at gatherings like this one. There was never anything *not* to like about them, until now. She knew what growing up around them had been like for Brandon, but, at that moment, Regina knew she could very easily hate Sofia.

It was irrational, she knew. Sofia had never been anything but sweet to Regina, but it killed her to know Sofia was the cause of Brandon's first broken heart. Regina knew now that Sofia had used him to alleviate her curiosity, but if she'd been the least bit interested in him in any other way— she'd been his first choice—Sofia might be here with Brandon instead of Regina. The only reason Brandon had even noticed Regina to begin with was because she'd reminded him of Sofia.

What's past is prologue. What's past is prologue.

Regina closed her eyes for a moment in a desperate attempt to calm herself. She reminded herself that if things had gone differently in her life, she, too, might be here with someone else, her *husband,* Ryan. Regardless of why and how things had come about between Regina and Brandon, everything happened for a reason, and that's why he was here with *her* now.

Brandon tugged her hand. "Your sister's calling you, babe."

Regina snapped out of her thoughts to turn in Pat's direction. She was standing with her cousin Claudia and Ricardo, motioning for her to come over. *Great.*

Forcing a smile, she turned to Brandon, who'd now snapped out of the stupor Sofia had put him in. He smiled back at her in what felt like a hopeful smile. Hopeful of what? That she hadn't caught the gazing exchange between him and Sofia? Or that she still hadn't picked up on who she was? Starting toward her sister, she pulled Brandon along with her. "Come on. It's time to meet Ricardo."

Ironically, coming here today, she'd thought this might be the most uncomfortable moment she and Brandon would be dealing with. Pat wore a mischievous grin. Before she could say anything, Regina shook off the unnerving thoughts of Brandon and Sofia. She smiled big and hugged Claudia. "Hey, where have you been hiding? I haven't seen you in so long."

"I know," Claudia said, pulling away. "I've been so busy trying to get my business going. It's been crazy." She turned to Ricardo, who was smiling nervously at Regina, and wrapped her arms around his arm. "This is my boyfriend, Ricky. Honey, this is my cousin, Gina."

Regina had met Ricardo the year she decided to take the summer off school and came home. She spent most of her time on the beach where she met the former US Junior Surf Team member trying to go professional. He was working as a part-time surf instructor in the meantime. While he was very nice on the eyes and made for an exciting summer fling, other than trying to make the US team, he truly was a beach bum. He had no real aspirations of doing much else with his life, and her sister Pat had been the first to point that out.

Pat was probably the reason why the fling went on longer than it might have. Unlike her sister Bell when she first brought Romero around to her unimpressed older sister, nothing was more satisfying to Regina than seeing Pat's disapproving face whenever she walked into a family gathering on the arm of her eye-candy beach-bum boyfriend. Maybe if Regina had been serious about him, it might've bothered her. Instead, she got a kick of annoying her sister to pieces.

She and Ricardo had both agreed neither was looking for anything serious, and Regina knew her stay in Southern

California was only temporary. By the end of the summer, the fling had run its course, and Regina had the perfect excuse to end things. She was going back to New York. They agreed to keep in touch, and they had for a few months, until all communication had slowly tapered off.

Regina smiled, holding out her hand and waiting for *Ricky* to either come clean about knowing her already or pretend not to. She'd already decided if that was the card he wanted to play she didn't care either way. She saw her cousin once or twice a year, and they'd never been close, so it didn't matter to her. Not surprisingly, Ricardo cowardly chose the latter. "Nice to meet you, Gina," he said, reaching out his hand.

Regina went along, introducing them to her boyfriend while her insides still roiled about the real elephant in the room. After some small talk, they got back to the topic of Claudia's house cleaning and landscaping business and how she and Ricardo had met when he applied as a landscaper. Pat immediately gave Regina a knowing look.

"That was way back when I was first trying to get things going," Claudia said.

"Yeah," Ricardo added as if Regina really cared. "I was just looking for a job on the side, but I was still doing surf lessons at the same time."

"Now he runs the landscaping part of the business, and I run the housekeeping side," Claudia said proudly. "We stay real busy."

Brandon gave Ricardo as much attention as he deserved since he was such a complete nonissue. He glanced away often, though Regina had to wonder if his indifference with Ricardo was intentional or if he truly was too distracted with *other* things to care much.

Glancing behind Ricardo, Regina's eyes met with Valerie's. Valerie, who was standing with Sarah, smiled big. She tugged Sarah as they both made their way toward her and Brandon. Regina wondered how much about Brandon and Sofia either knew. Sarah smiled as big as Valerie when she saw Regina, but there was no missing the way her mouth fell open when she saw Brandon. Both she and Valerie spoke in voices too low for Regina to hear as they approached, but the big smiles were back once they were close enough to reach out and hug her.

Pat was busy grilling Claudia about the business she'd started up, so Regina could focus on Valerie and Sarah.

"Oh my God, you look so good," Valerie said, hugging her. "Isabel told me you were moving out here. You're staying for good, right?"

"Yes, I'm pretty sure," she said, pulling away from Valerie's tight hug then hugging Sarah. "The job I'm working on now will take at least a year, if not longer, but I like being close to the family, so I think I'll stay."

They both turned to Brandon. Before Regina could figure out whether she should introduce him as if they didn't know him, Valerie turned to him. "Isabel said this was her first time meeting your boyfriend. I take it this means you and Brandon are an item?"

Regina nodded, her knotted insides getting tighter. She wasn't sure how she should address the fact that, unlike her and Ricardo, Valerie was not going to pretend not to know Brandon. "Yes, we met on the base two months ago."

"Oh," Valerie turned to Regina, still smiling but her brow lifted significantly. "So it hasn't been long?"

Without giving Regina a chance to respond to that, Sarah turned to Brandon. "What a small world." She smiled sweetly, turning to Regina for a moment. "Brandon and Angel and his brothers grew up just a few houses away from each other and went to the same schools." She then turned back to Brandon. "How've you been, Brandon? Obviously, life in the Marines suits you well."

"Always has," Brandon said with a small smile. "And I agree," he added, looking around, the already small smile waning a bit. "It's a very small world. But I've been good. It looks like the family is really growing."

Just then one of the twins ran over to Valerie, screeching as *The Taz* caught up to her, holding something out with an evil laugh that made the little girl scream even louder. Even Valerie braced herself. "What is *that*?" she asked, her face contorted in disgust.

"It's a worm!" his sister screeched, hiding behind Valerie.

Out of nowhere, Alex swooped down and lifted him easily over his head and onto his back. "Boy, didn't you promise you were gonna behave?" he asked the now-laughing-hysterically Taz. "Drop the worm," he ordered, trying to sound firm, but Regina could see he was holding back a smile.

With the worm dropped, Alex began putting him down, tapping him on the behind. "No more worms, you hear me? Go take care of your sisters."

Just behind him Angel now approached, also putting down his own son, who quickly took off after The Taz. They were both headed at top speed toward Mandy's outdoor playset.

Alex kissed Valerie then turned to Regina with a smile but addressed Brandon first. "Billings?" he said. His smile wasn't quite as bright as when he smiled at Regina. "Long time."

Brandon nodded, glancing around. "Yep. Long enough. I see the second generation of Morenos is growing fast."

"That it is," Angel said, wrapping his arms around Sarah's waist from behind. "What about you? Any kids yet?"

Brandon shook his head, and Sarah smiled then winked at Regina. "You never know though. He and Gina have been dating for a few months now."

Bell and Romero approached them. As usual, Romero wore a huge grin. "Isn't this crazy?" Romero asked. "Gina and Billings. I never thought I was gonna see this guy again. Now we just may be related someday."

"What is that you guys always say," Pat suddenly chimed in. "*Easy!* They've only been dating for a few months, and Brandon hasn't been made to jump through all our hoops yet."

Feeling Brandon tense, Regina turned to Pat, trying not to sound as annoyed as her comment made her. She hoped Brandon didn't think she meant all of them as in the Morenos as well. Regina knew Pat meant her family, but with all of them standing there, it could easily be construed as all of *them* as well. The last thing she needed today was for her sister to add to the already mounting tension. "Pat—"

"You see here," Romero's uncle Max stuck his phone in Pat's face. "That was me back in high school."

With a frown, Romero suddenly scoffed. "Will you stop trying to convince her you were good-looking once upon a time."

"*Once upon a time?*" Max lifted his collar on both sides. "I'm a fucking chick magnet. What are you talking about?"

They all laughed, and for a few minutes while Romero, Max, and Pat went back and forth, the attention was off Regina and Brandon. The phone got passed around to the guys, who all laughed and poked fun at Max for the clothes he was wearing in the photo.

"Check out the Fonz." Romero laughed.

Sal and Grace arrived. They came over and chatted and said hello to Regina and Brandon. Much like the other two brothers, Sal was civil but not overly friendly to Brandon. They were the only couple who arrived without kids.

"You don't have any kids, Sal?" Brandon asked, and he seemed to have loosened up just the tiniest bit like Regina, but neither was completely relaxed.

Sal and Grace smiled at each other. Then Sal patted her belly. "Third one is on the way, and the other two are with her sister and my cousin Vince. They're married but holding off on the baby making for now, so they often take our two rug rats for the day or even the whole weekend. But, yeah, we have two: boy and a girl. They should be here in a few."

"Where did Sofie and Eric go?" Bell asked, looking around. "I saw her earlier, didn't I?"

With the exception of Romero, Max, and Pat, who were still caught up looking through the photos on Max's phone, there was an obvious shift in the mood of the group. Alex's jaw actually tightened as he, too, looked around.

Sarah cleared her throat. "Last night she told me the baby had been real colicky this whole week. She and Eric might be inside with him."

The subject was changed, and then Bell announced the food was ready. Time seemed to move in slow motion as they all served themselves and sat down to eat. Fortunately, they all had their hands full, trying to serve and feed restless kids and dealing with babies. The novelty of Brandon, their old neighborhood acquaintance, being Regina's boyfriend wore off for the moment. Regina and Brandon sat with her mom and a couple of aunts instead of at the table with the Moreno clan.

"Why didn't daddy come?" Regina asked her mom.

"He's been real tired this week," her mother explained. "The doctor switched his medication, and it makes him sluggish. We got up early and attended the Mass, but when we got back home, he said he wasn't feeling up to coming. I told Bell I'd stay and eat, but then Pat's taking me home."

"But he's okay, right?" Regina asked, feeling a bit worried.

"Yeah, yeah." Her mother patted her hand. "It's just gonna take some time for him to adjust to the new medication. He wasn't feeling ill or anything, honey." She smiled. "He was tired and not in the mood for crowds. I left him on his recliner, watching TV. He even reminded me twice to be sure to bring him back cake."

Regina smiled, feeling a bit relieved, but she didn't like to hear that her once-active dad didn't even have the energy to attend a family function. It wasn't like him.

Trying not to over think things, Regina ignored the fact that when Sofia and Eric had finally made it out into the yard again they sat at the furthest table from her and Brandon. It was understandable that they might feel a little uncomfortable. Then the one time she thought her and Sofia's eyes had met Sofia quickly looked away without addressing her. After finishing up eating, Regina excused herself to use the bathroom inside. Once out of the bathroom, she made an unexpected detour towards the baby's room when she heard him whimpering.

"Oh, Romeo, Romeo, wherefore art thou, Romeo?" she whispered as she turned the corner into his room.

He was already standing, holding the rail, and his little whimpering face brightened the moment he saw her. Like she'd seen him do so often before, he screeched, jumping up and down. He stood there with the biggest but near toothless smile as he held out his little arms to her.

"Just like your daddy," she said, picking him up out of the crib and kissing his bald head. "Always smiling and laughing."

Knowing Romeo's diaper likely needed to be changed, Regina walked over to the changing table and laid him down. He kicked wildly, making the loudest noises as she began undoing the onesie he wore.

"Shhh!" She giggled. "Seriously, must all you Romeros be so loud?"

Still smiling, she leaned in and kissed him again on the forehead. She loved that she'd been able to convince her sister to go with her first choice and name him Romeo. Bell had been worried he'd be teased mercilessly in school. Both Regina and Pat had laughed and had reminded her who this kid's father was.

"If he's anything like his dad," Pat had sneered, "*no one is gonna be teasing this boy.*"

She turned when she heard someone at the door. "Hey." Sofia smiled a bit awkwardly. "I heard him screech and thought mine had woken."

Regina's sudden cheery mood deflated at the sight of her. Sofia looked as perfect as ever. It was disgusting.

Stop it.

"No," she said, trying to sound as normal as possible and turned back to face Romeo. "This little guy is ready to go join the party. I'm just changing him first."

"So how've you been?" Sofia asked, coming to stand next to her by the changing table.

"Good, good." Regina nodded as she finished wiping Romeo clean. "I moved back to California, so I'm happy about that."

"I heard," Sofia said while tickling the bottom of one of Romeo's feet. "That's good you get to be near your family. I can't even imagine being so far away from mine." She cleared her throat and went on. "And you're with Brandon now." It was a statement, not a question, and it took Regina by surprise. She froze for a moment then turned to face her. Sofia smiled a little less awkwardly now and more genuinely. "He's a good guy."

"I know he is." Regina turned back to finish changing Romeo and did her best not to sound bitchy, but her response was already too quick.

If Sofia even tried to bring up her past with him, she'd snap for sure. Regina did not need to hear about how Sofia rejected the man she was now in love with, especially now that she knew Sofia's presence alone still had such an effect on him.

To her surprise, instead of saying more, Sofia reached out for Romeo, who Regina had finished changing. "Can I hold the little chunkers?" she asked with a big smile.

Regina let her pick him up, and to her relief, they moved on to small talk about Romeo, Sofia's baby, and his colic as they made their way back outside. Brandon was engaged in a conversation with another Moreno, Sofia's younger cousin Vince, the one who'd been watching Sal's kids today. From what Regina knew Vince was a career military guy too. This was probably why Brandon seemed so at ease talking to him. She also doubted Vince knew anything about Brandon's past with Sofia, since she also knew he hadn't grown up in the same area as the other Morenos. They were likely talking about their lives in the military, exchanging stories like the ones she'd often heard her own father exchange growing up.

The ease in which he'd been talking was gone the moment he looked up and saw Regina with Sofia.

"He woke up?" Bell walked up to Sofia, forcing her to look away from Brandon's piercing stare.

"Yeah," Regina said. "I changed him already."

"Thank you, sissy," she said with a smile as Romeo practically jumped out of Sofia's arms at the sight of his mommy. Bell held her arms out to him with a big animated smile. "I'll take my baby boy now," she said to Sofia. "I need to get him fed before he gets cranky."

As soon as Regina was back at Brandon's side, he leaned into her ear after slipping his hand in hers. "How much longer we gonna hang around?"

Relieved that she didn't have to be the one to suggest ducking out early, she shrugged. Normally she would've hung out much later, but her shoulders had been so tight and tense from the moment she realized who Sofia was to Brandon, she could hardly wait to get out of there and have a glass of wine or two. "Well, you've met everyone except my brother and dad, but neither are gonna make it, so you can meet them another time. If you want, we can leave now."

They made their slow, steady exit, saying good-bye to everyone. Sofia, once again, conveniently disappeared, and Regina couldn't be more relieved. They'd almost made a smooth exit, except for Bell's ill-timed request that Romero snap a few photos of the three sisters before Regina left. She then asked Valerie, Sarah and Grace to get in the photo too.

"Wait," she said after Romero had already taken a few. "Where's Sofie? She needs to get in here too."

The entire time they'd been there Brandon and Sofia had been as far apart from one another as possible. Usually, the entire length of the backyard had been between them. Now Brandon stood but a couple of feet away from the group of women taking photos. And Pat was looking in the back door calling out for Sofie.

Within minutes, both Sofia and Eric walked out together. Neither looked particularly thrilled, and Regina *did not* miss the deadpan way Eric looked at Brandon. It wasn't a glare, but it certainly wasn't welcoming. Sofia lined up with the women. Romero wasn't the only one taking the photos now. Regina's mom had gotten in on it, and that meant they were going to be there a while because she took *forever* to take her photos and was very demanding about everyone staying put until she was done.

Finally, they were done. Then her mom suggested that the guys line up this time. To Regina's horror her mom turned to Brandon. "You too, hon. Anyone my kids bring home, whether a friend or more, is automatically welcomed into the family, so get in there."

Brandon turned to Regina, who had nothing for him except a rueful smile. This would be over soon enough, and then they could get out of there. Regina squeezed his hand and tiptoed to kiss him as they walked past each other. Instead of escaping back into the house as Regina thought Sofia might do, she came over and stood by Regina and the other girls to watch the guys line up.

Of course, Brandon stood off to the side on the opposite end from where Eric stood.

"Stop with the faces, Moe," Manny said from where he was sitting. "Swear to God, this guy . . ." He turned to his wife Aida, shaking his head, then back to Romero. "For all the laughing and goofing off you do, you'd think you'd do it for one stinkin' photo. How many more pictures of you looking like mug shots do I need on my walls! Smile, will ya?"

Regina was glad there was no one heckling Brandon about his rigid expression. While he wasn't making hard-ass faces like Romero, he certainly wasn't doing any smiling. Still she couldn't help but feel warmed that he was being such a trooper. Just coming here today to meet her family had to have been hard enough for him. She'd felt his unease mounting as they'd driven there. And then for things to turn out this way, she was certain he was regretting having come here at all. She just hoped it was *all* he regretted.

After giggling, Sarah turned to Regina, who couldn't quite take her eyes off of Brandon. "Wow," Sarah said. "I still can't believe you and Brandon are together. I mean what are the odds that of all the marines you could've hooked up with down at that base, it would be Brandon?"

"I know, right?" Valerie said, leaning in and lowering her voice. "Is he always this serious?"

They all turned to look at him just as he glanced their way, and Regina turned away quickly, hating how obvious it was they were talking about him.

Grace turned to Regina, lowering her voice as well. "He's very handsome, Gina." She leaned into what now looked like a little gossipy circle of women. "But is he as intimidating as he appears to be?"

Regina smiled, and if Sofia weren't in that gossipy circle with them, she might be tempted to tell them just how intimidating Brandon had really been when she first met him. She hadn't had the chance to gush about him to anyone but Janecia, and even then she'd been limited in doing so. He'd been by her side every night or within hearing range when she was on the phone, and the only time she'd really gotten to talk to Janecia was when they got together on their date nights. Even then, with him there, she could only do it when he happened to walk away for something or they excused themselves to the ladies' room.

Her sisters didn't know all the details either. She'd refrained from telling them too much before they had a chance to meet him for fear they might judge him unfairly.

With the men's photo shoot over, they began to disperse, and Brandon started toward them. Regina was about to respond to Grace when Pat tugged at her arm. "We'll have to talk later, Gina."

"Yes," Valerie said, glancing at Sofia then Gina and finally giving Bell a strange cautionary look. "He was always a little *different*. I'll call you tonight, Isabel." Regina didn't even have time to make sense of what that might mean when Sofia pulled her aside. She glanced guardedly over Regina's shoulder. "You still have my number?" she asked quickly. Regina nodded. "Call me, please, if you need to talk about *anything*. I mean it, okay?"

Before Regina could even respond, she walked away in a rush. Not a second later, Brandon was at her side. He stared at her for a moment, his eyes as cold as they ever got. "Something wrong?"

"No." She nodded, still confused about Sofia's bizarre behavior.

What would Regina possibly want to discuss with Sofia? Brandon? *Hell no!* The last thing Regina wanted was to hear Sofia's explanation of why Brandon wasn't good enough for her or, worse, details about that moment they shared long ago.

"Are you sure?"

Regina must've looked as befuddled or maybe even as annoyed as she felt because Brandon was staring at her as if expecting a better explanation for her sudden change in mood.

"I'm sure," she said then turned to the girls.

Sarah and Valerie had already walked away, tending to their little ones, and Pat had been called away by her mom. Regina smiled at Bell and Grace, hugging them both goodbye again. Bell told Brandon once again how nice it'd been to meet him, and they finally made their way out of there.

As expected, the mood was a bit tense in his Jeep. Regina hadn't decided if she'd wait for Brandon to admit that Sofia Moreno was *his* Sofie from his past or if she'd bring it up on her own.

To her surprise, Brandon got right to it. "Did it bother you?"

She almost blurted out yes! She absolutely *hated* that the beautiful sexy Sofia with the curves to die for and those annoyingly adorable dimples was *the* girl from his past. But she took a deep breath and thought it better if she asked him to clarify exactly what he was asking. Did it bother her that it was Sofia or his reaction to seeing her? She still wasn't sure which was worse.

"Did *what* bother me?"

"That your ex pretended not to know you."

Disappointed but glad she asked for clarification, she shook her head. "Not at all." She was surprised that after everything else that had come to light today he'd think she might be concerned about *that*. That was the least of her worries. "I had a feeling he might. My cousin Claudia can not only be annoying she can be a real bitch. If he's been with her long enough that they've gone into business together, I'm sure he's seen that side of her already. He probably figured she wouldn't be thrilled that he dated her cousin, even if it was a long time ago."

"Does he still look the same?" Brandon asked, lifting an eyebrow but stared straight ahead.

If this day had gone any other way, Regina might be tempted to smirk at that. But she was fairly certain that Brandon knew just how insignificant seeing Ricardo today was. It had nothing on the strangling feeling of knowing they'd be getting to the topic of Sofia and he might admit to feeling more for her than he'd actually first admitted.

"He does actually," she said as indifferently as she could, glancing out her window. "His hair's a little shorter now, but aside from that, he's still the same as I remember."

"So what happens if she marries him and he's around for years? You ever gonna come clean?"

Regina shook her head, feeling a little annoyed that he was focusing on this when there was something so much more pressing she wanted to get to. "I see her once or twice a year if that. We've never been close enough that I'd feel compelled to tell her. Besides," she said, turning back to him, "he's a very inconsequential part of my past, someone I hadn't even thought of until the other day when Pat called. We went out one summer, and when it was over, it was over. He wasn't anybody that made a real difference in my life."

She stared at him, waiting for a reaction to that. He had to know what she was trying to imply. After today, there was no doubt in her mind. The entire summer she'd spent with Ricardo had nothing on that one moment he and Sofia had shared so long ago.

"Good to know."

That was his only response, and they were quiet for a while. Was he really not going to address the Morenos and their sister? It wasn't as if it were something she was looking forward to discussing, but it would kill her wondering why—*if* Sofia still meant something to him.

She waited for what felt like a very torturous, long, few minutes for him to say something more about today. *Anything.* She could get creative and somehow bring it back to subject of his unexpected reunion with these people, but he said nothing.

Deciding she wouldn't bring Sofia up specifically, she didn't want to beat around the bush for too long, so she sat up straight and went with something close. "So that was interesting, huh? Bet you weren't expecting to see all your old friends from back when."

"They're not old friends, Regina," he said, staring straight ahead as he drove. "I told you about my neighborhood when I was growing up. I didn't have friends. And you heard what your brother-in-law said. We didn't exactly get along."

Shrugging that aside, Regina reminded him of one thing. "Romero seemed excited about seeing you again after all this time. And everyone was very cordial." He continued to stare straight ahead and said nothing, so she continued. "The girls said you were handsome but thought you looked a bit intimidating."

They came to a stop, and Brandon unclenched his hand on the wheel then clenched it again tightly. He finally turned to her. "Is that right? What else did they say?"

His chilly demeanor confused her. Was it possible he didn't realize she knew who *Sofie* was? Shouldn't *she* be the one feeling a little perturbed about his reaction to seeing her? That after all these years he was obviously still feeling something for her.

"Valerie said you were always different."

The light turned green, and he was back to staring straight ahead. "Valerie is Alex's wife, right?"

"Yes," Regina confirmed. "The petite blond one." He chuckled dryly, continuing to stare ahead, and Regina peered at him. "What's funny?"

He lifted a shoulder. "Before today, I don't remember ever exchanging so much as a word with her."

Regina watched as his jaw clenched, still confused why *he* was acting this way. "And that's funny?"

"Yeah, it is," he turned to her, but there wasn't a trace of humor in his eyes. "Because she knows as much about me as I do about her." Bringing his attention back to the road, Regina noticed how he clenched the wheel again. "Not a goddamned thing."

Clearly the fact that Valerie would make such a harmless remark was offensive to him. But Regina wasn't buying that *this* is what had him all worked up, and it made her insides wild with jealously. As much as she tried to calm herself, she couldn't help but just put it out there. "Sofia said you're a good guy."

Instantly, it felt as if the air had been sucked right out of that Jeep, and they both sat there in suffocating silence.

CHAPTER TWENTY-ONE

Brandon

The phone rang, and without looking at who it was, Brandon sent it to voicemail. He had a feeling the moment he realized what he was in for today that before the day was over someone would get to Regina about him and Sofie, but he hadn't expected for it to be *her*.

"You asked her if I was?" he said, staring straight ahead because he didn't dare look at her.

He could feel her eyes digging into him. The whole time he'd been stuck standing up there taking those damn pictures he'd seen her with all the yentas and wondered what they were filling her head with. That Sofie would say he was a good guy surprised him. If he weren't so paranoid about all of them, maybe he would have been glad instead of suspicious.

"No. She just brought it up all on her own," she said then added. "It actually came out of nowhere."

He fucking knew it.

His phone rang again. This time he looked down to see who it was, but he didn't recognize the number, so he sent it to voicemail again.

"Out of nowhere, huh?" he said, pulling onto the freeway exit. "What else did she say?"

"Is there more . . .?"

She stopped before finishing, but the sound of uncertainty in her voice made his heart speed up, and he turned to her. "More what?"

"More to you and Sofia you didn't tell me?"

Looking in her worried eyes now for as long as he could before he had to look back at the road, he didn't see any anger or distrust—just apprehension.

"Why? Did she say there was?"

"Was there?"

His fucking phone rang again. It was the same number from before, but he'd be damned if he were answering it now.

"No, there wasn't." he said nearly through his teeth. "Now answer *my* question, Regina. Did she say there was?"

He turned to face her again, and she was peering at him now. The suspicion was undeniable now. "Why?" she asked, the uncertainty she'd spoken with earlier replaced with a more demanding tone now. "*She* didn't say anything else, but is there something you're thinking or worried she might've?"

Brandon gripped the wheel even tighter. His heated pulse was thrumming in his ears. "*She* didn't? Did someone else?"

His brain raced, trying to remember if Regina had been alone with Alex or maybe Eric. Had the girls fed her any bullshit about how things had gone down between him and Sofie?

Once again his phone rang. *Fuck!* He was in no mood to talk to anyone right that second. He could barely contain the heat rising within him, enough to keep the conversation he was having with Regina under control.

Looking at his phone, he saw the same damn number on the screen again.

"Is that the same person calling again?"

Brandon nodded unable to even look at her at that moment. Thoughts of what someone might've told her inundated him. But the fact that she was sitting here questioning him with obvious distaste was what really pissed him off.

"You should answer it," she said. "It might be important."

Only because he thought giving his mind a break from his infuriating thoughts might help him calm, he hit the button on his earpiece. "Hello?"

"Brandon. Oh my God, I was about to give up and just call Regina. Is she with you?"

The female voice was familiar, but he couldn't immediately place it. "What? Who is this?"

"This is Pat," her sister said. "I didn't want to call Regina because I don't want her to freak. She plays it off pretty well, but I know when it comes to Daddy she just might. He was unconscious when I got my mom home." Pat's voice suddenly broke. "We have no idea how long he's been out, but he was rushed to the hospital. They think he had a heart attack. I'm just getting here now. Is she with you?"

"Yeah, she is," Brandon said, glancing at Regina, who was looking out the window.

Feeling the fear suddenly overcome him, fear of seeing Regina freak out replaced every ounce of anger that had started building just minutes ago. Suddenly, he couldn't care less about any of that.

"Can you please bring her to Mission Hospital?" She rattled off the information about where it was. Then her voice broke again. "Don't tell her he was rushed here, okay? Just say he wasn't feeling well so we brought him in. We'll tell her when she gets here."

Brandon hung up and turned to Regina, dreading his next words to her. Her brow was arched a little too high, and he knew her interest in the phone call was zero—she was still thinking about whatever it was she'd been told about him and Sofie.

"That was Pat," he said, and her expression changed immediately. "Your dad's not feeling well, so they took him to the hospital."

"*What?*" The panic was immediate. "That was Pat?" she asked, instantly digging in her purse. "Why did she call *you*?"

Brandon had no answer for that. He wasn't even aware Pat had his number. "I don't know, babe," he said, reaching his hand out over her knee to try and sooth her. "She just said he wasn't feeling well. Relax. It might not be anything."

Regina's hands were already beginning to shake as she dialed her sister.

"Pat!" she said. "What happened? What's wrong with Daddy? And why didn't you call *me*?"

She was quiet for a moment as Brandon jumped back on the freeway. He listened to her trying to get more out of Pat, but it sounded as if Pat wasn't giving her much. "What do they mean you don't know? What was he complaining about? Was something hurting him? Is he running a fever?"

As casually as he could, Brandon stepped on the accelerator. Talking to Pat seemed to have calmed her some, but apparently she wasn't satisfied because she called her sister Bell as soon as she hung up.

Brandon listened quietly without saying a word, and he was glad she took his hand when he reached out for hers. Her hand still trembled a little, but it wasn't shaking like when she'd first pulled her phone out.

"Are you sure you're not keeping anything from me, Bell? Pat said she tried calling me first, but I had no missed calls, yet she called Brandon four times in a row."

Glancing at the clock, Brandon wondered how long her dad had been out before Pat and her mom got there. He didn't want to even think it, but if it had been a massive heart attack, her dad might already be dead. He'd hate to think of what Regina might do—how'd she'd react—if they got there and he was gone. Ever since she'd told him about her family not knowing a thing about her breakdown in New York, she'd reiterated how important it was that they never see that side of her. For whatever reason, it was something she was completely ashamed of. And worst yet, she was still insisting she didn't need her meds.

By the time they got to the hospital, Regina had calmed considerably. Talking to both her sisters had done the trick. She explained to Brandon why Pat had his number.

"She asked for it the last time I had brunch at my parents. She said it was just in case there was ever an emergency. You'd be the closest one to me, especially since I mentioned how often I spend the night at your place." This seemed to embarrass her, and he actually smiled when she added with a whisper, "My mom and Bell have it too."

As soon as they were out of the car in the hospital parking lot, he came around and cradled her face with his hands then kissed her. "No matter what, baby, you can handle this. Okay?" He looked into her still-frightened eyes as she nodded. "I love you."

"I love you too," she whispered back, and after seeing the suspicion in her eyes earlier, hearing her say it with such sincerity was music to his ears.

~~~

Fortunately, her father was alive, but he was in surgery when they arrived. It almost felt as if Regina had gone numb. She didn't shake or freak out when she was told that her father, in fact, had suffered a heart attack. He was in surgery to have three stents inserted and would need to have more surgery to have two more inserted on the other side.

The hysterical Regina who'd begun to lose it in the car when she was simply told her father wasn't feeling well sat next to her mother the whole time, assuring her mom that her dad was going to be okay. Romero held Bell a few times when she'd broken down and cried, and Pat sniffled the whole time. Meanwhile, Regina remained composed and focused on keeping her mother calm.

At one point, Brandon followed her out into the hallway when she excused herself to use the ladies' room and pulled her aside.

"How you doing?" he asked, looking into her almost glazed-over eyes.

She nodded, glancing away. "I'm okay," she whispered. "He's gonna be okay."

"He is," Brandon agreed immediately and then said the exact opposite of what he'd always been taught to believe. "It's okay to cry, babe. If you're worried or afraid, you can let it out."

Shaking her head, she smiled weakly. "No, I'm fine."

He let her go, and she rushed away to the ladies' room. Brandon actually hoped she was going in there to cry. He knew hearing her dad was in surgery because he'd had a heart attack had to be terrifying.

I've never dealt well with loss.

Remembering her story about nearly using a gun to help her deal with the loss of her late husband, made Brandon squeeze his eyes shut. He shuddered to think of how she'd deal if her dad didn't make it.

The doctors seemed to think they'd caught it in time and he was safe. They'd insert the stents tonight. He'd be monitored for a few days in the hospital, and then he'd see his regular doctor and be scheduled for the second surgery to have the other two stents inserted. The most severely blocked arteries were being taken care of tonight. And while the other two were more than seventy percent blocked, they still could hold off on those so he wouldn't have to be out so long and they could keep the surgery less invasive.

Brandon was in awe the entire night of how well Regina kept it together. Even after the doctors inadvertently mentioned the ambulance ride to the hospital and Pat and her mother had no choice but to tell Regina the truth that he'd been rushed there in cardiac arrest, she stared at them in silence but didn't lose it.

By the time her dad had made it safely out of surgery and they'd all gotten a chance to go in and see him, it was early morning. Only two people were allowed in the ICU at once, and Regina asked Brandon to go in with her. The moment she laid eyes on him, Brandon saw it. For the first time since they'd gotten there, her face scrunched up, and for as much as she tried, she had no control over her quivering lips.

"He's gonna be fine," Brandon whispered, hugging her and kissing her head.

She clung to him and, to his relief, finally cried against his chest. He slid his hands up and down her back and continued to kiss her head. "Let it out, baby. It's okay. You'll feel better."

As she continued to cry quietly against his chest, Brandon almost resented the fact that her sisters were willing and able to cry openly in front of Regina and she felt the need to be the strong one. Why?

Brandon had never been a religious person. He couldn't even remember the last time he'd prayed. But seeing how long and how despondently Regina cried against his chest scared the hell out of him. Her dad had gotten through this, this time. Brandon was now actually praying he'd be fine after the next one.

Hiding the impatience, Brandon kept to himself what he was feeling as he watched Regina clean her face up. She'd refused to walk out of the ICU with any evidence that she'd broken down. He wanted to tell her Pat mentioned she knew Regina played it off, that she knew she could freak. She had the right to. This was her father—her *daddy*. Why couldn't she be allowed to fall apart? But he knew this was not the time to argue about this, so he waited silently as she reapplied makeup and powdered her red nose.

She looked up at Brandon from where she was sitting and smiled. "Is that good?"

"That's perfect," he said, reaching his hand out to her. "Let's go."

Regina stood, hurrying over to her father's side one last time and kissed his forehead then shook her head and waved her hands in her already welling eyes.

"Stop, stop, stop," she whispered to herself.

"You don't have to." Brandon finally addressed the issue, but she shook her head and walked ahead of him out into the hallway of the ICU.

On the way home, Regina explained that her Grandpa Boot was her daddy's father. She also mentioned her father was the one who had labeled her the brave one early on. "My sisters were always so shy compared to me. Neither ever took chances, and while I wasn't wild or anything, I did like having fun and trying things they never would. When I was younger and the boys would play baseball outside during the summer, I was the only girl who asked to play with them, and it was because of my dad's encouragement. He said I was probably better than most of those boys, and he was right." She smiled. "When I decided I was gonna go to school clear across the country, all my siblings stayed close by, and when I told him I was thinking of applying at Cornell instead of asking, 'Why so far,' like my mom did, he immediately smiled and said, 'Good for you.'" She lowered her voice to an almost whisper as if there were anyone around that could hear her. "My sisters always refer to my dad as a bit cold and indifferent, but I never got that from him. Like with my grandpa, we always had a special bond."

She was quiet for a moment, and Brandon turned to see if maybe she was crying again, but to his relief, she'd fallen asleep. Since she slept the rest of the way home, Brandon had plenty of time to ponder the day's happenings. With Regina's dad being in the hospital for what probably would be the rest of the week, Brandon was fairly certain any talk or even thoughts of Sofie and her family were the last things they'd be discussing in the coming days. As much as he wanted to know exactly what Regina had been getting at just before her sister called, he wasn't anxious to feel what he'd begun to feel during that conversation. Infuriatingly, somehow his past with the Morenos was coming back to haunt him.

~*~

Regina

Walking into her parents' dining room, Regina was surprised to see Alex and Romero there now too. When she'd stepped into the bedroom to see her dad almost a half hour earlier, only Valerie had been there with Bell.

Regina got the distinct feeling that whatever they'd all been discussing was cut short when they heard her coming. It was oddly quiet for a moment; then both Alex and Romero greeted her with Romero walking over to hug and kiss her. "How is he?" he asked.

Frowning, Regina shrugged. "Asleep now, but I got to talk to him for little while before he knocked out. He's doing better, I guess." She turned to Bell. "Why does he seem so listless?"

"Gina, he's recovering from major surgery," Bell reminded her, motioning for her to take a seat at the table with them. "You can't expect him to be all chipper so quickly. Mom said the meds make him sleepy too."

Regina frowned, taking the seat next to Bell and Romero across from Valerie and Alex. Bell poured her some coffee. "Thank you," Regina said, reaching for the creamer and sugar. "How's Mom doing?" she asked, turning to Bell.

She'd driven out to see her dad several times this week but hadn't been there yesterday. Today was only her dad's second day home. Her brother, Art, took their mom to the supermarket today while Bell and Regina stayed and watched over their dad. Pat was on her way as well. It'd been this way the whole time. Her mother hadn't been left to deal with this alone even one day, but Regina still worried. Her mother had her own high-blood-pressure issues, and stress only added to it.

"She's hanging in there," Bell said, nodding as she sipped her coffee. "You know her. She's like you, a real trooper during a crisis."

Regina refrained from frowning, and after inquiring on whether her mom was taking her own meds, she reminded Bell she'd be willing to take time off if they needed her to come and stay with her parents for a few days. Bell assured her they had it all under control. Then Bell changed the subject to something Regina had given very little thought to all week.

"Did, uh . . ." She cleared her throat and glanced at Alex and Valerie. "Did Brandon tell you about him and Sofie?"

Him and Sofie. God, she hated how that sounded. She stirred her coffee, preparing herself to not sound defensive or jealous, though she was suddenly feeling both again.

"What about him and Sofie?" she asked then lifted a shoulder quickly meeting Alex's eyes. "I mean I know way back something happened between them that didn't exactly go over well with you, your brothers, and Eric since she was already with Eric, but I didn't ask for details."

"But he *did* tell you then?" Bell asked, sounding a little relieved, then gave Alex an I-told-you-so look.

Regina studied Alex's strange expression for a moment then glanced back at her sister. "He'd told me about a girl in his past." Regina thought about how Brandon said Sofia hadn't even been a girlfriend. Yet she'd left such an impression on him. "He said it was someone he grew up around and later they'd had an experience. But it wasn't until the baptism that I realized it was Sofie." She turned back to Alex. "He had no idea either that I knew her or that he'd be running into all of you guys again." She shrugged. "Like Romero said that day, 'Small world, huh?'"

Valerie touched Alex's arm, who frowned in reaction to Regina's response. Then Bell spoke again a bit cautiously. "Did he mention what that *experience* had been exactly?"

Regina eyed Bell, feeling a little uncomfortable, especially given Alex's reaction. Thoughts of Brandon and Sofia had lingered most of the week, but her father's health had taken front and center in her mind.

"It's been years, Gina," Alex said suddenly. "I'm sure he's a different guy now. And like I told Bell, as smart as you are, your judgment of character is likely spot on. I'm sure you wouldn't get involved with someone unless you knew exactly what you're in for. I wasn't even gonna say anything, but it just didn't feel right to not at least mention it."

Regina peered at him curious now. "Mention what?"

Alex glanced at Bell as if it might be better if she told her instead of him. "Did he mention that he and Sofie's brothers never got along?" Bell asked again, her tone a bit too cautionary. Regina was torn between being nervous or annoyed by that.

"Yeah," she nodded. "He said something like that."

The Morenos had always been sweethearts, as far as Regina was concerned. She didn't want to tell them that she knew the main reason they'd been upset with Brandon was because they wrongfully blamed him *alone* for the indiscretion he and Sofia had had while she was already seeing Eric. From what Brandon had told her, Sofia had been just as willing. If they chose to be delusional about their sister's innocence, that was one thing. She wouldn't even go there unless she was forced to. But if they thought they were going to point fingers now and she'd sit there and allow it without defending Brandon, they had another think coming. So she braced herself for what Bell or Alex might *mention* to her next.

"Alex was just concerned because growing up it seemed Brandon's character wasn't always the most honorable," Valerie explained, her tone as cautious as Bell's, and now Regina decided it *was* annoying.

"It's not even about the way he was when we were kids." Alex shrugged. "None of us were perfect, and people grow out of stuff like that. It's what happened later when he got back from the Marines after having been gone a few years. We all thought he'd gone on the straight and narrow and then . . ." He paused, and before he went on to say what Regina knew was coming, she interrupted because she didn't want this to get ugly.

"He told me, Alex." Regina informed him. "He and your sister shared a moment—a kiss—even though she was already with Eric." She shrugged to show it was nonissue for her. "He thought they'd made a connection, especially since she allowed it." She made sure she got that part in but wouldn't harp on it. "He was wrong, and she admitted they'd made a mistake."

"Honey, are you sure he didn't have the faintest idea that you knew the Morenos?" Bell's cautious tone was even gentler now. "That being with you would give him possible access to being around Sofia?"

"What?" Regina asked, completely insulted now. "No, of course not. He had no idea. When he told me about her, he mentioned her name, but it's a common name. It never even dawned on me it might be *this* Sofia." She turned to Alex now, attempting only for Valerie, her sister's longtime friend, not to glare at him. "And there was no way he would know I had any association with any of you."

"Sweetheart, I never said—"

"No one is accusing him of anything, Gina," Bell interrupted Alex, touching Regina on the arm. "And Alex never once insinuated that this was the case, hon. It was just something that occurred to me just now."

"Well, it's not," Regina said, no longer holding back her irritation.

She saw Valerie and Bell exchange glances, and then Bell took a deep breath. "Did he tell you that, even after he was warned to stay away from Sofie, he followed her to the beach to insist on talking to her? Then when she told him *again* that he needed to stay away, he showed up at their home, insisting on seeing her?" Bell asked with a wince. "That he was completely drunk and caused a huge scene just outside their home? And only after he'd been beaten pretty badly did he finally leave?"

Now Regina was stunned silent. She turned to Alex and Valerie. Both looked at her with *sympathy*. "Brandon stalked Sofia?"

That was a far cry from the tidbit he'd shared with her about this.

"I wouldn't call it stalking, G." Alex said. "We never heard from him after that day." He shrugged. "He was drunk. People do all kinds of stupid shit when they're drunk."

"I heard that." Romero laughed.

Alex turned to Valerie. "It's not that big a deal really, but Valerie didn't feel right not saying anything. Like I said, it's been years. We've all made mistakes in our past." He shrugged again. "Shit happens." He turned to Bell as he pushed his chair back, and Valerie begun to push hers back as well. "I seriously doubt he had a clue Gina knew us. Brandon's no dummy. If he's with your sister, it's because he knows what a catch she is."

Alex winked at Gina, and under normal circumstances, she would've felt flattered. Instead, her mind was swimming with questions. Mostly she wanted to know if there was more she didn't know. Alex and Valerie may've wanted to make sure Gina knew about this, but neither seemed eager to share anymore.

"Thank you for letting me know," she said, standing to see them off, since they were obviously leaving.

They both nodded and then hugged her good-bye. Alex once again reminded her that what they'd just told her was a long time ago and even said that if her gut told her Brandon was a good guy then he probably was.

Romero started in on Alex about their new SUV. Bell had already mentioned to Regina that she and Romero were in the market for a new SUV as well. Just like that, the subject of Brandon was axed as the two couples began talking about Alex and Valerie's Escalade.

Regina excused herself to the bathroom, saying her final good-byes as the two couples walked out the front together. They were now completely engaged in the conversation about how much room the back of the escalade had for the strollers and other baby things they constantly traveled with.

After using the bathroom, she peeked in on her dad again. He slept soundly, and she smiled, but her mind was still on Brandon. Romero and Bell walked back into the house just as she walked out of the hallway.

"Come sit and talk some more, Gina." Bell said, pointing at the dining room table.

"I'm gonna call my uncles," Romero said, turning back to the front door. "I wanna make sure everything's still cool with the kids." He shook his head. "I told them to just stay home. I'm surprised those two ain't banned from Chuck E. Cheese yet."

Bell laughed, turning back to Gina. "The first time they took Mandy, Max got stuck in one of the tubes. Another time they nearly got in a scuffle with a dad whose kid was hogging one of the games she wanted to play."

Regina smiled, glad that Bell wasn't jumping right back into the subject of Brandon. She was still trying to digest everything they'd just told her. She didn't think she could take anymore.

Just minutes after Romero walked out, Pat walked in, holding a pie. "I just missed them?" she asked with a frown.

"Alex and Valerie?" Bell asked then nodded. "Yep, they left just a few minutes ago."

"Oh well," Pat said. "More pie for us. It's Razzleberry, Bell. Your favorite." She turned to Regina as she set it down on the table. Bell was already on her way into the kitchen. "I'll get chocolate cream next time, babe."

Regina smiled big at the pie. It was just what she needed to get her muddled mind off Brandon and Sofia. Bell came back with plates and silverware.

"Seriously, Gina," she said as she set the plates down. "I hope you don't think I was trying to insinuate that Brandon was in any way using you for his own ulterior motives. He seems absolutely love-struck with you. Even Mom and Pat thought so, didn't you?" she asked Pat as they both took seats at the table.

Pat nodded but looked confused and turned to Regina. "Why would you think Bell was insinuating he was using you?" She then turned to Bell even more quizzically, lifting a brow. "What ulterior motives would he have?"

God no! The last person she wanted to be having this conversation was Pat. She tried getting Bell's attention so she could give her a look that would make her stop. If anyone knew how critical Pat could be, it was Bell. Already she'd questioned Regina a few days prior about Brandon's rank and if he was planning on moving up or if he was happy where he was.

Over the years and after a lesson well learned with her scumbag ex-husband, Pat had eased up a bit on butting into her siblings affairs, but she could still be quick to judge. Regina was in no mood to hear her take on Brandon allegedly taking advantage of Sofia—no matter how long ago it was. She'd enjoyed riling Pat in the past with Ricardo the beach bum, but this was Brandon. She'd be damned if she would let Pat speak badly of him.

Unfortunately, Bell was too busy slicing pie to catch Regina's pleading expression. "Regina's Brandon and Sofie had a thing once upon a time." Bell said, handing Pat a plate with a slice.

"What Sofie?" Pat took the pie but peered at Regina.

"Alex's sister," Bell said, handing Regina a slice.

"It wasn't a thing," Regina reminded Bell, knowing full well she was now sounding defensive, but she didn't care. This entire topic was beyond annoying.

"Wait," Pat said. "Sofie and Brandon? When? How long ago was this?" She turned to Bell with a frown. "I thought Sofia and Eric were one of those couples that have been together since childhood?"

Once again, the reminder that Brandon had been the only one to tempt Sofia *ever,* not to mention the fact that he'd refused to stay away from her—even took a beating for her—was not helping Regina's growing insecurities. She'd now have to deal with seeing them *react* to one another every time her sister had something where all the Morenos were invited, and that happened *a lot.* There was no question now that Brandon was an equally significant part of Sofia's past as she was in his.

Even though this subject had made her lose her appetite, Regina ate quickly. She was so over talking about this that all she wanted to do now was leave.

"This was a long time ago," Bell explained, "before Sofie and Eric got married. Brandon grew up in the same neighborhood, so she'd known them both just as long."

Of course Pat pressed on as Regina continued to inhale her slice of pie. "So Eric and Sofie weren't always together? She was with Brandon before Eric?"

Regina pushed her chair back, unwilling to hear more about Brandon and Sofia's longtime relationship. It obviously ran far deeper than Brandon had made it sound. She stood up, picking up her coffee cup. "I gotta go."

Bell looked up at her, instantly apologetic. "Oh, honey, I hope you're not upset. I didn't mean to—"

"Upset about what?" Pat asked. "If it was that long ago, what does it matter?"

"It doesn't," Regina said, trying to sound as assuring as she could. Then she forced a smile, glancing back at Bell. "And I'm not upset. I just have to go. I didn't realize how late it was."

She knew Pat well enough to know she wouldn't be letting this go. They could talk all they wanted about Brandon and Sofia when she left, but Regina didn't want to hear another word about it.

The whole way home she replayed everything that had been said. Then she replayed the conversation that had begun to escalate between her and Brandon on their way home from the baptismal party, before they were interrupted by Pat's call. All week she'd pushed it to the back of her head, slowly convincing herself she didn't have to continue that conversation *ever*.

Now she wanted the truth. The *whole* truth. She believed Brandon when he said he loved her. She felt it in the way he looked at her, held her, and *kissed* her. But after today's revelations, she just needed something that would confirm he was completely over Sofia, because now she wasn't so sure Sofia was over him.

Brandon grew up in the same neighborhood, so she knew them both just as long.

Was it possible Sofia had grown up torn between Brandon and Eric? Could seeing him after all these years have reawakened feelings from the past? Had she actually followed Regina into Bell's house that day so she could try to find out more about her and Brandon? Shaking her head, Regina decided that was crazy. But she knew herself all too well. This would fester away inside her if she didn't at the very least finish that conversation she and Brandon had started after the gathering. What had him so worked up that day? There was only one way to find out. She'd ask him.

CHAPTER TWENTY-TWO

They still hadn't talked about downsizing their living arrangements to just one place. There was no rule yet either as to whose place they'd be staying at each week. It just sort of happened. Regina was buying her place while Brandon was leasing, so it was likely that when it happened they'd end up in her place. This week they'd been at her place all week. Brandon had driven there after they'd gone to the hospital because Regina had mentioned she needed to get some things from her place, and they'd stayed there all week.

Brandon was in the shower when she arrived. She plopped onto her sofa, feeling completely exhausted. This week had been such a drain on her emotions. Just as she drove up and saw Brandon's Jeep in front of her place, she'd started having second thoughts about bringing up the whole Sofia thing again. Did she really want to have this discussion this week? From the way he'd acted on the way home from the gathering, she knew there was potential for it to get ugly. But that was just it. The Morenos were a major part of her sister's life, and Bell was a major part of Regina's, so it was inevitable that they'd be running into Sofia and Eric again and again. Regina wanted this behind them. Whatever happened between Brandon and Sofia or whatever they had was in the past, but she didn't want any surprises. Every new thing she discovered today alone had been a blow, and she was ready to just rip the bandage off once and for all—get it all out in the open.

Bell had called her twice on the way home, but Regina wasn't up to talking about what she knew her sister was likely calling about. She'd let both calls go to voicemail, and she saw she had one now, so she hit the voicemail button to listen to it.

"Gina, please don't be mad at me. The only reason I brought up Brandon and Sofia again was because I wanted to make sure you knew I wasn't trying to insinuate anything about him. Everyone agrees it was all in the past and you have nothing to be upset or worried about, okay, sissy? Call me, please. I wanna hear you tell me you love me and you forgive me. I'll be waiting."

Regina smiled, hanging up and hitting speed dial. As soon as her sister answered, she said exactly what she wanted to. "I love you, and there is nothing to forgive because you didn't do anything wrong."

She heard Bell let out a sigh of relief. "Oh good, you know I hate it when we fight."

For the first time that she could remember all week, Regina laughed. "I'd hardly call this a fight, and how could you hate it when we never do?"

"You know what I mean," Bell said, laughing softly. She must've been home now because Regina could hear Romeo in the background, squealing loudly. "Seriously, I wouldn't have even asked Alex and Valerie to come over and talk to you today if I knew it would upset you. Sofia is a sweetheart and all and completely devoted to Eric, but the news was kind of a shock to me, so I figured it would be for you too. Alex was fairly certain that Brandon probably hadn't told you anything about it. I hated for someone to mention it one day and catch you off guard. That could be uncomfortable. Even from what Valerie finished telling me today on the phone after you left, there isn't a whole lot to the story, but still, if it were me, I'd hate for something like that to be brought to light in a crowd with me being the only one who didn't know. It could make things very awkward, and I just didn't want to risk that happening to you."

Regina sat back slowly. Even hearing Romeo's squealing laughter, which usually made her smile, couldn't shake the ugly feeling she suddenly had. Valerie had called her back and told her more? She glanced up at the stairway and listened for the shower. It was still going.

"Belly Bell?" she started very apprehensively, but if she got all the information she needed to know from her sister, maybe she could avoid having to have this conversation with Brandon at all. "I'm almost afraid to ask, so please be gentle with how you lay it on me, okay?"

"What?" Bell asked, no longer laughing and also sounding as nervous as Regina.

"All he told me," she said, lowering her voice when she heard the shower upstairs turn off and she got off the sofa, "is that they had a moment—a kiss."

She heard the bathroom door open upstairs, so she started for the front door. Once outside, she continued. "He said she took it back right after and that was it." She squeezed her eyes shut, afraid to ask her next question, but she had to. "What else did he leave out?"

Bell exhaled dramatically, and Regina knew that wasn't good, so she held her breath, chewing the corner of her bottom lip. "Okay, so she called me back to tell me what she couldn't say in front of Alex. Sarah told her it was a little more than a kiss. But you can't say anything, Gina. Sofia confessed this to Sarah only. Her brothers and especially Eric don't know this."

Feeling the same irrational anger she'd felt on that ride home begin to simmer inside her, Regina gripped the phone. "How much more? Did they sleep together?"

"No," Bell said quickly. "Well, at least I don't think so." Bell lowered her voice as Regina braced herself. "Valerie said it was an actual slip that Sarah even told her what Sofia had shared with her. Apparently, it'd been so long since Sarah had even thought about Brandon after you guys left Sunday, she and Valerie started talking about the incredible coincidence and how awkward it was to see Brandon for a moment there. Then Sarah mentioned how guilty Sofia had felt about the whole thing back then. Hold on," Bell said and went quiet for a moment. Regina heard a door close and suddenly Romeo's screeching was gone. "I came out onto the porch because I don't want Romero to hear. Anyway, Valerie said when she asked Sarah why Sofia felt so guilty over just a kiss it was as if it dawned on Sarah that she hadn't actually told Valerie everything. She made Valerie swear not to say anything, but even then, Valerie said it seemed as if Sarah backpedaled and toned it down. All she said was that the kiss Sofie and Brandon shared was a little longer than she'd first admitted. It actually took place in his bedroom, and Sofie confessed to Sarah that she enjoyed it more than she should have. Val says she thinks maybe there was more to the story, but it was obvious Sarah felt bad about what she'd already let slip."

Bell paused for a moment, and the very thought sunk into the frothing cesspool of jealousy at the pit of Regina's stomach. Of course Sofia enjoyed Brandon's kisses—but maybe there'd been more?

"What Sarah did tell her, and again, this was strictly between her and Sofie, was that before Brandon reported back to duty," Bell paused again almost as if she hesitated to go on but then she did, "she ran into him one last time, and he told her he was in love with her."

The door opened behind Regina, and she turned to see Brandon standing there shirtless and wearing a pair of basketball shorts ,the kind he always put on at night before getting in bed and stripping down to nothing. This look usually excited her, but at the moment, she felt nothing but utter seething jealousy.

"Hey," he said, looking a bit perplexed. "I thought I heard the door close. Why are you out here?"

Val says she thinks maybe there was more to the story. He told her he was in love with her.

Regina pointed at her phone but said nothing as Bell's words played back over and over in her head. Brandon's brows came together for a moment before he nodded and went back inside.

"Was she in love with him too?" she whispered as soon as the door closed.

"Shit! I didn't even think to ask," Bell said, sounding irritated with herself. "I think Valerie would've mentioned it, but Gina you have to promise you won't say anything to Brandon. Valerie said it was obvious Sarah felt very uncomfortable about having let it slip. The only reason Valerie even told me is because, like me, she agreed if it were her it would definitely be something she'd want to know, and she thought you should."

"I won't say anything to him about that." Regina assured her, though she wasn't making any promises. "Is there anything else?"

"No, that's it. Honey, you're not upset, are you? It really was a long time ago."

"No, no." Regina shook her head. "I'm fine. It *was* a long time ago, but like you said, it's better to know everything upfront, right?"

The call was cut short when Romeo's squealing started up again and it turned into whining. Bell had to tend to him. Regina was getting ready to pull the plug anyway. She knew Brandon was probably already wondering why she'd taken the call outside—something she hadn't done once since they'd been staying with each other.

She walked back in to find him sitting on the sofa. It immediately felt odd because he was just sitting there doing nothing but waiting, yet already he appeared on edge.

"How's your dad?" he asked.

"Better, I guess."

He sat up closer to the edge of the sofa and patted the spot next to him, but she turned the opposite way toward the kitchen table to put her things down.

"What do you mean you guess? Something wrong?"

With her back to him, she took off the light sweater she wore, placing it on the chair and was startled when she felt him touch her. She turned with a flinch, and he backed away, looking at her confused.

Regina shook her head, bringing her hand to her forehead then reached out and touched his arm lightly. "I'm sorry. I was just . . ."

"What happened?" He reached for her hand, slipping his into it, and searched her eyes. "What's wrong?" He glanced back at the door. "Who was that you were on the phone with out there?"

"My sister, Bell," she said, already changing her mind about bringing up Sofia.

She hated how instantly things felt tense because she was incapable of hiding the unease that the revelation of knowing he'd been in love with Sofia made her feel. Regardless of what else might've happened in his bedroom that had Sofia feeling so guilty, it shouldn't matter. It was a long time ago. Regina had been in love before him too, but it *did* matter because she couldn't forget how, even after all this time, Sofia's presence alone could change his demeanor so drastically.

He was still staring at her, waiting for more. "I just wanted to ask her one last thing about Dad before I called it a night."

Clearly that answer was not satisfactory because he continued to peer at her suspiciously. "Did something happen today?" he asked, looking down at her hands, and she clenched them in case they did the stupid shaking thing when she was feeling unnerved.

Too chicken to just address the damn subject of Sofia, she shook her head.

"I was getting worried," he said. "You were gone later tonight than the other nights."

His eyes appeared to still be searching for some kind of clue in hers. If he looked too deeply, he just might find it because the visual of him and Sofia gazing at each other the way they had at the gathering, coupled with Bell and Alex's words that were now roaring in her ears, was going to give her away.

"No," she said as casually as she could. "Valerie and Alex were there tonight, so I sat and talked with them and my sisters a little longer."

The tiny flicker in his eyes and his nodding seemed to indicate that answered *something,* but his eyes continued to scrutinize her. "Maybe next time you drop me a text and let me know you'll be a little late? If you hadn't been here by the time I got out of the shower, I was gonna call you and see if you were okay."

She nodded, and normally his concern for her would warm her, but she got the feeling from his tone he was worried about more. One of his regular questions all week when she'd got back from seeing her dad had been "who else was there?" This time she'd given him the answer without him having to ask, and it was the first time all week that someone besides her siblings and her mom had been there. Even with the hunch that Brandon was bothered by the fact that she'd been late because she'd been talking to Alex and Valerie, she wasn't prepared for his next question.

"So what did Alex and Valerie have to say that compelled you to stay and chat longer, Regina?"

His tone was hard—accusatory—and it had her taking a step back. Brandon's eyes widened slowly and glanced down at her feet.

"My sister, actually, just asked if I knew about you and Sofia."

Instantly, he jerked his head up to glare at her. "What about me and Sofie?"

The sound of those last three words, especially coming from him, and the fact that he'd said "Sofie" despite her deliberate choice to avoid the now too-cute-to-stomach nickname, may as well have been a piece of wood grinding against rock. It ignited something within her, but she attempted to remain calm. She *did not* want this to turn into an argument, though given the look in his heated eyes, it already felt inevitable.

"The same thing you told me," she said, lifting her chin. "That you two shared a *moment* once upon a time. She is the same *Sofie* you told me about, right? Or is—"

"No," he said, his brow lifting. "She's the same one. What else did they say?"

"What else do you think?"

That flicker she'd seen earlier in his eyes was an all-out flame now. "I don't know. Your sister wouldn't know much, but if Alex was telling you, I can only imagine. I doubt his spin on how things went down between me and Sofie was favorable to me." Those blue eyes burned into her now with conviction. "I told you Sofie's brothers never liked me."

"You may've not gotten along with them Brandon, but from what I know of them, they've always been very sweet and fair."

Brandon scoffed. "I'm sure they were with you. They didn't hate *you*."

"The word hate never came up once today," she explained. "As usual, Alex was very sweet when he explained the whole thing. Since it was so long ago, he said he wasn't even going to bring it up. He said that it just didn't feel right not saying anything."

Those piercing eyes went darker and harder with every word she'd said. "Yeah, I'm sure his ass was in no hurry to give you his bullshit version of what happened."

"So why don't you tell me your side, then?"

Both his brows shot up, and he dropped her hand. "*My* side?"

"I meant—"

"There're sides now, Regina?"

"No!" she said, reaching out for his hands, but he backed away.

"What else did he tell you?"

"That's it," she insisted, her heart racing. Then she changed her mind, so she shook her head and watched as his already heated eyes narrowed in on hers. "He told me a lot more than you did, and," she paused, lowering her voice, "I know now things were different than how you explained it."

"And you believe him?" His words were laced with anger and exasperation.

She stared at him, torn between telling him what Bell had asked her not to or keep it to herself. "Brandon, it's not that—"

"You believe him?"

His expression fell, and this time there was only one thing she heard in his lowered voice—pain. She didn't think Sarah or Valerie had made up what Sofia herself had admitted, and it was so long ago, so she didn't understand why he'd be so wounded by her believing it.

"Is there anything you left out?"

He stared at her for a moment, shaking his head, still incredulous, and she was suddenly filled with regret. Had Sarah gotten it wrong? Was it possible that, just like she'd forgotten that she'd never told Valerie Sofia's secret, she'd gotten her facts wrong too?

In a flash, the hurt in his eyes changed. It wasn't gone, but it was now accompanied by disgust. "I fucking knew it!" he said, backing up. "They got to you."

"What?" she said, walking toward him, unable to believe how angry this made him. It only made him speed up, and he was already at the bottom of the stairs. "No one got to me. What are you talking about?"

"Is that why you took your sister's call outside, Regina?" He pointed angrily at the front door. "To make sure I didn't overhear your conversation? Since when do you do that?"

She shook her head, feeling like an idiot that she didn't think her going outside to talk to Bell would set off any alarms. This was Brandon. He picked up on the smallest of details. "This is crazy. Why would they be trying to get to me?"

"Did he tell you what a worthless loser I am too?"

"No! Brandon, stop this. I'd never believe something like that anyway. I know you're not."

He came to an abrupt stop halfway up the stairs and stared at her for an achingly long silent moment. "But you'd question if . . ." He shook his head and started up the rest of the stairs.

Regina brought her hand to her mouth, feeling the lump at her throat growing by the second. How had this gone so wrong? Just when she'd decided to follow him up, he rushed down wearing a T-shirt now, holding his shoes in one hand and his keys in the other.

Her heart plummeted. "Where are you going?"

"Home and you know what?" He turned to her. If she didn't know any better, he'd lost some color in his face. "Don't worry about taking sides, babe, because I'll tell you right now," he said as he flung the front door open, "I won't be pleading my case to *anyone*, not them or you. That family can kiss my ass, and if you believe the bullshit they're feeding you, then you can too."

Before her rattled brain could wrap itself around his words, she flinched at the sound of her front door slamming shut. She was frozen to that spot for too long before she finally sat down at her kitchen table.

"What just happened?" she whispered to herself, bringing her trembling hand to her mouth.

She replayed the whole argument back in her head, trying to pinpoint the exact thing that set him off.

Sides.

He thought she was taking sides, and that they'd gotten to her. About *what?* With her heart still at her throat, as much as she wanted to go after Brandon or at the very least call him, she decided it'd be better to give him a little time to cool off. She picked up her phone ready to call Bell again instead. Just before hitting speed dial, she changed her mind. Bell had told her everything she knew. She scrolled down her contact list, looking for Sarah's number. She could swear she'd exchanged numbers with all the girls at one point.

Her stomach tightened as she scrolled down quickly and saw Sarah Moreno. Chewing the inside of her cheek, she mulled it over whether she should call her or not. What would she say to her? That first Valerie and then Bell had passed on Sofia's secret—something she'd trusted Sarah with? And now Regina was calling hoping to get even more from her?

Clicking the back key, she stared at her contact list again. Unlike when she searched for Sarah's name, she scrolled further down, slowly this time. Then she saw the name she was looking for: Sofia Diego. Did she dare?

Call me please if you need to talk about anything. I mean it, okay?

Regina remembered it feeling so odd when Sofia had said that to her. It almost felt as if there was something Sofia wanted to talk about—Brandon. Of course, Regina had no intention of taking her up on the offer, but given the circumstances, she now felt as if it were something she needed to do.

Worst case scenario, they slept together. But that still didn't explain why he would think they were trying to get to Regina or that she would be taking sides. Sides to what? That her brothers might still think Brandon had taken advantage of Sofia? So what? Sofia obviously not only went along with it she admitted to enjoying it. And Sofia naïve? That was a joke. From the moment she met the spunky Moreno sister, naïve was the last thing Regina thought her. Somehow Regina didn't buy that Sofia would be that naïve even way back then. Regina remembered hearing some of the funny stories the girls told while sitting around having martinis and wine in past gatherings. Sofia might be sweet, but she'd been a sneaky one. Those brothers of hers didn't know the half of it.

The truth was that their sleeping together wouldn't be the worst-case scenario. What if Sofia had always been secretly in love with him? What if that's what Sarah had kept from Valerie? Regina knew firsthand how easy it'd been to fall in love with Brandon, how sweet and wonderful he could be. The thought of him reverting back to the cold Sergeant Billings she'd first met choked her up. She needed to get to the bottom of this now.

Would calling Sofia make this worse? She debated about it, going back in forth on whether to try Brandon first instead. One thing was for sure. She needed answers now. There'd be no sleep for her tonight if she didn't get them.

CHAPTER TWENTY-THREE

Brandon

The keys slammed so hard against the glass coffee table it cracked. Brandon's phone rang for the second time, but he refused to answer it. He couldn't talk to her right now. He didn't even want to hear her voice, yet he was dying to. How the fuck did that even make sense? Sitting back on the sofa, he brought his hands to his face, and he slid them both down roughly, taking in an angry breath. He wasn't even sure if he was more angry or hurt.

All week he'd been afraid something like this might happen. From the moment he realized the Morenos were a part of Regina's life, he'd wondered how that would affect their relationship. He could deal with seeing Sofie if he had to. Like Sunday it might be uncomfortable, but he'd since decided it was a sacrifice he'd be willing to make for Regina. Any feelings he may've had for Sofia had been dead and buried for years. He knew now after experiencing real love that what he felt for Sofie had been nothing more that infatuation and maybe a desperate need to feel cared for as he thought she might.

As tempted as he'd been to bring up the subject this week, he hadn't. Regina had already been dealing with turmoil since her dad's heart attack. He didn't want to add to it. He knew talking about Sofie and her brothers and the shit they might tell Regina about him would be a sore point, but he didn't realize how infuriating it would be. The thought of them possibly poisoning her mind about him had bothered him all week, but a bigger part of him was confident she'd be immune to any bullshit they might feed her. He couldn't be sure, but as far as he knew, today was the first time this week she'd heard anything more about him and Sofia, and already she was acting suspicious. Not once since her first reaction to his questioning her about her therapist had she been secretive.

One conversation with Alex and Regina was already having her doubts about him. That's all it took, and he could only imagine what being around them longer would do. She believed what they said already. He saw it in those hesitant eyes. He couldn't deal with this. He *wouldn't*. She wanted his side of the story? Why? All this time around him—knowing him—falling in love with him wasn't enough to prove that things hadn't gone down the bullshit way Sofie's brothers said they did? She expected him to plead his case to her now?

"Fuck that!" he said, flinging his phone across the room where it hit the wall and slammed down on the floor in one piece.

He wondered for a moment if he'd be making a trip tomorrow to the wireless store for a replacement until he heard the text message alert go off. He sat there, staring it at it without moving until it went off again. With the amount of close friends he had, he didn't get many texts, so he knew it had to be her. Unable to fight the curiosity of what she might have to say to him, he got up and walked toward it.

The phone might still be working, but the screen was cracked. He frowned, clicking on the envelope.

We really need to talk. Can I come over tonight? Can't end it like this.

End? Was she serious? He reread the confusing text again. He'd known this would be an issue, one that might take him days to get over, but she was talking about ending things over this?

He didn't even realize he'd brought his hand to rest over his chest until he felt the pounding heart against it. He almost hit the dial button to call her when another text came through.

I just want the truth, the whole truth. I can handle it. I promise.

Because what he'd told her wasn't the whole truth? He started to respond, but he was so pissed he had to retype some of the words because like her first text they were all over the place.

Sounds like you already know the truth, or you wouldn't be promising to be able to handle it. Have Alex tell you the WHOLE truth. Why the fuck do you need to hear it from me if you've already made up your mind whose side you're taking?

He almost kept typing everything he wanted to say to her: how stupid he felt for thinking she'd automatically dismiss all the bullshit for what it was and how disappointed and disgusted he was that she hadn't. Then he changed his mind and deleted the whole damn thing. He wouldn't give her the pleasure of knowing what this was doing to him.

His dad's words about the sacredness of his deep emotions came to him out of nowhere, straightening him out and pulling his head out of his lovesick ass.

No one has a right to know what you're feeling deep inside but yourself. Showing it is a sign of weakness.

It would probably be the hardest thing he'd ever do in his life, but he'd been alone long enough. He knew he could do it again.

Don't come over. I don't want to see you anymore. Handle this, Ms. Brady. This CAN end like this. It just did.

He sent it then turned off the phone and tossed it on the table, feeling an all-consuming and unbearable ache in his heart. Stopping at the door of his bedroom, he wondered if he'd just made the biggest mistake of his life. For one very weak moment, he considered grabbing his keys and racing to her place to give her what she was asking for—swallow his damn pride and give her his side of the damn story—the whole truth. He could plead his case and beg her to believe him. But he shook his head.

"Never," he whispered, feeling numb as he continued into his bedroom. "Not even for you, princess."

~*~

Regina

Each time Regina read the text her heart plummeted even further. She stared at it until her eyes were too blurred with tears to be able to see it clearly anymore. He couldn't be serious. He was ending things just like this—via a text?

She hit speed dial, feeling completely incensed, ready to tell him off. How dare he? This is how much she meant to him? One argument was all it took for him to just dismiss everything they had?

The call went directly to voicemail, and she grabbed her keys, ready to charge down to his place and face off with him. Then she had a terrifying thought. What if seeing Sofia again after all this time is what had made it so easy for Brandon to dump her just like that? Maybe there was something that ran much deeper between him and Sofia. Maybe there was more to their story than anyone but the two of them knew. It had to be something big for Brandon to be this livid with her, but what?

Putting her keys back down, she scrolled through her phone quickly until she saw Sofia's name. With a trembling breath, she pulled herself together and hit the dial button before she could change he mind. She paced around her front room, not even sure what she'd say to her, but she had to get to the bottom of this.

"Gina?" Sofia's voice sounded guarded.

"Yes, Sofia it's me. Can you talk?"

"Um, yeah, give me a sec." The line went quiet for a moment then Sofia spoke again.

She asked Regina about her dad and let her know she'd keep him in her thoughts. Regina thanked her then got right to it. "Listen, I spoke with Alex and Valerie tonight at my parents' house. They told me a little bit about the things that happened between you and Brandon before you were married. Brandon had already told me a little also, only I had no idea you were the same Sofia he had mentioned."

She wanted to make sure Sofia knew Brandon hadn't left her completely in the dark about this, but it scared her to death to wonder what else he'd left out—what else Sofia might've confessed to Sarah about that made her feel so guilty. Regina was fully prepared now to hear they'd slept together—more than once even. What scared her more was the possibility that Sofia was the real reason why Brandon had decided he never wanted another attachment again. Maybe seeing her again reminded him of the fact that she was someone he'd never get over.

"I mentioned it to Brandon when I got home, and he got really upset. I get that he and your brothers didn't get along, but I don't understand why he'd get this angry. He stormed out of here and . . ." She decided to leave out the fact that Brandon had just up and dumped her. Regina wouldn't accept that things were over until she'd at least spoken with him. Trying to keep it together and not break down, she spoke again, but she lowered her voice to a whisper in an effort to keep it from breaking. "He's just really, *really* angry, and I'm trying to understand why."

She heard Sofia inhale deeply. "This is why I was hoping you'd call. First of all, what exactly did Alex tell you?"

Regina told her, and Sofia was quiet for a moment. "He didn't tell you Brandon took advantage of me?"

"No." Regina's voice was a near whisper now. "He didn't, did he?"

"*No*," Sofia stressed immediately. "He didn't, not at all. It just surprises me that Alex wouldn't tell you Brandon had. It's what I was worried about and why I wanted to talk to you. I had a feeling that story might get back to you, and I wanted to set the record straight. It's why I told you at the party that Brandon was a good guy."

Regina thought about that for a moment, and her worries about Sofia secretly being in love with Brandon doubled over. "Brandon told me everything that happened was consensual," she whispered. "But he did leave a lot out." She closed her eyes, her hand clutching the phone tightly. "Is there more?"

Sofia's sudden silence was enough to spike Regina's heartbeat, and she squeezed her eyes even tighter. "Sarah was the closest thing to a sister I had back then. So she's the only one I ever told, but even she doesn't know the whole truth. I had to deal with the guilt of Brandon taking all the blame for what happened for years. None of us had talked or even thought about this for years, and I wasn't sure how my brothers or Eric would react to seeing him after all this time. I am surprised but happy that Alex didn't go there again and make Brandon the bad guy." She paused before going on then took another deep breath. "You're the only one I'm going to tell, but I need to know this will go to the grave with you. I'm only doing it because Brandon didn't deserve to take all the heat like he did back then. I certainly don't want to be the cause of any problems for him now."

She was quiet, and Regina assured her she wouldn't tell a soul. In a lowered voice, Sofia began again. "You know all about my brothers and what they were like when we were growing up, right?"

"Yes."

The thought actually made her crack a smile. She'd heard so many stories. She'd also heard the stories about how Sofia and Eric had sneaked around right under their noses. What was worrisome was that Sofia admitted to have been the instigator in all those stories. She wondered now what else she'd done with Brandon that no one knew about.

"I could make all kinds of excuses, Regina, but the truth is I was young. I'd never been kissed by anyone but Eric, and the bottom line is I was attracted to Brandon. So when he decided to kiss me, I let him. What nobody knows is that he gave me the opportunity to walk away. He literally told me to tell him to stop before he did it and that he would, but I didn't. I wanted him to." With another deep breath, she added, "Eric was already so hurt when I confessed what had happened I couldn't possibly tell him that I could've easily avoided the kiss but chose not to. The worst thing was my brothers and Eric all blamed him. They made me out to be this naïve *stupid* little thing," she said, her voice dripping with irritation, "who had been taken advantage of. As much as I wanted to scream at them, that I'd given into a moment of weakness of my own free will, I didn't because I was terrified of losing Eric. His following me to the beach and then showing up drunk at my house was all because he was afraid I was actually buying into what my brothers were saying."

That thought suddenly woke Regina. "Was it just the kiss, Sof? Nothing else ever happened?"

"Nothing else *ever*."

Feeling an enormous relief, she still had to ask one more thing. "Were you ever in love with him?"

"No," Sofia answered immediately and with conviction. "That was one area I had far more experience than he did even back then." To Regina's surprise, Sofia touched on the very thing she was thinking. "He confessed just before he left that he was in love with me, but I'd been in love with Eric for years. I knew what true love really felt like, and there was no way Brandon could have felt that for me. *No way.* We never had that kind of connection if that's what you're thinking."

Smiling, Regina knew that, even with this information, she still had to fix things with Brandon. Like Sofia he likely thought Alex had badmouthed him—made him out to be a villain.

Sides.

She couldn't have him thinking that by asking him to explain his side she'd meant the story of his taking advantage of Sofia. All she'd been asking for or ever cared about was whether or not there was more to the story of him and Sofia, something Sofia had just confirmed. No, there wasn't.

Thanking Sofia for all her honest and upfront information, she hung up and tried calling Brandon again. This time it didn't go straight to voicemail, but he didn't answer anyway. Knowing that at least his phone was on now, she sent him a text.

> If you don't answer, I'm coming over.

She wouldn't even wait for him to respond. Grabbing her keys, she headed for her car when she got his text response.

> I'm not giving you my side, Regina. So don't waste your time.

At the very least, he was responding now. Frowning, Regina texted back as fast as she could, standing right outside her car.

> I don't want your side. I spoke with Sofia. I just want to talk to you now.

She waited before she got in the car in case this was all he was going to give her. She didn't want to be driving if they were going to go back and forth via text. Startled when her phone rang, she was even more surprised to see it was him, but she smiled, answering immediately.

"Hello?"

"You spoke with Sofie?"

Irritated by his insistence of calling her that and not thrilled about his extra chilly tenor, she frowned. "Yes. I called her—"

"You called her?" His voice went up a notch, bordering on the explosive now. "*Why?*"

"Because I needed to know the whole truth, but not—"

"Because *my* truth wasn't worth shit?" He practically spit his words out, and she was certain now what he was thinking. "Whatever Alex put in your head had you questioning me *and* calling Sofie?"

"You wouldn't answer your phone, Brandon. I tried calling you first."

"Go to hell," he said coldly, and the line clicked.

Her jaw dropped as she pulled the phone in front of her to confirm he'd actually hung up on her. With the confirmation that he had, Regina got in her car, throwing her phone on the passenger seat. She understood why he'd be so pissed, but he could at the very least have given her a chance to explain.

"How fucking rude!" she growled as she turned her car on.

Her phone rang, and she snatched it up, hitting the answer button. "How dare you?" she said loudly, already feeling choked up.

But the male voice on the other end wasn't Brandon's. "What?"

She shook her head, feeling a little stupid. "Art?"

"Yeah, who'd you think it was?"

Not wanting to get into it with him and in a hurry to get to Brandon, she played it off. "A friend of mine. I was just being silly. What's up?"

"Bad news, babe. Dad's back in the hospital." Her heart tanked, and she gripped the wheel. "It's not looking good. They want us all down there ASAP. I'd just gotten home when I got the call. I could swing by and get you."

"No!" she said, the lump in her throat nearly unbearable, and her voice gave. "Not looking good?" she cried as she pulled out of the parking space. "What does that mean?"

"I don't know. They just told me to get there as soon as I could and to get you on the way. Gina, you shouldn't drive like this."

"Too late. I'm already on my way. I'll just meet you there."

As soon as she hung up, she let out a sob, banging her steering wheel. "Daddy, wait for me, please!"

~~~

The moment she arrived at the hospital, she knew she was too late. Bell tore herself away from Romero, whose chest she was latched on to, and ran to Gina.

"Sissy, he's gone! Daddy's gone!" she sobbed, wrapping her arms around her.

Regina nearly collapsed, but she held onto Bell with a shuddering bawl. She allowed herself to fall apart for just a few minutes as she and Bell clung to each other. When she walked into her father's room where her mom was sitting holding his lifeless hand praying, it took everything in her, but she held it together. Pat stood next to her mom, crying softly, and Gina hugged her then leaned over and kissed her mom on the head.

"How are you feeling, Mom?"

Her mom didn't answer. She didn't even look up. She just kept praying and brought her husband's hand to her cheek.

Instantly, Regina was all business. "Have they checked her blood pressure?" Bell and Pat exchanged blank glances. "They need to," she said, heading out.

Just as she'd been afraid of, her mom's blood pressure had spiked. Regina's grief turned into utter dread. She'd just lost one parent. The last thing she wanted was to have to worry about her mom making herself sick over this. Not surprising, her mom hadn't remembered to take her medicine lately as she should. Her mom took it and was taken out of the room so she could sit somewhere and relax away from the sight of her dead husband until her blood pressure went down. Regina sat with her and her siblings, and they spoke calmly about the good times with her dad, remembering only things that made her mom smile even if both her sisters were a mess.

Bell held onto Romero, burying her face in his neck. Art held Pat, comforting her as Regina continued to speak to her mother soothingly. After about an hour, they were allowed back in her father's room for a final good-bye. Both Pat and Bell said they'd stay the night with her mom. Regina needed to leave—needed the luxury of falling apart like she really wanted to. She took the long numbing drive home where she'd now spend her first night without Brandon, grieving alone.

~~~

Afraid of giving into the temptation of calling Brandon, Regina dropped her cell phone on the floor and then proceeded to bang on it with the bat she'd pulled out of the closet. When she was satisfied it was completely nonfunctional, she proceeded to smash the mirror on the wall and then the lamp on the table next to it. Little by little as she obliterated everything in her sight she fell on the floor, taking another big swig straight from the wine bottle, and sobbed.

This was exactly why she didn't want to be tempted to call him. She didn't want anyone, but especially Brandon, to see her this way. The excruciating pain of losing her father manifested itself and was quickly becoming too overwhelming. It was making her feel as if she was losing her mind—she could barely breathe, and she no longer had the will to fight the temptation to pull the gun out of that trunk. If Brandon caught her this way, this may be the last time he ever saw her, and she'd be damned if she wanted him to remember her this way.

She hated feeling so weak, but she was. Any strength she needed to try and get through this subsided with every second that passed. "*Why!*" she screamed, agonized.

It was a question that just poured out. She didn't even know what exactly she was asking, or maybe she did. Why was she so weak? Why the *fuck* couldn't she deal with pain like normal people? What was wrong with her!

The vision of her father lying lifeless in his hospital bed with her mother sitting by his side hit her suddenly. It felt as if someone had taken her bat and pummeled her with it.

"No!" she screamed, shaking her head as if the louder she screamed the more she could will the vision and the reality that her father was gone. "No!"

Scrambling onto her knees, she scurried toward the wooden chest, spilling the near empty bottle of wine on the floor in the process. Flinging the chest open, she grabbed at things—old pictures, Ryan's baseball glove, everything she hadn't wanted to look at in over a year—and flung them all aside until she saw it: the gun.

Her heart pounded against her chest, and she began shaking, but she reached for it. She reached for the box with the ammunition too and took it in her other hand. Holding the cold gun in her hand brought back all those memories of that dreadful day, the day she'd been interrupted. "Not today," she said with conviction and stood up shakily.

She made her way up the stairs to her bedroom, nearly tripping along the way. Thoughts of Brandon and how her fall had brought them together came to her, and she nearly smiled. Then reality slammed into her mercilessly, and she felt her face crumble again.

Rushing now, she opened the door to her bathroom and walked in, locking it behind her. She'd do it this time, and the world would be rid of her pathetic ass once and for all.

She sat on the cold floor for a moment, silently, as the tears continued to roll down her cheek with one thought: Brandon. How naïve she'd been to think his love could make her better—his presence in her life could somehow make her stronger. She was hopeless. Even her beautiful Brandon hadn't been enough to give her the strength to fight through this suffocating pain.

Setting the gun on the floor, her hands nearly shook out of control as she reached for the box of ammo and took a single bullet out. It was all she needed.

CHAPTER TWENTY-FOUR

Brandon

Glad that it was Friday, Brandon had arrived at work that morning, somewhat dreading to see Regina. He'd been both surprised and disappointed she never showed up or even called him back last night. Twice he'd almost given into the temptation of calling her. Even arguing with her would be better than going the whole night not seeing or speaking to her.

Mainly he'd dreaded seeing her today because he knew how badly it would hurt if she did or said nothing to try and rectify the situation. Clearly, she didn't care enough to call him back last night, and he knew telling her to go to hell had a lot to do with it. He'd actually been disappointed when he realized she hadn't come in to work today.

He thought of her anxicty issues. The possibility that maybe this fight and his telling her it was over could have made her lose it, had him calling her by noon. He'd put it off, telling himself she was fine and that she was probably just being melodramatic by not showing up today. Even he had considered staying put today—calling in sick—something he'd so rarely done in all his years in the Marines. He'd seriously considered it today, not to be melodramatic but because after tossing and turning nearly the entire night he'd been tired as shit this morning. He knew he'd be a zombie all day. The only thing that got him out of bed and to work was the possibility of seeing her.

Regina had ignored all his calls, but he left no messages. Even though a small part of him worried that she might not be well, an even bigger part was still pissed—pissed that she'd gone as far as calling Sofie to get the *whole* truth. It still burned him up that it'd taken one conversation with the *sweet and fair* Alex Moreno to trigger enough doubt or suspicion that she'd be acting like she did when she got home. *One* fucking conversation. She'd even flinched at his touch! It'd been such a huge blow—such a huge disappointment—he still couldn't get over it, and he doubted he would any time soon.

He'd actually driven around his block twice after work, talking himself out of driving down to her place, because he could hardly stand going another minute without seeing or hearing from her.

Deciding he'd call her again, he frowned when the line beeped just as her line rang. He glanced at the screen on the off chance it might be her, but he didn't recognize the number. He waited for her line to ring again, but it didn't. Like all the other times, it went to voicemail. Then suddenly it hit him. The phone number on the screen was familiar, and he remembered Pat had his number. He glanced at the number on the screen and cursed himself for not saving her number that day.

Remembering why Pat had called him last time, he hit the answer button, dreading why she might be calling him again if this was her. "Hello?"

"Is Gina with you?" Pat asked a little too quickly—too panicked.

"No why?" he asked, turning left towards Regina's place as his heart sped up.

"I've been calling her all day. So has Bell. She hasn't returned our calls. None of us remember her saying if she was going into work today or not. She was fine last night when she left the hospital, but—"

"The hospital?" he asked, punching the numbers into the keyboard at the entrance of the closed gate of Regina's community gate. "Is your dad sick again?"

Pat went quiet. "She didn't tell you?"

"No," he said, speeding towards her condo, the sheer panic spreading like fire "What happened?"

"Daddy had another heart attack last night," she said, her trembling voice breaking. "Only this time he didn't make it."

It wasn't until he was at Regina's door that he realized he'd dropped the phone without so much as telling Pat he was sorry or even good-bye. To his enormous relief, the door wasn't locked, but the relief was short lived. Her front room was ransacked. The sight of everything in it smashed including the mirror nearly stopped his heart.

He went cold when his eyes zeroed in on the empty wine bottle on the floor next to the big open chest in the corner. It looked as if it'd been rifled through.

I never got rid of the gun. It's buried in there somewhere.

The instant it hit him he shot upstairs like a madman. "Regina!" he yelled out. Seeing how she'd trashed her room as well only panicked him further as he searched around frantically for her. "Baby, where are you?"

CHAPTER TWENTY-FIVE

Regina

Hearing Brandon's voice made her shaky hands move faster and she began to whimper. The sudden bang against the door made her flinch. The door knob rattled, and Regina's head jerked up to make sure she'd locked it. "Regina baby, open the door!"

Her whimpering got louder until she couldn't hold it in anymore. What little calm she'd managed so she could load the damn gun was gone. Brandon's voice alone was enough to make her even more emotional. "He's gone, Brandon!" Her words were a bit slurred to her own ears. "My daddy's gone! I didn't even get to say good-bye to him!"

"It's okay, sweetheart," he assured her, rattling the door knob again. "Just open the door and let me in, please."

She sobbed louder now, the cruel reality once again slapping her in the face and squeezing her heart. "Oh my God, he's gone! He's really gone. I can't take this, Brandon. I can't. It hurts so bad. I just wanna die."

"No, you don't!" he yelled as she felt him push against the door. "Your dad wouldn't want that either. Listen to me, baby. It's gonna be fine. *You're* gonna be fine. Just open the door, okay?"

"I just want this pain to go away. I finished all my wine—"

"I'll get you more!" he yelled, continuing to push against the door. "Just promise me you won't do anything crazy."

Suddenly, his voice was level with her, coming in from crack in the door very close to her ear. "Baby, *please,* let me in. I wanna hold you. I wanna make you feel better."

She touched her fingers to the door where she knew his face was just on the other side. "I don't wanna feel anything anymore." She sobbed.

"No! No, don't say that!" The nearness of his voice against the door was gone, and she imagined he was back on his feet. "Regina." His panicked voice broke in a way she'd never heard it as he rattled the knob in vain. "Please don't do anything right now. You're not well. You're upset and you've been drinking!" He went silent for a moment, and then he spoke again in a near whisper. "Do you have the gun in there?"

"Yes!" she screamed. "Because I'm a fucking coward and this is the only way I'll be able to deal with this! I'm not strong like you."

"Yes, you are!" he yelled. "You can do this. Let me help you."

"No, I can't. I can't!" she cried. "I'm sorry, Brandon. Tell my family I'm sorry, but I just can't do this."

She was sobbing uncontrollably, but she could still make out what he was yelling. "I'm not telling them, Regina, because you're not gonna do this. You're gonna be fine. Stay with me, babe."

She pressed her lips together in an effort to not scream out anymore because she hated to hear him so panicked. She managed to speak again without sobbing.

"I love you, Brandon. Never forget that."

She felt him lunge at the door again and heard it crack. "No, baby, please! *Please,* I'm begging you," he cried. *Cried.* Brandon was crying. Hearing how tortured he sounded did something to her. "I'm not strong. I need you. I *need you,* baby. I can't live without you, Regina," he wailed through the crack of the door, banging against it some more.

Something snapped in her head, hearing how tormented Brandon sounded all because of her. She struggled to get up, still holding the gun in her hand. She thought of Ryan and what his loss had done to her. How could she be so selfish? He loved her as much as she loved him, and she loved *him* more than *anything*. If he did this to her, she'd be instantly destroyed. How could she even think of doing it to him? She was a complete idiot! With clarity setting in, it felt as if the heavens had opened up and she'd finally seen the light. Fumbling with the ridiculously big gun, she nearly fell as the room moved sideways and her head spun a little. "Brandon, I'm so sorry!"

CHAPTER TWENTY-SIX

Brandon

"*No!* Don't do this to me, please. I love you so much. I'm sorry about yesterday. I'm sorry about everything. I'd do anything for you—"

The sudden and unforgiving earsplitting sound of the gun going off and then the thud of her body hitting the floor took his breath away, and he stood there, shaking. His mouth fell open as he felt his heart shatter. The tears continued to flow down his face, and when he was finally able to speak, he cried out. "Regina?"

There was complete silence on the other side of the door, and the next sound he heard was out of his own mouth as he let out an agonized wail. "*Noooo!*" He fell on his knees against the door, sobbing and refusing to believe it. "No!"

The pain was like something he'd never felt in his life. He knew now why she'd be so desperate to make it go away. It was ruthless, and part of him, the child in him, still wanted to believe this hadn't happened. This was just a nightmare he'd wake from.

Moving his head numbly, he looked down, expecting to see blood dripping out from under the door, but there was none. He blinked, still not able to believe what just happened, and then his insides began to warm. This wasn't like when his parents had passed. He wouldn't just get over it this time and move on with his emotionless life. He knew now he *did* feel. He felt a lot, damn it, and what he was feeling right now would *never* pass.

He hadn't lied when he told her he couldn't live without her. Remembering the gun on the other side of the door, he sprung to his feet. With the adrenaline blazing through him now, he cursed God as he kicked the door.

"This is the life you handed me!" he yelled as he slammed his body into the door and heard it crack again. "Are you fucking mocking me?" He kicked it even harder, and this time it finally cracked open. "Well, I don't want it! You hear me? I don't want this fucked-up life anymore! I won't live without her!"

Pushing the door open, his anger subsided as he saw her body on the floor, blocking the door, and he was inundated with pain again. He struggled to get the door open with her lifeless body blocking it, but he finally managed, and he dropped to his knees next to her and sobbed.

At first, he was so consumed with grief all he could think of was looking for the gun because he couldn't take another agonizing moment of seeing his beautiful princess like that. He could hardly see straight as he continued to sob like a child, taking her body in his arms.

~~~

It was first time since the day of the burial Brandon visited the cemetery. He'd been so bitter back then he swore he'd never return. He'd told himself there was nothing here for him, no reason to come back ever, but now it was time and he had to.

Kneeling down in front of the small tombstone, he laid the single daisy over the grave. It was time to say good-bye once and for all to the belief that he didn't need love—that he didn't need friends and family—that he was strong because he didn't cry, didn't show emotion, and didn't beg. He knew now just how much he needed all those things that for years he'd said he could happily do without. He'd never be that man again.

Feeling the gentle touch on his shoulder, Brandon looked up at his beautiful Regina. He was thankful now and would be every single day of his life that he had her in it, because he *needed* her. He couldn't live without her, and he told her as often as she'd let him. He touched her hand then brought it to his lips and kissed it. She leaned over and kissed his head. "I'll give you a moment to be alone with your dad, okay? I'm gonna be over at that bench." She pointed.

Brandon nodded. "I won't be long."

She walked away, and he turned back to the tombstone: *Stephen Billings, husband and father*. For years, he hadn't bothered reading or going through his parents' things. It wasn't until after Regina's incident when he sat with her while she went through some of her father's and her late husband's things that he decided to do the same with his parents' things. He'd buried them in a box he'd kept in storage for years, right there in San Diego.

After reading through some of his mom's journals, Brandon realized what those demons his father had were. Like Brandon himself, Stephen had had a father who was cold and impenetrable. Unlike Brandon, he didn't have a mother to protect him, ever. But he'd had a younger sister, a sister who his mother said his father had once upon a time shared his feelings about. Katie was the only person to ever show him love, and she looked to Stephen to protect her. He was all she had and she was his world.

Katie had died at the hands of a father who then turned the gun on himself, leaving Stephen completely alone at the age of seven. More than loneliness, Brandon's father had lived his entire life with the agony of not having been able to save his sister. He'd failed her, and he'd never forgiven himself.

His parents met in foster care. They'd grown up together, fell in love, and married. Like Brandon, his father had sworn he'd never have children. He didn't want to fail them as he had his sister. Then his wife got pregnant.

Stephen was beside himself. In hindsight, his mother wrote in her journal that his father was a man in desperate need of psychiatric help. In her notes, she also said she saw the love Stephen had for Brandon in his eyes but that he fought it tooth and nail. Then the phobia began. The same phobia Brandon had lived with for years: that he would turn into his father. His father's phobia of turning into the man who'd taken his world away manifested, getting worse over the years and turning him into the hateful man Brandon remembered.

If Brandon hadn't gone years with the same fears, he was certain he wouldn't understand. Brandon swore he'd never live in fear of his demons again because there was something much bigger he was terrified of now. Losing *his* world—losing Regina. He'd lived through the excruciating pain of thinking he had, and he knew with all certainty nothing, *absolutely nothing,* would ever be worth risking that. He'd been a changed man from the moment he first kissed Regina. But after that horrific experience, he'd live every day of his life thankful to have been given a second chance and doing everything he could to make her happy.

"I forgive you, Dad," he whispered.

It's what his therapist had told him he needed to do. She'd been right. It felt good to finally forgive his father. It didn't right any of the things his father had done: All the miserable years of growing up feeling different—unaccepted—the freak of the neighborhood. All the years of not living after both his parents died because he'd been afraid. He was only glad now that he'd managed to overcome that fear when it was most important, when he'd decided to open up his heart to Regina.

She brought all this change into his life, including talking him into seeing a therapist and letting out all that he held in, all the pain he numbed away after both his parents' deaths. It did feel better to let it out, and he knew now needing a therapist didn't mean he was weak. He was healing, and it felt damn good to let it all out.

~*~

Regina

Watching Brandon kneeling at his father's graveside was almost unbelievable. He'd come such a long way. She'd been surprised when he agreed to join her in seeking the therapy to help them deal with the things they were both obviously still dealing with. It was only once every two weeks, but it was already helping. Brandon had told her more than once that the day he buried his father he'd said good-bye forever and he'd never come back here again.

She knew he'd been nervous about coming here today, but she was proud of him. This was a huge step for him.

Her family still didn't know about what happened that day in her condo. She wasn't sure she'd ever tell them, but they'd since moved her out of there. Seeing the patched up bullet hole in the ceiling of her bathroom was a constant reminder of what she'd put Brandon through, and she didn't want to be reminded of it anymore. Neither did he.

Shaking her head, she still couldn't get the memory of hearing him become so hysterical out of her mind. In her haste to get up and open the door to comfort him, the ridiculously powerful gun she'd bought to make sure it got the job done had gone off in her hand. The force had been so much that she'd flown back against shower tile and had been knocked unconscious.

She'd woken to Brandon's sobs. He'd been cradling her in his arms, but they'd been sobs of joy. He later explained that, before he was able to break the bathroom door in, he really believed he would find her dead in a pool of her own blood. He also confessed that his only thought the entire time was to take the gun and turn it on himself.

Smiling suddenly, she watched as he stood up and began walking toward her. She too stood and met him halfway. "How do you feel?" she asked tentatively.

"Good." He smiled. "The therapist was right. I needed to do this."

Regina wrapped her arms around his waist. "I'm proud of you, baby."

"How do you feel" he asked, pulling away to look at her. She looked up at him, smiling big. "Excited."

"Me too." He kissed her. "Let's go do this."

~~~

Bell set the birthday cake on the table. It was considered in bad form to do any celebrating while still in mourning, but it'd been over three months since their father had died, and their mother insisted it was time. Her father wouldn't have wanted them to mourn for weeks or even days much less months.

Romero sat in front of the cake with Romeo and Amanda on his lap, smiling big as they all sang happy birthday to him.

Once Romero finished blowing out the candles, Regina took ice-cream duty as Bell set slices of cake on plates. She smirked, watching Pat, who was once again engaged in an ongoing debate with Romero's uncle Max on the loveseat in the living room. Those two were always going at it lately, and if Regina didn't know any better, she'd say her sister enjoyed arguing with him a little too much.

Bell caught Regina smirking and then leaned into her and whispered, "Don't you dare tell her I told you, but she's had him over to her place a few times."

Regina's jaw fell open. "You're kidding me."

Bell giggled then shushed Regina as she continued slicing the cake. "The first time it was supposedly to settle a bet about making tamales." She rolled her eyes but laughed.

"She had him over, and they made a few dozen tamales together, so you know he was there for hours. Another time she said he'd offered to take a look at her dryer because she'd mentioned the timer wasn't working, but she insisted that's all he'd done. She thinks she's being sneaky, but she doesn't know Manny tells Romero everything, and according to Manny, she's all Max ever talks about these days. He also says they get together way more often than Pat's admitting. Pat and Max!" Bell covered her mouth, laughing. "Can you even imagine?"

Looking up at Pat, Regina saw her sister place her hand on her hip, suddenly looking completely appalled at whatever Max had just said. She then stood up and walked off toward Regina and Bell. "Uh, oh," Regina whispered. "Looks like trouble in paradise."

Both Regina and Bell went back to quietly filling the plates with cake and ice cream as Valerie and her girls helped pass them out. Pat came over and picked up two plates: one for her and one for Max, no doubt. She eyed Regina, who couldn't wipe the smile off her face.

"What are you smiling about?" Pat asked suspiciously.

"Nothing." Regina shook her head. "I'm just in a good mood. That's all."

Bell placed another slice of cake on the plate Regina had just scooped ice cream onto. Then Bell stopped. "Wait a minute," she said, pointing at Regina's hand. "What is that?"

Pat eyes were instantly on Regina's hand as well. Regina smiled big but said nothing. She glanced over at Brandon, who was now sitting with Romero, Angel, and Manny, laughing at whatever story Manny was telling them.

She was so relieved that any awkwardness between him and Sofia's brothers seemed to wear off even more every time they were around them. They'd all been around for her father's services, and then later they'd been invited to Alex's home for Sal and Grace's baby shower. Even Eric had been civil enough, and while he wasn't going out of his way to chat with Brandon, they'd been in the same circle of guy talk more than once.

"Gina," Pat asked, setting down the two plates of cake she had in her hand then picked up Regina's hand to get a better look at her ring. "Is that what I think it is?"

"I don't know," Regina teased and turned in Max's direction. "Is *that* what *I* think it is?"

The smile on Pat's face instantly went flat, and for some reason that made Regina laugh. "Oh come on! What's the big deal?"

Pat looked around wide-eyed, pressing her lips together, and waited for Valerie to walk away with another two plates of cake. "Don't be ridiculous," she practically hissed, but Regina caught the humor in her sister's eyes. "We're barely friends. The man is incorrigible."

Regina smirked. "Ah huh."

"Never mind that," Bell said, coming around the table, and took Regina's hand in hers. "Are you engaged?"

With a giddy smile, Regina nodded. "We weren't going to make a big formal announcement, but I was waiting for you to be done with all the formalities and sitting down to relax to tell you guys and Mom."

Pat hugged her first, congratulating her, then Bell, which caught the attention of Valerie and Sofia, who were walking by. "What's going on?" Valerie asked.

"Gina and Brandon are engaged," Bell nearly squealed.

"Oh wow! Congratulations," Valerie said, reaching out to hug her.

Next came Sofia, who smiled big. "I'm so happy for you. You two are such a sweet couple."

Regina barely had a chance to smile and thank them when both Pat and Bell whisked her away. They walked over to Brandon and practically tackle-hugged him. Then they rushed over to where Regina's mom sat with her aunts eating cake. Within minutes, it was all everyone was talking about, and Brandon and Regina were besieged with hugs and well wishes.

~*~

Brandon

"*¡Ay qué guapo!*" Regina's elderly Aunt Benny held Brandon's hand in her fragile little hand, nodding with a big smile. "*Bien venido a la familia—*"

"*Tia Benny.*" Regina smiled and glanced back at Brandon. "*Brandon no habla Español.*" She turned back to Brandon. "She's says you're very handsome and welcomes you to the family."

"Oh," Brandon said, turning to her aunt with a smile. "*Gracias.*"

He was grateful he remembered one of the few Spanish words he knew. He wasn't sure what Regina had said to her aunt, but he was fairly certain she'd once again reminded her he didn't speak Spanish. Regina had warned Brandon about her aunt ahead of time. "No matter how many times I reminded her Ryan didn't speak Spanish, he'd had to sit and listen to her long stories in Spanish many times. She's probably worse now since she's gotten older. Ryan always just smiled and nodded."

Brandon did the same thing now. He smiled and nodded as her aunt nodded back and smiled then she glanced back at Regina. "*¿Le dieron pastel?*" She then turned back to Brandon with a concerned look. "*¿Comio pastel? Está muy bueno.*"

Again Brandon smiled and nodded. Regina smiled at him and shrugged. "She wants to know if you had cake."

"Yes," Brandon smiled, touching his stomach. "It was very good."

Regina's mother came over, and the three women began talking way too fast for Brandon to keep up with his very limited Spanish. Casually, he walked away over to the big aquarium in the next room. This was his first moment alone since they arrived, and he took a deep breath then exhaled slowly. These visits with her family with the Morenos around were getting a little easier. It was always a bit tense at first, but after a few minutes, he'd begin to feel more comfortable.

"Congrats."

Brandon turned, surprised to see Sofie smiling at him. "Thanks," he smiled, trying not to look as uncomfortable as he felt.

So far all the other times he'd had to be around her, especially since he'd been busy consoling Regina at her father's services, she'd been the only one of the Moreno clan he had yet to speak to. He figured it'd happen eventually. He just didn't think it'd happen when they were alone.

"Gina's a great girl. You two should be really happy." She glanced in the direction where Bell and Romero sat with her brother Art and his wife. "Her family really likes you too, as they should."

Brandon smirked, nodding. "Yeah, Aunt Benny says I'm handsome."

Sofie laughed sweetly. "Aunt Benny knows what she's talking about."

Feeling the smirk diminish, he took a sip of his beer, not sure how to respond to that. Sofie glanced around, a bit guarded.

"Listen, Brandon," she said, lowering her voice a bit. "I didn't think I'd ever get a chance to, but now that I have it I want to make sure I apologize."

He stared at her confused. "For what?"

"Everything that happened in the past. It wasn't fair that you took the blame for it all when I'd willingly gone along with it. You have no idea . . ." She stopped and smirked. "Well, actually you probably do have a *very* good idea what it was like to deal with my brothers."

Brandon couldn't help but smirk either. "Yeah, I have a pretty good idea."

"I want you to know I did try to explain to them that it wasn't all you. I even tried explaining it to Eric, but after everything that happened and given the history they had with you, it was impossible to get them to think objectively. They just weren't seeing it. As far as they were concerned, no matter what I said, I was being naïve and it was all you." She rolled her eyes. "I gave up trying to convince them, and after you left, I figured it didn't matter. Even though that was a long time ago, I've always felt bad about it."

Of course, he'd never tell her how much she'd affected him and for how long. In hindsight, he knew now it wasn't so much what happened between them but *when* it happened. The timing couldn't have been worse. Aside from the horrific incident he'd gone through with Regina, that year was one of the most devastating of his life. Because things had gone down with her that same year, he just always associated her with the worst period of his life. He'd been swept up into that memory, but really, the memory of the first girl he thought he had feelings for and didn't reciprocate shouldn't have been so tragic.

He'd since come to another conclusion, and *that* he would tell her. "I was angry about that for a long time, but you know what? I'm glad things happened the way they did."

Smiling, he thought about the tattoo on his abdomen, and for one very foolish moment he considered lifting his shirt and showing it to her. He almost had to laugh, knowing that, while seemingly no one appeared to be paying attention to them, if he did, he'd be tackled on the spot.

"Shakespeare said it first, but then a very wise woman said it to me later. 'What's past is prologue.'"

Her eyes widened, and she seemed almost embarrassed. "I'm still no good at deciphering poems or whatever things that deep mean."

"It just means my past set up my present, and I'm presently one very happy man."

Regina walked up to them suddenly, slipping her hand into his. "And I'm one very happy woman."

Sofie smiled genuinely. "And I'm very happy for you both."

A crying baby got Sofia's attention, and she excused herself. Regina turned to look at him, squeezing his hand and lifting a brow with a smirk. "I was jealous for a moment there when I saw you two chatting alone," she whispered, poking him in the ribs with her elbow. "You don't even know how lucky you are I walked up at just the right moment. You would've had one crabby brat to deal with for the rest of the night."

"Crabby brat?" He grinned. "Not my princess," he said, leaning his forehead against hers. "And trust me. I know just how lucky I am."

~*~

Regina

"I'd say your family's excited." Brandon smiled, kissing Regina as he opened the car door for her.

Regina was still walking on air. She couldn't believe what a difference a few months made. The first couple of weeks after her dad's death had been incredibly depressing—something she'd never thought she'd get past. Luckily, she had Brandon to help her through it. With each day that passed the world got a little brighter.

She was even beginning to deal better with knowing Janecia was now also engaged to a man who owned a motorcycle—one she'd been on more than once. Though secretly she knew her dealing better with it had everything to do with the fact that Janecia was pregnant now. Not only had she told Regina there was no way she was getting on a motorcycle while she was pregnant she'd also mentioned Clay had been the one to bring up trading in his "Hog" for a better suited family SUV. It wasn't a done deal yet, but Regina had her fingers crossed.

She turned to Brandon and took his hand between both of hers then leaned her cheek against it, feeling so blessed to have him in her life. Brandon glanced at her and smiled. "Chocolate for your thoughts."

"Deal!" she said, smiling big.

"Chocolate-chocolate-chip waffles?" he asked, switching lanes suddenly. "They serve them all day."

"Yes," she said quickly with a giggle.

That made her even more excited. She'd never been into carrot cake and that was the kind Bell had gotten for Romero. Regina had barely touched her slice.

"Okay, so let's have it," Brandon said. "What's that dreamy smile about?"

She didn't want to kill their happy moment, but she wouldn't lie either. "I truly believe you and I were meant to save each other." They came to a stop, and he turned to stare at her but said nothing. She immediately felt choked up, but she had to continue. "I never told you this, but that day you found me in my bathroom hysterical, I had every intention of putting that gun against my head. My heart felt so hopelessly broken it literally ached with every beat. But it wasn't until I heard your cries . . . It wasn't until I *felt* how much I'd be hurting you in the process that I instantly regretted having so much as thought of doing something that would devastate you like that."

Brandon was staring straight ahead now, his own eyes tearing up. "I've had some bad days in my life," he whispered. "But that was by far the worst one ever."

"Medication or not, I can promise you this with absolute certainty. Those thoughts will *never* cross my mind again. It's not about just me anymore. I live for you, Brandon. And I'd never do that to you. *Ever.*"

She kissed his hand and he pulled her hand to him gently. "Good," he said, kissing her hand too. "Because I don't know about *me* saving *you*, but I *know* you saved me." He shook his head as a single tear slid down the side of his face, and he leaned in and kissed her. "I live for you too, baby.

EPILOGUE

MRS. BILLINGS
MY WIFE
MY PRINCESS
MY LOVE
MY WORLD

Lost for a moment, still staring at the tattoo he'd gotten on his upper arm just over a year ago, Brandon's train of thought was derailed as Regina gasped and Buddy, their six-month-old beagle, barked.

"Artie baby, not so fast!"

Brandon glanced up at the tall slide his son was now rushing up the ladder of. He tugged on Buddy's leash to calm him then smiled. "He's all right," he assured her, wrapping his arm around her from behind and rubbing her pregnant belly.

"He wants to keep up with all the other boys, but he's the littlest one," she said.

Brandon watched as his son effortlessly climbed the ladder and reached the top, holding his hand out for him to see. He gave his son the thumbs up and smiled. A few years ago, having a family of his own was the furthest thing on his mind. Now here he was with a wife, a son, another one on the way, and a dog.

Artie grabbed hold of the pole on top of the slide and swung himself out over the open slide, laughing and making Regina gasp again and pull away from Brandon.

"Arturo Stephen Billings, don't you dare do that again!"

Brandon made eye contact with Artie and shot him a warning look. His son sat down on the slide and slid down hands in the air. He came down so fast he flew into another boy at the bottom and they both fell into the sand. The other boy, at least two years older and twice his size, got up then shoved Artie back into the sand. Artie rolled around, laughing.

Regina started to charge. "Hey! That's not nice!" she said to the other boy who'd already started walking away but turned to look at her.

"Relax," Brandon assured her again. "He loves that shit. It's just horseplay, baby. It's what boys do."

Artie was already running back to climb the ladder of the slide. One of the other boys pushed him aside and climbed up before him.

"No pushing!" Regina yelled out, glaring at the other boy.

Artie didn't even flinch as he rushed up behind the other boy, laughing. Brandon watched, chuckling and calming Regina the whole time. It was the same thing every time they came to the park. By the time they packed things up, Brandon could see his son wouldn't even make it out of the parking lot awake. As usual, he made Dad proud, playing hard and keeping up with the big boys the entire time.

Brandon chased him down and tackled him on the grass. Buddy joined in the fun, jumping all over them both. This was something he'd never had the pleasure of doing with his own dad, and it was something he knew Artie loved. It was now one of his most favorite things to do with his boy—wrestle and see how much Artie enjoyed their time together.

"Time to go," he said as Artie tried to squirm away, laughing hysterically, and Brandon tickled him. "I said it's time to go. Hey," he said as his son continued to squirm. "Who loves you?"

"Mommy!" Artie laughed.

"Who else?"

"Buddy!"

This was a game they played, and Artie loved teasing him. "Wise guy, huh," Brandon tickled him even more making him squeal loudly. "Who else?"

"You!" he finally screeched. "You love me, Daddy."

"You bet your butt I do," Brandon said, standing up and pulling him up with him. "You have fun today, champ?" He asked him as he sat him on his shoulders.

"Yeah, fun!" Artie said, and Brandon felt him kiss him on the head.

"Next time maybe we leave Momma Bear home," Brandon said with a smirk, and Regina peered at him menacingly. "She doesn't get it."

"No, Mommy come too." Artie said.

"All right, all right," Brandon said with a conceding smile in Regina's direction. "I guess she can come with us next time."

Once they had Artie in his car seat and they both sat up front, Brandon checked his rearview mirror and could see his son was already having a hard time keeping his heavy eyelids open. When he saw Brandon looking at him, he opened up his eyes wide in an effort to fight the inevitable slumber. His big blue eyes stared at him for a moment before the lashes came down again slowly.

"I don't know why he tries to fight it." Brandon smiled as he pulled out of the parking lot.

"I don't know why he tries so hard to do *everything* those other boys do." Regina frowned. "They're all so much bigger than he is. Maybe there's a park somewhere else for just little kids his age."

"No way," Brandon said, smiling. "He loves it. Besides, if we go somewhere with little kids, he'll be doing all the pushing. Then you'll have to hear it from all the other momma bears."

"He's not a bully!" she said.

Brandon laughed. "I know, but he doesn't know his own strength. He just bulldozes through a crowd of kids, so it's better that it's a crowd of bigger kids than smaller ones."

"That's your fault for always wrestling with him. It's all he ever wants to do, even with my brother and sisters—*girls*."

Again Brandon couldn't help laughing. "Well, we'll just have to teach him some manners with that. It's not okay to push girls around, but with boys, it's fine, even bigger ones."

Regina sighed, rubbing her swollen belly, then groaned. "I can't even imagine two of them."

"Yeah, that's gonna be fun," Brandon agreed with an even bigger smile.

Regina's brother had given up trying for a boy after three girls. Regina mentioned it would've been nice if her brother had had a boy and they'd named him after her brother and her dad. So when their son was born, Brandon insisted she name him after her dad. She then insisted if they were doing that his middle name would be after Brandon's dad. Now that they had another boy on the way, she'd already told him this one would be named Brandon. He'd agreed, though she'd balked at the suggestion that if they ever had a girl she'd be named Princess.

"No way," she'd said. "Girls are evil. She'd probably have a miserable time in school with all the other jealous girls hating on her just because of her name."

As much as Brandon had talked shit about families like the Moreno's who were way too overprotective about the princess in their family, he already knew he was going to be a total hypocrite about it. He made no apologies. How the hell was he supposed to know what it felt like to love someone so much you'd be ready to kill if anyone messed with him? He felt this way about both Regina and Artie already, and he was damned sure it'd be even worse with a little girl.

Now that they were going to have two bulldozing boys, maybe if their third was a girl, he could convince Regina that, with brothers like Artie and little Brandon, no one would pick on their daughter, not even girls. Brandon still had time to work on her.

They got home and started their nightly ritual. Regina finished changing their half-asleep little boy into his jammies, saying she didn't have the heart to put him in the tub now as sleepy as he was.

"He can take a bath in the morning," she said. Artie stood a little wobbly, holding on to Regina with one hand and rubbing his eye with his other. "Say goodnight to Daddy."

"Goodnight, Daddy," Artie said.

"Goodnight, champ." Brandon smiled, his heart swelling as it always did when his little boy smiled at him. "I love you."

"I love you too," Artie said as he took Regina's hand and they began to walk away.

Brandon waited to see if his smartass kid would ruin the tender moment like he always did by saying something to take from it. As young as he was, Artie already knew how to make a funny, but Brandon thought he might be too sleepy. Just when Brandon thought he was home free and he'd gotten an "I love you" from his son with no follow-up wisecracks, Artie turned and smiled.

"And Buddy too."

Brandon jumped from the sofa, making Artie squeal and take off running to his room. He heard Regina groan as he ran past her to catch Artie.

"Brandon!" she whined. "He was almost out for the night. Oh my God, I *already* have two of them."

Brandon laughed as he tackled Artie on the floor, shushing him because he was suddenly wide awake. "I think we're in trouble," he said as Artie scrambled to his feet.

Just seeing his son's bright smile as he leaped into the air to make a flying tackle onto him had him smiling big. Artie landed on Brandon's stomach, nearly knocking the wind out of him, but he still had to laugh. "Good one!" he said with a groan.

Maybe they would be in trouble, but this was totally worth it.

ACKNOWLEDGMENTS

As always, I need to thank my family first: my husband Mark and kids Marky and Megan. Thank you for your continued love and support. Without you guys, none of this would mean anything to me .I love you all and appreciate your patience when I go into "the zone" and hear nothing of what's going on around me. Thank you for understanding it's not something I do on purpose. It just happens.

To my beta readers, Dawn Winter, Judy DeVries, Emily Lamphear, and my *commadre* Inez Sandoval, you're all just an amazing group of women, and I feel so blessed to have you all on my team. I thank you for continued dedication and for not having gotten tired of my endless questions. I look forward to working with you on *all* my other projects!

I'd also like to thank the many bloggers out there who have supported me and pimped, reviewed and participated with my cover reveals and announcements. You guys have been a HUGE part of my success, and I thank every single one of you from the bottom of my heart!

To my one-stop superhero beta reader/editor/formatter and listener to all my whiny rants/vents and obsessive worrying Theresa (Eagle Eyes) Wegand, you have truly been God sent, and I'm so, so glad I found you. As always, your work is impeccable, and I can't say enough about it. I hope to be working with you for years to come! Thank you so much!

I want to give a special shout out to "my girls," my very special group of incredibly talented and superstar authors. Without you, I think I'd be insane by now. I'm so glad our bond has withstood the test of time. You really are the only ones who truly, *truly* get it. Thank you for the support, love, and *always* being there, ready to say the perfect thing when I need to hear it most. I hope to be including you all in my acknowledgments even when I'm on my 50th book! I love you all!

I'd also like to thank my new cover artist, Sarah Hansen of **Okay Creations**. From finding the models, to putting together the photo shoot to creating the beautiful cover of Breaking Brandon, you're awesome, and your work speaks for itself. I'm so excited about working with you on future projects!

And, of course, my incredibly awesome readers! Thank you so much for your continued support, emails, messages, and comments, which always seem to come at the most perfect time, making me smile and sometimes even tear up. I've had the enormous pleasure of meeting and chatting with many of you, and I really hope to meet you *all* one day! I love you guys, and I can't wait to get the next one out to you!! I wish there were more ways I can show you all my appreciation. I hope to have a few surprises for you guys in 2014 just to show you that I really am listening and reading ALL your messages and comments!

ABOUT THE AUTHOR

USA Today Bestselling Author, Elizabeth Reyes, was born and raised in southern California and still lives there with her husband of almost twenty years, her two teens, her Great Dane named Dexter, and one big fat cat named Tyson.

She spends eighty percent of time in front of her computer, writing and keeping up with all the social media, and loves it. She says that there is nothing better than doing what you absolutely love for a living, and she eats, sleeps, and breathes these stories, which are constantly begging to be written.

Representation: Jane Dystel of Dystel&Goderich now handles all questions regarding subsidiary rights for any of Ms. Reyes' work. Please direct inquiries regarding foreign translation and film rights availability to her.

For more information on her upcoming projects and to connect with her--she loves hearing from you all—here are a few places you can find her:

Blog: www.ElizabethReyes.com

Facebook fan page:http://www.facebook.com/pages/Elizabeth-Reyes/278724885527554

Twitter: @AuthorElizabeth

Email EliReyesbooks@yahoo.com

Add her books to your Good Reads shelf

She enjoys hearing your feedback and looks forward to reading your reviews and comments on her website and fan page!

Printed in Great Britain
by Amazon.co.uk, Ltd.,
Marston Gate.